DELAYED
GRATIFICATION

DELAYED GRATIFICATION 180

Jessie McAna

Copyright © 2012 by Jessie McAna.

Library of Congress Control Number:		2012914905
ISBN:	Hardcover	978-1-4797-0126-1
	Softcover	978-1-4797-0125-4
	Ebook	978-1-4797-0127-8

All rights reserved. No part of this book may be reproduced or transmitted in any form or by any means, electronic or mechanical, including photocopying, recording, or by any information storage and retrieval system, without permission in writing from the copyright owner.

This is a work of fiction. Names, characters, places and incidents either are the product of the author's imagination or are used fictitiously, and any resemblance to any actual persons, living or dead, events, or locales is entirely coincidental.

This story was originally presented as "Punishment" by arianawhitlock. The author holds all rights to the series that was previously posted on fanfiction.net.

This book was printed in the United States of America.

To order additional copies of this book, contact:
Xlibris Corporation
1-888-795-4274
www.Xlibris.com
Orders@Xlibris.com

Contents

Prologue   Intense 9

1   Becoming Daniel's Master 15
2   Moving On 26
3   Cupid 32
4   Master of Multiples 37
5   Unworthy 43
6   Punishment 49
7   Transition 56
8   Acceptance 61
9   Comfort Zone 69
10   Frustration 77
11   Needy 89
12   Respect 102
13   Regret 125
14   Foot in Mouth 137
15   Concern 150
16   Angels of Justice 166
17   No Such thing as Paradise 173
18   Denial 197
19   Lessons 203
20   Stress 212
21   Truth Be Told 222
22   Jealousy 230
23   Crazy 243
24   Safe Words 250
25   Trust 259
26   Strike 265

27	Initiation	272
28	Monster	283
29	Broken	286
30	Starting Over	295
31	Destruction	310
32	Painful Endings, Delightful Beginning	337
33	Heart to Heart	348
34	Cry for Help	358
35	Drama, Drama, Drama	374
36	Panic	387
37	Kidnapped	396
38	Choice	398
39	Cost	401

Epilogue Surrender 407

To my best friend, you have been standing beside me since the beginning and I could not be luckier to have you.

Prologue
Intense

Daniel's Point of View

I'm waiting for him. Kneeling on the padded floor, naked, waiting. I'm mentally exhausted from my day-to-day life and am grateful to be here; here, where I'm able to shut it all off, to relax, to find inner peace. Soon, my mind shuts off; the rhythm of my breathing is steadying. I have achieved the edges of subspace.

I feel my master's hands in my long, dark brown hair. I break formation to look him in his deep blue eyes before I fall into submission. When his fingers leave my hair, I don't hear him walk away from me. I wait for his instruction, ready to please him, only to be surprised by the tool he drops into my line of sight.

"Thorn, Master," I reply, remaining still.

"Good," he praises, and I realize he's testing me. My first lesson with my master involved my three safe words: *rose*, which means I want to end the session, *petal*, which means we pause the session until I am comfortable, and *thorn*, which means I have reached a hard limit. Honestly, I'm not in the mood to be tested today. I want the illusion of surrendering. Safe word tests and requests from my master break this illusion. I am aware that as the sub, I am in the one in control of what is and is not done with my body. But it is a reality that is easily forgotten when you are playing the game. I trust my master, I trust that he will not hurt me. I crave the illusion; the illusion allows my mind to be free, to float in subspace.

I feel him drag a finger slowly across my shoulders. Then I feel him press into the pressure points on my neck while he pulls it gently upward. I find it painful at first, but my muscles soon relax into his touch.

"There's my Daniel," he praises.

I'm pleased my master knows me so well. I'm sensing tonight is going to be intense.

"Crawl to the X-frame," he orders. I follow his instruction and kneel, waiting. "Arms spread to your sides," he instructs. I stretch them out level and wait. Time passes, my arms are aching, but I refuse to break formation, keeping them level. I allow my mind to focus on this one simple task, nothing else. Nothing in the outside world matters in this moment; all that matters to me is that I please my master. This small exercise allows me to fall deeper into submission.

"Daniel," my master states, bringing me to the edges of reality by touching my face, "look at me." I raise my eyes to his. "It pleases me so that you trust me. You are already in subspace?"

"Master?" I ask, keeping my position.

"I've asked you to rise." He smiles kindly.

"Master, my apologies."

"No need for that. You are very obedient. I know where your mind was." He smiles. "Now rise."

I carefully balance myself onto my feet, keeping my arms outstretched. That's when I feel the leather cuffs, laced with wool, my master has secured onto both my wrists. Just as I did not hear his initial command to rise, I did not feel him putting them there.

The first time subspace blocked out my reality so completely I found myself shouting petal, my pause word, and questioning him. He had smiled widely and said, "Welcome to subspace, Daniel." I was astonished that something like that could happen, but I soon learned to crave it. At first, it took time to reach these heights in a single session, but as my master and I have grown closer and our bonds of trust continue to grow deeper. I find that if I allow myself, I can fall easily. However, doing so does not always prove to be effective, for I am here to please my master as well, by respecting and obeying him.

My master hooks my arms and ankles to the frame before I feel his hands on my ribs. "Are you with me, Daniel?"

"Yes, Master."

"Safe words," he demands.

"Rose, petal, thorn," I reply instantly.

"When do you say them?" he asks, while running his hands down my back and cupping my ass.

"When I have reached my limits or am uncomfortable, Master," I respond with a shaky breath, feeling him run his index finger over my puckered hole.

"Good." He smiles. Silence falls into the room while he continues to tease me. I fight back from whimpering as my dick slowly becomes painfully hard. "I want to push your limits tonight, Daniel." I swallow hard, waiting for my master to continue. "Do you get punished for safe wording, Daniel?"

"No, Master," I respond, trying to keep my voice steady. Then I see a second tool placed in my line of sight. I can't stop the gasp from slipping through my lips. The tool drops to the floor with a thud as my master's hands run through my hair.

"Permission to speak freely, Master." I request.

"Denied," he responds. "I know your reasoning behind this limit, Daniel. You will not be punished if you choose to safe word. But my role as your master is to bring you to your limits and push you past them. With that in mind, and how far we have come in our relationship as Dom and sub, I am asking that you reconsider. The choice is ultimately yours, Daniel. Know you will be rewarded greatly if you accept the challenge and you will not be punished if you decline." He waits patiently for me to decide as he continues to run his fingers through my hair. He knows I find this to be extremely satisfying and is rewarding me for considering his offer, no matter what my choice may be.

"Yes, Master," I decide, "I will allow this."

He drops his hands while pressing his smiling lips on my neck. "You please me so much for trying." The statement makes me proud. "Safe words," he insists again, stepping away to pick up the discarded tool.

"Rose, petal, thorn," I answer, feeling the first bead being pushed past my tight ring.

"When do you say them?" he asks, gently pushing a larger second bead inside of me.

"When I have reached my limits or am uncomfortable."

"Do you need to say them, Daniel?" he asks, pressing an even larger third bead inside of me.

"No, Master," I respond while I concentrate on breathing and not fighting my restraints. When the last of the five in the strand is being introduced, I lose my concentration and pull back on my wrists. "Petal," I gasp. Immediately, the pressure stops, but the beads are not removed.

"Would you like to say thorn Daniel?"

"No, Master. Please, just give me a moment."

"Relax, Daniel. It has not escaped my notice you are fighting your restraints."

I take a few deep calming breaths. When I am relaxed, my master notices. He does not speak; he wants me in subspace and knows that could break it. Instead, he waits patiently before completing his task. I focus on keeping still. My master has chosen to restrain me, but it is not something he wants me to rely on. He wants me to stay in any position he places me in, with or without bindings. I gasp when I feel the vibrations. *When did he put a three-bar vibrating cock ring on my dick?* The sensation forces me to stay focused in order to avoid cumming. My dick had softened to a semi while Master was introducing me to a new tool, but it was quickly awakened. I breathe loudly through my mouth and moan when I discover the anal beads also vibrate.

"Safe words!" my master demands.

"Rose, petal, thorn . . ." I pant. "Petal, Master, please."

He quickly moves to turn the vibrators off, while I work on staving off my orgasm. *Fuck me!*

"Talk to me, Daniel," Master encourages, running his fingers through my long hair.

"Intense."

"Do we need to stop?"

"No, Master. I'm better prepared."

He waits a moment longer before he turns all the vibrators back on. Then he places nipple clamps on, and I hold back a curse when I realize they too vibrate. He is driving me mad! The only option I have of not being a cum whore is to fall back into subspace. Something my mind escapes to eagerly. I vaguely feel my master's hands slapping me across my ass cheeks, but soon, even that becomes irrelevant. I am free. I have achieved ultimate subspace. Time is meaningless.

The only thing that brings me back to reality is my master's firm order in my ear. "Cum, Daniel." Instantly my seed coats the X-frame and floor. I cry out, falling onto my restraints. "Rose, Master," I grunt, my legs giving out.

Quickly, my master releases my ankles, then my wrists, from my restraints and removes all toys. "Can you walk?"

"With help," I admit, leaning on him.

He takes me out of the playroom and onto his couch, where he sits me down gently. "Wait right here. I'll be only a moment." He assures before coming back with a candy bar. "Eat."

"Sorry?" I ask.

"I know we are equals right now, Daniel, but you need to eat that." He frowns, pulling me into his body.

I decide not to question him and eat the candy bar. When I am finished, I turn to him teasingly. "Want to tell me why you are messing with my diet?"

"It helps," he smiles, running his fingers up and down the side of my arm. "That was an intense session, Daniel. The risk of subdrop is high. I'm trying to prevent it."

"You think I can drop from that?" I ask in disbelief. I have heard of subdrop. It was another thing my master was constantly educating me on, though I have never fallen personally nor have I come close until today. His touch is comforting, and I know that he is using it to bring me back to reality slowly. Had he not been such a trusting, caring master, he could have made sure my sea legs had gone and sent me on my way. Instead, he is making sure the immediate dangers of a heart attack and stroke are gone by keeping a close eye on my heart rate and eye dilation.

"You almost blacked out in there," he worries aloud. "I need to make sure you are okay to drive and that your adrenaline and endorphins are regulated before you leave."

"It was a good pass out." I smile.

He gives a small laugh. "Don't care. I'm going to keep you safe through this."

"Thank you." I smile wider. "I am pleased to call you Master."

"And I am honored to have you, Daniel." He smiles before kissing my hair. I lean into him for about an hour or so before I sit up.

"You will call me in the morning," he orders.

"Yes, Master." I smile, gathering my clothes to dress. He walks me to the front door, handing me one more candy bar, knowing that I will eat it. When I get to my car, I sigh. Too damn bad my falling for him would break our contract, because if I'd let my heart, that's exactly what it would do.

1
Becoming Daniel's Master

Clayton's Point of View

I need a new sub; mine has broken our contract. He has fallen in love. God, I hate it when this happens. It makes my life complicated. Frowning, I realize I am going to have to tell him this is over. I fight back an instant headache; I'm not looking forward to this.

Picking up my phone, I leave him instructions:

Meet me at my house seven, kitchen chair, remain clothed.

I hit send, waiting for a panicked call. The overly attached ones always call, and sure enough, this is no exception. I stare at my phone, waiting for my voicemail to pick up. Yes, definitely time for a new sub.

Voicemail finally kicks in, and I dial an all-too-familiar number.

"Clayton, angel, what do I owe the pleasure?"

"Master."

"Oh, please, Clayton, I haven't been your master in a very long time. Call me Alec or I'm hanging up."

"I'm looking for a replacement, Alec." I frown, not looking forward to telling him why.

"Replacement? But I thought Bobby made you happy?"

"He fell in love." I blurt out, knowing it's going to hurt but helpless to it. At least it was me and not a master that wouldn't mind. Alec still has a chance, that's why I took Bobby to start with, to ensure when Alec was ready he had a chance at ultimate happiness, assuming I could convince

Alec's stubborn ass to mix. I figure I can get him and Bobby to play then I could nudge him toward a relationship. *One step at a time Clayton.*

"Oh," he says taken off guard, "I'm sorry to hear that Clayton." He clears his throat and I close my eyes wishing these two's timing would work out, instead of one being in a contract while the other is looking. "You're in luck. I do have some prospects for you, Untouchables who are looking for a trusting Dom outside of Chloe's playhouse. I'll warn you, they are a little *untrained*."

Alec always did like the type who knew how to please him instantly. "I was untrained, Master." I smile.

"True, but you were different somehow." Alec muses. "I'm on the hunt myself. These prospects are good, but they are not quite to my standards. You have more . . . patience." I can't help but laugh at that. Alec is not known for patience. "Meet me the day after tomorrow at eight." Alec continues. "I'll introduce you."

Hanging up the phone, I smile. This is perfect, Alec's hunting. Now I just have to figure out how to get him to accept Bobby as a sub. Assuming Bobby has not fallen too hard for me. I moan at the thought, getting through the next two hours is going to suck. But then, I too am on the hunt. My cock twitches at the idea, and I vaguely wonder if I should take just one sub this time. Maybe multiples would be nice for a change, less chance of them falling in love . . .

While I debate and wait for Bobby, I take a shower and do some light cleaning. When seven o'clock approaches I unlock my front door, knowing Bobby will be here soon and smile when I hit the hallway, hearing the front door open, always punctual. I ignore his arrival at first, letting him wait. Dreading this, I sit on my bed listening to Bobby tap his foot on the floor for a good fifteen minutes before I decide it's time and make my way to the kitchen. Normally, I would reward him for his promptness. But this was far from normal. When I sit myself down across from him, the first thing I notice is that he's been crying. This only affirms my decision to let him go, for he should not have any shame. He has done nothing but please me.

I stand and walk behind him, kneading my fingers into his tight shoulders. It's the only affection I have ever shown him, but I knew he craved it; and tonight he needs it.

"I'm sorry, Bobby, but it's time to part ways."

"Have I not pleased you well, Master?"

I give him a reassuring squeeze. "This has nothing to do with your discipline, Bobby."

"I don't understand, Master."

"You've developed forbidden feelings for me, Bobby. I've warned you of the consequences of that." He doesn't deny it; instead, he drops his head in acceptance. Moving to face him, I squeeze his hands in a reassuring manner. "You know Alec well, and you know I hold the highest respect for him. In time, Bobby, when you are ready, he is a very good contact for you, when you decide to find another."

He gives my hands an accepting squeeze and rises to his feet, thus breaking our Dom/sub connection forever, for I did not give him permission to leave. "Thank you, Clayton," he whispers, touching my cheek with teary eyes, then swiftly makes his way to my front door. His reaction was what I was hoping it to be so I call out to him.

"Bobby wait!" He turns to me, hopeful. "Alec's looking." I smile, biting my lower lip.

He lets out his breath and leans against my door. "Alec doesn't mix."

"Mix?" I ask believing he meant professional verses personal, as Bobby and Alec work together. But there's something in his eyes.

"We're dating." He shrugs. "Sort of, we're not exclusive . . . yet. We're taking it slow . . . and he hasn't told you, has he."

Fuck me! Shoe leather anyone? "Not yet, no." I frown trying to gain my composure from the shock. I knew Alec had feelings but no damn clue he finally acted on them. "But I'm sure it's just a matter of time." I assure Bobby who is looking a little pale. Honestly this is perfect, they belong together and they are halfway there on their own. "Do you mix Bobby?"

"Always wanted to try it." He shrugs looking at me with sad eyes.

"He's my best friend." I point out, ignoring his implication. "I don't want to get your hopes up but if you're willing to fight for it, I'm willing to help you."

"Why?" he asks skeptical.

"Because you two are made for each other." I smile, shrugging. "Don't deny it. We've all hung out enough, it's obvious."

"What do you have in mind?" he asks studying me.

"Give me some time." I tell him. "That is if your feelings for me won't make things awkward or hurt him."

He grins. "Let's put it this way Clayton, if I had a choice between the two of you. It'd be Alec every single time. No offense."

"None taken." I laugh in relief. "I'll call you."

He nods and says goodnight. Knowing that it will take time for Alec to come around to this, I pretend I am still in the dark about their dating relationship and send Alec a text:

What about Bobby? He's well trained.

Two days later I make my way to Alec's, arriving promptly. The moment he opens the door, I downcast my eyes. "Master."

He wraps his arms around me. "I've missed your touch, Clayton," he whispers, kissing my lips gently. "If only I didn't fall in love with you."

My touch he might miss but me not so much, we are after all best friends. I can tell he's feeling lost, partly because he's on the hunt, partly because of Bobby, so I pull him into me and hold him for a moment. Alec may have fallen into the trap of falling in love, but I denied myself from making such an error. When the time came, he admitted it to me, and we ended our Dom/sub relationship. What he wasn't expecting was for me to ask him to train me as a Dom. It took him three days to give me an answer, but when he did, he introduced me to a world beyond my wildest dreams.

He pulls away and runs his fingers through my hair. Not wanting to give away the fact I know about him and Bobby I decide to keep my eyes cast to the floor. "You are not a sub, Clayton. Stop acting like one," he snaps, walking away and toward his personal playroom. I bring my eyes up to his retreating form, following him wordlessly. "The moment we walk through these doors, you must treat me as your equal. You understand?"

"I understand, Alec."

He smiles, "Good."

"Alec."

"Yes, Clayton."

"I want more than one."

He stops, turning to me. "Are you nuts? The dynamic of multiple subs is so draining."

"Less risk of them falling in love." I shrug. "Lost two that way. Don't want it to happen again."

"Maybe you're the problem? Maybe you show too much affection?" he ponders, crossing his arms over his chest.

"I've done what you told me to do. Appreciate them, for they are giving themselves to me. One display of affection, only as a reward, never kiss them, and if you can't resist that, then at least make sure they are bound, which, by the way, I have never kissed a sub. How am I doing so far?" I snap, annoyed that he accused me of such a thing.

"Maybe you're just too irresistible for your own damn good," he mutters, turning back to the doors. "I know I thought so. Anyway, be warned. Like I said, they are untrained."

The moment we walk through the doors, we are greeted with ten subs kneeling almost naked before us. I immediately discarded four in my mind based solely on the fact that they could not stop moving. Alec had tied numbered silk belts over their torsos. I made a comment to him. "Two, five, six, and seven do not interest me." Immediately, they rise to their feet and exit the room.

I've never based my selection on looks; I found it to be too messy. I want discipline or at least for the potential as such. Yet I can't stop myself from walking over to the brunet man with shoulder-length hair, kneeling before me.

"Number Three, stand."

He does so effortlessly, keeping his eyes trained on my feet. I stand there for a good two minutes just staring at him. His eyes never leave the floor and he remains still. I'm impressed. Walking away from him, I grab the first toy in the cabinet that I see and come back to him. I trace his muscular torso with the flogger in my hand, impressed that the only movement he makes is his breathing. Then I hit him with it, and he makes the most delicious sound. However, he does break formation for just a moment before correcting his error.

"I can work with this one," I tell Alec.

"I thought you might like him Master Clayton. He does show great potential."

"Any others that might strike my interest? I really don't feel like wasting time with those who are too scared to follow rules."

"He is the most disciplined of the bunch. Please tell me. What are the things you really don't want to train?"

Turning to the subs, I use my most authoritative voice. "I demand complete and utter stillness. While I don't mind the use of bondage, I do not want you to depend on it to keep your position. If this is something you know you can't do, then you know where the doors are."

Four and Eight stand and exit the room.

I walk over to the remaining three. *How many subs do I really want out of this? Four?* I was thinking more on the lines of three. Yet, I really am not sure how long I can maintain even three. Alec is right, it's exhausting to handle more than one. Not to mention, needing to please more than one man in a night can be draining, but I really don't want to go back to just one. *Decisions, decisions.*

"I am a master of multiple subs. If you cannot handle that, I suggest you leave."

Number Ten exits the room. Three. I can work with that. "Assuming you want to come with me, know that this is a temporary arrangement unless you can prove yourself worthy."

"Yes, Master," they all say out of unison. I cringe from all of them speaking out of turn. I really do have my work cut out for me.

"Get dressed," I command, exiting the room with Alec on my heels.

"Are you sure about this?" he asks. "Number Three really would make a great solo sub."

"He has potential," I admit, walking to the kitchen and pulling out a beer.

"And the other two? You didn't even test those," he grips, grabbing a soda for himself.

"Not here," I respond, popping my can. Then the doors opens, and two of my three subs walk out of the room. I slam my beer on the counter so hard it slouches out of the can and onto my hand which only annoys me further. "Explain yourselves!" I demand, sucking the beer off my skin, approaching them.

Both realize their mistake immediately and drop to their knees, lacing their fingers behind their back. "Sorry, Master."

"You will be." I seethe, turning to Alec, "Master Alec please give them my contact information and dismiss them."

He nods, and I turn back to the playroom, where I find Number Three kneeling on the floor just as he was before, except in clothes.

"Why didn't you follow them?" I ask, approaching him.

"You didn't give the command to leave."

I stand behind him and comb my fingers through his long, soft hair. He breaks formation and leans into me, staring into my eyes for the first time. I'm taken aback at how green they are and surprised at the fear in them, before he corrects his position. "It's alright," I find myself saying. *It is?* "We can always start this way, if you'd like." *We can?*

"If it pleases you, Master."

"Why didn't you stop them?" I wonder, making my way to the other side of the room where I left the flogger.

"You didn't give us permission to speak." His voice goes straight to my cock.

"No, I didn't, did I?" I ponder out loud. He's observant. I like observant and obedient.

"What's your name, Number Three?" I ask, walking back to him, flogger in hand.

"Daniel, Master."

"Tell me, Daniel. How do you feel about becoming my sub?"

He doesn't answer me right away, and I slap the flogger in my hand.

"May I have a moment to put it in words, Master?" I nod my acceptance, waiting. "I think I feel excited the most."

"I'm asking for all of your feelings, Daniel," annoyed that I have to clarify my question.

"My apologies, Master. I feel excited, aroused, determined, and disappointed."

"Disappointed? Do I not please you in some way?" I ask with an edge of anger.

"No, Master. That's not it at all." He rushes, "It's just that, well, I want to be enough."

My eyes narrow at that. "I gave you the option to leave when I told you I wanted multiple subs."

"You did."

"Then why didn't you?"

He bravely lifts his eyes to mine. "I've never met anyone so skilled with that instrument before. It's exciting and worth the sacrifice." He casts his eyes back down. "If you'll still have me, I will make you proud."

— 21 —

I drop the instrument to the ground and walk up to him. "You want to make me proud, Daniel?"

"Yes, Master."

"Then pleasure me," I demand, freeing my swollen cock from my jeans.

His mouth is surrounding me instantly, and I have to bite my lower lip to keep from crying out while his skilled tongue works its magic. *Fuck me! This is the best damn blow job I've ever had, and that's saying something!* He swallows me down his throat and begins humming, causing me to run my fingers through his long hair and tug a little, resulting in even more moans. I begin fucking his face, and not long after he started, I find myself at my climax. "Swallow!" I demand, giving him the only warning he needs to accept my seed down his awaiting throat. I force myself not to support my weight on his shoulders as I come down from my high. *Fuck. Me.* When I pull out, he leans in to lick me clean, greedily taking every drop that I have given.

I pull back and zip my pants, moving to stand directly behind him, stroking his long hair as a reward. This time, he doesn't break formation. This man can be my undoing if I'm not careful. I realize that I cannot maintain my role as master if ever I were to have other subs in the room when he is with me. Fuck! I'm hiding from him now just to gather myself from that unbelievable orgasm! I need this guy alone. It's the only way it's going to work. Besides, knowing he wouldn't practically care for a multiple-play scenario himself gnaws on my conscious. He could easily walk away from me, and I don't want that.

"I am going to reward you well for your obedience tonight, Daniel." I smile. He did give me a reason to reward him after all. "Although I do plan on maintaining multiple subs, you did express your disinterest in it, so I will keep our sessions solo."

"Thank you, Master."

"You're time here is finished tonight. The moment you stand, we are equals. Understood?"

"Yes, Master."

"Stand," I instruct, and immediately he does so, turning to face me and looking me in the eye.

"May I have your phone?" I ask.

"Of course." He smiles, digging in his pocket, handing it to me.

I program my phone number into it along with my real first name and alias last name. "You're sure about this arrangement?"

"Yes."

"Call me tomorrow at exactly 7:00 p.m." I smile, handing his phone back to him. "I will give you my address then."

He nods and looks at the doors, raising his eyebrow in a silent question. I like the respect, even though we are equals, and answer him, "You may go."

He blushes a little, turning to leave and I follow. When we are halfway to the doors I surprise myself, stopping him by wrapping my arms around his waist. My voice works without my permission and I find myself whispering in his ear, "As your master, I want to make it clear that *all* of your orgasms are mine."

He stops, and I can hear his breathing falter, so I drop my hands down to his hardened member, smiling to myself. "Yes, Master," he manages, turning a delicious shade of pink before he walks out of the room. I give him adequate time to leave Alec's home before I join my old master for a drink.

"He's trouble, that one," Alec cautions. "Almost kept him for myself, but it's too risky. He reminded me way too much of you."

"Have you thought about having Bobby for your own?" I wonder, picking up my abandoned beer.

Alec frowns. "Clayton, I'm sure he's delicious and well trained." I smile at his compliment. "But having Bobby as my sub would be extremely complicated."

"You're making a mistake if you let him go," I warn, taking a swig. "From the little I've seen, you work well together. Got to admit, there is an untapped chemistry there." *Untapped my ass!* I want to call him out but I'm waiting for him to admit it to me.

"Clayton, we work together. Besides, I'm his boss, for fuck's sake. Tell me how that would work. It would mimic a 24/7 Dom/sub relationship, and you know how I feel about those," Alec protests.

"You could always keep us separate," I remind him, being that I am his silent partner in his Youth-In-Need center.

"And look how that turned out. I fell in love and feared I lost you," he argues. "I've made that mistake once, Clayton. I won't make it again."

"You're mistake is letting him slip through your fingers," I counter. His eyes meet mine, and I can see the discussion is over, at least for now; I'm not giving up that easily. I can also see the hint of pain. He's aware of what I am thinking, and it would mean he accepts us both moving on past each other. It's been almost two years since we broke our Dom/sub relationship and anything else that didn't resemble friendship but I know he still hangs onto the hope that I will change my mind.

Looking away, I change the subject, not wanting to dwell on painful memories. "So how untrained are these guys anyway?"

He shrugs, "They've graduated from the Untouchables, which means they understand and respect our culture, and their blood tests are updated. All off them have expressed interest in a sexual component in a male Dom. Personally, I'm going to keep searching but admittedly these are the best prospects. I just hate all the damn work."

I give him a look, wanting to bring up Bobby's name again but stop when I realize he's turned his back to me.

"Delayed gratification?" I ask instead.

He shakes his head. "All three could use help in that department." I moan. "I warned you," he chuckles.

"Yes, that you did." I agree. "What do the other's think of them?"

"Chloe and Rachel have had their fun." He shrugs turning back to me but still avoiding eye contact. "Kyle showed interest in Daniel but changed his mind. I think he might have his eyes on a long term sub whose contract just expired with Chloe. He seems very hopeful."

I give a small laugh, knowing Kyle the sub must be smoking if he's willing to pass up Daniel. It doesn't escape my attention that Alec's fidgeting a little, which is unusual for him but I chalk it up to nothing more than being uncomfortable about Bobby, so I don't pry. "I have tickets to the game." I smile. "Want to go?"

"Sure, on one condition."

"Anything."

"Careful, Clayton," he warns with a glare. I just wink at him. "Trust my background checks on these guys, okay." He shrugs, throwing me a curveball. "Don't look at me like that. The less you know about your subs' personal lives, the better."

"You got a point, never care to know who they fuck in their personal lives." I laugh, giving him a verbal jab about Bobby even if he's not aware of it, adding. "Guess it's fair they know me as an alias."

"Thank you."

"I trust you." I smile. "So six o'clock."

He smiles. "See you then."

2
Moving On

Clayton's Point of View

"Boss, Alec is on Line One," my assistant, Mike, buzzes in, interrupting me. Normally, I would be pissed about this, but Alec is on a very short list that Mike has the right to disturb me, no matter what I'm doing.

Smiling to myself, I pick up the phone. "Hello, Alec."

"Clayton," he answers, and by his tone, I can tell he's debating something.

"What's on your mind?" I ask, glaring at Mike walking in the office, interrupting me further with a delivery that I need to sign for personally.

"You know me too well, Clayton." He laughs as I take the signature pad from Mike's hand.

"Just as you know me." I smile, handing Mike a pair of scissors, which he takes and proceeds to open the package.

"It's Bobby," Alec admits while I sign my name.

"What about him? You change your mind?" I ask, watching Mike lift the lid and I try to avoid gagging from the smell of dead roses covered in maggots accompanied with a dead rat. He slams the lid back on quickly while fighting back nausea.

"I want him to join Angels of Justice," Alec whispers, and I freeze. After some silence, he speaks again, "Clayton?"

"I'm here," I whisper. "Give me a moment," I add, quickly putting him on hold and looking up at Mike, who rolls his eyes at me.

He snatches the box and signature pad from my desk. "Sorry, Boss, I'll dispose of this." He cringes. "And don't worry. I'll hold your calls and cancel all your appointments," he adds, walking to the door. "Why on earth you two aren't dating is beyond me," he chuckles. "Do yourself a favor, Boss. Leave through the back entrance. Your next appointment is Cassandra."

"Thanks," I smile "You keep treating me so well you might get a raise."

"If I have to keep deterring Cassandra, I am going to demand one." He laughs and then frowns. "Just kidding, Boss." *And you had a backbone for thirty seconds. Had you not retracted, I would have given you one.* "Drive safely," he adds.

I quickly gather up my things and pick the phone back up. "I'll be there in fifteen minutes," I tell Alec before hanging up abruptly and exiting out of my private passage; grateful for it at times like this when I really want to avoid horrid clients. True to my word, I am walking through Alec's front door exactly fifteen minutes later.

"You're not talking me out of it, Clayton." Alec sighs the moment I sit down on the couch next to him, grabbing his hand.

"Are you fighting against him on a personal level because he's the one?" I ask timidly.

"I think he could be," Alec answers sadly. "But I thought the same with you once, which is why I'm not confident about risking it. He doesn't know that I'm a member of Angels of Justice, if he can't accept it then what's the point of trying anything personal."

I can't stop the selfish pain, Angels of Justice is something that Alec and I do as a team, a Dom/sub team and to hear that he wants Bobby, hurts. "You're ending us." I whisper in a pained voice.

"We ended us a long time ago, Clayton. You ended it," he reminds me. "And I think Bobby would be good for this cause. We had this case at work. This kid was so black and blue. Turns out he ran away from his step-father. I got the police involved. But Bobby's reaction, wanting to do more to that low life . . . he'd be perfect for this, Clayton."

"So you're replacing me?" I ask, rubbing small circles on his hand trying to accept the hurt.

"No," he whispers. "No matter how unhealthy it is, I can't do that."

"So you want to *add* Bobby?" I ask, biting my lower lip, half relieved, half tortured, I don't want to share him.

"Yes."

"I know you're dating him Alec, he told me." He turns away from me. "Does he know you love him?" I ask, causing him to snap his eyes to mine. I keep his stare, letting him know that I am aware of his feelings, that I know he would only allow another to join us if he truly cared for the man.

"So he can run like you did?" Alec growls.

"Bobby isn't me." I smile softly. "He's not afraid of commitment."

"Please, Clayton, give me some time here." Alec begs of me. "I'll tell him, if he can handle this. But when he's ready for a new Dom in his personal life, it won't necessarily be me. Just as it is with you, I will be his 'Grand Master'." He glares at my frown. "I know your feelings about it, Clayton. Keep them to yourself. As I said, it's complicated."

Silence falls between us. "We would never work, you know," I eventually argue.

"So you keep telling me." He sighs, "But we never really tried."

"I can't lose you, Alec. You mean too much."

"When will you admit that you love me, Clayton?" he asks. I quickly drop his hand and look away. He takes a deep breath before he speaks again. "If he's accepting, we will initiate Bobby on Friday."

"I'll be here," I agree, standing up.

"Clayton, wait," Alec calls, jumping to his feet, grabbing my wrist and pulling me to him. "Don't stay away from me like last time, please," he whispers in my ear. "It killed when I thought I lost you. Don't walk away, please. Let our friendship be strong enough for this."

"You love Bobby, Alec. What does this matter?" *Why does this hurt? This is what I wanted. Why can't I breathe?*

"It matters, Angel." He whispers tenderly, kissing the skin on my neck. "Promise me you won't shut me out again. I know you've carved a piece of your heart out for me, just as I have you."

"It's not enough, Alec," I whisper as tears fall out of my eyes, realizing this is the closest I've ever come to admitting my feelings to him.

"I know, Angel, I do." He whispers, gently running his fingers down my chest. "Please, Clayton, I need you in my life." He opens his hand showing me the scar that I made when we vowed to always be in each other's lives in some way.

I turn in his arms, meeting his eyes. "It hurts you, Alec, which is the last thing I ever want to do."

"It hurts more when you keep your distance." He frowns. "Please, you said it wouldn't change things."

"Yet *you* want to add another sub to Angels of Justice," I counter.

"Are you jealous, Clayton?" he asks, raising an eyebrow.

"Yes," I admit openly. The thought of sharing my master right before my eyes . . . "But if this is what you need, who am I to deny you?" I ask, lacing my fingers in his, pressing our scars together. "I'll stay as your sub Grand Master, but only part time. Only when you need me. I'm sorry, but anything other than that hurts too damn much."

"I understand," he answers, swallowing back tears.

"I should go," I whisper.

"Please stay," he pleads, pulling me tighter, letting me feel his erection.

"Alec," I whisper in argument.

"Please, it's the last time we can ever be, Clayton. We have no personal commitments to anyone else, Bobby and I aren't yet exclusive, but when I admit my feelings . . . if he doesn't reject me, it will be too late."

"You love me more," I whisper, decrypting his omission.

"Always," he growls, before crashing his lips to mine. His taste is always so amazing, so perfect, and I want to get lost in it, in him. But when he breaks away from my lips and kisses my neck while his hands fight with my shirt, I plead with him.

"Alec, please."

"Please, Clayton?" he asks, impatiently lifting my shirt over my head.

"This is going to hurt you in the morning," I warn. "We don't feel the same."

He grunts in frustration, pushing our hard cocks together. "Tell me you don't want this, Angel, and I will stop. Tell me that you don't want us to be us one last time and we won't."

Our eyes meet. I barely register the task of ripping his clothes off as he leads our way back to his bedroom. By the time we make it there, we are both naked, and I find myself falling on his bed while remaining lip-locked.

Our hands travel down each other's familiar muscles, and we both moan when he grips both of our cocks in his hand, starting the perfect pace.

"Goddamn, Alec, my angel, feels so fucking good!" I gasp, bucking my hips as my eyes roll in the back of my head.

His lips are at my ear instantly, "This is our last time, Clayton. Please be patient with me."

I turn to kiss him, "You've taught me well, my angel. I can hold out as long as you want me to." I moan as our tongues meet between us before our lips collide again. He pulls back with a smirk, gripping my hips and flipping me upside down. Before I can react with much more than a gasp, his dick is hovering over my lips, and mine is being swallowed down his throat. *Fuck!* I open my mouth willingly and wrap my lips around his perfect mushroom head. I slowly take him in. I know when I am delivering the perfect amount of suction when I feel him release a deep throat moan that vibrates my cock. I smirk and start my tongue dance that always drives him mad, soon my wet cock is hitting cold air as a beautiful symphony of curses slip through his swollen lips that ends with, "Best fucking blow jobs of my life!" I can't help but lift him up and chuckle softly. Which causes him to grunt and begin his magic on me, soon I'm the one cursing, needing to take him back in my mouth if only for a distraction.

When I can't take anymore, I signal him to stop by gently sucking his swollen balls in my mouth. He drops my dick as he begins putting weight on his knees, worshiping my body with his tongue as he kisses his way up my stomach and starts to pinch my nipples while kissing me upside down. I lace my fingers through his dark brown hair enjoying his teasing before I drop my head back and flip over, taking his dripping cock back into my mouth. After a few moments, he grips me by the arms and lifts me up to his lips. We kiss for a while before he leans forward causing me to lie down on my back.

I moan when I see his muscular arm reach for the nightstand. Not much longer, the distinct sound of a lube cap is being popped, and his cold wet fingers are at my entrance. He looks at me with a raised eyebrow, I whisper my consent, moaning when I feel him slip in two fingers. By the time the third stretches me, I am close to losing all coherent thought. He senses my relaxed state and switches out his fingers for his cock. While he slowly presses into me I wrap my legs around his hips, allowing deeper access. Our dark blue, lustful eyes meet, and the air around us fills with passion and a hint of tension from unspoken words. I plead with my eyes that he can see that I care for him, that he knows I would never want to hurt him, that I surrender to him. When it gets too much, he lets out a deep throat growl and starts to pound into me.

"Fuck! Yes, Alec!" I gasp in pleasurable surprise. He moans, shifting me slightly. "Yes, Angel, right there! Please, fuck me hard right *fucking* there!" I growl dragging my nails down his scarred back, loving the feeling of the ride, truly amazed that no other man has ever been able to make me feel this fucking good in my entire life, honestly believing that no man could ever come half as close, especially to my heart. After what feels like hours passing, I cry out as the most intense orgasm of my life screams for release, "Fuck, Alec, please angel, I need to cum."

"So soon, my angel?" he asks in a pained voice, slowing slightly.

"I'm so sorry," I whisper. "But we can't go on forever."

He closes his eyes to my words and orders in the most painful growl I have ever heard him make, pounding me faster, harder, "Cum for me, Clayton!" I can't deny his demand as my trapped dick releases my fluids while my ass clinches around his pulsing cock. I can't see anything but white. As I am riding my high to Mars, I barely hear the whisper, "I love you, Clayton. All you have to do is ask Angel, and I'm yours forever."

I shake my head as the earth begins to fall around me. *It's your imagination. He loves you, but he's not in love with you. He wants Bobby.*

He pulls out gently and sits up, keeping his back to me.

"Would you like me to stay, Alec, or would it be easier if I left?" I ask, rolling onto my side, watching him.

His body is slightly trembling, but his voice is steady. "I think it best if you go, Clayton. I will see you Friday. Please, don't let this come between our friendship."

I pull him to me and kiss him with all the feeling I have for him, when I break away, my lips are on his ear. "It won't. I swear. But know this, the moment we add Bobby, we are no longer each other's angels. The choice is yours, Alec. I just want you to know my terms."

"Then I guess this is goodbye, Angel," he whispers as tears fall from his eyes and his lips press to mine. "But hello, Clayton. Yes?"

"Always, Alec. Always."

⇒ 31 ⇐

3
Cupid

Clayton's Point of View

At Bobby's initiation it was more obvious to me than ever that him and Alec were meant to be. I tried to mention it again at another game but Alec shut me down quickly and filled me with more baseball statics than I ever really wanted to know. So after some debating I have decided on a more radical approach, I'm setting Alec up. He just doesn't know it yet.

Confident, I call Bobby and tell him my plan. I won't lie, it took a little convincing, considering we both know it's drastic and risky. After promising him I would take all the heat if this went sour and assuring him that he could play the shocked card, Bobby eventually comes around. Smiling, I tell him to meet me at Alec's.

Determined to make this happen I head over to Alec's place. I knock on his front door and immediately cast my eyes down but force them upward. I am on a mission, and my slips won't help this. When he opens the door, I smile and meet his eyes. "Alec."

He raises his eyebrow at me, as though he is surprised I didn't slip and call him master, but invites me into his home anyway. "How are you, Clayton? What brings you by?" I make sure to keep his front door open so that I can see through his storm door, hoping he doesn't notice, before I make my way to the kitchen and grab two beers from his fridge handing him one. "Why do I have a feeling I'm not going to like this much?" he asks, looking at the can. Alec rarely drank but keeps his fridge stocked for company.

"How's the hunt going?" I ask, popping the top of my can and grabbing a seat on a nearby barstool. I can hear him sigh audibly before he follows my example sitting down next to me. He doesn't answer my question. We both know his impatience with training makes finding a sub difficult and his flexing jaw tells me he's figured out why I'm here. "Bobby's perfect for you, Alec," I argue again after a long stretch of silence.

"Is he?" Alec's voice cracks. "Cause I thought that about you once upon a time."

"Alec," I whisper, taking his scarred hand into mine. "What we had, have," I find myself correcting, "is something beyond special." He squeezes my hand and I can see he's fighting tears. "But we've been through this; it's not enough. You know that." He squeezes his eyes shut and releases our connection. "Alec, please, you mean so much to me. We still have each other in our lives, unless you don't want that."

His eyes shoot open in shock and he stares at me. "I need you in my life, Clayton. I've told you that."

"I'm right here," I assure him, hating we are having this conversation again but knowing it's necessary. "But if my presence prevents you from happiness, Alec, I don't see how it's fair I stay."

"It doesn't," he assures me in a firm tone.

I find myself flinching, casting my eyes to the table. I'm grateful for his resistance to my offer; it would kill me to walk away. Trying to hide the slip, I turn my attention to my beer. "Then why the hell are you holding out on Bobby?" I ask. "You can't be blind enough to not know that he's in love with you too."

"Love doesn't fit into the playroom, Clayton. I thought you and I both agree on that," Alec snaps. I know he's right, I'm pushing against my own standards. But I want him to know unconditional love. And I know the only way he can do that is to accept someone both inside and outside the playroom. And Bobby and him have this chemistry . . .

"You know why I took Bobby on as a sub?" I ask, trying to keep on track.

"No," Alec frowns, taking a deep swig of his beer.

"It wasn't to hurt you, Alec," I assure him. "It was to help you."

"What the hell are you talking about?" he seethes.

"I was helping him wait for you," I respond. "You weren't ready when he was looking, and I was damned if he found a new Dom that would risk you losing him. I figured that if I filled that role for him, it would help both of you come together in the end."

"He fell in love with you, Clayton!" Alec growls.

"You rather it have been some other Dom?" I ask, "Kyle perhaps? Damn it Alec he told me he'd sign another contract with Bobby, one that allowed it to get personal. Where would that have left you?"

He's quite for a moment, staring at his beer. "Do you love him?"

"Not the way you do."

"Typical answer for you, Clayton," Alec snaps.

"He doesn't love me the way he loves you, Alec," I argue. "We are best friends, for fucks sake. We mirror each other in some ways. You trained me to be a Dom, Alec. You have to see the similarities here."

"You think he is deflecting?" Alec asks in surprise.

"Unconsciously, yes," I respond. "Which is why he never really admitted any feelings to me." I turn to face him full on. "Alec, he's the one you've been waiting for." I can see the protest in his eyes, wanting to tell me I'm a stubborn fool. "He can love you unconditionally, Alec" I whisper, hurt filtering in my voice. We both knew that was why I held back. "You deserve unconditional love." Tears streak down Alec's face, and I quickly wipe them away. Bobby's knock distracts him to the storm door, and Alec's eyes snap back to mine as though I had just slapped him in the face.

Ignoring his silent accusation of betrayal I let Bobby inside. "Glad you decided to join us, Bobby." I smile, taking him by the hand and leading him into Alec's playroom. Alec watches in pure shock as my drastic plan unfolds before him. I ask Bobby to accept me as his master for one last night, and he agrees. Then I order him to kneel in the center of Alec's playroom. He obeys me effortlessly.

I leave to reenter the kitchen where Alec hasn't moved. "Will you join us, Master Alec?"

"Angel?" he whispers, swallowing more tears.

I approach him and wrap my arms around his beautiful body. "He's the one, Alec. You are both ready. Please join us. Embrace your happiness."

"Are you sure?" he asks, intertwining our fingers and squeezing with all his strength.

I meet his eyes, knowing I have to be strong. I have to do this; he deserves this. "I'm sure," I respond, causing him to drop his forehead onto my chest.

We stand there frozen for a few moments, before he lifts his head and releases his grip to dry his eyes. "So be it." With that, he walks into the playroom. I follow him inside and stand in front of Bobby.

"You have been a very pleasing sub, Bobby." I smile. "Despite that you and I have ended our contract, I would ask that you allow me to give you one final reward." I step out of the way, allowing Bobby and Alec to stand in front of each other. "I have one of the most skilled Dom's looking for a well-trained sub, Bobby. Would you be interested in being his?"

"Yes, Master Clayton," Bobby replies.

"Master Alec," I address, "Bobby is a very disciplined sub. I can give you a list of his limits if you are willing to accept him as yours."

Alec's eyes flash to mine one last time before he directs his attention to Bobby. "I would be willing."

I smile. "Then it's settled." Without another word, I leave the playroom and finish my beer. Both of them following after me a short while later.

The tension in the room is thick, and I break it by pulling out two tickets to tonight's game. "Starts in a few hours." I shrug, ignoring Alec's glare of being set up. "You two enjoy." I wink, heading for the door.

"I love you, Clayton," Alec responds, stopping me in my tracks. I turn to him slowly, unsure what to do. "You want me to move past you and find happiness, then I will," he continues calmly, "but I will be damned if I don't get this out in the open for both of you to hear." Bobby's face is starting to pale, and Alec's is set in stone. I stand in silence, trying to find words. This is something that I'd rather not have verbalize but obviously Alec needs it. "Bobby," Alec continues saving me from a response, "I am not trying to hurt you. I just need it known that I love Clayton."

Bobby gives a half smile. "I know that, Alec. But does that mean you can't ever love me?"

"No," he responds, reaching for Bobby's hand. "But I can't have unspoken feelings if we are going to try this."

Bobby gives him a nod. "I can respect that. Since we are being brutally honest here, I love him too." I find myself squirming a little, but they don't seem to notice. "Alec," Bobby continues, "I know I could love you more."

Then he leans into Alec's ear. I can see the shock of whatever words he says, and then I see the kiss. My heart stings at the sight of it, but I know I am doing the right thing. Figuring they are distracted, I take my cue to leave and go to my car, praying I did the right thing for Alec's heart.

4
Master of Multiples

Clayton's Point of View

It's been three months since I took on my new subs. Daniel has surpassed my expectations by far and has rapidly become my favorite. I find that he's the only one I cannot bring myself to gag because the beautiful sounds he makes go straight to my cock. The other two are more of a headache, and I'm beginning to wonder if they have grown feelings for each other. If so, I will be forced to let them go.

When I started this new project, I had two introductory meetings. One with Shawn and Wade and the other with Daniel; both sessions started as usual. My subs were clothed and told the rules. My three biggest pet peeves were failing with safe word usage, falling in love, and being cum whores. The rest I could work with. The sessions did not end the same however. I found myself dismissing Shawn and Wade easily after they agreed to my terms and I agreed to theirs. Daniel's, on the other hand, ended slightly differently. I had just stated my rules and we established his safe words.

"Do you have any terms of your own, Daniel?" I ask. It's a general question in these types of things.

"Terms, Master?"

"Things you absolutely hate," I clarify. "As your Dom, my duty is to pleasure you, Daniel, not torture you."

He ponders the question for a moment before he answers, "Handcuffs are always uncomfortable. While I don't mind being restrained, I hate the pinch of handcuffs."

"Anything else?"

"Not being able to pleasure my master every chance I get."

I glare at him for a moment, but there is no cockiness in his voice and he isn't smiling. "I don't normally allow that during the first meeting," I respond evenly.

"Master. May I ask you something?"

"Go on," I respond, half curious.

"Would it be too bold of me to ask why you are taking on new subs?"

"My last one broke the rules," I respond. "He fell in love."

"I see." He's quiet for a moment before looking at me. "Will you break the first meeting rule for me?" he asks, his eyes almost pleading before he catches himself and casts them down to the floor.

"It pleases you to pleasure me?"

"Yes, Master."

I want to badly but I decide against it. I did not allow my other subs to do this; he will not be an exception. I did however concede just a little. Standing up, I walk behind his chair and begin to lazily comb my fingers through his long hair. "When you go home tonight, I want you to think of all the ways you will please me, and when you cum, I want you to scream my name."

"Your name, Master?" he asks, surprised.

I tug on the roots of his hair. "Do not question me!"

"Yes, Master, when I cum tonight, I will be screaming your name."

"Good, now go," I growl, releasing him. I'm surprised that he doesn't rush for the door, but he does get up to leave.

"Master?"

"Yes, Daniel?"

"May I call you while I do it?" he asks, again without cockiness.

Fuck me! "Yes, Daniel, you may call me."

That night was the first of many of phone nights with Daniel. I had never in my life shared a Dom/sub relationship like this one, and I was quickly becoming addicted. I was getting annoyed with myself that every time he spoke to me, my dick twitched.

Frustrated, I concentrated more on my other subs, ignoring my suspicions that they were falling for each other, trying to make sure that I didn't make Alec's mistake. I told myself it was necessary because they were the weakest links in this whole mess, and they had very little discipline. Shawn was the first to disappoint, shortly followed by Wade. It was frustrating, to say the least, especially when they didn't seem to feel shame or guilt in their actions; although they acted as such.

The first time Daniel lost control, he gasped in horror, shocked that his body betrayed him, and he blushed dark pink. "I'm sorry, Master. You deserve better." Normally I would have kicked him out as punishment, reminded him of our contract and demanded a renewal, just as I had with Shawn and Wade, but I couldn't bring myself to do so. Not the first time. Instead, I'm finding myself standing behind him, combing my fingers through his long hair, while he tries to hold back his sobs.

"I can tell it was an accident and you feel shame, yes?" I respond calmly.

"Yes, Master," he answers with a cracked voice.

"Why didn't you use a safe word, Daniel?" I frown.

"I was enjoying it," he whispers in shame.

"Your safe words shouldn't just be used for displeasure and pain, Daniel. If you know you will disappoint me, then I suggest you have me stop before you reach your breaking point," I demand, tugging at his hair.

"Yes, Master. I'm sorry, Master."

"Get dressed, Daniel. We are done for tonight. I will not let you off easy for this," I add, frowning to myself because I know I already have. I promised myself to be harder on him, to treat him just as equally as Shawn and Wade, but that was a promise that was going to prove to be difficult to keep.

By the six month marker, I realized that I needed to drop Shawn and Wade. Although they had come a long way, I was not getting the same satisfaction out of them as I was with Daniel, and I knew that they deserved a better master than me. When I broke the news to them, they both seemed disappointed, thanked me and left holding hands. I frowned at that. They knew better. That's when I swore off multiple subs.

I postponed my next session with Daniel, using the time to redo the playroom for just him. I even went as far as buying new tools that had his name on them. I tried to convince myself I did it to reward him, to let him know that his submission was appreciated; but at the back of my mind, I had this fleeting thought that it was something more, something I did not

— 39 —

quite understand, just as I didn't understand my desire on the first day to claim all of his orgasms. I've never done that before. I really didn't care how many times my subs jacked off when they weren't with me. And I sure the hell didn't care who they fucked as long as it wasn't each other and they displayed updated test results to me every session. I never asked Daniel to do so. I greedily claimed his orgasms and trusted that he obeyed. I was going to have to correct this error. He need only to be loyal to me in my home, nowhere else.

Frowning, I dial his number.

"Hello?"

"Daniel?"

"Yes, Master." That was my cue that he was alone and able to talk. If he called me Clayton, I would give him a set time to call me back.

"I need to apologize to you, Daniel," I start, noticing his breathing change but he knows better than to speak, which only causes me to smile. "I realize that I've attempted to claim you outside of my house, and the more I think about it, the more I believe it is unfair to you."

"I don't find it unfair, Master."

"Daniel, I've asked that we stay exclusive. You deserve the right to date."

"My personal life doesn't give me that luxury, Master," he informs me and I can tell he is frowning. "I'd like to keep our current arrangement, if that is okay with you."

"No, Daniel, it's not. Our arrangement will be changing." His breath hitches, but he remains quiet. "Meet me at my house on Friday, seven, usual position but in my living room. I'll explain then."

"Yes, Master," he answers in a strong, almost forced voice. I almost feel bad for making him squirm, but I am pleased that he didn't cry or beg. He was staying emotionally detached, just the way I like it, except he refuses to date. I frown at that, wondering how much of his personal life was getting in the way and how much he did it just to please only me. I push the thought aside. What he did and did not do in his own personal time was not my business. If he wants only to be satisfied by my caring touch, who am I to argue?

Friday approaches slowly, and I can't help the excitement that our new toys are bringing every time the UPS man comes to drop them off. I have the room prepared by Thursday, and when Friday comes, it's all I could do to keep my emotions in check when I hear Daniel walk through my front door. I remain in my room, giving him time to strip naked and get into position. When I finally emerge, I can feel the tension in the atmosphere. He's worried. Smirking, I stand behind him and comb my fingers through his long hair. He falls out of formation and leans into me, looking into my eyes. I notice his aren't puffy. He hadn't been crying; he was still staying emotionally detached, just as I should be.

"I've made a change, Daniel," I start feeling him tense underneath my touch. Smiling, I continue. "Open the drawer of the end table," I instruct. He shuffles over on his knees and opens the drawer. "Stand up, take the flogger from the drawer, and inspect it. You may be my equal after you do so."

I watch him stand and take the flogger, turning it over, freezing the moment he sees his name. I watch his body tense, and then he abruptly turns to me.

"I don't understand."

"It's your favorite, yes?"

"Yes," he answers cautiously.

"Follow me," I instruct, weary of his cautiousness at this point. When we get to the playroom, I smile encouragingly, "Close your eyes, Daniel."

He lifts an eyebrow at me for a moment, which is allowable as an equal, and then follows my instruction. I take him by the hand and walk him over to the cabinet. "Open the doors Daniel." I can tell once again he is surprised. I have never let anyone see my personal cabinet before.

He opens them and stares at the tools hanging inside. I find myself holding my breath, waiting for his reaction. "May I?" he asks, reaching.

I shrug trying to breathe normally, "Of course."

He studies a few pieces, each has his name inscribed, and then brings his attention to the room. It's a different color than before and all the equipment is new. "What about the others?"

"What others?" I ask, unable to resist a smirk.

His eyes meet mine, and his jaw gapes open for just a moment before he closes it. "You mean?"

"I'm your only master, and you are my only sub," I answer, trying to keep my excitement from showing.

— 41 —

"May I ask why?" he questions, replacing the last piece of equipment he had been holding.

"You have pleased me the most."

He drops to his knees instantly. "Thank you, Master."

Just when I thought that our relationship couldn't get more perfect, Daniel surprises me. From that night onward and for years to come, he relaxes into a new form of submission that I haven't had the pleasure of experiencing as a Dom. I knew the level existed; I was able to achieve it myself when I was Alec's sub, but to have someone give themselves so completely to me . . . I barely use bondage anymore; it's unnecessary. Over the years, Daniel very rarely disappoints me, leaving me with the desire of more each and every time. I force myself to keep our meetings at once a week, but I crave more. I want him daily, and to my shock and surprise, within the past six months, my fantasies are beginning to involve Daniel in not such a submissive state. But all good things, they must end.

5
Unworthy

Daniel's Point of View

I'm being punished. I am kneeling here in this cold room, naked, next to a no-name male who is also kneeling naked at my side. It is my fault that he is here, for I am a failure. I have failed my master and this is my punishment.

~Six Weeks Ago~

I had been pleasured by my master's skilled hands for hours; the feel of his touch on my body is divine. My cock is hard and leaking. It's taking every bit of concentration I have not to cum. I'm exhausted. I've thought about safe wording, but I fear I will leave unsatisfied, and I am not allowed to satisfy myself without his permission. No, I need to endure this pleasurable torture, and I will be rewarded.

I feel my master untie me. "Crawl on your knees to the middle of the floor," he instructs in an authoritative tone. I do as he says, crawling across the padded floor, and wait.

When he approaches, I can't help but lick my lips as his pre-cum drips to the floor wasted. I want to taste him, I want to pleasure him, to be pleasured by him.

"Open your mouth, Daniel," he demands. Instantly I am rewarded with his cock in my mouth. I hum around him, working my tongue around his flesh, delivering the perfect suction, causing him to moan and gasp while pulling on my hair. I'm aroused, too aroused, I need to calm myself, but I can't . . . shame washes over me the moment I lose control and spill my essence onto his calf. He pulls out of my mouth instantly in surprise.

"I'm sorry, Master. Please," I cry, staring at the floor.

"Get your clothes and go," he replies coldly, turning his back to me. I do as he says.

~Four Weeks Ago~

Two weeks pass without a single instruction from my master. But the moment the text message comes, shame washes over me, as I relive my failure in my head. I need to apologize.

"Delayed gratification," my master states, as he strokes my hard cock, two days later, after we renewed our contract. "It's a skill really, one that I thought you had mastered," he growls.

I don't reply as I lean against the chains that have me standing before him. I've lost the privilege to apologize with words, so I do my best to express myself with every privileged touch he allows. My purpose here tonight is to endure his skills and not cum. If I am good, I will be allowed to pleasure him.

For the past two hours, I had fought my body's natural instinct as he brought me on edge and left me there. I was beginning to regain my confidence. That is, until he brought out my favorite toy.

"This will end your punishment, Daniel," he tells me, slapping the leather across the left cheek of my ass. I fight to hold back so hard that I am screaming, begging for my release, but he denies me as he continues his pleasurable assault on my skin. Tears begin to spill over my cheeks, and in that moment, I know I am going fail him. I scream out my safe word, and my body's essence spills out of me. Almost immediately, he lowers me to the floor, removing his equipment. He doesn't say a word as he places my clothes next to me and exits the room. I sit there broken for a moment, feeling nothing but shame and guilt. I know he deserves better than this, better than me.

~Two Weeks Ago~

Relief washes over me the moment I check my caller ID and see my master's name displayed on the screen. Unfortunately, it is completely replaced by fear the moment I answer my phone.

"Daniel?"

"Yes Clayton." I answer, letting him know I can't talk.

"Meet me at my house at 7:15 sharp. Sit in a kitchen chair and remain clothed."

It was the first time he has asked me to stay clothed since our first meeting together. I knew this was bad. By the time I am sitting in his kitchen chair, I'm a ball of nerves. He studies me for the longest time, not saying a single word, which makes it so much worse.

"I'm sorry," I eventually crack.

"You don't have permission to speak to me, Daniel," he warns.

I nod my head and wait.

"I'm not sure what to do," he admits. "You disappointed me twice in a roll, Daniel. The second time, however, you used your safe word before you lost control. I don't punish the usage of safe words. You know that." Tears begin to streak down my face as his words hit my eardrums, thick with disappointment and disgust. "You also know that you do not have the permission to cum inside or outside these walls unless I tell you to," he growls. "Tell me, Daniel, what do you feel?"

"Shame," I answer instantly. "I'm a failure."

"Yes, that you are," he confirms. My tears fall faster. "Do you have any new stresses in your personal life I should be aware of?"

"Nothing I can't handle."

"Obviously you are wrong on that," he snaps, then sighs. "I've been punishing you by keeping you away, Daniel. You don't seem to be able to make it two weeks without my touch. In this new contract, I'm increasing our sessions," he states, "Work your personal life around me if you want this to continue. We normally meet once a week. I think that we need to meet twice. Is this acceptable?"

"Yes, Master."

He stands, "Get on your knees."

I follow his instruction immediately clasping my hands behind my back; he unzips his jeans and displays himself to me. "Pleasure me," he demands. I instantly swallow him down my throat, sucking and swallowing while I swirl my tongue, giving him maximum amount of pleasure. He doesn't hold himself back, quickly falling victim to my talented tongue. "Swallow!" he cries as his cum coats the back of my throat. I greedily suck every last drop out of him before I release him from my lips.

"Stand." I rise to my feet, keeping my eyes trained on the floor. "Go home, Daniel, and when you get there, strip naked and call me. I want your hands free. Use the earpiece I gave you."

I do my best to keep disappointment from showing as he steps aside, giving me no reward, no affection that I truly crave. I exit his house slowly, but the moment I am out of his sight, I break down and cry. Not wanting to fail him further, I go directly home, strip naked and call him with my earpiece as he instructed.

"I want you to touch yourself, Daniel." I do as he says. "Now stroke slowly." I let out a small hiss, I am still sensitive and aroused from having the privilege of pleasuring him tonight. "Don't pick up your pace," he warns after some time and the desire to do so becomes known. I force myself to stay slow. "Good, I can tell by your breathing that you are being a good sub." As I continue to stroke myself, he begins to talk dirty to me, after twenty minutes of this slow pace, I'm whimpering from being on edge, trying to hold off my orgasm while I continue to stroke myself.

"Stop. Drop your dick and lace your fingers behind your head," he instructs. I can't help the cry of agony that escapes me as I do what he tells me. "You're a dirty cum whore, Daniel. You do not deserve to cum tonight."

Tears spill down my face, "Yes, Master."

"Careful Daniel, I have not given you permission to speak. Now stay on the line. I want to hear you suffer through the blue balls," he states through a smirking tone. He does not help the situation in the slightest as he continues his dirty talk. When my breathing finally stills to a pace of his liking, he instructs me to meet him at his house two days from now and warns me not to seek any release until then.

The next two sessions are torturous, as I am allowed to pleasure him, but he refused to let me release. I was able to control myself though. I wasn't sure, nor would I admit, if it was his touch that was getting me so hot I couldn't control my urges, or if my personal life was somehow getting in the way. Either way, it left me with a lot of running, as I tried to deal with my sexual frustration.

The third and final punishment session is set for tonight. I wait for my master like an eager whore, unable to achieve even the edges of subspace. He keeps me waiting for almost an hour before he makes his appearance. He approaches me from behind, running his fingers through my hair. I break formation to lean into him. He smiles down at me. "If you're good, I will let you cum tonight." I can't help the spark in my eye at the thought of finally having a release. He gives me a small chuckle. "I take it you want to be good?"

"I want to please you, Master, make you proud," I answer falling back into formation.

He hums his approval, walking away from me, only to return with some leather cuffs. "Stand," he orders. I obediently rise to my feet. He restrains my wrists behind my back before coming around to face me. Then he does something unexpected; he kisses me. I gasp in surprise, and he pulls back a few inches. "Do you want to safe word, Daniel?"

"No, Master," I breathe, and his eyes flash to mine while he slowly leans back to my lips. The moment our lips touch I'm on fire, I want to touch him, I *need* to touch him, and I let out a whimper because the damn restraints won't let me. He seems to understand my predicament, pulling away. "No, Daniel, you can't touch."

"Yes, Master," I sigh, keeping my eyes to the ground.

He smacks my ass for talking out of turn. "Look at me," he demands. I do so, only to be assaulted by his intense stare and his lush lips. The flames return, and my body gets too excited, too worked up. This was new. After three years of being his sub, he was giving me a part of him that I didn't know I wanted or needed until this moment. There was no going back for me; I wanted this forever. For the first time in three years, I let a fleeting thought bring hope, *This could become something more.* I'm so distracted by the idea I lose touch with reality and my body betrays me.

The instant he feels it, his eyes harden in anger and he chastises me. *Fuck!* I don't dare move or speak when he steps away. "This isn't going to work, Daniel," he all but cries, and I can tell he's trying to keep his emotions at bay. He walks behind me, releasing my arms. "It's best if you go and don't return."

"No, Master, please, no," I beg, dropping to my knees. "I'll do anything. Please, don't leave me." Tears are streaking down my face, and I make a daring move of making eye contact as I continue to beg. Now that he's shared every part of his body with me, I crave more. But if I can't have more, I at least need him; whatever he is willing to give me I need.

"Silence!" he yells and I do my best to keep my dry heaving sobs at bay, stilling my tongue from pleading. "You don't know what you are asking for, Daniel." He frowns, keeping his distance. "I'm afraid at this point, the only way to express to you how to act is by showing you."

My stomach twists in knots as his words wash over me. *I've failed him; he wants another.*

"Are you willing to endure such a harsh punishment, Daniel? Or do you think it best if you just leave?" he growls in frustration.

"I don't want to leave you, Master. I want to please you," I answer, maintaining eye contact.

"If you can't take it, then know that it will be the last time you will ever see me," he warns.

"I can take it."

"I don't want to do this, Daniel. We should end this now," he pleads.

"I can take it," I repeat and make another bold move, reaching out for his wrist. "Please, don't leave me."

He pulls his wrist away harshly as he stares down at me. "Get dressed and go. I will send you instructions in a few days."

"Yes, Master." I frown, standing to gather my clothes. "Thank you, Master," I add before exiting the room to dress in the spare bathroom.

6
Punishment

Clayton's Point of View

I'm confused. Why is he willing to go to such extremes to stay with me? Doesn't he realize that he can get a new master and end this torture? His words come back to me. *"I don't want to leave you, Master. I want to please you."* Just me? No one else? Has he developed the same forbidden feelings I have? Do I dare hope?

I call Alec for guidance.

"Do you have feelings for him Clayton? I only ask because had he been Bobby or anyone else, you would have ended it by now."

"Nothing I can't control."

"You're not being fair to him, Clayton. You should let him go," Alec advises.

"I don't think I can," I cry into the phone.

"Clayton . . . Just because you left me, doesn't mean he will leave you. You will tell him, Clayton. In your next meeting. Understood?" he demands.

I know he hates being harsh with me, but it is what I need. I thank him as my master and ask to borrow his sub. He questions my judgment on choosing Bobby, but I explain that Bobby knows my style, what I can and cannot deal with. He assures me he will ask Bobby and let him decide.

Three days later, Bobby shows up at my door alone. "Come in," I smile.

He walks in and plops down on the couch. "So you got yourself in a bind with a sub?"

I sit down next to him, frowning. "Something like that."

"Is it really true, man?" he asks in astonishment. "Someone finally got to Clayton Reynolds's heart?"

"I'm not that cold, Bobby," I frown. "I do love people."

He looks at me for a moment before pointing out, "True, you just don't normally take chances, Clayton. You are risking losing him."

"You in or out?" I snap, not wanting to get all analytical about this.

I see a flash of something before he responds. "He would be stupid to tell you no, Clayton."

"Bobby," I frown, realizing after three years, he still harbors feelings. *God, I'm a prick for asking this of him.*

"No, don't, really. Alec's good for me, very good. I'm happy both inside and outside of the playroom."

"You sure?" I ask, cautious.

"If I wasn't, I wouldn't agree to this," he assures me. "Now tell me, what's the plan?"

I fill him in on the details, and the next day, I go to a local sex shop and purchase a few tools that I plan on using for this hell. I couldn't stand the thought of using Daniel's tools on another man. I gave those to him, for him and him only. Frowning, I realize that I may be back in the near future if he walks away from me.

When the dreadful night arrives my stomach is in knots. Daniel and Bobby are in the playroom, kneeling naked, waiting for me. This really, really sucks. The moment I walk through the doors and see them side by side, I need to be grounded. So I walk up to Daniel and run my fingers through his long hair. Guilt runs through me when he refuses to break formation.

"Do you know why he's here, Daniel?"

"Yes, Master," he answers as tears of shame streak down his guilty face.

"Do you understand the extra weight safe wording has tonight?" I had told him that if he does it's over. *God, please don't let him end this.*

"Yes, Master," he answers painfully. This is going to be harder on him than I thought. I fight with the pit of my stomach as I force myself to continue.

"I really wish I didn't have to go to this extreme with you, Daniel," I sigh, dropping my hands from his hair. "All my past subs have not had the privilege I am giving you tonight. Rest assured, I would have ended it with them. But you begged me, Daniel, and I have trouble denying you." I frown. He really has no idea how much power he has over me. "Not that I won't." Wanting to make myself abundantly clear I decide to reiterate our phone conversation. Moving in front of him I lift his chin with my index finger. He closes his eyes to prevent meeting mine, respecting our roles. "Enduring this is your choice. As you know, you can use your safe words at any time, and with the exception of your pause word, doing so will prevent renewal of our contract. But I want to warn you, if you are a cum whore tonight it will also end our relations. Do you accept these terms, Daniel?"

"Yes, Master," he whispers.

I think I catch a glimpse of his features twitching when I walk over to Bobby, but when I look at him, his face is masked. I place my hands on Bobby's shoulders. "Do you understand your purpose here?"

"Yes," he answers turning his head toward me.

"While in these walls, you will call me Master." My eyes flash, and he stares at them for a moment before he falls back into his submissive posture and role.

"Yes, Master."

"Good," I praise, giving him my first instruction of the evening. "Shuffle on your knees and kneel before him facing me." This puts both Bobby and me in Daniel's line of vision. I watch as Daniel forces himself to stay still, but he can't fight the fact that his skin just turned a shade lighter.

"I'm going to let him pleasure me, Daniel," I tell him, "while he does so, you are going to count the number of times I lick my lips while he gets me off." I can hear him swallow, and he is starting to look a little green as he sways momentarily in his position. "Do you want to safe word?" I ask gently. *Please don't, please stay.* I count seventeen heartbeats before I get frustrated with his silence. "Answer me, Daniel," I snap.

His words come instantly, "No, Master."

"Good," I reply in relief and pain all at the same time. "Bring your eyes to my face, Daniel."

He meets my eyes just for a moment and I give him a silent apology before turning my full attention back to Bobby. "Open." He does, and I shove my cock in his mouth, receiving instant pleasure. I'd forgotten how skilled he was at this, but he was not nearly as skilled as Daniel. I could stave off my orgasm and that was the plan. Daniel needs to see delayed gratification but not from Bobby, he needs to see it from me. I do my best to continue to lick my lips and ignore the pain that is streaking down Daniel's face while I make him watch me be pleasured. When it gets to be too much, I turn, causing Bobby to drop me out of his mouth, and face Daniel dead on. His eyes are full of hurt, shame, jealousy? I step away from Bobby to approach Daniel, hopeful.

"Are you jealous, Daniel?"

"Yes, Master."

Relief washes over me, but I know I still need to play my part. "Look at his dick, Daniel. He's hard but he hasn't cum on my calf like a whore." He follows my instruction, causing shame and despair to return to his features before he can mask them again. That's when I notice he's soft. "It didn't please you to watch me pleasure?"

"Not by another, Master." His answer takes me off guard, and I have to walk away from them both before they catch the fact that I am smiling at that statement. "How many?" I ask retrieving my desired item from my cabinet, walking back over to Bobby.

"Twenty-six."

"Good." I praise, placing the newly purchased wool cuffs on Bobby before ordering him to stand and direct him over to the horse. I bind him to it, all the while keeping an eye on Daniel, who I can tell is conflicted and hurt. I am wondering if this is going to be too much, but he doesn't move. He doesn't safe word. He doesn't leave.

"Crawl over here, Daniel," I demand enjoying the fact that my dick twitches while I watch him crawl on his hands and knees toward me. "Stop," I order, moving to situate him into the best position for him to watch me perform.

Walking over to the cabinet, I take out a newly purchased flogger, and hear a gasp, turning my head toward it I see Daniel fall out of position with wide eyes. "Pet-al Mas-ter." Daniel stammers, covering his face with his hands.

I'm at his side instantly. "Shh . . . it's alright, take a closer look," I tell him gently, displaying the flogger for him, turning it over and over until he realizes the instrument isn't his, all the while staring at his beautiful face. His eyes snap to mine, and I give him a small smile running my fingers through his long hair.

"This is a hard lesson, Daniel. I'm aware of that. But please know that I am not cruel. I would never use anything that is yours. I care for you, Daniel. If that wasn't so, you wouldn't be here." His lower lip quivers a little and I nod, "Look at the horse, Daniel."

He reluctantly does so and his muscles relax when he sees the wool covering, which is also new.

"Thank you, Master." he whispers, "I'm ready Master."

I give him a half smile when his eyes cast back down to the floor and he moves back into position. His sweet breath is hanging in the air around me, I want to comfort him, to feel his lips on mine one last time, in case he does decide to walk away. So I kiss him lightly, savoring it as I bring my lips to his ear. "Notice that I didn't cum for him, Daniel."

I stand before I can lose any more control, walking back over to Bobby. "Now I want you to watch as he takes it like a man, Daniel," my authoritative tone returning, "not like a cum whore."

Before I start, I insert a gag ball into Bobby's mouth. Once again, this is new, but I did purchase the one that I knew Bobby liked, for this was not the first time I have ever gagged him. In the corner of my eye, I catch Daniel's surprise and pride while he watches me tighten the gag. But the moment I turn to him, his face is masked once more.

Throughout the next hour, I cannot stop the arousal that Daniel's intense stare is causing. I make sure I perform for him the way I would if it were his body. I'm giving him a gift of letting him watch me pleasure someone the way I would pleasure him. Yet I believe that his jealousy has returned and his cock stays soft. *Is he jealous? Or is it me that he's not interested in?*

Frustrated with the damn insecurity in my head and the fear that Daniel is going to walk away even after enduring this session I release Bobby from his binds and remove his gag, turning him to face directly at Daniel. "Touch yourself," I instruct while I go and retrieve a towel, handing it to him shrugging, "whenever you're ready." Then I walk behind Daniel and ideally comb my fingers through his long hair, trying to comfort him and steady myself while we both watch. When Bobby finally cums, I nod, "You've fulfilled your purpose."

"Thank you Master, it's been a pleasure." Bobby smiles while he gathers his clothes, and leaves us alone.

After a few more strokes of Daniel's hair, I step in front of him, maneuvering so that my dripping dick is in front of his face. "*This* is how one delay's gratification, Daniel," I moan, touching myself. I resist a smile waiting for it all come together in his head. When it does he looks up at me in bewilderment. "You have no idea how hot you were making me."

"Master?" he asks confused.

I frown insulted. "You think he did this to me?"

"Yes, Master." He answers, correcting his gaze.

"No, Daniel. You did this." I assure him, "The feel of your stare was incredible. The fact that you now know exactly what I do when I pleasure you, it's erotic." I pause then add, "Now stand for me."

When he does, I notice his cock is still soft and battle with my insecurity. *Why didn't watching me turn him on?* "Do you not ever watch porn, Daniel?"

"Yes, Master."

"Does it not arouse you?" I ask wearily.

"Yes, Master."

"Then why hasn't this?" I demand.

"Because you were with someone else, Master." He hurtfully whispers.

His statement hits me like a freight train. *This isn't in my head. He feels it too.* "You've grown forbidden feelings for me?" I ask in such a whisper I am not sure he heard. I think he does though because his breathing has faltered, either way, he doesn't answer. "Daniel?" I ask, touching his cheek. "Look at me." He turns his head to face me, keeping his eyes closed. "Don't make me tell you twice."

He gasps when his eyes meet my intense stare. I can't help but search his soul while I ask my next question, "Is that why you are having such difficulty being with me?"

He doesn't answer verbally, he doesn't have to; his eyes are telling me everything I need to know, everything I feared was not true. He's not going to walk away from me, not without breaking his heart too. I can tell he's scared that I might end this if he admits his feelings, so I try to encourage him. "You are not the only one to blame, Daniel." I fight back my fear, forcing myself to say the next statement, whispering in his ear, "I have grown forbidden feelings for you too."

My heart breaks with his reaction of stepping back from me, biting his lower lip. I can only pray that he doesn't leave, but it's not my choice. It has never been my choice. Fear crashes over me and I remember him saying his personal life doesn't allow him to date. I try to push the thought in the back corners of my mind and offer myself to him willingly.

"If you're interested in exploring this, meet me in my bedroom. It's the last door on the right."

As I exit the room, I hear his sweet voice ask, "What about this, Master?"

I shrug, "Who says we can't have both?"

He doesn't move. I want him to so badly, so I add the only thing I can think of. Letting him know I would see him as my equal if he joined me outside of this room. "And, Daniel?"

"Yes, Master?"

"If you do come to my room, call me Clayton."

7
Transition

Daniel's Point of View

    I'm frozen, my heart is pounding, my mind is racing, and my feet are stuck to the floor. My master just asked to change our relationship, which according to our contract, is an irreversible request. I honestly don't know what to do. The day he gave me the gift of a solo sub was one of the happiest days of my life, for I had served him well. But being a sub was easy for me, something I've grown accustomed to over the past three years, something I craved.

    While I will admit the idea of having my master as something more intrigues me, it also terrifies me. I have always failed in relationships, and since he has become my master, I had stopped trying all together, for he requested my every orgasm, and I gave it to him freely, almost in relief.

    The question I am facing now is, have I in fact fallen in love with him? Did I crave his touch? Yes, immensely. Did I crave his praise? Yes. Did I crave his heart? Did I crave his soul? Honestly, I do not know.

    Slowly, I get dressed, while my stomach twists at the realization that this may be the last time I am ever here, and it is tainted with another. I have a choice; I can go to him or I could leave. I desired neither option, but the idea of leaving makes my stomach turn more for the thought of *my master* pleasing another. I shake off the distasteful images and make my way over to his cabinet, opening the doors to his vast collection of tools, almost all inscribed with my name. I grab my flogger and make my way slowly to his room. The door is closed, so I take a few calming breaths to steady myself before I knock.

"Come in, Daniel," he calls. With sweaty palms I turn the handle, terrified of what awaits me. The first thing I notice is that he is fully clothed with wet hair. He must have taken a shower in the time it took me to debate. That gesture makes me more comfortable, for he has washed off the no-name male he sent to punish me. I notice that he's nervous, and more relief washes over me, because I feel the same way.

"Clayton," I manage, leaning against his dresser.

"It feels weird, doesn't it?" he muses, walking over to his bed, sitting down in the middle with his legs crossed. I am half relieved, half hurt when he doesn't offer me to sit. "I've never had this happen before," he admits to me. "Well, that's not exactly true. My master had fallen in love with me, but I didn't feel the same."

"What happened?" I ask.

He takes a deep breath, avoiding my eyes, "I left him. I couldn't go back, so I trained as a Dom. Now I'm sure you understand why I was so adamant about my subs falling in love. It changes things."

"How long have you had forbidden feelings?" I frown, not sure I really want to know the answer to the question.

"I think it started the day we met, but I didn't recognize it for what it was until about six weeks ago. Yes, I knew I had feelings for you. I'm sure you figured that out on some level yourself. But I thought I could control them. I thought that you were my favorite because you had such a strong desire to please, and you please very well, Daniel."

"But when I started to fail you?"

"The second time you failed me, I called my master for advice. He told me to end it. Most masters would have. That is why I had you come clothed. It was my full intention to do so. Yet I couldn't. I berate myself to no end for taking advantage of you the way I did during that time. You have given yourself to me so completely, and here, I can't admit that I've grown forbidden feelings because I was terrified you'd leave."

"Is that why you kissed me?"

"Yes." He admits, "I was trying to express to you without words . . . I felt guilty that I couldn't explain, but my anger at your lack of control got the better of me. I knew I should have ended it sooner and I tried that day. I really did."

"But I begged you not to."

"Yes."

"Can I ask you something?"

"Of course you can, Daniel. We should have no secrets between us. Not after all of this." He gives a half smile but fidgets with his hair. He's still nervous.

"How did today's session make you feel?" I ask, almost in a whisper.

"Guilty, like dirt, painful, yet somehow aroused by the thought of you watching."

"I did not like it," I admit in a distasteful tone.

"I know," he sighs. "You weren't really meant to."

"I am good to you, Master. I very rarely fail you. And to endure such a harsh punishment. For what?! The choice of bringing us together or tearing us apart! How is this fair?!" It's the first time I have ever raised my voice to him, and I can tell he's slightly surprised.

"You have every right to hate me," he frowns with a shudder.

"Yes, I do," I agree, "but I can't bring myself to do it. Master, please," I beg, dropping down to my knees before him, "don't end this. What we have is perfect. I don't want this to end."

"Stop calling me Master, Daniel, for I am not your master. Not anymore. I failed you," he climbs off the bed, reaching out for my arm and pulls me to my feet.

"I can forgive you. Your rule was that I never fall in love. You never mentioned anything of yourself falling. Please," I beg.

I can hear his breathing change, and I can tell he's fighting his emotions. "There's no going back, Daniel."

I wrap my arms around him for the first time pulling him to me. "I'm not sure I can move forward. The thought of us moving past each other makes me ill, but the thought of being something more . . ."

He pulls back slightly, brushing his hand through the side of my hair. "What, Daniel? You can tell me."

"I'm terrified," I admit.

"So terrified that you won't express your feelings for me? Or terrified of displeasing me because you do not feel the same?"

"I don't know," I answer. "I do know that I could never do this with another."

"May I kiss you?" he asks. The question surprises me, for my master has never asked to touch me. But he's not my master any longer. He's Clayton, a man who believes he is in love with me.

"I don't know how to do this," I admit with a blush.

"Neither do I."

I crash my lips into his, and we stumble just for a moment, unsure of who wants to take the domination. I pull back from him, nervous, but before I can speak, he gently presses his lips to mine, once, twice, three times, and soon I am opening willingly to him, he retreats his tongue slightly, giving me the chance to kiss back, making us equals. I moan my appreciation as our tongues dance, while our hands glide down one another's body. When we break away, we are both gasping for air, and I vaguely register that was the most intense kiss of my life.

"Will you admit your feelings now?" Clayton asks, pulling me back into him. "There's no going back either way, Daniel."

I let out a small sob, "I've hidden them so well, for so long. I'm not sure how."

"Shh," he whispers, physically relaxing. "There's no need for that now."

I pull back and stare at him for a long moment. "This is going to get complicated fairly quickly. You know that, right?"

"Yes."

"It won't be easy for me to see you as an equal."

"You won't always have to," he assures me. "We can adjust slowly if you want."

"How?"

"Let's keep our meetings as is, except when you come over, let's start out clothed in the kitchen chairs." he offers.

"I'm really no good at the whole dating thing." I warn with a frown.

"We'll take it slow," he promises. "I know your body completely, Daniel. Let's start with you learning mine, on your own terms. And we can talk, get to know each other."

"So what does this make us?" I ask confused.

"There's no need for labels." He smiles.

"But we're equals?" I clarify.

"Of course," he answers, confusion crossing over his features.

Before he can ask any questions, I take his wrists and pin them behind his back, bringing my lips to his ear. "If that's the case, I expect that you still own all of my orgasms, and now I own yours."

"Fuck me," he whimpers.

I don't know what's come over me, but I continue, keeping his wrists pinned and free one of my hands to stroke his obvious boner. "Not tonight." I release him with a smirk, "I'm pretty sure you know what delayed gratification is."

He raises an eyebrow at me and is about to say something but quickly changes his mind. "It's going to take me a while to adjust to this too," he confesses, bringing attention to the flogger in my pocket. "May I ask?"

Smiling, I pull it out of my pocket, tossing it to him. "It's missing a name."

"A name?" he asks, in shock.

"I want to become your Dom," I clarify. "As long as I can keep the sub role too. I really do enjoy it." He stares at me, and I can clearly tell he's uncomfortable. Shrugging, I head for the door. "Those are my terms. Think about it. You have my number."

8
Acceptance

Clayton's Point of View

~Six Years Ago ~

Hello, Clayton, meet me at my place at eight. Kitchen chair, clothed.

Confused, I replay the message on my voicemail several times. My master's voice didn't seem angry, not that it should; I haven't done anything wrong. Yet I can't seem to place it; it almost seems sad somehow. Frowning, I replay the words in my head; he's ending it; that much is clear. I just don't understand why.

When he finally sits across the table from me, he seems to be lost for words as he studies my calm features. Yet his eyes confirm my suspicion. What we have is over. Frustrated and pissed, I decide to make this ending easier for him and end it myself.

"I just have one question, Alec." His eyes narrow at me, for I am not allowed to call him Alec to his face while in this role, not to mention I'm talking out of turn. "What did I do wrong?"

His body falls limp as he slouches back in his chair. "Nothing, you're perfect, Clayton."

"Then why are we here? Ending this?" I frown. "Alec what we have . . ."

"Is special Clayton," he interrupts with a half-smile, "But I can't do this anymore sweet angel."

"Why the hell not!?" I demand, my emotions getting the best of me as tears fill my eyes.

"Because I'm in love with you!" he snaps back, fighting his own emotions.

"Master?" I ask in shock, for this was not one of the possibilities that was running through my head.

"I'm sorry, Clayton," he sighs, reading my features. "I know you don't feel the same. I'd like to stay friends and if you wanted to try this with someone else I could give you a few contacts."

"No. I can't see giving myself to someone else so completely." Silence falls between us for a moment and I take his hand, the one I scarred not that long ago, placing it in my equally scarred hand, "This won't end our friendship Alec, I vowed forever and I meant it."

He squeezes my hand back tightly, relief visibly washing over him while he smiles, "Me too."

I let go, leaning back into my chair, trying to keep my own feelings at bay; realizing I don't want to leave this lifestyle. "Will you be my teacher?"

"Teacher?" he asks surprised.

"Teach me your skills, Alec." I smile.

"My skills? . . . Let me think about it, alright."

Fallen for me? I'm still sitting in his chair trying to absorb this, wondering if the feelings I have could be labeled as love? *It's the closest thing since Ryan . . . but it's so different and if I risk it . . . No, I can't, I just can't . . .* I swallow my emotions and stand to leave. "I look forward to your lessons." I smile. "Thank you for being honest with me, Alec. You have earned my fullest respect."

I make it through his front door, shutting it tightly before I collapse on his front porch. Who was I kidding? I fucking loved him too. "Fucking fuck! I hate you, Ryan!" I turn my face to Alec's door and softly cry into it, "I love you too, Alec, so much, too damn much to lose you." I force myself to walk away then and have never acknowledged those feelings again. Instead, I've developed the closest friendship of my life, one that I would never trade or risk for the world.

~**Present Day**~

"Master?" I cry into the phone.

"Clayton. What is it? What's wrong?" Alec panics on the other side of the line.

"I need you," I cry, dropping the phone as I curl in on myself in the middle of the bed. Daniel had to ask for the one thing I really don't know if I can give. I'm going to lose him. I'm not sure how much time passes, but I vaguely register my name being called, although I do not answer it. It doesn't take my master long to find me.

"Clayton," he sighs, climbing in the bed and pulling my back into him. "Hey, it's okay," he whispers, caressing my hair lovingly, which only makes everything so much worse because they are not the arms I am truly craving. "Tell me what happened."

"I don't know," I cry into my pillow.

"Did you tell him?"

"Yes."

"And?"

"He was angry. He even yelled."

"Yes, well that was to be expected, Clayton. Bobby told me how he seemed to react. Your goal was to teach him a difficult lesson and you achieved that."

"I shouldn't have done it. I should have just ended it," I cry.

"Did he leave after he yelled?" he asks and then adds, "I'm assuming he yelled after you made it clear that your current relationship was over."

I pull Master's arms closer to me. "Yes to both."

"Come on, Clayton. Stop making me pry this shit out of you. Explain what the hell happened after Bobby left," he demands in frustration, wiping my tears from my exposed cheek.

"I realized he had feelings too," I cry. "He didn't deny it, but he didn't confirm it. It gave me the strength I needed to tell him how I felt."

"That's when he yelled?"

"Not right away. I told him to meet me here, in my room, if he was interested. He took so long, I took a shower and almost gave up with him coming at all."

"But he did," my master smiles.

"Yes. That's when he yelled, when he realized there was no option of going back," I sniff. "He didn't exactly express his feelings the way I did, but his kiss told me everything."

"So why are you crying like it's the end of the world?" he asks, shaking me in frustration. "You scared the hell out of me, Clayton!"

"He wants to change things."

"Things already changed." Master states in confusion.

"No, you don't understand. He wants to be equals. Both outside and inside the playroom." I clarify in shame.

"He wants to be your master?" he asks, shocked.

"I've never known anyone but you," I cry. "I don't know if I can, but if I can't, I've lost him."

"I'm not your master, Clayton," he sighs. "I'm your friend, and if you ever call me master again, outside of Angels of Justice, I swear this friendship will end."

I know immediately what he was doing. He is stepping aside for Daniel. Although we had parted ways all those years ago, with a small exception, I could not help myself from calling him Master. He never really minded much, especially when I was upset, knowing I needed to be taken care of in that state of mind. Today was the first time he has ever reminded me of this so harshly. Usually it was just him rolling his eyes and handing me a beer. But he's never once hung our friendship in the balance over it.

"You think I should try this?" I sulk.

"What's the worst that's going to happen? You two don't work out? You will hate yourself if you don't at least try, Clayton. Trust me, if in the end you part ways, your heart will hurt a hell of a lot less if you at least tried."

"Do you and Bobby switch?" I ask sitting up.

"No," he winces. "It's not how we work."

"But you think *I* should try it?" I ask over my shoulder.

"I have never been a sub, Clayton, and I don't plan on starting. You, however, are great at both roles." I give him a 'yeah right' look, "Don't look at me like that. You know I am a major league player in this world. I'm very aware of the grapevine, Clayton, you are viewed highly. Even Bobby was excited to be pleasured by your touch again."

"Alec," I frown, "I wasn't trying to —"

"I know Clayton, don't worry." Alec assures me, "He didn't exactly come out and say it. But I know why you two ended things. I just don't think you realize how hard it was for him when you ended your contract." He shrugs. "I think he found peace in it though, knowing you are happy. He told me that much, that no matter what happens between you two, you'd be a fool not to fight for him. It was obvious to him how both of you feel."

"We've agreed to take it slow," I moan, unsure if and how this is going to work.

"I think that might be best." He smiles, climbing off my bed. "You know I'm here for you, Clayton, but I think you're just scared. Stop thinking so much and just feel. Once you guys get comfortable, maybe we can hang out or something."

"Was it easy? You and Bobby adding the playroom?"

"Not at first, no," he admits, "but it slowly came along."

"Would you like anything from me, Alec?" I smile knowing he wouldn't, but it would feel wrong not to ask, after he so willingly let me use his boyfriend.

"You already gave it, Clayton." He smiles. "I think Bobby can let you go now. That's why I agreed to it in the first place."

"I didn't know." I frown, standing and walking out of my room into my kitchen, grabbing a beer for me and a soda for him. "God Alec, I've been hanging out with you two for years."

"Didn't know what?" he frowns following me into the kitchen.

"How strong his feelings were. I wouldn't have done it."

"I did that on purpose, you know." He shrugs, taking a drink. "I know Bobby told you he was happy with me, that you've seen our relationship develop, but I don't think you understand it. It's not like we sit around and think about you. We're both happy with each other but there's still that ping now and again. Truth is, I wanted him to see you with Daniel. It was selfish and fucked up, I know, but it was a perfect opportunity for him to close his past. What kind of man would I be denying him that chance?"

"Have you talked to him? Told him why you agreed?"

"Yes."

"And?"

"He wasn't happy with me but understood. It's nothing we can't work through."

"In the end, you and I are good, right? No jealousy, no worrying that Bobby and I will run off or any complicated shit like that?" I ask, taking a drink.

"No, we're good." He smiles, looking me in the eye. "It helps, Clayton, that you found someone. And not just because of how Bobby feels."

I give him a nod, letting him know I understand. Moving on I smile, clicking my bottle to his can, shaking my head. "Glad you got my back Alec, because I need your help on where to start with this shit."

After Alec and I talk about my fears of transition and he reminds me my limits with Daniel will not be the same limits I had with him, I decide to accept Daniel's offer. Not wanting to appear like an eager whore, I allow one week to pass before I call Daniel, and the moment I do, I'm angry at myself for not doing it sooner.

"Hello, Clayton," he answers.

"Daniel." I smile; it felt good to hear his voice.

"Have you thought about my offer?"

"That's why I'm calling actually. Are you alone?" I ask timidly.

"Yes."

"I want to invite you over, but our room isn't quite ready. That is, if you still want to," I rush worried. A week is way too fucking long. He probably gave up on me.

"The offer is still extended." I can tell he's smiling.

"Daniel," I start, biting my lower lip. *Alec better be right about this.*

"Yes, Clayton?"

"I need to cum," I whisper, surprised at the amount of pleading that my voice held in those four words.

"You called for my permission?" he muses seductively.

"Well, yes, but also to accept your offer. If you don't mind, I can go with the standard stop, pause and hard limit as a safe words until we have a chance to talk about it," I answer with a cracking voice. Why am I freaking out? God, when did I turn into such a mess? Why can't I be bolder to him? *Because you don't want to; you want him to be.* The thought surprises me a little, because I can't really deny it.

"Are you hard, Clayton?" he asks, lust clear in his voice.

"I wasn't," I admit, "until you started talking to me like that."

"What are you wearing?" he muses with a small laugh.

"Jeans and a shirt," I answer cautiously.

"Lie on your bed, unbutton your jeans, then pull the zipper down slowly," he instructs me, my dick twitches at the realization that I *might* get some fucking release. The thought stops me dead.

"Wait."

"Hmm?"

"Promise me I can cum."

"Clayton?" he says still in his seductive voice, "I'm surprised at you. Has it really been so long you've forgotten *how* to be a sub? You do realize that you are in no position to make demands, don't you?"

"Yes," I answer in a rough voice. "I'm sorry, this is just so new."

"Hmm, so it is," he agrees. "Yet, you will still be punished for it, but not tonight. Have you followed my instructions, Clayton?"

I moan at his authoritative tone and quickly unbutton my jeans but slowly unzip the zipper. "Yes."

"Are you going commando?" he smirks.

"Always." I smile.

"Not the next time we meet," he snaps. "Consider that a light punishment for questioning me." I groan; I really did hate wearing underwear. "Slide your pants to your knees," he orders, I do so eagerly. "Roll your balls." I follow his instruction. "Now I want you to go to your nightstand and grab your lube."

I cringe. "Small problem."

"What?" he asks irritated.

"I don't keep it there."

"You do now. Go on, go get it, and keep fondling yourself," he demands.

I hurry and grab it out of the shower where I had left it after getting so fucking hard from his eyes on me. "I have it. May I go back to the bed?"

"Yes."

I lay back down quickly, hoping that the ill location of my lube hasn't disturbed the mood. "Okay," I whisper.

"Kneel on your bed and lather your fingers," he instructs.

Thank the heavens I thought to call him with my handset. "They're silky for you, Master." *What? Wait, did I just call him Master?*

"Slide two inside yourself and start pumping," he moans, "but don't stop fondling your balls."

I follow his instructions, setting a steady rhythm. It feels so fucking good and is so fucking painful because my leaking dick, that is so goddamn hard, is being neglected.

"Please," I beg.

"Please what?"

"Can I touch myself?"

"No, I'll let you cum but only with your current movements." I can't help the whimper that escapes my lips, and my rhythm starts to pick up as I force my hands not to touch my needy cock. "Imagine my lips around you, Clayton," he whispers with his lustful voice returning. "Imagine the warmth of my tongue stroking you, the suction I'm creating while I greedily lick every ounce of cum you give me."

"Fucking hell, Daniel, please" I beg, truly at the edge.

"Hmm . . . I'm sorry I didn't hear that," he chuckles.

Fuck! Fucker liked the Master slip. My internal debate gets overridden by my body's natural desire. "Master, please," I beg again, trying frantically to stave off my orgasm.

"Please what, Clayton? What do you need?"

"Please, Master, I need to cum, *please!*" I beg, sweat dripping off my skin from my desire.

"Alright, cum for me, Clayton." The moment the lustful command leaves his lips, I collapse on my hands from exhaustion and my dick pumps cum all over the sheets. *Holy Shit!*

"Are you okay?" he asks in a concerned voice.

"Yeah, fucking great," I breathe, still trying to slow my heartbeat.

"When will our room be ready?"

"In a few more days. I'll give you all the details once I get to return the favor?" I smirk.

"Favor?" he asks amused. I know he damn well knows what I'm talking about.

"I suggest you start calling me Master if you want to fucking cum tonight." I all but growl. *There I am.*

His breath catches in his throat, and once he gains his composure, he pleads, "Please, Master."

This is going to be interesting.

9
Comfort Zone

Daniel's Point of View

The room is ready and the moment I get the text, my dick twitches. I cannot express my relief and fear that was pulsing through my veins when my master had called me. At first, I was afraid he wanted to end it, but then he asked me for release and I had to swallow hard. The sound of him pleading with me was so erotic, the feel of this new power was consuming, and I could not keep the grin off my face because I had my master begging.

It was fucking hot to tease him, the way he had been teasing me for the past fucking three years, and when he called me Master . . . I had to bite back a groan. That shit is fucking addicting. I could tell he was still uncomfortable when he tried to set the terms, but I wouldn't let him. He even tried to compromise with just my name, but I wouldn't allow it. He has to know how serious I am.

I have to admit, though, the moment he took charge, I almost came; for as thrilling as it is being his master, being his sub is what I secretly desired most. I love to pleasure him, yes I love to please my master, my Clayton.

When I arrive at his place, I am surprised at my nervousness from finding Clayton's front door locked, forcing me to knock for the first time. Not long after, he opens it with a smile.

"Hey."

"Hey."

"Well, come in," he smiles, stepping aside.

"This is new," I comment with a blush, walking into his house.

"New good or new bad?" he asks cautiously.

I bite my lower lip. "Good, I think," blushing redder.

"This makes you nervous," he notes, "If it's too fas—"

I cut him off by pulling him into me and pressing his lips to mine, pulling away with a smile. "Overthinking makes me nervous," I whisper.

"Sorry." He smiles, blushing for the first time.

"So how do you see tonight playing out?" he asks, running his fingers through his messy blonde hair walking to the kitchen.

I give a small smile. "I was going to ask you."

His eyes flash to mine while he licks his lips, and then he sighs, throwing himself in his chair. "Fuck."

"What?"

"I'm freaking out," he admits. "Not the whole talking thing, but the whole playroom thing."

I walk up behind him and run my fingers through his hair and am surprised how soft it really is. "How about tonight we do what we do in the playroom, but before we start, we make out like teenagers?"

"Wow, you really are better at the whole boyfriend thing than you give yourself credit for," he smirks.

I let out a hearty laugh stepping away from him. He stands up grinning so widely his sexy dimples show and small laugh lines crease at the edges of his eyes. I'm so struck at his beauty that I can't help but stop and stare.

"What?" he asks subconsciously.

"You're beautiful," I whisper, pulling him to me. I can hear a small gasp escape his lips, and then our tongues are dancing. I can't stop my hands from gliding down his back and cupping his ass before I slide them up under his annoying cotton T-shirt that is keeping me from his skin. We break away when I feel him fight with my shirt too, tossing them aside hurriedly as we search for each other's lips again. I let out a moan when he gently sucks my tongue while my hands trail down his naked abs for the first time. I've always wanted to touch them, and now that I have, I never want to fucking stop. We stand there half naked, chest to chest, swelling our lips while our hands explore for way too short of time before I pull away gasping.

"Daniel?" he asks in concern.

"I can't, I need to," I pant. "Fuck, it's been so long."

"You need to what?" he asks cautiously, his eyes searching mine in fear.

"I need to breathe for a second," I explain, "unless you want me to fucking cum, which would so not be my fault because your fucking tongue is so goddamn talented," I bitch. "Fuck! It's hard to concentrate."

His body relaxes as understanding dawns on him. "I see." He smiles slowly. "Well, maybe we should stop that for tonight. After all, we are taking it slow."

"Yeah, alright." I smile back, breathing heavy.

"Good, now strip," he demands, raising an eyebrow. I realize immediately that we have fallen into our playroom roles. I can't help the teasing as I slowly retract my belt and zipper. "I didn't ask for a show, Daniel. You will be punished for that." My dick twitches in response, but I'm able to hold back the moan while I quickly step out of my clothes.

Once I am naked, he offers his hand leading me back to the playroom. "I've rearranged a few things and added some new pieces that I think we will enjoy." He smiles, opening the six-panel double doors. I'm curious, but I keep my eyes trained to the floor. "You may look around Daniel."

"Wow!" I gasp in shock.

"I was hoping you'd like it. Come, be my equal for a moment. I want to explain the new things." As we walk, I notice that the horse has been removed. I'm kind of glad. It just wouldn't feel right after last time.

The first thing he takes me to is the corner of the room, where there are two padded walls and a bench with multiple hooks around it. "This is a standard bondage booth," he explains. "I thought you might find this useful, when the time comes, to explore my body. Once upon a time, I was an expert at stillness, Daniel, which I demand of you, but I don't know how easy it will be for me to get back to that role. I thought this piece could ease the frustration of the adjustment."

Not far down from that is the padded wall rack that I know very intimately already. He takes me over to the other wall, to his cabinet of toys opening it, revealing equipment with both our names. I smile but I do not comment at it, still embarrassed that I had the balls to ask for it to begin with. Past the cabinet is the bondage block and next to that the bondage table, both of which I had spent some time with. On the third wall there was my X-frame, except it had two separate bolts. "We are about the same height," he explains, "but our arm span is different." I nod my head.

In another corner is an elaborate system of pulleys and ropes. My eyes widen, and he smirks. "I couldn't resist," he explains. "I've had training on them, I'm sure you will enjoy them, in time. I won't push you, though. It is quite an experience." He smiles, walking over to the last piece of furniture against the wall that we came in on. "And this I am very excited about."

"A coffee table, Master?" I ask, uncertain.

He chuckles. "That is one of its functions, yes. But watch." He grins and starts flipping bars and what not, suddenly, the middle of it rises up into a round shape but leaves plenty of flat space on both sides. "Come." He smiles, and I approach him with uncertainty. "Climb to the middle and straddle it," he instructs, I do so, finding that my knees are comfortable and my ankles don't hang over the edge. "Now lean forward on your stomach and put your wrists over the edge at the sides." I comply and he quickly moves to cuff my wrists in leather, hooking them to the bench. "It's a doggy-style bench." He winks, walking back to the cabinet. "Or a spanking bench, as some call it. Tonight, we are going to be crimsoning both names."

He walks up to me with the flogger in hand. "Would you like that, Daniel?" he asks, running his fingers through my hair.

"Yes, Master. Please, Master," I whisper casting my eyes down, truly aroused at the idea of finally getting laid.

"You've pushed yourself to your limits for me, Daniel. You will be rewarded," he says, walking behind me. The feel of the leather straps stinging my flesh over my parted cheeks from the flogger is unexpected, I let out a loud moan in surprise, unable to fight back from tugging at the restraints, grateful they were there. "That was for talking out of turn earlier," he growls, slapping me again. This time, I am ready and am able to stay still. "That was for giving me a show." He gives me another full ass slap, harder than the last two. "And that was for being the eager whore you are, fighting against restraints. You know better, Daniel," he says in disgust, swinging the flogger again.

"Please forgive me, Master," I beg, earning another full cheek swat, making me even more aroused. After that, he starts to alternate sides, making my skin burn in desirable flames. It doesn't take long before I discover the disadvantage of this new piece. "If you hump yourself, you will not cum tonight," he growls, reading my mind. I close my eyes, forcing my body to stay still while I continue to get pleasured by his skilled hands.

Eventually he stops, dropping the flogger to the padded floor with a dull thud. In my limited vision I see him move in front of me. "Are you comfortable enough to kiss me from this position?" he asks timidly.

"Yes," I answer, clearing my throat, "Master."

He smiles and leans into me. "Good, because I want to kiss you before I fuck the hell out of you," he growls in my ear, kissing down my jawline. "And I want you to kiss me back, just like we were earlier," he whispers, crashing his lips to mine, kissing me to fucking oblivion, and he knows it.

I'm the one who has to break away, panting. "Petal," I whisper quietly. "I can't kiss you like that," I whimper, dropping my head down into the table, hiding my face with my hair. "I can't fucking concentrate, and I'm serious about not ever wanting to disappoint you again."

"Daniel."

"Master, please," I beg, near tears.

"Look at me," he demands. I force myself to look up at him. "I don't find it an insult that you have a hard time kissing me, quite the opposite actually," he muses. I give him a skeptical look before I can stop myself and quickly correct my features. "I owe you an apology, Daniel. I should have never reacted the way I did when I kissed you the first time. Although I don't really consider that a kiss, I was dominating you at the time." He presses his lips lightly to mine, "Please, don't feel shame that you enjoy being with me."

"Can I punish you for it later?" I smirk, allowing just a little edge of cockiness in my voice to snap him back to the here and now so he will stick his dick up my ass, where it fucking belongs.

His eyes narrow immediately before he steps out of my line of sight. "That will be up to you, but for now I'm calling the shots," he growls, *like a moth to a flame*. I hold back my smile when I feel lube dripping down my ass crack. "You're such a good sub, Daniel," he says slowly, pressing a slick finger into my entrance. "You know your limits and you don't push yourself too far so that you won't disappoint," he praises, slipping in a second finger and begins to stretch me slowly. "You listen well, Daniel, using your safe words not only for pain but for keeping me happy." He starts to twist and bend his fingers inside of me.

"It really fucking turns me on how well you please me, Daniel," he moans, his voice filling with lust.

I'm moaning as he prepares me, taking in his words of praise with pride. *This is how it's supposed to be. This is how my master's supposed to feel. Happy, proud to claim me as his.* His fingers disappear, and I don't have a chance to whimper at the loss, because he's pressing into me. *Fuck Yes.*

"So fucking tight," he moans, I can't help but cringe against the pressure. It has been so long. "Daniel, are you alright?" he asks, stopping his movements as he caresses my hair.

"Yes, Master," I whimper. "More please."

"Daniel?" he questions again.

"I'm ready, Master, please," I beg, getting past the burning and the desire for his movement becomes overwhelming. He must hear the truth of my words in my voice and I feel the pressure of him burying the rest of himself deep inside of me. I moan, forcing myself not to buck my hips and wait for him. I have a feeling he's not teasing though, just trying to adjust himself.

"Daniel?" he asks in a calm voice.

"Yes, Master."

"May I cum at will inside of you tonight?" he asks lustfully.

"Fuck, yes," I growl, which causes him to start pumping me, slowly at first before he finds a faster rhythm of his liking. He shifts me slightly, perfectly, knowing my body as intimately as he does, which causes his cock to slam into my prostate with each inward thrust. I moan out in pleasure as he hits it over and over. My balls are tightening, the twist in my stomach is there, but I fight back my release, not just because I don't have permission, but also because this feels so fucking good I don't want him to stop. My voice has other ideas though, and soon my moans are turning into whimpers while I fight back my body's will. "Please, Daniel, just feel," my master moans, running his hands down my back. I let out a deep throat moan of desire because the only touch he has ever allowed before now during fucking was his hands on my hips. But now, now, he could touch me wherever the hell he wanted when he fucking wanted to.

"Master, *please*," I beg, unable to hold off much longer before my pleasure turns into pain. He seems to understand and lets out a small scream, "CUM, DANIEL! FUCKING CUM!" he demands, thrusting himself inside of me with each word before he lets out his own release. Our dicks pulse in unison.

The moment he withdraws, I collapse, fully content on not moving a muscle. I feel him rub the cooling gel into my skin some time later, as he always does during our wind down, before he releases my wrists and says, "Rose," thus ending our session. When I sit up on my knees he kisses me passionately. Pulling back he whispers, "Thank you."

I climb off the table and we go to retrieve our clothes in the kitchen, we dress in silence, and it doesn't escape my attention he's wearing boxers. When it starts to become awkward I run my fingers through my long hair with a smile and decide to break the ice.

"I enjoyed that. And I love what you did to the room."

"Maybe next time, we'll do dinner or something?" he asks.

"I'd like that." I smile, pulling him to me, dropping my lips to his ear. "And next time, you will be calling me Master."

He goes rigid for a moment, then he swallows.

"Don't worry, Clayton. I won't push you at all." I assure him, running my fingers through his hair. "I know we are taking it slow, okay. I promise, what I plan to do to you, you will enjoy."

"What are you planning?" he asks cautiously.

I just smirk stepping away. "You'll see."

"You're leaving?" he asks with a frown.

"I have to, Clayton."

"Why?" he asks.

Well, this hasn't been an issue before. "I have a 5:00 a.m. flight tomorrow. I need to sleep."

"What?" he asks shocked. "How long will you be out of town?"

"No longer than usual." I frown, hearing a boyfriend question from my master is definitely an adjustment.

"You do this all the time?" he asks, and then his face falls into one of those "ah-ha" moments. "That's why you don't date."

"Promise me you won't get needy." I cringe.

He lifts his hands up in the air. "Nope, not me." Then he bites his lower lip. "But I do have a few requests."

"Oh?" I ask hesitantly.

"First, now that I know you are tempting fate by fighting gravity, as your boyfriend, I would feel more comfortable knowing your flight numbers so I don't have to freak out when I hear about some freak accident," he laughs nervously.

"I can do that." I smile. He's worried; it's kinda cute.

"Second, knowing you are so far away and inaccessible is going to turn me into a horny mess, so I would appreciate it if we could keep up our phone sex."

"Anything else?" I ask with a chuckle.

"Yeah, next time, pack your bags before coming over so you can stay the night in my arms," he answers matter-of-factly.

"You're going to be the death of me, Clayton." I frown. "I'll text you my flight info in the morning, and when I am lonely in my hotel room, I'll call you, assuming you will be available."

"Well, I won't be waiting by the fucking phone, but I will be looking forward to it," he smirks.

"Good night, Clayton. I'll see you soon." I promise him, giving him one last tender French kiss before I leave.

Texting him flight numbers, fuck, he really is my boyfriend.

10
Frustration

Daniel's Point of View

"Your ass is way too fucking perky for a 5:00 a.m. flight," Ben complains, rubbing his face.

"Just had a good night is all." I smile pulling out my phone and texting Clayton my flight numbers.

"You mean you got laid." He smiles knowingly.

"Something like that," I admit.

"You ever going to tell me about your mystery man, Daniel?" he asks with a smile. Ben and I have been friends since college, and though he is straight, he never really had a problem with my gender preference. He only gets stupid when he is drunk and some idiot makes a comment or whatnot, but that has all but diminished seeing as I have not dated in a little over three years. Well, we were close enough for him to realize that I was getting some, but he accepted my explanation of 'he's just a fuck buddy, nothing special.'

"His name's Clayton," I answer, causing Ben to give me a double take.

"Clayton," he repeats. "Wow, there's a first."

"Yeah, well, now he's my boyfriend."

"You're shittin' me!" he grins. "You're dating your fuck buddy!"

I laugh with a smile. "At least I know he's a good lay."

"Wow, Daniel, what brought this on?" he asks as we make our way past security.

"We realized there's potential for something more." I shrug.

"So when do I get to meet him?"

I cringe. "Not right now, Ben. This is all so new."

"Don't tell me you're nervous about dating the guy." He scolds.

"Yeah, I kinda am."

"Why? Afraid you will fuck it up or something?"

"Something like that."

"Oh, hell no! Daniel Kingsley is *not* in love!" he about shouts, causing my face to turn a deep shade of red.

"Shut up, Ben, before I make you do this fucking shoot by yourself," I threaten.

He drops it while we make our way to our gate and onto the flight. Right before I turn off my cell phone, I notice I have a text message from Clayton.

Thank you, please be safe.

I chuckle at the message and briefly wonder if the man has ever flown in a plane before. Yawning, I put my head phones in and close my eyes while the flight attendant goes through the in-case-of-emergency protocols while the plane moves to the runway. I'm almost asleep after takeoff, when Ben pulls one of my headphones out of my ear.

"Seriously, you're in love?" he asks with a grin.

I peek and eye open. "It has potential."

"Okay?" he says slowly. "What kind of answer is that?"

"Have you ever desired something unobtainable?" I ask, turning to him.

"Um, hello, have you seen our job descriptions?" he laughs, causing me to roll my eyes.

"Not like that." I scuff. "This is different. I mean, he was a fuck buddy right? There was no complications to it, just a booty call. That didn't stop me from enjoying myself, and I quickly realized that it was *him* I was craving, not the sex. But at the end of the day, I could never really explore the possibility for something more for fear he would detect it somehow."

"So what changed?"

"He did," I smile, biting my lower lip. "He told me that he has feelings for me, that he thinks he loves me."

Ben raises an eyebrow. "Well you didn't end it, so that must mean you have feelings too."

"Yes."

"Would you call it love?"

I pull my eyebrows together. "I don't know. I don't think I've ever been in love before."

"Man, promise me he is nothing like needy, whiny Brad." Ben cringes with the memory. "God, that guy was so over the top I wouldn't have put it past him to try to fuse your hips together or some weird shit."

I let out a small chuckle. "Yeah, he really did destroy it for a lot of men out there. Needy, insecure types are so not my thing."

"Why did you keep him around so long anyway?" Ben wonders, smiling at the flight attendant giving us our sodas. She doesn't even need to ask us our preferences anymore, having them memorized a long ass time ago.

"He was wet clay in the sack. I could do what I wanted, when I wanted, and how I wanted to do it."

"Now that sounds fun." Ben laughs, "Guess I can forgive you for making me suffer through eight months of him."

I shrug, pulling out my laptop for a distraction. "It got old."

"Kingsley, you are fucking crazy." He laughs, grabbing his laptop as well, both of us spending the rest of our flight working.

The moment we get off the plane, we are greeted by suits to take us to our destination.

"You ready for this?" Ben asks, rolling his shoulders.

"That depends how skilled they are," I grumble. I absolutely hate people who can't follow fucking orders. To my utter frustration, we find ourselves wasting five fucking hours to get through something that should have taken less than twenty fucking minutes.

"How'd you talk me into this?" I bitch after we call it a day, before somebody ends up with a black eye.

"Oh, stop your ragging. You'll love it in the end."

"Yes, by then, they will fucking know what we want and we will let them all fucking go," I mutter.

"Not all. We always have our repeats."

I moan, "Call Ethan again. Beg him, offer him double, just get his ass here so he can work with these idiots."

"I'll see what I can do."

Not long after, our car pulls up to the hotel and we check in. When I get to my room, I collapse on the bed in complete exhaustion. *Fucking idiots.* I decide to gear my thoughts to happier things like Clayton. Last night was so fucking perfect, and I would give my left nut right now for him to be my master. I smile at the idea and call him.

"Hello, Daniel," he answers with a smile, "how was your flight?"

"Can't complain."

"You sound exhausted."

"Just a long day of bullshit," I yawn, "along with another cold night of hotel sheets and shitty food. Nothing new really."

"How often do you travel?"

"Hmm, about eighty-five percent of the time." I hear his breathing stop, so I add. "Usually, it doesn't last more than a day or two, and I do get use out of my house."

"What do you do?"

"I'm a film director. Sometimes short stories, other times big productions. This time, I'm working a movie that involves a lot of dancing and idiots can dance but *really* suck at acting. It's draining, to say the least."

"Well, that answers a few questions." He laughs.

"Such as?"

"Why you prefer a sub role. You get sick of being in charge."

"You have no idea."

"You get back on Thursday, yes?"

"Looked up my flights?" I chuckle.

"Too much?" he worries. "I do have a legitimate reason for it."

"Oh?"

"I want to make you dinner," he answers quietly.

I let out a frustrated moan, "Now you're just making it difficult to be away from you."

He laughs. "I'll cook the food, you bring the wine."

"Deal." We fall silent for a moment. "So what do you do to pay for that house of yours anyway?"

"Have you ever heard of Blackboard Entertainment?"

"The record label?"

"Yeah, well, I'm the co-founder and CEO."

"You're serious? You're the one who discovered the *Eyes of Seduction*?" I ask surprised.

"Yeah, Lilly and Monica are good friends of mine from college, and they lost a fucking bet with me. I was a radio announcer for the college at the time and I put on their smash hit, *Dazzle,* the station got slammed with requests. After some convincing on my part, we invested some cash and we all got rich."

"Are they in charge of any of the new groups?"

"Occasionally, they'll put their two cents in, but for the most part, I'm the one people have to impress."

"You have a good ear." I smile. "*Gone a Blur* is brilliant."

"Thanks. They're a work in progress, but for the most part, I like them."

Knock, knock, knock!

"Hold on," I grumble. "Sign says do not disturb!" I call out.

"Ahh, come on, man. I need a beer and I hate drinking alone," Ben calls.

"Hold on," I mutter again to Clayton, opening the door for Ben. "I'm exhausted. I just want room service and sleep."

"One beer," he begs.

"No, Ben," I argue, shaking my head at him. That's when he notices the phone in my hand, and his eyes light up. Before I can react, he's swiped it from my hand.

"Clayton?" he asks, pushing me away to keep me from grabbing the phone back. I can only imagine what is going on in Clayton's head right now. "So you're the fuck buddy turned boyfriend."

"Give me the fucking phone, Ben!" I growl as we continue our childish struggle.

"Dude, we so have to meet," Ben laughs, before he can say anymore, I have him pinned to the bed, and rip the phone out of his hand. Taking a few calming breaths, I put the phone to my ear, keeping Ben trapped beneath me.

"I'm going to have to call you back, Clayton."

"Okay . . . are you alright?" he asks cautiously.

"No." I frown before I hit the end button.

"You are a fucking asshole!" I growl at Ben.

He gives me a shit-eating grin. "I know."

"One beer," I concede, shifting my weight off him. "I'll meet you at the bar."

"Thanks." He smiles, rolling his eyes as he heads for the door, laughing on his way out.

I call Clayton back immediately. "I'm so sorry," I groan before he can even say hello.

"For what?" he asks almost in surprise.

"Ben." I frown. "He's sort of known about you since the beginning, but he has no idea of the BDSM, just the fact that we were sort of together."

"So you called me your fuck buddy to avoid questions and dating pressure."

"Pretty much," I laugh. "Sorry if you find it offensive."

"Why would I?" he asks. "You tell him a lot yes? After all, he called me your boyfriend."

I smile. "He won't stop bugging me until we agree to a double date."

"Oh?"

"Don't worry, no pressure. I can hold him off for a month or two," I rush, realizing what I just said.

"I'm sure we'll work something out," he answers almost dryly. Then his voice changes to a seductive tone, "Are you alone now?"

"For now, but I promised his ass a drink at the bar. We really did have a long fucking day."

"He's a director too?"

"Assistant director, yes," I confirm.

"I won't have time later," he yawns. "I have an early meeting and really need some sleep."

"Maybe tomorrow?"

"Yeah," he agrees.

"Have a good night, Clayton."

"You too, Daniel."

I hang up the phone and make my way to the bar. Ben and I end up sharing two drinks and a meal together and we both almost fall asleep at the table. We drag our tired asses to our separate rooms and call it a night. I'm so tired I honestly don't remember my head hitting the pillow.

The next day is full of the same bullshit, and by the time I am out of there, I am beyond frustrated.

"You're skipping out, aren't you?" Ben asks.

"Thought's crossed my mind," I admit, almost in tears I'm so frustrated.

"Ethan promised to show up at noon the day after tomorrow. Be back by then, alright?" He was used to my sudden disappearances during a shoot. Usually it was because Clayton had texted me a time, but not today. Today was so fucking different.

Not bothering to check out of the hotel, I have the driver take me directly to the airport. It's fucking ten o'clock at night, and the only thing I want to do is sleep. The moment I board my unexpected flight, I'm out before the plane takes off.

Once I arrive back in town, I go home and smile when I notice the UPS package has arrived. This only makes me more eager and I text Clayton.

Noon, your house—no excuses. M.D.

Checking the clock I decide to attempt a few more hours of sleep. Upon waking I quickly take a shower, get dressed, wrap the package, and head for his place. When I arrive it's about five minutes after noon and I try his front door; it's unlocked. Walking in I find a very surprised Clayton sitting clothed in a kitchen chair. He seems to catch my mood and casts his eyes to the floor.

"I have something for you, baby." I smile, setting the black box on the kitchen table. He gives a small smile but doesn't speak. "I can't stay, Clayton. I just needed to see you." He brings his eyes to mine and they are full of worry. I raise an eyebrow and he quickly corrects himself. "This is going to take longer than originally planned." I frown. "I probably won't be able to stay until Tuesday or Wednesday of next week, depending on Ethan's magic."

"What can I do, Master?" he asks timidly.

"Careful Clayton." I warn, rubbing at my headache, he didn't have my permission to speak. "I just really need someone who can follow fucking directions, you know." He shakes his head in understanding, I stand behind him and comb my fingers through his hair. "I realize this will be a unique experience for us, Clayton, and I want to make you as comfortable as possible. I'm not going to push you hard today."

"Thank you, Master."

I smile, tugging on his hair for his insubordination. "About that. There is something that happened last time that bugged me." I sit down in the chair and look at him. "Be my equal, Clayton."

"What did I do that made you uncomfortable?" he blurts out, extremely worried.

"You asked my permission to cum." I frown. "It felt wrong somehow."

"But I thought . . ."

"No, it's alright. I just think that if we're in the playroom, then the Master should have full reign during that time."

He looks at me for a moment. "I can agree with that."

"You can open that, you know." I smile, trying to hide my nervousness.

He smiles while lifting the lid carefully, finding black tissue paper, which he pulls back to reveal a dark blue, soft leather collar that has the inscription *Daniel's,* sewn in white leather. He lifts it out of the box, raising both eyebrows, showing surprise.

"I know we never collared before, but considering the circumstance, I thought it might help us fall into the appropriate rules," I explain answering his unspoken question. "I went with a simple, soft leather strap because well, I found it the most appropriate without being demeaning. If you don't like . . ."

I'm cut off with his lips pressed to mine. "With the explanation, I love it. How long before you have to leave darlin'?"

"My flight leaves at 2:00 a.m." I frown. He smiles, handing me the collar. I take it from him, and join our lips, kissing him until we are out of breath. When I break the connection, Clayton falls to his knees. Smiling, I carefully attach the strap to his neck. "Comfortable?"

"Yes, Master."

"Go to the playroom and get into position, unclothed," I order. He slowly stands and disappears. I force myself to hold back a smile; it was the first time anyone has followed my directions properly in two fucking days. I give him time to undress, when I enter the room I find him exactly where I want him.

"I'm not going to be using any tools today, Clayton, I am not appropriately trained on them and will not risk hurting you," I start, standing behind him. "Stand up and close your eyes." Again, he follows my directions perfectly. "Lace your fingers behind your head." Once he's in position, I lightly brush my fingers down his body, starting with his neck and ending at his heels. Using my flat hands I slowly rub them up the front of his body, intently skipping over his genitals, caressing his beautiful, muscular torso with care. I've always wanted to touch him like this, to feel his skin, to see his body react to me. His body does not disappoint, and I can tell he is enjoying this. When I get to his nipples, I take the time to tease them before I drop my hands, stepping back.

"You're so beautiful," I whisper into the air, admiring his form. There's so much that I want to do to him, but I'm not exactly sure what he's ready for. The longer I stare, the more uncomfortable I become. Sighing, I give him his final instruction, "Kneel." He does so, and I step behind him releasing his collar. He raises an eyebrow at me but doesn't argue as I help him to his feet.

"You hungry?" I ask with a smile. He shrugs. "I'm going to go raid your pantry," I grin leaving him to his thoughts while he redresses.

I find some bread and make my way to his fridge, happy to discover that he has all the supplies for some good sandwiches and begin making them.

"I'm confused, Daniel," Clayton says joining me in the kitchen, pulling a beer out of the fridge for both of us. "Were you being cautious because you are unsure of my limits or yours?"

I shrug, passing him his sandwich. "A little of both," I answer honestly, "but I was satisfied with the outcome."

"And what outcome is that exactly?"

It's my turn to raise an eyebrow at him. "I'll take that as a master-to-master question and not a sub questioning his master?"

He chews on his food for a moment before he answers me. "I'm sorry. You're right. I have no right to ask you the purpose of that exercise."

I shake my head. "I already told you the purpose. I just wanted someone to fucking listen to me."

"Is work that stressful?" he asks, concern coming across his features again.

"Yes," I admit, swallowing. "I wasn't in the right mindset to push either of us today."

He gives me a genuine smile. "Thank you, Daniel. That really means a whole hell of a lot."

I smile back. "So I was thinking we can make out like teenagers and maybe watch a movie or something. After you get home from work of course."

"I am home from work."

I frown in disapproval. "I don't want to disrupt your day too much, Clayton."

"My boyfriend is leaving town for about a week, and you want me to leave him when I get so few hours before his departure? I think not."

We start talking about everything. I find that he's a great listener, and he really is worried about the stress of my job. He even went so far as to offer that up as a possible reason why I was having errors lately. I tell him it's a part of the territory and I will be fine. After lunch, we agree on a movie from his vast collection, but we don't spend time watching it because he starts to lick the back of my neck with open-mouthed kisses. I lose all interest in the movie and begin to kiss him, exploring his body in ways I could only fantasize about until now. We end up in his bathtub, where I melt into his fingers kneading into my back. I don't remember falling asleep, but I guess I did because I wake to Clayton drying me off in an empty tub and bringing me to his bed. I vaguely catch the fact that he slides next to me with his arms around me before I lose consciousness again.

I'm awakened to the smell of chicken. I frown when I look at the clock: 10:00 p.m. I make my way to the kitchen, after I find my clothes, and give him a small pout. "Why'd you let me sleep so late? I would have rather spent the time with you."

He smiles at me, putting the food on the table. "You needed to rest," he explains. "Ben called me, but he said it wasn't urgent, just that Ethan had to cancel or something like that."

I groan, falling into my chair. "Fuck!"

"What does Ethan do exactly?" he asks, joining me at the table with our drinks.

"He's a great crewman who is born to lead," I explain. "We pay him a hell of a lot of money, but we keep him in that title so that the new actors aren't intimidated, like they are with me and Ben. We don't use him all the time, just with really tricky cases like this, where we know our authority is what is freaking these guys out, even though we have never raised our voices at them. But believe me, I've come close. It's been a long time since I've had to deal with such untrained group."

"You're not going to be back by Tuesday, are you?" he asks sticking a fork full of food in his mouth.

"Probably not," I sigh, picking up my fork "but I might drop by again, if that's alright. You can text me when it's a good time for you."

"I just might do that." He smiles bringing another bite to his lips. "So you gave Ben my number?"

"No." I laugh, "Fucker swiped my phone at dinner the night you two talked. If it bothers you I can tell him to lose it."

"No it's good." He smiles. "I don't mind being friends with your friends . . . when we're ready."

We eat the rest of dinner asking about small details of each other's lives, and once again, we find ourselves shirtless on his couch swelling our lips, exploring each other. When I can't push it off any longer, I give a small whimper.

"I have to go."

"Let me take you," he offers, kissing me again.

"It's ok, Clayton. You don't have to do that," I argue against his skin.

"I want to."

"You promise not to make a habit out of this?" I frown, remembering Brad.

"You taste so fucking good," he whispers, and I'm lost in his touch again.

Five minutes later, I am forcing myself to move. "I seriously have to go."

"Alright, but I'm driving," he insists, throwing me my wrinkled shirt.

The drive is short but that's mainly due to no traffic this time of night. When I step out of his car at the passengers drop off, Clayton calls after me. "Daniel?"

"Yes, Clayton."

He licks his lips. "Just so you know, I'm not against giving head."

I smirk. "I'll keep that in mind."

He kisses me tenderly before whispering, "Be safe."

"Stay out of trouble," I retort, kissing him again and slamming the car door closed before I miss my flight.

I can't keep the smile off my fucking face as I head to the gate. Yeah, I really do think this whole boyfriend thing could be something good.

11
Needy

Clayton's Point of View

"I'm worried about him." I frown into the phone while I look over a potential contract for a new band.

"It's not the first time," Alec points out.

"This is different," I argue.

"How so?"

"I know what's wrong," I mutter. "He flew three states just to see me."

"And you're complaining because . . . ?" he asks, trailing out the word 'because.'

"He was so frustrated. We even had a session, and he didn't really do anything but order me around."

"That bothers you why?" Alec asks. "Because you were used to giving him orders?"

I chew on the inside of my cheek. "I thought I would at least be able to pleasure him. But he's taking it slow, too slow."

"That's not your call, Clayton," Alec reminds me. "What about outside of the playroom? How is that coming along?"

I cringe. "It's awkward at best, unless we're sucking face, which we do a lot."

"Give it time. You'll get there," he assures me.

"I'm still worried."

"Does he know?" Alec sighs, trying to pacify me at this point.

"I think he senses it. I'm just scared to push it."

"Why?"

"I don't want to come off as needy," I whine. "Apparently he's against that."

"You're against that," Alec laughs.

"I know, but this is different. I can't explain it, Alec. I've been on edge since he left."

"What's really bothering you, Clayton?" He presses. "You know you can tell me anything."

"No, Alec, I can't." I moan. "But you will know the moment you see us together, if you agree."

"Agree to what exactly?" he asks cautiously.

"Agree to teach Daniel," I propose. "He's admitted that he's clueless, and while I'd be happy to bring in a sub again, I don't think it's the best of ideas. I should be the sub, and if that's the case, I would only submit to the both of you."

"Have you talked to him about it?"

"I thought I'd run the idea by you first."

"I'll think about it." Alec groans. "Now tell me what's bothering you, Clayton."

I bite my lower lip. "Out of context, you are not going to like it." I explain, trying to soften the blow. "In context, it makes sense, I guess."

"Stop prancing around," he snaps.

"He bought me a collar," I answer in a rush. Alec falls silent for so long I check my phone to make sure we're still connected. "It's not elaborate or anything. On the contrary, it's a simple, soft leather," I bite my lip nervously. "It's really not all that uncomfortable, different but not uncomfortable."

"You're right, I need the context," he answers simply, with an edge to his tone. I know how Alec feels about collars, and that's always made me apprehensive about using them, let alone submitting to them.

"It gets a little confusing," I admit to him. "One moment we're us, and the next, we're in our roles."

"So you're sloppy," he almost growls.

I close my eyes in shame. "Yes, Mas-, Alec."

"I can see why he would want to collar you. As a master, I'd consider doing the same," he mocks in anger, though I know he would dismiss a sub before he'd ever consider collaring them.

"It's different," I argue. "We're different. Besides, he gave it as a gift. There was no annoyance."

"You're stumbling, Clayton," he cautions.

"Which is why I'm asking for help!" I snap at him. "I'm sorry," I immediately add in a quiet tone; I rarely speak to him like that.

"Alright, alright, I'm in. But I'm only doing it because it's you, Clayton," he's quite for a moment. "So did you agree to this collar thing?"

"Yes."

"You realize that means you are going to have to get him one too." I groan at the thought. "This is why Bobby and I don't switch," he mutters. "Call me tomorrow and let me know when."

"Thank you."

Hanging up the phone, I call Mike to tell him to hold my calls and cancel my meetings for the rest of the day. I am in no mood for company. Frowning, I turn to my computer and Google the words 'submissive collars' cringing at the images that come up. *No thank you.* Thinking about it, I guess as far as collars go, I got lucky. Still, if I wasn't so damn sloppy to start with, I wouldn't be in the market for one *ever*. Alec was right; I deserved this punishment, even if Daniel had no idea he was giving me one. I want to give him a similar collar like mine, no ability ever to attach one's hands to their neck or tie them by the neck like a dog.

I find what I am looking for and have a high suspicion that this is probably the same place Daniel purchased mine, mainly because it was the most respectful site I can find. I place an order for a dark green collar with white embroidery of the word *Clayton's* on it. I can't help the knot in my stomach while I fill out my credit card information that I know by heart, having it sent to the attention of Justin Lake.

I am way too important socially to be buying this shit with my real name, so I had my lawyer make me a fake identity with a credit report and everything, just in case. Plus, if my nosy neighbors get to it, they won't freak about the label on the box, if ever there is a company stupid enough to do that again. I laugh to myself at the memory of purchasing my first horse. Stupid thing had to be signed for, my neighbor offered and freaked when she saw the label. She told the driver there is no way that I was into that shit, refusing to sign, pointing out that I was Clayton Reynolds and some crazy wannabe was pulling my leg. The guy took it back, and it took me three weeks to get it all worked out. After that, I paid off the UPS driver to drop off all said boxes even if I wasn't home. Then I contacted my favorite stores and threatened my business if they were ever disrespectful like that again. I want a box, no letterings or logos with a P. O. Box address. Period. I have to admit, throwing out Alec's name was helpful in those conversations as well. Let's just say I'm on the VIP list.

But this, this was a fucking new company, and I really didn't have the slightest clue how it would come, so I filled out their additional information box with my request, ideally wondering if I should have just gotten a UPS box at one of their stores a long ass time ago.

When I finish that tedious task, I become restless, very restless. I clear out my browser history on my computer and decide to leave for the day, hoping a run will take the edge off. It doesn't. I go home and stretch, turning on some light music with some wine, I even pick up my guitar but that doesn't work either. I try reading, but that blows; I try watching TV, but I find myself channel surfing; I even try doing laundry, but nothing helps.

Annoyed, I realize that nothing will help, not until I talk to Daniel. I can't just call him, needing to hear the sound of his voice. God, that would terrify him. Hell, it terrifies me! What the hell is wrong with me? *You're worried about him.* "UGH!" I scream, pulling at my hair. Why did he have to fly in to see me when he couldn't stay? What did he want? Was it just to boss someone around or to be with me? Why is my world spinning out from underneath me like this? Why did my heart have to go and make this so fucking complicated?

Right when I'm about to cave and call him, my doorbell rings. Frustrated, I go and answer it. Alec and Bobby are on the other side. I can't stop myself from jumping Alec the moment my mind registers he's there, I cling to him for dear life. "How did you know? What the hell is happening to me?"

Alec picks me up off my feet and takes me inside to my couch, but he doesn't answer me. Instead, he cradles me in his lap, allowing me time to become grounded. "I don't understand what's happening to me," I cry. "I'm not weak like this. I can go days without calling my boyfriends. Why is he so damn different?"

"You're boyfriends were never your subs," Alec smiles, running his fingers through my hair. "As a Dom, it's your job to take care of your sub above anything else, even yourself. You are trying to do that in both of your relationships with him, and if you don't find a balance, Clayton, you are going to go crazy."

"I don't understand," I cry, realizing I should be ashamed at my tears soaking his shirt but not giving a damn at the moment. This is so not me and I hate it.

"Let me ask you this." He smiles, scratching my scalp a little. "Had Daniel just showed up as your sub yesterday what would you have done?"

I bring my eyebrows together. "It's happened a time or two."

"Okay and what did you do?" he asks kindly.

"I gave him what I thought he wanted, what I thought he needed."

"And did he seem satisfied when he left?"

"Of course," I answer almost in insult.

"What happened yesterday?" he asks gently.

"I let him call the shots." I frown. "I listened and let him deal with his issues his way."

"Which didn't involve you taking care of him," Alec points out.

"I gave him a back rub, let him sleep, made dinner, even took him to the airport." I argue. "Neither one of us wanted him to leave."

"Clayton, what you two are doing . . ." he stops, deciding to choose his words before he finishes, "Well, it's complicated. Giving up your Dom role and submitting to him is challenging enough for you. Then you add the fact that you are worried and you get this," he indicates me, by waving an open hand up and down.

"So what should I do about it?" I ask, pulling away a little.

"Nothing. You need to adapt. You could try talking to him, but if he's worried about needy, I'd suggest you offer to listen some more. Most of the time, people just need to vent, after which they are fine. Careful with how you react to that, Clayton. This ball of nerves is really not healthy."

"How did you know?" I ask again.

"Besides him being an excellent therapist?" Bobby speaks up. "Dude, he's been there. Give it time. You'll adjust. And talk to Daniel. He needs to know what you are feeling."

I frown at his advice. "How am I supposed to explain it to Daniel when I don't understand it myself?"

"Like I said, give it time." Bobby smiles. "Pizza should be here soon. Pick out a movie, and I'll raid your fridge for the beer."

"There's an extra case downstairs." I smile.

"Why doesn't that surprise me?" He chuckles.

We spend the next few hours watching a movie and eating grub, but I find that I am still fidgety. It's getting late, and I'm surprised that Alec and Bobby haven't left, but I think they are waiting for the same thing I am—Daniel's phone call.

"I'm fine," I insist after the clock turns to 11:30 p.m. "Go home already," I bark, tapping my thumb on my knee.

Bobby rolls his eyes, keeping his thoughts to himself, which winds me up more. "Aren't you glad I ended it? Now that you know what I'm like, I'm sure it's a total turnoff."

His eyes widen in shock and he shifts them to Alec for help.

"You are not like this, Clayton. You never have been in the past," Alec counters, saving Bobby from a reply. "He just has you all tangled up in your underwear is all."

"What underwear?" I snap.

Bobby laughs and Alec fixes his shocked expression before he too rolls his eyes.

That's when my phone finally rings. I stare at it frozen, unsure what to do now that he actually called. Do I answer it at such a late hour, or do I let it go to voicemail? Before I can make a decision, Alec is answering the call.

"Clayton's phone," he laughs. "Umm, yeah, I think he's taking a leak. Hold on." He places his hand over the mouthpiece. "Yo! Clayton! Phone!" he yells out unnecessarily loudly in his New York accent.

I catch on quickly. "Who is it?" I yell back.

"Who is it?" he asks Daniel. "Your boyfriend!" he yells again.

I smile, asking in a whisper, "Did he say that or his name?"

"His name," he whispers back, handing me the phone.

"Hey." I smile.

"Hey. This a bad time?" he asks and I can tell he's upset.

"Umm, no, not really," I answer, the smile disappearing off my face. "I was just hanging out, no biggie. I can ditch my friends for a few."

"I don't want to put you out, Clayton."

Crap. "You sound tired," I note.

"You have no idea," he whispers and his voice cracks. *Shit.*

"Give me a second, okay," I mutter into the phone, before putting him on mute. When I'm sure he can't hear me, I flop down on the couch. "He's crying. Fuck."

"Shit, Clayton, I was trying to help you with the not waiting for his call gag. I wouldn't have done it if I knew he was upset," Alec panics. "Tell him that you've stepped away. He doesn't need to know that we're here. Make him think you were at a party or something."

"You don't have to stay," I answer, giving him a pointed look.

"We're staying, so keep the damn phone sex to a minimum, unless he won't let you."

Sighing, I take the phone off mute and head down the hallway. "Hey, you alright, darlin'?"

"It's nothing. I'm just tired. Go hang out with your friends. I'll talk to you in the morning," he answers dismissively.

"No," I respond firmly. "Daniel, I want you to tell me what's wrong."

"Clayton . . ."

"Don't make me punish you," I warn, not sure if I'm pushing it or not.

"Ethan quit," he answers in defeat. "He got a better offer and didn't know how to tell us."

Now I just want to reach through the damn phone and wrap my arms around him. "I'm so sorry. Is there anything I can do?"

"Find me another organizer," he laughs without humor. "No, seriously, you're doing it, Clayton. I just really needed you tonight, *so much so it's almost scary*," he whispers the last words, and I'm not sure if he intended for me to hear them. Regardless, he's feeling vulnerable and I want to help.

"Would it freak you out to know that I've been chopping at the bit all day?" I ask timidly. "I was using my friends as a distraction. I couldn't really explain it except somehow I knew you were upset and I wanted to call but . . ." I stop, biting my lower lip.

"But?" he whispers.

"I didn't want to come on too strong or appear needy," I confess. "I'm not needy, Daniel. I never have been, but to quote you, this has gotten complicated fairly quickly."

"I wouldn't have minded," he tells me, and my body relaxes under his words.

≈ 95 ≈

"I think I need your definition of needy," I laugh shyly. "But not tonight. Tonight, I want to be holding you close to my body and running my fingers through your hair."

"That sounds nice, baby."

"Can I ask you something?"

"Of course."

"Where exactly is this shoot of yours anyway?"

"Near Death Valley at the moment. Why?"

"Are you getting enough water?" I ask. "Is your crew?"

"Yeah, we're all good." He smiles, "Thanks, though. I appreciate the small worry."

Yep, definitely need a definition of needy. "I wasn't worrying," I counter. "I find that people are easier to work with when they are comfortable. I was trying to help."

"Oh, well, thank you for that too," he adds.

"Get some sleep, Daniel. We'll talk in the morning."

"Clayton?"

"Yes, Daniel."

"Thanks for having a life and not sitting around waiting for my call."

I bite my lower lip. "You're welcome." I answer hanging up the phone. "AHHHH!" I grunt out in frustration, throwing myself onto my bed. Bobby is the first through my bedroom door, followed quickly by Alec. "If this guy is anymore flip floppy, he'd be a fish out of water," I complain.

"Why? What did he say?" Alec asks, concerned.

"Oh, you know, the usual. He needed me and wished I would have followed up on my instinct and called him. He was happy that I was worrying but doesn't want me to. Oh and the best part, he was disappointed that he couldn't have me alone but was thanking me for having a life and not sitting around the phone waiting for his call!" I groan. "Help."

"God he's worse than a woman." Bobby laughs.

Alec smacks Bobby in the shoulder. "Why was he crying?"

"He had a good employee quit," I mutter, "but that, that I can fix."

"Do you think that's a good idea Clayton?" Alec asks cautiously.

I roll my eyes at them. "It's late. You should go. You're both going to be shit tomorrow if you don't."

"Alright, but don't do anything stupid." Alec glares.

I shake my head, waving them both off, "Don't plan on it. Now go away, you know where the door is."

"God, to think he treats all his friends like this," Alec mutters on his way out.

The next day, I get up and go straight to the office telling Mike to contact my favorite choreographer in the entire planet. I love her but I'll be the first to admit, it doesn't hurt her career choice that she's a total bitch.

"Boss, Amber Mallory, Line 2."

"Thank you, Mike."

"Clayton Reynolds, to what on earth do I owe the pleasure?" she squeals, the moment I say hello.

"I'm cashing in the favors you owe me, sugar," I laugh.

"Shit, I knew those were going to haunt me," she giggles. "Alright, hit me."

"I need you to go to Death Valley and look up one Daniel Kingsley. He's a film director who is about to go out of his mind with a poorly organized crew."

"Umm. He's the director. Shouldn't he be doing the organizing?"

"There are a LOT of extras," I grumble, not liking that she pointed out a weakness.

"Define a lot."

"Amber," I snap, "get on a damn plane."

"It will cost ya."

"Like I'm worried."

"Should I tell him you sent me?"

"Yeah, tell him that I'm sending the best because I can't do it myself."

"Flattery will get you everywhere," she giggles again. "Can I have his contact info?"

Hoping I'm not pushing it, I give her the contact information and warn her to be nice to him. She just giggles and lets me go. In attempt to soften the blow of her arrival, I send a few back and forth texts to Ben.

Hey Ben, I have a surprise for Daniel in a few hours. Do you mind rolling with me here?

Daniel doesn't exactly like surprises Clayton.

I know. Trust me alright, you will both be thanking me for this.

For what exactly?

Her name's Amber, she'll be calling you soon. She's a bitch but she's the best.

Clayton man, don't hate me for saying this but you shouldn't have. Thanks for the warning I'll do damage control.

Lol. Thanks. Talk soon.

I spend the rest of my day listening to demo tapes of the 'best and the brightest' and begin to worry that the world has gone to shit, when one of the *Gone a Blur* members barges in my door.

"Heard of knocking?" I snap.

"You're assistant was busy." She shrugs, putting her feet up on my desk.

I push them off and jump to mine. "Don't forget who feeds you," I snarl. "What do you want, Cassandra?"

She stares at her nails likes she's bored. "I'm cancelling Atlanta."

"Why?" I ask cautiously, holding back my temper.

"I just am." She shrugs.

"Let me make this perfectly clear. You finish out your tour, *then* you quit the band, as you oh so desperately want to. If you hang me out on this, I can guarantee you that you will not sing for any record label again."

"Please, don't over dramatize. You don't own me," she scuffs, rolling her eyes.

I glare at her, pulling a file out of my drawer and sliding it over to her. "I have copies." She opens the folder and sees herself in an extremely compromising position and looks up at me in shock. "Finish the tour. If you decide to quit after that, I will give you all the copies. If you don't, I have a direct line to *The Enquirer*." She closes the folder and clears her throat trying to gain some dignity. Stalking out of my office without another word.

After work, I go for a run, and when I get home, I'm almost completely exhausted. Realizing my phone is dead I place it on the charger. Hunting through my fridge I find some leftovers and plop down on the couch, turning on the TV for background noise, content on finishing my plate and going to bed. I'm so fucking beat that when my phone goes off, I honestly debate on whether I am going to get off my tired ass to get it, being that it is on the other side of the room. Moaning, I decide to push myself up and grab it before it hits voicemail. Before I answer it I check the caller ID. At least, it was worth getting up.

"Hello."

"I don't know whether to love you or hate you," Daniel growls.

I cringe. "Too much?"

"Yes, believe me when I say you are in trouble, Clayton," he answers firmly. Then he laughs. "You realize we might try to keep her, right?"

"Does this mean I get to see you soon?" I ask hopeful.

"Maybe, I'll talk to Ben, see if I can get away. He's ecstatic, by the way."

"Glad to hear it." I smile.

We fall silent for a moment. "You sounded tired when you answered the phone."

"I'm on the hunt," I explain. "Every time I look for the new and exciting, I find a shit-load of crap before a singer hits me. Today was just crap."

"I see."

More silence.

"Daniel?"

"Yes, Clayton."

"I want to ask you something, but I don't want you to answer me tonight. And I want you to listen to the reason behind my request before you comment, okay?"

"Why do I have a feeling I am not going to like this?" he moans.

"I don't want to train you," I rush, "not that I don't want you to be trained, just that I can't be the one to do it. I don't feel comfortable adding another sub to our arrangement . . . not after . . ." I cut off, unable to say it.

"I'm listening," he encourages after a few moments.

"I want Alec to do it. Do you remember Alec? He was the one who introduced us. He's very good at this, Daniel, and I am willing to submit to both of you."

Silence.

"Daniel?"

"Clayton, as your master, I'm going to ask you a series of questions. I expect honest answers with a yes or no." I agree with my silence. "Alec is your previous master, yes?"

"How did you . . . ?"

"Yes or no, Clayton."

I swallow hard. "Yes."

"This said master is the same master who fell in love with you?"

I close my eyes. "Yes, but we're still very close friends."

Silence.

"I said yes or no."

"My apologies, Master. Yes."

"You will be punished accordingly. This is the same master who taught you?"

"Yes."

"Has he agreed to this?"

"Yes."

"Did you think about what you were asking of him emotionally, offering yourself to him as a sub?"

"No."

"Now that I've brought it to light, does it change your request?"

"No," I answer, closing my eyes. Fuck! How the hell am I going to explain Alec to him? Never mind I can't ever tell him about the exception of Angles of Justice. The exception is why I didn't even flinch when asking Alec to do this. I've kneeled before him less than two months ago. If Alec had a problem with me submitting to him, I would know it.

"Ask him again, with this new information. If he says yes, I'll consider it."

"Yes, Master. Thank you, Master." I'm forced to keep my thoughts to myself. Angels of Justice survives because of secrecy, it is a must, and I don't know how much I can trust him. Fact is, Daniel is not one of us, and because of that, he can't know.

"Now, it's time for your punishment for the following: not following directions, sending Amber without asking first, and not taking Alec's feelings into consideration. Drop your pants to your knees right where you are standing." I drop my pants. "Start masturbating, while you do it, I want you to constantly rub your finger over your sensitive tip." I follow his orders, my breathing staying steady. When it hitches a little, he continues, "Take the finger you are using on your tip and collect your pre-cum. Keep stroking yourself with your other hand." Obeying, I spread my legs a little to keep my pants at my knees and balance my phone on my shoulder. "Now, suck the cum off your finger," he orders, "and thrust your dick harder." I obey while he stays silent, listening to my breathing and moaning. Not much longer, I am forcing myself to hold back the desire to cum, and right when I think I'm going to lose it, he orders, "Grip the base of your dick hard and cockblock yourself." I scream out, following his painful instruction. "Stay standing and support your own weight," he growls, causing me to be even more uncomfortable while I force my body to calm in the most painful way possible. For phone sex, it was a harsh punishment.

"You will call me tomorrow after you talk to Alec, and if you two are still comfortable, you will have him call me," he orders.

"Yes, Master."

"Clayton?"

"Master?"

"No. Dang, we need a transition word."

"I also need a new safe words," I point out, wanting something more personal, but not wanting to use the ones I use with Alec.

"Hmm . . . looks like we need a kitchen conference."

"You're coming back soon, aren't you?" I smile.

"Amber bought the ticket before I even met her, saying something along the lines of needing to thank my man because she doesn't come cheap."

"Well, no, not usually, but I cashed in a few favors she owed me."

"I'm serious. I really think Ben is going to try to keep her," he warns. "I made him hold off on any offers until I talked to you about it."

"Only if I can borrow her now and again." I smile. "I really am glad it worked out."

"Me too, I have an early flight tomorrow. I should get going."

"Be safe," I whisper.

"I will," he promises.

We say our goodnights, and right after we hang up, he texts me his flight number. Even though I'm sexually frustrated, I sleep better than I have in the past two nights, knowing I was able to put a smile on his face, where it belongs.

12
Respect

Daniel's Point of View

"Welcome back, Mr. Kingsley." The flight attendant winks, passing me my drink and a napkin.

"Thanks." I smile pulling out my tray. That's when I notice a note.

You are so fucking hot! Call me 281-555-3825—Jeremy

I can't help the blush that crosses my face as I read the message. I have known this guy professionally for over three years, he chooses now to come on to me! I guess Clayton is affecting me more than I realize. I find a pen from my bag. *Sorry, taken.* Then wait to hand it back to him when he comes to collect my trash.

The flight takes longer than I remember, but I'm sure it has something to do with my nerves. My mind has been reeling since last night. I have to admit I never really thought about the *actual* training part before. But Clayton had and though I really hate to agree with him, a no-name sub wasn't an option. That bridge was torched in a very large flame, leaving us with only one option. Clayton being the sub, which was not easy for him; *I am pushing him by asking for it in the first place.* His solution is reasonable in the grand scheme of things. He's comfortable and I will be taught by the best. I just wish the best wasn't in love with the same man I was.

~Three Years Ago~

My flesh is raw from the flogger; my dick is dripping with cum. I'm tied to an X-frame, my back to my master. This is the second time he has used this device. I was nervous last time because it was the first time I've had my back to him; he made it as comfortable as possible by showing me the items in which he was going to use before he used them. This time, however, he's pushing me a little more by surprising me with his objects. He started with a riding crop, then the flogger. Now I'm waiting for the next item, waiting, waiting . . . WHAP! A hard leather paddle smacks across my sensitive skin.

"Rose!" I scream, unable to take it any longer. All movements cease immediately, and my master's fingers are in my hair.

"I'm going to release you Daniel, but I need you to talk to me. Tell me what you're feeling." His hands leave my hair and move to my wrists.

"I . . . can't, I just . . . too much," I stammer out, dropping my wrist that my master has freed, watching as he unties me from the rest quickly, offering his shoulder to help me to keep steady. When I start to walk, my knees betray me, causing me to stumble, but I'm caught by his strong arms.

"Take slow, deep breaths, Daniel," he tells me, pulling me close to his body. I fill my lungs with air, hoping the room will eventually stop spinning. I feel weak. My master helps me to a spanking block and sits me down.

"Are you okay to sit here on your own?" he asks, worry etched in every inch of his face.

"Yes, Master."

He nods stepping away. "I'll be right back."

I take the time to gather my wits about me, putting my elbows on my knees, placing my face in my hands, still trying to maintain slow breathing.

"Wrap your arms around me," my master says, bending down so I can grip his neck. He lifts me up into his strong arms, caring me out of the room into the spare bathroom. The moment we walk in, we are hit with steam, from a freshly drawn bath. "Get in," he instructs. The hot water feels good on my muscles but not so great on my skin at first, that is, until it goes slightly numb. The tub is a Jacuzzi-style, big enough for two; still I am slightly surprised when my master strips down to join me. "Show me your back, Daniel," he instructs.

I shift around to do so, feeling his hands fall to my shoulders, kneading my muscles.

"I'm sorry I failed you, Master," I whisper as tears of shame come over me.

"Failed me, Daniel?" he asks surprised. "You have not failed me."

"But I had to stop. I couldn't appreciate your skills."

"Daniel, had you not stopped me, and you were suffering, then you would have failed me. Using your safe words does not mean you failed me. You just met your limits tonight. I will warn you, I will bring you here again, then I will push you past them. It will take time, but in the end, you will thank me."

"Why are you doing this?" I ask. "I have done nothing to pleasure you, yet this feels like I'm being rewarded somehow."

He sighs but does not stop. "Daniel, I am your master. My job is to put you above all else, including my own pleasure. I pushed you tonight, just as I will every time we meet, but I will not forsake you. I will be there through everything, including helping you down from your limits."

I fall silent for a while, thinking about his words and really enjoying this massage. "Master?"

"Daniel."

"I'm confused."

"Feel free to ask me, Daniel," he encourages, dropping his hands.

"Last time," I swallow hard, "last time, I failed you, I was abandoned."

"Look at me, Daniel." I turn to face him. "Do you remember our contract?"

"Yes, Master."

"What are my three unforgivables, Daniel?"

"Misuse or lack of safe wording, falling in love, and cumming without permission."

"Did I push you to your limits on the day you are referring to, Daniel?"

"No, Master."

"And what happened?" he asks, I can tell he's trying to keep his voice even.

"I broke our contract," I admit in shame. "But you allowed renewal."

"Do you see the difference, Daniel?"

"Yes, Master," I answer, casting my eyes down.

He lifts his hands from the water and combs his fingers through my hair. "I'm proud of you, Daniel. You serve me well."

"Thank you, Master."

~Present Day~

I am your master. My job is to put you above all else, including my own pleasure. I frown at the memory but appreciate it all the same. Stepping into this role is going to be harder than I initially thought, especially since Clayton has expressed his limits. I have to put my insecurities about Alec aside and let him train me, for Clayton, for us, but that doesn't mean I have to like it.

We're still very good friends. Clayton's voice echoes in my head. I moan out loud. Alec is a package deal with Clayton whether I like it or not. I will not choose his friends, but I will feel more comfortable speaking with Alec alone before this goes any further.

When I get off the plane, I smile at the flight attendant on the way out. "No hard feelings."

He shrugs, "I can be patient."

I chuckle. "Don't hold your breath. I think he may be a keeper."

"Only time will tell," he laughs, giving me a wink.

I roll my eyes and head for the luggage carousal. The shoot is basically over. We had our main characters' roles performed to satisfaction by the time that Amber had gotten there. We just had a few scenes with the extras that were driving us up the damn wall. There was this dancer who could only do one thing—dance. You ask anything else of her, and she's close to tears. Ben and I thought about firing her, but we loved her dancing style, so we tried to work with her over and over and over . . . then Amber shows up and she nails it in three takes. That's when Ben told me he wanted Amber's personal number as he vividly pondered her other skills. Since he was so distracted and Amber had already bought a one-way plane ticket, I asked Ben if he would mind taking the rest of the shoot by himself. The grin on his face was divine. "No, Daniel. I don't mind if I have Amber's undivided attention."

So here I am in Texas, waiting on my damn luggage. Seriously, what the hell is taking so long?! I'm getting impatient watching bag after bag until finally the last one is pushed through, which is mine. At least they didn't lose my luggage. Grabbing it, I walk out of the airport with the reality that my car is parked in my boyfriend's driveway. Cringing, I head for the cab line.

"Need a ride, darlin'?" a familiar voice calls.

"Clayton?" I ask in surprise.

"You gave me your flight number," he says smiling, "and I am holding your car hostage, so I thought I would be nice."

I bite my lower lip, walking up to him. I'm not one hundred percent sure how to react to this because I really don't want this to become a trend, but at the same time, I really appreciate it. "Thank you," I whisper, pressing my lips to his.

"You're welcome, but don't get used to it."

I try not to show my relief. He insists on taking my luggage from me, arguing I have the laptop and just got off a long flight and it's the least he can do. I try to protest, but he gives me a look causing me to fall silent immediately. Then he smiles, grabs my hand, and takes me to his car.

When he pulls out of the parking garage, he frowns. "I have to get back to the office, darlin'."

"Not a problem. You can just drop me off at my place." I shrug with a smile.

"Actually, I'm going to drop you off at mine," he answers, biting his lower lip, indicating he's nervous.

"May I ask why?"

"Two reasons, the first being that I don't have keys to your car, so I think you might like it back."

"The second?"

"Alec wants to talk to you in person," he answers, staring at the road in front of him.

"I see." Tension in the car builds as silence falls between us. "Pull over," I finally instruct, pointing to an exit ramp. He doesn't question me and exits the highway. Once he gets past the lights, he pulls into a commuter parking lot and parks the car.

"Look at me, Clayton." He closes his eyes for a moment before slowly turning to face me, keeping his eyes cast downward. "No, Clayton. *Look* at me." He lifts his eyes to mine, and I can tell he's freaking out unsure as to what is coming next.

"I've been doing some thinking since we last spoke," I start, seeing his body tense. "I'm not sure if you realized exactly what you asked of me last night, Clayton. I'm not sure if you see things the same way I do, but that's your boyfriend talking. As your master, I realize I have to step into a different role. You explained it to me once, saying a master must put their sub above everything else, including themselves. Last night, you set limits, Clayton, and though they are uncomfortable to me personally, I feel that as your master, I need to fulfill this request."

"Thank you, Master." He smiles then holds up a finger, meeting my eyes. "Daniel?"

I realize he's transitioned on me and I smile, letting him know it's okay. "You're about to question me on my insecurities about Alec, aren't you?"

He nods. "You do realize there is nothing to worry about, right? I mean Alec is happy with another. We're just all really close friends."

"I'm getting that impression." I frown. "I'm just, I don't know. We barely know each other socially, and we have these feelings, this history and it's so complicated. Then you have a friend who admitted he was in love with you . . . not to mention he knows you better than I do."

"You're jealous," he concludes obviously upset.

"Yes," I admit. "But not the 'I don't want you to be friends with him' kind of way, more of the 'envy, I want that to be us' way."

He gives me a smile, reaching for my neck, pulling me toward him. "You silly, silly man, don't you realize what we have is so much more than what I've ever had with anyone one else?" He presses his lips to mine. "I love you, only you," he whispers, kissing me again. Then he puts his forehead on mine. "Do you trust me, Daniel?"

The question surprises me; trust is the last thing I want him to question. I grip his hair at the back of his neck. "Completely, always," I whisper back before our lips collide and our tongues dance. When we break away for air, I look at him. "Never doubt my trust, Clayton, please." He shakes his head, trying to kiss me again, but I hold him firmly by his hair. "I'm not ready to say it, not yet. Please be patient," I whisper. He gives me a small smile. "I really do suck at relationships," I admit. "And this master gig is a lot harder than I initially realized."

"Daniel, if you're uncomfortable, we don't have to . . ."

I kiss him lightly on the lips, silencing him. "I want to try it, Clayton. If it doesn't work out, it doesn't work out." I can see a small amount of fear come into his eyes. "Not us," I clarify. "I want us to work, and if it doesn't, well, I really don't want to think about that." I press my lips to his again, still holding him to me, hoping to express to him what I feel in ways words seem to fail me.

Passion ignites between us, he starts kissing down my jawline, reaching for my belt. I pull back in surprise, but the flare in his eyes leaves me no room to argue, I moan, meeting his lips again. The feel of his naked hand on my cock is amazing. He breaks the kiss long enough to growl, "I want to fucking swallow your cum." Then his hand squeezes my dick. I wiggle my pants off my lap, looking around to see if there is anyone there to notice. The place appears to be deserted with empty cars, before I can get a full assessment, my dick is in Clayton's warm mouth.

"Oh my fuck," I moan, gripping at his hair while his tongue swirls around my cock. He moans in response to my gasp, gently tugging on my balls, causing a string of profanities to escape me while I struggle to stay in my seat. His tongue is just as talented with my dick as it is my mouth. I'm on edge at an embarrassing quick pace. To my defense, I can't count the number of blow jobs I've had since I met Clayton, because there aren't any to count. I haven't received head in over three fucking years. "Clayton, baby, I'm gonna cum!" I warn, which only causes more pleasure from him swallowing my dick down his throat. "MAS-CLAY!" I scream as I fall over the edge, giving him my seed to swallow.

When my dick goes soft in his mouth, he pulls away, licks it clean, and then busts up laughing. "Mas-Clay?"

I start laughing as well. "Sorry about that. I was floating."

"No biggie. Thanks for the Clay," he laughs, again putting the car into drive while I redress, winking at me he adds, "But I do prefer Clayton."

He pulls into his driveway about ten minutes later, and we make a date for later that night. "Thank you for understanding, Daniel," he whispers, before kissing me again.

I nod, getting out of the car. "Thanks for the ride. I'll see you tonight."

He smiles and I close the car door, nervous as hell to go inside. Taking calming deep breaths, I choose to try the front door knob and not knock. It's unlocked, so I let myself in.

Alec is sitting on the couch, watching the latest baseball game.

"Rangers or Cardinals?" I ask, making my way to Clayton's fridge, hoping there is beer.

"Cardinals," he mutters unhappily. "We're down by seven."

"Ouch."

"Too many errors," he bitches. "We pay these guys way too much for such a poor performance."

"I'd have to agree with you there." I smile, handing him a beer.

"Thanks," he says, not really looking at me.

I sit down in the opposite side of the couch, starring at the screen, watching our home team get our asses kicked, while waiting for the inedible conversation. After almost a half hour, I figure he's waiting on me.

"So you seem to be my boyfriend's best friend," I start, "at least, that's the impression I'm getting."

"We're close," he confirms, taking a swig of beer.

"How close?" I ask, keeping my nervousness out of my voice.

"Closer than most of his past relationships have been comfortable with," he answers. "I mainly try to stay out of the scenes to avoid the whole jealous boyfriend bit. It gets tiring and I'm not going anywhere."

I bite the inside of my cheek, working to keep my attitude in check. "Are you still in love with him?"

He turns to look me in the eye, "Yes, I am."

I give a small smile. "I was expecting you to deny it."

"Not my style," he answers, turning back to the game.

"Does he know?"

"On some level, I'm sure he's always known that, but it's not like we talk about it or anything." He shrugs. "I was actually surprised when he asked me about it today, but I realized quickly that you were the one who made him ask."

"What did you tell him?"

"Same thing I'm telling you," he answers turning back to me. "I know he still feels the same way he always has, and if he were to change his mind, I think I would freak." He rolls his eyes and curses at the screen as the catcher misses a fly ball allowing the man on third to slide into home. The game goes to commercial and he slouches back. "We would never work out in the end. I'm pretty sure he knew that way before I did. Besides, Bobby makes me happy, and we both love each other."

"How does Bobby feel about this training idea?" I ask, taking a drink of my beer.

Alec snaps his head back in my direction, appraising me for a moment before he answers. "He understands the situation for what it is."

"So he's about as happy as I am," I mutter.

"He expressed his concern but left the decision up to me," Alec answers, narrowing his eyes. "What about you? Are you going to deny Clayton this request?"

"I can't," I answer honestly. "As his master, my responsibility is to take care of him. He set his limits, I have to respect them. I don't have to like them, but I have to respect them."

"As his boyfriend?"

"I won't choose his friends, Alec." I assure him, "I'm hoping for a truce, maybe a night out on the town as a group or something. I'm willing to bend. I trust Clayton completely. Trusting you will take time, but I'm willing to give it a shot."

"I can see why he fell in love with you," Alec smiles, turning back to the screen. "You realize that your request for this 'switching' is one of the most uncomfortable things you or anyone has ever asked of him?"

"You don't approve."

"Not my business one way or the other." He shrugs. "But you seem to be doing it right. You understand the rules of the game, which is the main thing. But if you could do me a huge favor and explain to Clayton and myself for that matter what the hell 'needy' means, I'd really fucking appreciate it."

I cringe. "Mixed signals?"

"Understatement."

"Noted." I smile. "Thanks."

"You want to start tonight?"

"Clayton and I have some details to work out first, but tonight's good."

"We will start out as equals, Daniel, but in the end, *you* are Clayton's master. He will be following your lead."

"Thank you, Alec, for everything." I smile, standing up. "I need to get going. I'll see you tonight, say eight."

"I'll be here." He agrees. "Daniel?"

"Yes, Alec."

"You seem to understand me better than Clayton about this for some reason, and I'm not sure why that is. But since you will be his master when I'm around, can I ask that you two keep your personal relations private?"

"Personal relations?" I ask confused.

"Kissing, fucking," he explains evenly.

"I can do that as his master." I agree. "As his boyfriend, you will have to get used to the small public displays."

"I know." He shrugs. "Just please not while we're training. I don't need you to piss on your territory. I know what's yours."

"I think I can see why Clayton likes you." I laugh, heading for the door.

When I get home I realize that I left my luggage in Clayton's car, but I don't call him about it, figuring I would get it later. I make myself a sandwich and leave money on the side table for my cleaning lady. Then I take a nap before preparing for my evening with a fresh shower and a clean shave.

On my drive back to Clayton's, my mind drifts back through today. I feel better about this whole weird situation that I am being put in with Alec. And am grateful that Clayton didn't seem upset when I told him I wasn't ready to express myself in words. It means a lot to me that he was willing to wait for me.

When I get to Clayton's house my pleasant mood is burst the moment I walk through his door. He's obviously upset about something.

"Hey?" I ask in concern. "What's wrong?"

"What makes you think something's wrong?" he asks casually.

I raise an eyebrow at him, and he turns away from me. "Alright, something's wrong."

"Anything I can do?"

"An explanation would be nice." I look at him like he has three heads, unsure what he's talking about. "Don't be pissed, okay." Now I'm on edge. "My assistant pissed me off today, royally pissed me off," he growls. "I was angry and I wanted to show him who the hell he works for, so I made him do some dry cleaning."

"Dry cleaning?" I close my eyes, fighting back the instant headache. "My luggage."

"Yeah," he confirms. "I'm sorry if that crosses any lines, but I wasn't thinking clearly. Don't worry," he growls, trying to keep his temper, "it backfired on me when he handed me this. Apparently it was on top of your clothes. Forgive me for my assumption here but I was under the impression we're exclusive."

"We are." I confirm, completely lost, taking a piece of paper and a white bag that he hands me. *Thanks for the chance, sexy. Can't wait to hear from you. Enclosed is something I want you to wear on our date—Jeremy.*

"Fucking asshole," I bitch, pulling my phone out of the pocket.

"*Thank you for calling Mile High Airlines how may I direct your call?*"

"You can connect me to Martin Smalls," I snap.

"*I'm sorry, sir.*"

"This is Daniel Kingsley."

"*Oh, Mr. Kingsley. One moment . . . Martin Smalls, how may I help you?*"

"You can fire your fucking flight attendant!"

"*Who is this?*"

"Daniel Kingsley."

"*Mr. Kingsley, how did one of our flight attendants upset you?*"

"He fucking broke into my luggage and left me a note and a goddamn G-string to piss my boyfriend off!"

"*Mr. Kingsley, not to be condescending here, but can you tell me what proof you have?*"

I take a few deep breaths, trying to stay calm, vaguely registering that Clayton is watching me intently. "The proof I have is in my fucking hand, Martin. Never mind the fact he signed his fucking name! Don't tell me someone is setting him up, because I turned his ass down on my last flight, telling him I was dating someone. Now I can see why my bag was the last off the damn plane!"

"My deepest apologies, Mr. Kingsley. I'll see that your request is followed through."

"You better, or I'm taking my company and personal business elsewhere!"

"Understood. Once again, my sincerest apologies, Mr. Kingsley. Please take a complimentary Mile High flight for two anywhere you'd like."

I narrow my eyes. "I'll call you in a few days."

"Well, until then."

I snap the phone shut still working to calm myself. I make my way to Clayton's kitchen, find a bag to throw the shit in and toss it in the corner, just in case I need it for proof later. "Un-fucking-believable!"

"Well, that answers that," Clayton says with wide eyes. "I believe I know you well enough not get a stranger fired to save our relationship."

"I wouldn't put it past me," I smirk. "You are crazy sexy."

"Daniel."

"He gave me his phone number. I told him I was taken. I should have known he was up to something because he said he'd wait for me. I told him not to hold his breath, you were a keeper. He retorts with 'Only time will tell.' Fucking creep," I shudder, realizing I'm pissed again.

"I believe you." Clayton smiles. "You do realize you are fucking hot when you're pissed? It's taking every bit of restraint I have not to jump you right now."

"What's stopping you?"

"Pesky things like needing to talk before Alec gets here." He shrugs.

"I'm not in the proper frame of mind for that right now, Clayton. I need a distraction."

"That, that I can do." He smiles, walking up to me, rubbing his hand on my cock while he kisses me breathless.

"We're running out of time," I whimper, breaking away.

"Alright, let's get the pesky talking over with."

"Clayton?"

"Hmm?"

"How would you feel if I wanted to stay the night tonight?" His eyes flash into mine, I can tell he's fighting back a grin. "Good," I whisper in his ear, "because there are things I plan to do to you tonight that involves a lot of free time and privacy." He moans in response. "Clayton."

"Daniel," he whispers, kissing my neck.

"Your master wants you to go sit in the fucking kitchen chair."

He drops his arms away from me, silently agreeing to my request, but I can tell he's reluctant about it.

"Have you thought about your safe words?"

"Cherry, Seed, Stem."

"What about a transition word?"

"Red."

I laugh at his creativity. He's really put thought into it, seeing how both set of our safe words could be that color. "That's fitting. I like it."

"Is there anything you are against, Clayton?" I ask watching his body tense.

"I'm comfortable with the tools that we have in the room."

"Clayton? Don't shut me out or we will stop before we start."

"Red," he sighs, looking me in the eye. "Okay, I want to talk to you about this as a couple."

"A couple?"

He takes a moment before he explains. "It's the collar." He frowns. "I've never used one, and I understand the necessity of it. I do," he says, staring me in the eye, almost pleading that I don't get upset.

"But . . ."

"Promise me it's just for clarification purposes, and we will never use it as a restraint or add a leash or anything weird or degrading like that," he rushes in a timid voice.

I can't keep the shock off my features or the instant tears from falling out of my unblinking eyes. "Clayton, I would never . . . I can't even fathom . . . I'm sorr . . ."

I'm cut off by his tongue being shoved in my mouth. "I'm sorry. I know you gave it as a gift. It just freaked me out. I'm sorry. I should have said something sooner. I just didn't know how to react," he rushes.

"Breathe, Clayton," I interrupt trying to process but he's talking too fast.

"Daniel, I'm serious. I know you would not be cruel to me. I'm sorry. It's an overreaction to over-thinking. It's just, well, Alec's past kinda freaked me out on the whole thing, and fuck, I'm an idiot."

"Red!" I snap. "Sit down and shut the fuck up!" I yell, truly annoyed. *What the hell? I made him uncomfortable and didn't even know it!* "Damn it, Clayton!" I bitch, pulling at the roots of my hair as I lean back into the chair. "First, this is *not* a boyfriend issue. While I respect the fact that you want to speak freely, don't do that!"

"Yes, Master."

I glare at him for talking out of turn. "Second, I'm sorry that you were uncomfortable. That was not my intention, and you will be punished tonight for not bringing this to my attention sooner."

"Yes, Master."

"Stop that. I didn't give you permission to speak!" I snap again. He swallows hard but says nothing while he finally casts his eyes downward. "You obviously understand the true motive behind the collar, but I will not use it if you are uncomfortable. If you ask for it, that is one thing, but until then, it's off limits."

"Permission to speak freely, Master."

"Denied," I growl, still trying to collect my thoughts. "Go get into position, Clayton, but before you do, grab a pair of boxers. I'm sure you understand the need."

He shakes his head, leaving the kitchen. I take the time to try and calm myself, not much longer, Alec walks through the door.

"Are you ready?" he asks.

"No," I answer, my hands are still shaking. "I need a moment."

"You two have a fight?"

I close my eyes. "Not exactly. I just had two curveballs thrown at me. I'm shakin' up is all."

"Want to talk about it?"

"I had a flight attendant try to break up my relationship and my sub not be completely honest with me. You know, just a normal day." I laugh humorlessly.

"And what did you do about it?" he asks evenly.

"I went off on the airline," I dismiss not bothering with details.

"And the sub?"

"Nothing as of yet. I'm too angry."

"Where is he?"

— 115 —

"Where he's supposed to be," I answer a bit sharp. "Sorry. I just need a moment."

"What did he lie to you about?"

"I'm sure you know," I snip. "Apparently, there is an issue with collars that I had no clue about. And if that piece of information wasn't enough, he tries to talk to me about it as a boyfriend, not a sub! I don't want that shit to blend. That was the damn point of the piece of leather to start with."

"Did you give him the right to speak freely and explain the whole story?"

"I would have if he didn't already piss me off," I growl, crossing my arms over my chest. "I need help on how to calm down, Alec. I know that as a boyfriend, we could kiss and make up, but this, this is odd."

"Making him wait for you is always a good start." He shrugs. "You are doing the right thing by making sure your head is clear before you walk in there."

"That means a lot, coming from you."

"Did it feel good to tell the airline off?"

"Hell yeah!"

"Hang on to that feeling, Daniel. That is the frame of mind you are looking for."

"Clayton needs to be punished."

"I agree," Alec nods. "What do you have in mind?"

"For talking out of turn, teasing." I decide. "For omitting his feelings and allowing a session, short as it may have been, with something that clearly makes him uncomfortable . . . I'd like to use a whip or cane, but I don't want that to be how we start this out. I want to learn the pleasure tools. I hate punishment." I complain, running my fingers through my hair.

"Sub talking," Alec chuckles and then turns serious. "You have to learn all of them, and you will need the most lessons on the harder stuff. The last thing you want to do is hurt him," he falls silent. Then adds, "If it helps, I'm personally pissed about him keeping it from you too. This is a major thing, Daniel. It requires you to set him straight so you don't have this in the future."

"So what are your suggestions?"

"We punish tonight, I'd forgo the teasing, it doesn't fit with the lesson he needs to learn. I'll teach you the pleasure tools when he deserves them," Alec answers matter-of-factly.

"I thought you two were friends."

"We are," he answers firmly.

"So I'm not overreacting. This *is* a big deal."

"No, Daniel, you are not overreacting," Alec assures me.

"Good to know."

"Are you ready?"

"I want you to show me tonight." I tell him. "I will try it out, but for the most part, I want you to show me."

"Okay," he answers, standing up and walking toward the playroom. "You're calm, Daniel. It's time."

"Is it wrong to be dreading this?"

"No," he answers kindly, opening the doors.

Clayton is in position on the floor, I can tell that he has been crying. The emotion tugs at my heart, I look to Alec, who shakes his head no, and I frown. He's right. I can't comfort him. I can't tell him everything will be okay. He has shed tears of shame, as he should. I walk up behind him and run my fingers through his hair. He breaks position, leaning his head back, meeting my eyes.

"I'm sorry, Master," he whispers.

I drop my hands and step away. "I haven't given you permission to speak." He returns to his position, casting his eyes to the floor. "For being such a strict master yourself, Clayton, I am surprised at how sloppy you are as a sub." I circle him with honest disgust on my face. "Not being honest with me is an insult, and I am going to punish you for it; unless of course you want to bow out as a sub." I stop dead in front of him, standing there for a long moment. "Look at me, Clayton." His eyes meet mine. "Do you want to back out of this part of our relationship?" I ask sincerely, making the question clear that it would not be the end of all our relations. "Yes or no. Speak."

"No, Master," he answers confidently.

"Do you understand and agree that you need to be punished? Yes or no?"

"Yes, Master."

"Had we reverse roles, then you would not go light on me. I am going to treat you with the same respect. What are your safe words, Clayton?"

"Cherry, Seed, Stem."

"Would you be punished for using them?"

"No, Master."

"Good. Eyes down."

I walk over to the cabinet and pull out a silicon cock ring. Going back over to him I drop it in his line of sight. "This device would help you follow my instruction, but I am not going to use it. You *will* control yourself. You have lost the privilege to cum tonight. Stand," I order walking back over to the cabinet, retrieving the chains with leather restraints. I hit the automatic switch on the wall next to it, and a metal hook projects downward. Walking back to Clayton I strap the leather cuffs of the chains to his wrists before locking the chain to the hook. Then I walk back over to the switch. "Tell me when, Clayton." The hook starts to go back to its position in the ceiling until Clayton's hands are raised high above his head.

"When, Master."

Approaching him I test the chains, satisfied. "Good. Now, tell me in your own words why you are being punished."

"I failed you as a sub by not communicating my whole feelings."

"And?" I ask, after he falls silent.

"I allowed you to have a session even though I was uncomfortable," he cries. "I'm so sorry, Master."

"Anything else, Clayton?"

He's silent for a moment. "I'm having difficulties transferring back, mainly by talking out of turn or by wanting to fall out of submissive state to have my way."

"Don't forget eye contact." I add in disgust. "Are any of these actions considered respectable behavior?"

"No, Master."

"I'm asking you one more time, Clayton. If this is too difficult for you, I understand. I will not end our personal relationship if you cannot submit to me. Do you accept your punishment as a disrespectful sub, or do you want to end this part of our relationship?"

"I accept punishment," he answers firmly, keeping his eyes trained to the ground. I close mine, fighting back the knot in my stomach and look at

Alec standing next to the cabinet, which Clayton has his back to. He nods in encouragement.

"So be it." I walk over to the cabinet and Alec.

"I'm assuming the boxers are for my benefit."

I shrug. "His too."

"Then he will take this with his back." He hands me a slapper. "Warm him up with this." I raise an eyebrow and he smiles. "Hold out your arm." I follow his instruction. "Watch my wrist in slow motion." He demonstrates how to use the tool properly, and I nod in understanding after the second time. Taking the device, I walk over to Clayton, presenting the object in his line of sight.

"What do you see?"

"Our slapper, Master."

"Good, now please be a good boy and don't scream." I order, walking behind him, hitting him with it. The three layers of leather slap together giving an effective slapping noise, but his skin shows little response. Alec is next to me. "Pull back a little and hold your arm like this," he explains. This time, his skin flushes. Alec steps back, allowing me to continue on my own. All the while, I concentrate on the act of the swing and not on the reason for it, which allows me to stay focused, keeping Clayton safe.

After his entire back is flushed a beautiful shade of pink, I walk back to Alec taking the whip he hands me. "As far as these go, this is rather a soft selection," he observers. "I shouldn't be surprised. The man who ordered it was a sub once upon a time." I give him a pointed look, he smiles. "I guess he is now as well. Don't get me wrong. It has a bite, but the sting is nowhere near what it should be in my personal opinion."

Handing it back I ask him to show me, ignoring my flipping stomach. Alec demonstrates how to hold it, smacking the wall with it a few times, showing me his wrist action then has me try. When I've taken a few test blows on the wall, he encourages me to go to Clayton. Reluctantly, I do so and once again stand in his line of sight.

"What do you see, Clayton?"

His breath hitches, but he manages to keep his voice even, "Our whip, Master."

"Do you agree that you deserve punishment by this tool?"

He licks his lips. "Yes, Master."

I walk behind him, and Alec is once again by my side, showing me the stance and whatnot. I take my first swing, and Clayton cries out in pain the moment it makes contact. Alec's face balls up in anger, and I am almost ill from the sound. Alec pulls me to the side, whispering in my ear, "You told him not to scream. Obviously, from your reaction, I can see why. You don't have a gag ball in this collection, which is surprising. Threaten him with losing his dignity of underwear around me and use it as a gag to keep him quiet. Daniel, you can't effectively dole out a proper punishment if you are not committed to it."

I nod my head at him and position myself in front of Clayton, gripping his chin roughly in my hand. "I told you not to scream, Clayton." Tears streak down his face. "Do it again, and your boxers will be your gag ball while Master Alec admires the view." I release his face and step out of his line of sight. Then I stand behind him and wait. After counting to three hundred in my head, I snap the whip again. Clayton jerks, giving out a forced clench groan. "Better, but not perfect." I note.

"Same with you," Alec assesses. "May I?"

"Clayton, for the next few blows, I am going to be watching Master Alec use this tool. Does this make you uncomfortable?"

"No, Master," he answers in a whimper.

Alec starts to explain his stance and motions to me, when he's finished talking, he too waits before he delivers his blow, which is much harder than my two. Clayton falls back on his restraints, lifting his feet up off the ground for a moment but manages to keep from screaming. I'm worried, and immediately my hands are on his torso.

"Clayton, talk to me. Are you okay?"

"Yes, Master," he answers. "Thank you, Master. May I please have another?" He grunts, tears sliding down his face. Sighing, I step back signaling Alec to strike while I stand in front of him. I need to see how he reacts to this, and we don't have a mirror. Again, Clayton struggles but manages to hold his ground. The tears are the hardest thing to stomach. Staring at him now, it's hard for me to continue this, but I know I must. He must learn. "Again," I command, watching Clayton's body absorb the blow. I walk back to Alec and take the tool. I strike Clayton once more myself, and this one has a bite to it.

"Good," Alec praises while Clayton fights for control. He corrects me on a few small things, and by the tenth total blow between us, I feel comfortable with the tool. I do not feel comfortable with Clayton's back though.

Alec seems to catch my internal grimace and drags me back to the cabinet. He gives a small smile, handing me some leather cuffs and a hard leather paddle. "Perhaps something more intimate, yet humiliating, to finish off." I raise an eyebrow. Alec shakes his head, "I can't believe I'm going to tell you this, but this particular sub finds extreme humiliation in a knee spanking." I nod in understanding, trying to keep the smile off my face. I've always rather enjoyed it myself.

I hit the switch to lower the hook calling over my shoulder. "On your knees." I walk back to him, replacing his leather chain cuffs for the restrictive leather ones, effectively trapping his arms in front of him. "Stand," I command. Alec flips the switch to put the hook back. I guide Clayton over to our spanking block and sit down comfortably on it. "Bend over me," I command firmly. He hesitates for a quick moment but follows my instructions. "Are you alright, Clayton?" I ask lowering his boxers to his knees.

"Yes, Master."

"This has less of an impact," I note, showing him the leather paddle, "and I have not touched your ass tonight. Since that is the case, you will receive double the blows with this as you did the whip."

"Please, Master."

"Please?"

"Please punish me for my insulting behavior," Clayton begs.

"Now it's thirty," I snap. "You will not ask for punishment, Clayton." I slap his ass with my bare hand. He jumps in surprise but falls back into position. I continue with my hand until his ass is completely pink, then I pick up the paddle. "Start counting." He does so, when we reach seventeen, I can tell he's grown completely uncomfortable and the strokes are no longer pleasurable but painful. It doesn't help that he's rock hard and is forcing his body not to cum. By twenty-three, I am in agony, but I refuse to yield my consistent force, I am not weak. By the time we hit thirty, I'm close to tears myself, seeing the puddle of water from Clayton's on the padded floor. When I finally finish I rub his ass lightly before raising his boxers up to his waist. Then I resituate his restraints so that his arms are behind his back. "Scoot to the middle of the floor on your knees and wait for me," I instruct, he scoots himself slowly to where I instructed, bowing his head while he gets into position. I take the paddle back to the cabinet and indicate that Alec follow me out. The moment the doors close, I break down crying.

"Shh," Alec whispers, pulling me to his shoulder. "I know that was hard for both of you, Daniel, but it was necessary. He needs to view you as a Dom, not just a sub-boyfriend wannabe."

I can't keep myself from gripping onto this near stranger for dear life, trying to swim out of the water that seems to be drowning my lungs. "I know you're right, I do, but that, that . . . there are no words for how bad that sucked."

"I know," he sighs. "Come on, I'll show you what's best to use to help with his bruising," he offers, dragging me to the spare bathroom. He pulls out three familiar lotions from under the sink and explains the benefits of each one to me.

"When you go back in there you cannot be his boyfriend, Daniel. It's essential that you stay his master the rest of the night."

I frown. "I was planning on spending the night with him."

"Then spend the night with him." He smiles. "But don't transition until the morning. Trust me on this."

"What if he wants to?"

Alec gives me a raised eyebrow. "You're his master, Daniel. Do not give him the chance to do so."

"You mean deny him speech."

"Yes." He shrugs. "And deny any other comforting boyfriend technique you two have. You can hold him, Daniel, but don't be surprised if he cries. Don't go soft and kiss it better. Just let him absorb this lesson."

"Thank you again, Alec. Clayton really did do us both a favor by asking for this arrangement."

He gives me a kind smile. "Which is why I agreed to it. Goodnight, Daniel."

"Goodnight."

I take the time to wash my face and use some eye drops that I know are in the bathroom medicine cabinet before I can get the courage to walk back in there. Once I do, I avoid his face. I know what I will find. I just can't see it and remain strong. I walk behind him.

"Your punishment is over, Clayton. Please stand," I order in a kind voice, giving him that much, letting him know that this hurts me too. He follows my instruction. I release his wrists, dropping the cuffs to the floor. "Follow me." I don't look back to see if he obeyed. I know he will. I walk to the spare bathroom, turning on the shower and walking over to him, grateful that his eyes are cast downward so he can't see the pain in mine. Carefully removing his boxers from his waist I instruct him to step out of them. Then I check the water temperature before striping naked myself. Once done, I instruct him into the warm spray. I start by washing his hair then his body. This is a ritual he has done with me in the past after a difficult session, he deserves the same respect. When I am finished, I dry him off, ordering him to place his hands on the sink and spread his legs. He follows my directions. There in the light of the mirror's lamps, I see the complete damage that I have done to him. I check to make sure his eyes are cast down, but I know he hears my gasp.

"Master," he whispers. "May I speak freely?"

I close my eyes, remembering Alec's warning. "You may speak to me as your Master, but you will not be my boyfriend tonight."

His body shakes for a moment, before he whispers, "I understand, Master."

"Then you may speak freely as a sub." I encourage, taking the first of the lotions and rubbing them in my hands.

"I'm sure it looks worse than it feels," he says, his voice a little stronger as his eyes take in my face through the mirror.

"I wish it wasn't necessary." I frown, gently applying my lotioned hands to his skin.

He winces a little from the sting. "I'm curious, though. Whose idea was it, yours or Master Alec's?"

"Mine," I answer firmly. "I will never allow another to punish you for what they may or may not think is right."

"Thank you, Master." He smiles kindly. "You gave me the appropriate punishment and gave me exactly what I needed. I want to apologize again, Master. I did not realize that my actions were insulting you, that I was subconsciously pushing you, testing you. You are a quick study. I am proud to call you Master."

"Enough," I say simply, and his eyes fall back to the counter top. "Thank you, Clayton," I whisper, applying the last lotion. He shakes his head in response.

After his back and ass are treated, I take him to his bedroom. "You served me well tonight, Clayton. Thank you," I comment, pulling the sheets back and indicating he should lie down. "Would you still like me to stay tonight or would you rather me leave?"

"Please stay, Master."

I smile. "Okay. Would you prefer me to sleep on the couch?"

"No, Master. Please, I need you to hold me tonight," he begs, close to fresh tears. I give him a sympathetic smile, understanding exactly how he feels, and am happy that I am able to give him something that our previous arrangement did not allow. I find myself stroking his hair for almost an hour while he absorbs his lesson with tears of shame. Eventually, he falls asleep, and I lie there in pain, praying that I will never have to do that again.

13
Regret

Clayton's Point of View

What have I done? How could I be so insolent to a man I love? I never treated Master Alec this way even after we ended it. This is unforgivable. Had we not been in a relationship outside of this, I would have taken my well-deserved punishment and walked away.

I keep thinking about the day when my master presented the collar to me and it starts fresh tears. He's here now. I can't count the number of times I've awakened in the night, crying in shame, but he's here, soothing me with his fingers combing through my hair, but he doesn't speak; he just lets me be. I should have told him; I should never have worn it. Now, now I have to tell him how deep my betrayal to him really is. I tried to tell him before, but he denied me speech and now I'm not sure how to bring it up. I know I can't do it as his boyfriend; that's how I got disrespectful to start with. No, all things that involve the playroom stay between Master and sub. The question is which Master, which sub?

"Master?" I whisper, my voice breaking the darkness.

"I'm here, Clayton," he says soothingly. I close my eyes and relish his tone, knowing I'm about to make him angry again.

"May I speak freely as your sub, Master?" I ask, with a thick, pained voice.

"You may," he agrees, his fingers running through my hair over and over as he waits for me to continue.

"I made a mistake, Master, one that you are not aware of yet," I start, he freezes. I'm not even sure if he's breathing. "I was confused at the time, blending us with the flipping of Dom/sub, and it is a huge misunderstanding. I swear I wasn't trying to hurt you further."

"What did you do, Clayton?" he asks evenly, dropping his fingers from my hair.

I close my eyes, wishing the darkness would swallow me whole. "I'm so terribly sorry, Master. I-I purchased a collar for you too."

The silence is so strong my ears begin to ring, but I don't dare speak. After an endless moment, he growls, "Why didn't you tell me this before?"

"I was denied speech, Master."

"And when I asked you in our playroom what you were being punished for, why didn't you tell me then?" he asks through clenched teeth.

"I decided I wasn't going to tell you as my master. I did that as your master, and masters don't always tell their subs everything. If you think I am lying, please tell me the truth on how you felt giving me my punishment." My voice cracks through my little speech. "I'm sorry, Master. I am not trying to be disrespectful, just teaching."

"That's Master Alec's job, Clayton. You requested that," he snaps. "I'll forgive the teaching slip just this once, but don't test my forgiving mood." We fall quite for a moment. "Tell me, Clayton, how did it make you feel to purchase a collar for me?"

"It was . . . difficult," I answer honestly, "I would have rather purchased you a gag ball."

"I'm not going to punish you for it, Clayton," he decides. "I believe you have had enough of that particular lesson. Unless you prove otherwise in a future date, this lesson is complete. Actually," he adds in an afterthought, "turn to me, Clayton." I turn slowly, wincing as the bed presses on my sore skin, "I want to reward you for your honesty. Thank you for not taking advantage and using loopholes. I believe it will make us stronger in every way. I'm going to kiss you now, if you want to, I want you to kiss me back."

He finds my lips in the darkness, and I open to him willingly. I choose to let him dominate me, getting a feel as to what it is like to be his willing sub. My behavior seems to disappoint him, for he pulls back with a sigh. "I understand," he whispers. "I was the weak one for asking."

"No, Master, not weak, caring, but not weak," I whisper. "Goodnight, Master."

"Good night, Clayton."

When I wake in the morning, I am happily alone. My body is aching head to toe, and the moment I move, I grunt out in pain. I fucking hate whips, although they are better than canes. Even though I am fully aware that I got what I deserved, I am not beyond whining and being miserable when I am alone. This shit is fucking painful. I sit up on my ass trying to ease my back and let out a small scream, fuck that's sore too.

"CLAYTON!" Daniel cries, running into my room.

My eyes widen in shock. He was not supposed to be here, if I had known, I would have controlled myself. "Master, I thought . . ." I take a deep breath, casting my eyes down.

"Go on, Clayton."

"I thought I was alone," I answer simply, choosing to stand on my feet, because it was just too damn painful to stay sitting.

"Would you like to be alone?" he asks kindly.

"Yes and no, Master."

"Are you hungry?"

"Yes Master."

"Good, I will finish making breakfast then. Feel free to do what you normally do in the mornings or whatnot, but if you shower, wait for me in a presented position, back facing out and your hands on the sink in the spare bathroom before you dress."

"Yes, Master."

I wait until I am sure that he has left my room before I head to my personal bathroom. I adjust the mirrors in my three door medicine cabinet to take my first look at the damage and cringe. Sitting is going to fucking suck. I close my eyes in shame, not needing anymore reminders of my failure. I step into my multi-head shower and start making a mental list of things to do today, calling in sick is on the top. Being that it's Thursday, I reason I should heal enough to handle an office chair by Monday. I cannot look weak at work.

Once I'm finished with my shower, I shave and make my way to the spare bathroom to wait for my master at the sink, in the position he described. While I wait, I try to clear my head by falling into a submissive state, for I do not like being surprised by my master. Eventually, he comes in and rubs three lotions into my body. His hands are gentle, loving, careful. It takes everything in me not to meet his gaze through the mirror, to see what he is feeling; I have a suspicion, though, it's similar to the same things I feel when I've rarely have to punish him. My mind switches gears, and I know it shouldn't, but I'm restless from being a sub for so long, and I ideally wonder how my *boyfriend* feels right now. *Stop it, Reynolds!*

"I'm not going to apologize for this, Clayton, you deserved it," my master's voice breaks through my internal monologue. "I think we've had enough of the heavy," he says, stepping away from me, washing his hands. "You can relax, Clayton." I do so, still keeping my eyes to the floor. I see his feet head for the door, and right before he closes it shut, he says, "Red."

Relief overcomes me, and my legs give out. Until that moment, I wasn't completely comprehending exactly how difficult it was for me to stay in a submissive state. I let out a few sobs before I am able to compose myself. I go back to my bedroom, quickly dress and go out to the living room for my cell phone.

"Walker!" I growl the moment my assistant answers the phone. "I'm taking a long weekend, if you fucking bother me with nonsense, I swear you will have to find employment in a different country." I slam the phone shut, not waiting for a response.

Daniel is putting breakfast on the table. "Feel better?" he asks with small humor.

"Did I mention he pissed me off yesterday?" I answer, rolling my eyes.

"You did. You also mentioned you had him do my laundry for it," he answers with a shrug.

"Damn it, Daniel. What the hell does 'needy' mean?" I snap, which feels fucking good really.

He looks up at me for a long moment before he picks up his plate and leans against the wall, taking a bite of scrambled eggs. "Your friend told me that was bothering you. I was wondering when it would come up."

"Alec needs to mind his own damn business," I mutter following suit and standing while I eat.

Daniel laughs. "He doesn't seem the type, very protective that one. I'd go as far as stubborn too."

"Well, you know how to peg him," I admit, taking a bite of bacon.

"I wouldn't mind hanging out with him and his boyfriend, Bobby, if that's alright with you," he says, trying to be causal.

"That's a big step, Daniel."

"I know. I was just letting you know I'm ready." He smiles. "Oh, and I'm wondering if you have any vacation time coming up?"

"Why?"

"Well, the airline called back to verify that I was referring to a Jeremy Richards when I chewed them out yesterday, and then they offered two free tickets to the Virgin Islands." He smiles at me. "Well, to anywhere really, but I fly to the islands a lot. My grandfather sort of bought an island there."

My eyes widen in shock. "You're from old money?" I ask and then blush. "Shit, sorry."

Daniel laughs. "Don't worry about it, honest. We are both successful, so I don't think money and power will be an issue in this relationship. Besides," he shrugs, "I'm the black sheep. My sister Tasha is the rich, snooty one."

"You have a sister?" I smile. "Any other siblings?"

"Nope. You?"

"Only child."

"Vacation?"

I give a half smile. "Don't know. I'm working with a bitch right now, and I need to hold her goddamn hand. Let me see what I can arrange."

He shrugs. "No biggie."

"What about you? What are you going to do with yourself? Find another film to direct?"

"Yeah. I have a few boxes of manuscripts just itching to be read."

"You like the hunt just as much as I do, don't you?" I smile.

"I think I might," he answers with a glint in his eye.

"So what are your plans for today?"

He looks at me cautiously, "I was hoping to spend the day with you, but if you'd rather be alone, I completely understand."

I chew on my food for a while, thinking how best to answer him. "I think that I need a few hours to myself at least," I decide, "but I want to see you tonight."

"Alright."

"I also think we need some time off from the Dom/sub relationships," I add. "I'd like to take this weekend to get to know you."

He smiles kindly. "I'd like that."

"You haven't answered my question," I point out.

"Which is?"

"Needy?"

He bites his lower lip. "It's not easy to explain. It' just my ex, well, he was borderline obsessed with me and completely insecure. You don't seem to have either of those qualities, but if you ever met the boy, which I use the term loosely, then you would understand. Just let me be my own man, with my own decisions. I don't constantly need rides to the airport and whatnot, though at times, they are appreciated. I will end all of it immediately if you ever put a fucking care package in my luggage. Calling to say hi is fine, but don't freak if you get voicemail or if I answer but can't talk. I understand your request for flight numbers, and I have a feeling you have a fear of flying, which is why your pushing me off on this vacation, even if it is a legitimate reason. Just don't get obsessed or possessive or jealous or weird and we will be good."

"I'm sorry about the dry cleaning," I apologize. "I shouldn't have done that."

"No, you really shouldn't have," he agrees, "but if it helps, Jeremy Richards, would have been unemployed either way."

I give him a smile as I finish my last bite, placing my plate back down on the table. "Since you cooked, I will do the dishes."

"I can agree to that," he smiles, following my lead with his plate before walking up to me and carefully putting his hands on my hips. He leans in to kiss me, and I jump him, causing him to stagger while I wrap my legs around him. He finds a wall to lean on, grabbing me by the back of my legs, where he knows I'm not in pain. He kisses me back with as much fever as I am kissing him. "Warn me, next time," he grunts. "I don't want to risk hurting you. I'd never forgive myself."

"Sorry." I smile, reconnecting our lips, before I kiss down his jawline. "I want you," I whisper in his ear.

He moans, "Thought you wanted time alone."

"Please, Daniel," I beg, nibbling his earlobe.

"I don't want to hurt you," he answers, kissing my neck.

"You won't. I'll top."

"This time or every time?" he asks, nibbling my ear in return.

"Hmm . . . it's been so long since . . . too complicated right now," I answer, shoving my tongue into his mouth for a distraction, which I believe is working.

"Clayton," Daniel moans. "You realize you're asking for sex right? Nothing more?" I pull back, looking at him with surprise. "I haven't gotten there yet baby. I want to, but I'm just not there. I want that to be clear before you think we are making love when we aren't."

I sigh, wrapping my hands around his neck. "I'm about five steps ahead of you, aren't I?"

"Yes, but you seem to be willing to wait for the most part." He smiles. "I'll catch up in time."

"Will fucking me right now help or hurt that process?" I ask seriously.

"Hmm . . . it could never hurt." He smiles. "As long as we're clear where we are standing before we start."

"I'll admit it's not the best of circumstances, but considering our history, I can accept it." I smile.

"One small problem." I smile.

"What's that?" I ask, kissing on his neck.

"My orgasms belong to my master."

I pull back again. "Not when we're like this, agreed?"

He smiles, pushing us off the wall. "Fuck, yes."

Our lips join and Daniel heads for the couch. "No, bed," I argue, licking his neck.

"Clayton." He protests.

"I'm going to need room if you don't want to hurt me, Daniel," I argue, tracing his earlobe with my tongue.

He gives out a moan of defeat, taking me back to my room, thrusting his obvious boner into my nutsack. He sits down and scoots to the middle of the bed, causing my knees to find purchase in the mattress. When they do, I break away. "Wait." He pushes the hair out of his eyes, leaning back on his elbows to look up at me curiously. "I need to clarify something okay." He gives me a sad smile while nodding his head. "What we have, well, we're more than fuck buddies, right?"

Hurt crosses his features, but it's gone as quickly as it comes. "Of course."

"But this is just sex?"

He moans throwing himself on the bed, leaving me sitting on top of him. He rubs his face with his hands for a moment, collecting his thoughts. I give him time to think it through. "I wouldn't use the words 'just sex'," he finally says, looking up at me. "It's more than that, but it's not what you want it to be."

Relief washes over me and I smile, unable to keep my dimples from showing while pressing my lips to his. "Thank you."

He kisses me back while my hand finds the edge of his shirt looking for skin. I slide the cotton upward, revealing his sexy muscular torso, which I can never get enough of and haven't seen in so damn long, too long. I break away, tracing his nipples with my tongue, resulting in the moan I love to hear.

He lifts lightly on my shirt with more of a question than trying to remove it. I smile in understanding, climbing off him and we both stand to strip naked. I'm suddenly shaking because the realization dawns on me that this is the first time both of us have been completely naked for sex is in this moment. As his master I always had some sort of clothing on and he was never allowed to look or touch. He seems to read my thoughts and walks up to me, lacing my fingers in his.

"You're beautiful, Clayton," he whispers while his eyes travel down my body. My nervousness melts away as he gently traces my stomach muscles and then my 'V'. Unable to take his intense stare without blushing, I grab both of our hard cocks and start to stroke them. He gasps, dropping his lips to the crook of my neck, sucking lightly, but not enough to leave marks. My fingers fall into his hair with my free hand, and then our lips meet as the lust starts to build between us.

Daniel walks backward until his knees hit the side of the bed. I wrap my arms around him and he leans back. He repositions himself to the middle of the mattress and I crawl on top of him, caressing his muscles.

"I'm nervous," I whisper watching my dripping cock pool into his belly button.

"Me too," he whispers back.

I reach over his head to my nightstand, grabbing the lube.

"Are we sure we're ready for this?"

"I am. Are you?" he asks, rubbing circles with his thumbs on my hips.

"Yeah," I answer, "I've just never done this before." It was true, he's the first sub I've ever blended with. I can't say that in the reverse but some things are better left unsaid.

"Neither have I," he whispers.

I give him a smile, kissing him feverously while we both start dry humping in desperate need for friction. When I break away, my testosterone and adrenaline levels are off the charts, and my nerves are forgotten.

I slick my fingers with lube, and begin preparing him in the most intimate way. I know Daniel's asshole like a fucking map, and I'm annoyed when I don't get the moan I deserve, until I realize my map is fucking upside down, causing everything to be backward. It takes me a few strokes to adjust, but the moment I do, his eyes roll in the back of his head as he arches his back and curls his toes with the most sexy ass moan I have heard in my life; fuck me, I almost cum on the spot.

He relaxes into my hand surprisingly quickly. When I pull out to lube my dick, he whimpers loudly at the loss, and his eyes snap forward.

"Too soon? Would you like more time?" I ask worried.

"Fuck no, I just want to watch you," he answers huskily, pulling my lips toward his before I can aim my dick appropriately. I pull back with a smile adjusting so that I am at his entrance. "Please," he whispers, I push myself inside of him. Our eyes lock and both of us let out a moan while I bury my dick deep into his ass. I collapse on top of him, trying to stave off orgasm letting him adjust around me. He seems to be clueless about where to put his hands, settling with touching my arms. I appreciate that he is sensitive to the fact my back can't take a pleasuring touch at the moment.

When we are both ready, I begin slow, steady thrusts while I meet his hungry lips, kissing him until I am dizzy. Breaking our kiss, I reach down with one hand and grab his cock that is pressed between our stomachs, pumping him. "Cum with me, Daniel. I can't hold out much longer," I gasp my rhythm faltering into almost a violent pace. He screams out in pleasure, his hot seed spilling between us. I gasp as his ass clenches around me. "FUCK!" I yell, losing all coherent thought, cumming inside of him. When my body finally stills, my arms give out, and I collapse on top of him.

"Wow!" Daniel gasps.

"Yeah," I breathe, sitting up. "Fuck."

He turns to me. "Shower?"

"Sure."

He chases my ass to my personal shower, once clean, we collapse on the bed. Not long after, we're asleep.

When I wake a few hours later, I find a note from Daniel. *Have a few errands to run. I'll be back at eight, unless it's too late. Text me— D.*

I lay there a moment longer before I get up and make a quick sandwich. While I'm eating, I notice the clock is reading 4:16 p.m. and I realize I'm going to need a distraction, afraid of where my thoughts might take me if I don't. Yesterday is still too raw. I grab my briefcase and pull out some demo tapes that I brought home. Right when I'm queuing the first one up, my cell rings.

"Reynolds." I answer, not bothering to check the caller ID.

"How are you doing, Clayton?" Alec asks, concern deep in his voice.

"Are you asking as my friend or my master's trainer?" I answer cautiously.

"Come on. Don't do that, please," he begs.

"I'm sorry, Alec. I have to. It's the only way I can avoid the damn trap I fell into."

He's quiet for a long moment before he sighs. "Alright, I'll respect it. I don't like it. I find it a strain on our friendship, but I will respect it."

"Do you want to back out?" I ask fearful.

"No," he answers. "I think you both need me on some level, at least for now."

"I appreciate this, you know."

"I know."

"So do you want to hear me ramble about my boyfriend for a while because I have a shit-load to tell you." I smile.

"God, when did you turn into a girl?" he laughs. "Go on."

"Well, let's see. He cooked me breakfast. He asked me to take a vacation to his grandfather's private island in the Virgin Islands."

"What?"

"Yeah, I know, right?"

"Seriously, Clayton, you are turning into Cassandra. Knock it off!"

"If you were here, I would so deck your ass."

"What else?"

"He got a flight attendant fired for trying to set him up, he explained needy, and we fucked," I ramble on with my continuous smile.

Alec is quiet again for a moment and then starts to laugh . . . hard. "He got a flight attendant fired? I can see the attraction there, Clayton. You got yourself a man."

"The guy broke into his luggage." I defend. "He left him a G-strings and a note about a false date."

"He said it wasn't all you." Alec chuckles, catching his breathe. "He was pissed off when I got there. I let him vent to get into the right frame of mind."

"He's a natural at this, isn't he?" I observe aloud.

"More of a quick study, you being his case study," Alec answers. "So anyway, curious what the hell does 'needy' mean?"

"Obsessive, compulsive, insecure, attached at the hip." I shrug. "Nothing I care for myself. Oh, I was wondering if you and Bobby are up for a double tomorrow night?"

"Sure, on one condition."

"What's that?"

"You tell Daniel who the hell Bobby is."

Fuck me. "S-h-i-t! I didn't even think about that."

"I figured. Look, you can't avoid it, Clayton. Daniel really wants to try to be friends with your friends. The sooner you face this, the better."

"Fuck."

"I'm right on this, Clayton."

"I know," I groan.

"Let me know what he says."

"Yeah, but if I call crying, you'll be here, right?" I ask, getting freaked out.

"Always," Alec promises.

I hang up the phone, and before I can chicken out, I dial Daniel's number. I have an idea on how he is going to react to this, and I hate myself for it. Why, why did I do this? *You weren't expecting a relationship.*

"Hey, Clayton," Daniel answers happily.

My stomach flips. "Daniel," I manage but my voice cracks in the middle. *Damn it, stop crying.*

"Clayton, what is it? What's wrong?" he asks, immediately on edge.

"There's something I have to tell you, and I don't think you are going to like it," I answer, tears of fear falling down my cheeks.

"I already don't like it," he answers in a weak voice.

I swallow hard. "Alec called. I asked him about scheduling a double date for this Saturday. I was planning to ask you about it tonight, but I wanted to make sure they were available."

"And?"

"Alec reminded me that you don't know who Bobby is," I answer timidly.

"Alright," he answers, and I can tell he's freaking out.

"Well, he was," I take a deep breath, "he was my last solo sub." *Chicken! Come on, Reynolds, just tell him.*

"So . . . *both* of them are in love with you." I can detect a small amount of relief in his voice, but it's obvious he's jealous.

"Something like that, but I don't see it that way. I really don't. They're friends, nothing more," I defend myself.

"I think given time, I could learn to be okay with it. I appreciate the warning though."

"No, Daniel, you don't understand. There's more," I cry.

"More? Damn it, Clayton, just say it."

Holding my breath, I blurt out, "You met him."

"What? When?"

"Right before you became my boyfriend," I answer in a whisper.

Silence.

Silence.

Silence.

"Daniel?"

Silence.

Silence.

Silence.

"I'll call you back, Clayton."

"Daniel? Daniel?" But my pleading gets me nowhere. I'm talking to a dead connection and can only pray our relationship didn't die with it.

14

Foot in Mouth

Clayton's Point of View

Not long after Daniel hung up, I received a text.
I need some time to think. I'll call you when I'm ready.
I stared at it for a moment, numb inside before I texted back.
I understand.
I wanted to say more like 'I'm sorry, I'm an idiot, please don't end this, I love you.' But I kept it to a single non-needy text and waited for him to mull over this information. I still can't believe that I was stupid enough not to think about this sooner. *What the hell is happening to me?* I'm usually more attentive in my relationships, and I don't need my best friend every five fucking minutes. But this is different; this is terrifying.

About an hour later, Alec called, but he wasn't the one I wanted to talk to, so I let it go to voice mail. My phone had a text from him next, asking if I was alright. I knew if I didn't reply, he'd come over, so I told him yes, I was fine. I just needed to be alone.

All of this was three days ago. Now I am at work and truly fucking annoyed with Mike, who can't seem to keep his shit together, spilling everything from coffee to files when I walk next to him. The last time I told him to pull it together or post a want ad for his replacement, he turned a slight shade of green, nodded his head, and excused himself.

By the time I get home, I am beat, beyond beat. My ass is healed but my back was still sore and driving was proving to be a challenge. After grabbing a beer from the fridge, I turn on the game and lie on my stomach, searching for some kind of relief. That's when my phone rings. When I check the caller ID, I notice it's Daniel and debate whether or not to answer it. Quickly, my heart overrides my head and I say hello.

"Clayton, it's Daniel," he says, nervously.

"Hi," I answer.

"Look, I know that we have some stress between us right now, but I need a favor, you having a degree in sports medicine and all," he continues.

"I don't have a degree . . ."

"Yeah, you won't believe it. My sister, Tasha, walked into a wall."

My heart stops and I work to keep my voice steady. "How bad did he hurt her?"

"She's got a black eye and some swelling."

"Text me the address, I'm on my way. Keep it on ice and give her ibuprofen for the swelling. NOT acetaminophen, ibuprofen."

"Thank you." He whispers, hanging up the phone; a text with an address quickly follows.

"Shit!" I yell out, jumping up from the couch and running to my spare bathroom, searching my supplies for what I need. Then I grab my wallet and keys, barely registering locking the door and setting the alarm, before I drive to the nearest pharmacy for the rest of the supplies. Once I am satisfied that I have everything, I drive to Daniel's.

When he answers the door, I can see the worry etched in his face and I bite my lower lip. "Hi."

"Hey," he says. "I appreciate this."

"I know." I answer, with a weak smile. "I'll continue to give you your space. Thanks though for letting me help."

He nods, stepping aside for me to enter. I walk in and see the most beautiful woman I have ever laid eyes on. She has extra-long black hair, green eyes, the perfect heart-shaped face, with a stellar body, sitting in a bar stool chair. If I was straight, I would so be pleading for her number.

"Hi, I'm Clayton." I smile, extending my hand, and I can tell she's working not to flinch from it. I laugh it off, handing her the bag I'm carrying. "So tell me that the wall looks worse than you do."

She gives a weak smile, placing the bag on the island she's sitting at. "Daniel said you had a degree in sports medicine."

"Yeah, I do," I answer with a lie. "I can treat that, you will be good as new in about a week, but make-up will work effectively in about three days."

"Professional sports?" she asks, causing Daniel to roll his eyes behind her.

I smile. "Actually, I'm the co-founder and CEO of Blackboard Entertainment. My bands can get rough sometimes. I got the degree to make sure they look presentable at all times."

Her eyes light up with this information. "Well, it's about damn time my brother found a respectable boyfriend. I love the *Eyes of Seduction*."

I smile, pulling out some of my creams. "Maybe one day you could meet them."

"I'd like that." She smiles genuinely, wincing in pain.

"Here, I will try not to put too much pressure, alright." I assure her, holding up my hand, asking for silent permission before I touch her.

"Alright," she says and I begin to work.

"You'll find some vitamins and things in that bag. They will accelerate the healing process. I recommend taking one of each every day for a week." She doesn't say much to that, so I draw my attention to Daniel. "Could you please get me a cold washcloth from the bathroom?" He gives me a questionable look but leaves us alone nonetheless.

"Whoever did this to you, Tasha, was wearing a ring," I frown the moment we are alone.

Shock crosses her face. "I ran into a wall."

"No, you didn't," I argue gently. "You realize Daniel isn't going to give it a rest, right? You're his sister."

"It's not his business or yours, for that matter," she snaps.

"Who is he?" I ask as though she wasn't getting defensive.

"Fuck off!" she screams, jumping out of the chair and slamming a bedroom door down the hall.

Daniel comes into the room. "What happened?"

"I asked for his name," I answer, walking to the kitchen sink to wash my hands. "Whoever did it left his mark. Literally."

"I don't know how to get through to her," he admits in defeat, handing me the washcloth. I drape it over the sink, grabbing a dry dish towel to dry my hands.

"I know someone who can," I offer.

"If you say Bobby . . ."

"No, not Bobby. Bobby and I and you, for that matter, we're lucky. We've never had the displeasure of a cruel Sir." I frown, meeting his eyes. "There's a reason why Alec turned me off to collars, Daniel. He was a slave to one for many years." I watch shock and surprise come across his features while he searches my face in disbelief. "Don't bother asking him about it. He won't talk about it. But he happens to be a professional therapist." I omit the part that Alec usually refers his tough abuse cases to colleges, because he has a hard time with them.

"I . . . I don't know what to say to that, Clayton," he stammers as tears streak down his face. "I . . . why did you let me? Damn it!"

I close the distance between us. "I'm sorry. I'm truly sorry for everything. I should have told you, and I won't make a mistake like that again, I swear. I did it because I trust you. Please know that," I beg, wiping the tears falling from his cheeks. "I didn't think about Bobby. It didn't even occur to me, and I know it should have. But with you, I don't know. It's just so hard to think outside the moment. I wasn't waiting for the right time to tell you, Daniel. If it hadn't been for Alec, you would have found out in a bar or some shit because I'm a fucking idiot." I step away, pulling at the ends of my hair. "Goddamn it! This isn't like me. I'm better at dating than this, honest. I've only had one guy break up with me, but no one else even wanted to." I turn to him. "Are we cursed? Is there no hope for us?"

He stares at me for the longest moment, not saying anything, and then he says, "This isn't the time, Clayton. Tasha needs me right now."

I swallow hard. "I understand. Would you like me to call Alec, see if he can help?"

"I'd appreciate it, if he is willing."

"Okay," I agree, heading for the door.

"Please don't leave, Clayton," Daniel calls after me.

I turn to him meeting his eyes for a fleeting moment before he turns and knocks on the bedroom door that Tasha has locked us out of. Completely lost and vulnerable, I pull out my cell phone and call Alec.

"I've been worried sick, you know," he answers with a growl.

"Alec," I start and then stop. "We need you, just you. Can you come to Daniel's?"

"Clayton?"

"Please."

I give him Daniel's address and wait nervously in Daniel's living room. Alec is going to be so damn pissed at me for this, and I know it, but what choice do I have? Finally, the doorbell rings. Daniel steps out of the bedroom he had finally gained access to and opens his front door to Alec.

"Please come in," he says, stepping aside.

Alec gives him a small smile before he makes a beeline straight to me. "You have me worried sick. What the hell is wrong, Clayton?"

"Please don't hate me, Alec."

"Hate you?" he asks in confusion.

"This isn't about me or Clayton," Daniel steps in. "It's about my sister Tasha."

"Somebody abused her, Alec," I add weakly. "She's telling us she walked into a wall, but he left his mark on her face." Alec turns to me with wide eyes before his knees give way. I'm there in a heartbeat, catching him and cradling him to me. "I'm sorry, I'm so sorry. I know I've been asking the world of you lately, I do."

"Clayton, I, I can't," Alec cries, clinging to me for dear life.

"Please, Alec," I plead. "For me, I am begging you."

"You have no idea what you're asking of me!" he cries, putting weight back on his feet. "Of everything you have asked of me, you ask me this! Damn it, Clayton!"

"I know, Alec. I do." I answer pulling back to dry his face. "But Tasha needs someone Alec, please."

He laces his fingers in mine, squeezing to the point of pain. "Why do you have to beg me, Clayton? Don't you realize you are the only man in the world I could never deny anything?"

I close my eyes to that. I know I'm taking advantage of him. "Please."

"Look at me, Clayton," he demands. I open my eyes and stare at him. "I'm only going to do this because I love you, but if it's too much, I can't guarantee that our friendship will survive it."

"I don't want to risk that, Alec. I never want to risk that," I answer in a pained voice. "I love you too much to lose you like that. Please don't say that."

His eyes go wide with shock, and he steps back from me. "What did you just say?"

"I love you," I repeat swallowing back tears. "It's not enough. Come on, Alec. We would never work out. You know that. And when you first fell, I wasn't sure if I did, but as our friendship grew, well, you know how it is." He stares at me speechless. "Please." I beg, walking back up to him, taking his scarred hand in mine; tracing his, silently reminding him of our vow.

He looks at it for a moment before he balls his hand into a fist, "Fine, but I'm not above hating you."

"Thank you." I smile, turning to Daniel. He keeps his focus on Alec and directs him to Tasha's hiding space. I sit back down on the couch, overwhelmed with emotion, trying to put the last few moments in perspective. I don't register Daniel sitting next to me until he speaks.

"You didn't realize it until this moment, did you?" he asks kindly.

"Denial is a good policy when it comes to things like this. It doesn't change anything, so why does it really matter?" I answer bitterly.

"It matters," he says, taking my hand in his, tracing my scar. I can see the question but I'm not ready to answer it.

"I wasn't trying to hurt you more," I whisper, staring at the coffee table. "I think I've done enough damage. Maybe we aren't meant to work out."

"Don't say that," he scuffs. "Hear me out for a second, alright? Take a step back for a moment and look at the parallel here. Your master fell in love with you and you didn't allow yourself to, even though you became friends. As my master, you fell in love with me and I, well, I am trying to allow those feelings to surface, enough so that we're dating. I'm not hurt by how you feel for him, Clayton. If anything, I can relate." He shifts his weight to face me. "When you deny your feelings for three years, it's hard to just flip them on overnight. Well, at least it is for me." I turn my head to face him, but I don't speak. "The hardest thing I've had to live through since I've known you was my punishment with Bobby. The second hardest was our last session. I know both of these have to do with our Dom/sub relationships and shouldn't bleed into us, but that's proving to be impossible."

"I don't want to end this," I admit.

"Neither do I," he assures me. "But as a man, Clayton, I can't deny myself the release I crave from the other part of our relationship, and I cannot nor would I ever want to do it with anyone else."

"So where do we go from here?"

"I'm not ready to meet Bobby."

"I can respect that, and had we continued status quo, you would have never had to."

"True, but there's no going back, and I wouldn't want to anyway," he smiles. "I'm falling in love with you, Clayton. I've been falling for a long time. I'm just terrified to trust anyone with my heart."

"Who hurt you?" I ask gently.

"It's not the time for that," he answers, kissing my hand.

I want to tell him that it's alright, that he can trust me with his heart, that I would never break it. But I can't; not because of the timing, but because of everything that has happened between us so far. I'm honestly not sure if I can trust myself with his heart yet. I think we both need time; we both need proof before words like that can be spoken, so instead, I ask, "Can I kiss you?"

"Yes." He smiles, leaning into me gently, pressing his lips to mine.

"Well, at least something is going right," Alec laughs humorlessly. I pull away from Daniel quickly, facing him. He's as pale as a ghost.

"Alec," I cry, dropping Daniel's hand and going to him. "Are you okay?"

"No," he frowns, taking me into an embrace. After a long moment, he takes a deep breath before pulling away and sits down next to Daniel. "I couldn't get a name, but I can tell you this has been going on for a while. She didn't admit it, but the signs of frequent abuse are there. She keeps saying she deserved it, that it was her fault. I have a feeling he's smart, never hitting her where anyone would notice, until he got really pissed."

"Excuse me," Daniel cries, running to the kitchen sink, getting sick.

Alec turns to me. "Hire someone to follow her, Clayton. It's the only way you're going to get your answers."

"On it," I whisper, not really wanting Daniel to know this quite yet.

"I should go."

"You are in no condition to drive," I argue. "Let me take you home. I'll call a cab to get back here."

"You shouldn't leave Daniel," he argues.

"Then call a cab to come get your ass. I don't want you behind a wheel," I snap.

"My wheels?"

"I'll drop it off later. Stop arguing with me. Bobby would be pissed if he knew you tried to drive in your current condition, and I really don't want my ass kicked."

"Fine, I'll call a cab."

"Thank you," I smile, digging for my phone.

"Who are you calling?" he asks, grabbing his phone.

"Bobby," I answer, stepping outside onto Daniel's deck for privacy.

"I'm not going over there to get my ass kicked," Bobby says when he answers the phone.

"Good, he's not ready to meet you anyway. That's not why I'm calling. Look, Daniel's sister, well, she's in an abusive relationship."

"Fuck you, you did NOT go there," Bobby growls.

"I'm sorry."

"I'm kicking your ass."

"I deserve it."

"You can bet your ass you do. How is he?"

"Not good. He's calling a cab. I just wanted you to be prepared."

"You using him like this, Clayton, you know you're killing him right?" Bobby bitches.

"I know. But she's Daniel's sister, and I only trust a handful of people."

"Regardless, you're hurting Alec."

"I hear ya, alright."

"I'm kicking your ass," he growls again.

"He'll be there in less than thirty minutes," I deflect, "and Bobby, thank you for taking care of him in a way I never really could."

"Just send him back to me. I'll fix the damage, as always," he mutters, hanging up the phone.

A rock falls in the pit of my stomach; I truly am a selfish asshole.

"Hey," Daniel says, coming up from behind me.

I turn to him, gripping onto his solid form for dear life. "I need to be punished, Master, please," I beg, desperate to stop spinning, needing pain.

He pulls me away with complete fury and concern in his eyes. "You've done nothing wrong."

"I'm hurting the people I love," I argue, casting my eyes down. "Please, Master, don't deny me this, please."

"You'll explain yourself later," he demands, "but this isn't the time, Clayton. Red."

I do my best not to fall apart while he takes me back into his strong arms.

"The cab will be here soon," Alec says, stepping onto the deck. Him and Daniel exchange a look.

"I'm going to check on, Tasha," Daniel frowns, rubbing my arms. I shake my head to his unspoken question causing him to give me a long hard look before he leaves us be.

"What did Bobby say to you?" Alec asks.

"The truth as always. He's never been one to sugar-coat," I shrug. "I don't deserve your friendship, Alec. All I've been doing is taking and taking, leaving you in pieces for Bobby to glue back together so I can do it all over again."

"Harsh," he nods, flexing his jaw. "Shouldn't be surprised."

"He wants to kick my ass, and I think I'm going to let him."

"I won't," Alec growls. "I understand his intentions, but I won't let him hurt you."

"Figured you'd say that, but Bobby isn't my only option. There are other ways for me to be punished for it."

"That's between you and your master," he snaps, "but I won't be there to watch it."

I nod my head in understanding. "I understand if you want to walk away from me, Alec. I won't blame you one bit."

"I'm not walking away, Clayton," he groans. "But I need some time alright. This past month has been extremely difficult for me. I'll still be there for training if Daniel requests it, but you two really need to talk. Make sure he knows the difference between punishment and abuse. Daniel's going to question it after this. I'll help him in every way I can, but he's going to need you too."

"Thank you, Alec."

He takes my scarred hand in his and we stand silent for a while. "I'll call you, Clayton, when I'm ready," he promises, letting go and handing me his keys before he goes back inside.

I wait until I hear the cab honk before I go back in, finding a seat on the couch while I wait for Daniel to come back out of the room Tasha is still hiding in. When he does, I give him a sad smile, standing up. "I should go too."

"You don't have to, Clayton."

"Your sister needs you, Daniel, and I have a feeling afterward, you're going to need your master. I need to leave now so I can get in the right frame of mind."

"I can respect that," he nods. "Thank you for understanding my needs."

"I'm going to step out of our boyfriend bounds again," I warn him. "I'm going to find the bastard that did this to her. I'll get a name, Daniel. I'll leave the rest up to you."

"Clayton."

"No, I know you could do it, but she'll forgive you faster if it comes from me. Let me do this, Daniel, please," I beg, walking up to him.

"Fine, but just a name," he agrees, taking my hands in his.

"I need to know if we're okay, Daniel. Today has been a whirlwind, and I need to know that you and I are okay."

He gives a small smile, leaning into my ear with a whisper, "We're more than okay." He kisses me gently. "We have a few kinks to work out," he adds with a laugh, "but what relationship doesn't?"

"So we're moving forward?" I ask, staring into his eyes.

"Slowly," he answers, pressing his soft lips to mine again.

"Call me when you can," I whisper, kissing him gently again before I step away.

"Okay and, Clayton, that meeting . . . well I'll be anticipating a text for the time."

"Before or after we hang out as a couple?" I ask, unsure.

"Before."

"Alright, but if you can't get away tonight I still want you to call me. I'm worried about you."

"Will do." He smiles. "I should get back to Tasha."

I nod, heading for the door. "Daniel." He turns to me. "It's not the same, alright."

He nods and I quickly walk out into the fresh air, desperately needing to breathe. I make my way home in a daze trying to work out everything that has happened tonight. When I get there, I call my favorite PI and tell him what I need. Then I decide to meditate until Daniel calls to tell me that Tasha is staying the night. I let him know that I will be stopping by in a cab to get Alec's SUV but won't disturb them and that I have made arrangements with my investigator. I can tell he is still "iffy" to let her go home, back to him, and I can only reassure him that we will catch the guy. Telling him I gave my PI explicit instructions to make sure, above all else, that she's safe, even if he compromises himself to do so. Daniel thanks me and we say goodnight.

About an hour later I'm pulling Alec's SUV into his and Bobby's driveway. I didn't have the cab follow me here because I'm not sure how long this is going to take. I respect Alec's request for space but not without explaining myself, I just can't leave it like this. So here I am, standing at his front door. When I finally get the courage to knock, Bobby answers.

"What do you want? Haven't you done enough damage for one day?" he growls, blocking my entry.

"I need to explain," I answer in a small voice, holding up Alec's keys.

"You need to leave," Bobby barks, snatching the keys before slamming the door in my face. I deserved that, no denying it, but it didn't make it any easier. Frowning to myself, I sit down on their front porch and wait, all the while staring at my scarred hand, wondering if I lost Alec forever. Hours pass and the bright full moon is high in the night's sky before Alec takes a seat next to me.

"After all this time, you finally admit it," he sighs, looking off in the distance.

"I'm sorry." I frown, keeping my eyes locked on the ground.

"Sorry that you admitted it or sorry that it's not enough?" he asks with a humorless laugh.

"Alec," I manage, grabbing his hand, "don't you see it *is* more than enough." His eyes shoot to mine. "I was terrified. I still am, after Ryan . . ."

"*Ryan?*" he asks angrily. "You can love Daniel but not *me* because of RYAN?"

"Angel, please," I plead, fighting tears.

"Enough!" he snaps, freeing his hand from my grip, standing to leave.

"If I mess it up with Daniel, then it will hurt and life will go on. If I mess it up with you, my world would stop spinning."

"Newsflash, Clayton, you already have," he growls.

"No," I argue, scampering to my feet. "Please, Alec, don't end our friendship."

"We're more than friends, Clayton," he argues.

"Alec . . ."

"Please stop," he whispers. "We're happy with Bobby and Daniel."

"Not as happy as we could be with each other," I painfully whisper back, tears falling.

"No use in what might have been, Clayton. It's the past. This is now. We have who we love."

"So you won't run away with me then? There is no sunset or happily ever after for us?"

"There's no such thing as happily ever after," he answers with a small head shake closing his eyes.

"Still friends?" I ask timidly, when he starts to walk away into the shadows.

"Our vow still stands Clayton," he whispers, keeping his back to me while he touches his scar, "As you said, without you in my life in some way, the world would stop spinning."

"I love you," I whisper, wiping my tearful face.

"I love you," he responds, I watch as he fights with himself to not turn around and run to me. If he did, I would choose him in a heartbeat, but it was his turn to break my heart and force himself inside, into another man's awaiting arms. My heart has never hurt this much in my entire existence. I collapse to the ground crying. Ryan was a cakewalk compared to this. Losing love because of fear is the biggest regret of my life.

After some time, I feel Bobby's arms around me, and I sob harder because they aren't Alec's. Not long after, I am placed on a guest bed and my shoes are taken from me.

"Sleep," he says, heading for the door.

"Bobby," I call to him.

"I won't feel sorry for you, Clayton. Your stupidity is my gain. Besides, you found love."

"I wasn't going to ask for sympathy," I mutter. "I was going to ask you to be a better man than I could ever be and love him unconditionally."

He shakes his head knowingly. "Already there Clayton."

"Bobby."

"Yes, Clayton."

"Thank you."

When I close my eyes that night, my thoughts go straight to Alec, and I need my master more than ever, but I know that first my master will need me. I frown, thinking on when I will be able to fall into the proper frame of mind. I really hate to do it to Daniel, but I can't hurt him and I know that tomorrow will be too soon.

15
Concern

Daniel's Point of View

My life is spinning out of control. I am lost, alone, drowning. I need a constant; I need pain; I need to be grounded. My master has sensed this; he knows, and yet, he has not contacted me. I cannot lose him; I need him; then the realization hits; he needs me. Trying to solve both our problems, I pull out my phone, sending a single text.

Make yourself available to be alone within the next ten minutes. M.D.

I frown, thinking back to last week, when I realized that my sister is in an abusive relationship. I felt useless, but I knew Clayton could help with the bruising at least, so I called him. I had been thinking about calling to talk about Bobby that day anyway. I wanted him to know that I wasn't upset that Clayton used one of his friends, or even a former sub. I could understand and respect both those decisions. What bothered me is that I really didn't ever want to think about that night again, and now, not only did a no-name sub have a name, but he knew my shame and I am supposed to what? Eat dinner with this guy?

I'm grateful for Alec's warning to Clayton, and I called and thanked him personally. I'm really starting to like the guy, despite his history with my boyfriend. Hearing Clayton admit his feelings to Alec felt somehow relieving. I realize that most guys would have freaked when they stood and watched their boyfriend tell another man, a man who clearly loved him, that they shared love. But I am not most guys. I understand it. And when I confronted Clayton about it, he was honest. It really didn't change things;

they are close friends who both, at one point or another, admitted they are completely wrong for each other. It helps that Alec is so supportive of Clayton and myself as well. It also helps seeing Clayton acknowledge something he's denied himself, something I've denied for so long. Is Clayton my Alec? No, not really, in the end; he's more.

My phone brings me out of my musings.

"Hello, Clayton."

"Master."

"How are you feeling, Clayton?"

"Lost, Master."

"You've asked me for punishment, Clayton, and I don't dole out punishment without explicit cause. Please explain to me why you feel you deserve it."

"I am hurting the ones that I love, Master."

"Explain."

I can hear him swallow. "There are two people that I sincerely care about, and I have mixed their lives together in such a way that they are uncomfortable, yet they face these challenges because I ask them to."

"I will not punish you for your request of Master Alec's training, Clayton."

"No, Master, not you," he clarifies. "You have done me a great honor in accepting my request, and though I know it was difficult for you, I do not regret asking for it."

"Who are these two people, Clayton?"

"My best friend, Alec, and my boyfriend, Daniel."

"You're separating us? Master and boyfriend?"

"Yes, Master."

"Good. You will be rewarded for that," I smile, truly appreciating the separation. "Please explain how you hurt your best friend."

His breathing falters, "I can't, Master. It's between us."

"Then I can't punish you, Clayton. What about your boyfriend?"

"He's too forgiving," Clayton says snidely. "I hurt him and he didn't even get upset with me. At least, my best friend was hurt."

"I think you need to talk to your boyfriend, Clayton. I can't punish you for that either."

"I came without permission," he informs me desperately.

"Clayton, are you lying to be punished? Or did you do it to be punished?"

"Please, Master, don't deny me this," he begs.

"Answer the question, Clayton."

"The first, Master," he admits.

"I see." I bite my lower lip. "And you want punishment for lying."

"Please, Master."

"Be waiting for me at seven," I order, holding back my disappointment. I so don't need this right now, but obviously, he needs something, which terrifies me. He was so skeptical about falling back into this role, but once he accepted it, he seems to crave it.

"Thank you, Master," he whispers and I hang up the phone.

Frowning, I flip through my call log, dialing a now familiar number.

"Hello, Daniel."

"We need to talk. Meet me at the Stringbeans Coffee on Eighth in two hours. Don't drive," I stop, realizing my tension is causing me to be bossy. Taking a breath I warn in a softer tone, "Alec, you're going to need Bobby. Just have him keep his distance, alright?"

"The things that I do for that man," he bitches to himself. "Alright, I'll be there."

I make it there early and buy a cup of coffee while I wait. When I see them walk through the door I hold back an external cringe. Bobby gives me a small wave and smiles, approaching me. *Fuck.*

"Dude, I get it, but for what it's worth, no judgment on this end," he assures me, gripping my shoulder firmly. "You and Clayton love each other. That's what I got out of the whole damn thing, so whenever you're ready." I shake my head at him, unable to meet his eyes. He gives me a small smile and tells Alec that he will be sitting a few seats behind me if he needs him. They share a quick kiss, and Alec takes a seat.

"Thirsty?" I ask.

"Caffeine and this topic don't mix."

"Which topic is that?"

"Don't patronize me. I know what you want, Kingsley," he snaps.

"That's only part of it, Alec." I frown, rubbing my face with my hands.

"Who am I talking to?" he questions. "His boyfriend or his master?"

"I wouldn't go to you with personal relationship advice unless he was completely out of my reach," I explain.

"So his master then. What's bothering you?"

"He lied to me." I frown. "He asked for a punishment but wouldn't explain properly as to why he thought it was needed. I refuse to punish him without just cause."

"So he lied after you denied him?"

"Yep."

"What are you going to do about it?"

I shrug. "Same thing he'd do to me."

"Do you need me there?"

"Not tonight." I frown. "That's not what's bothering me."

"I'm listening."

"He was so cautious about this whole sub thing, saying he wasn't sure if he could do it. But now, it's almost as if he needs it more than I do." I take a drink of my coffee studying Alec's reaction to my observation.

"You're asking if this is normal of him?" Alec frowns, slouching in his seat.

"I'm just worried," I frown fidgeting with the lid of my cup.. "You two have been through a lot lately. I don't think you realize how much your friendship really means to him."

Alec looks away from me, taking the time to gather his thoughts. "Clayton's unique, Daniel," he finally starts. "Our friendship, well, let's just say since he's become a Dom, he's never asked me for anything until you two started . . . dating and what have you. But honestly, I can't count the number of times he's called me master after he walked away."

"When did that end?"

"When you stepped into that void," he admits.

"So he's never really let go of the role. He just stopped having sessions."

"I always corrected him, Daniel. I wouldn't let him fall victim to that. He called me Alec each time he slipped, but he did slip often."

"And now?" I ask, insecure.

"He knows our friendship will end if he ever does it again," Alec states simply. "You can judge me for allowing it as long as I did, Daniel. It's a huge 'don't' as far as a Dom is concerned, but I am a weak man."

"I've never viewed you that way," I correct him.

His eyes flash to mine. "You are one of the most complicated individuals I have ever met!"

"Why?" I ask taken off guard by his sudden temper.

"Your boyfriend told me he loved me right in front of you, and you didn't even react. Then your sub's previous master, the same man by the way, is telling you that he's never really let him go, and you still don't react. What the fuck Daniel? If you're not in this, leave now. I will not allow you to continue to string him along if you don't give a shit about him!"

I fall back into the booth. "On the contrary Alec, I love him, flaws and all. So you two have a complicated history, but you've managed to work around it. You're friends. I can't say I understand it, because I don't. I can respect it. When Clayton admitted that he loved you, I wasn't surprised. I knew it. Hell, you knew it. But you both said that you would never work, so what the hell is the point of being jealous? As you said, you're not going anywhere." I turn in the direction of Bobby. "You can't tell me that he and I aren't the same on some level here. He must know everything I do, and you two are still a couple. He hasn't walked out on you."

"That's different," Alec argues.

"How?" I demand.

"He knew, before we started anything, he knew," he explains. "And so did I."

I give a small laugh. "Clayton's hard not to love, isn't he?"

"Have you told him?"

"No."

He raises an eyebrow, and I take another drink of coffee avoiding his silent question.

"So this neediness is normal then?"

His eyes narrow. "I wouldn't call it needy. Nor would I say it's normal, expected, but not normal."

"What happened between you two?" I ask causing him to tense, and sit upright. "Not details, Alec, just an overview."

His eyes unconsciously fall to a scar on his hand, one that looks very similar to Clayton's, "I asked for a break," he admits.

Click. In that moment, everything comes into perspective. "I'm sorry. I should have never asked Clayton to call you when he offered. I was desperate to get through to Tasha. I didn't think of the consequences to you."

"I did get through to her, you know." He smiles, dropping his hands under the table, "She's at least talking to me, but if you say a damn thing to her about it, she'll shut down, so butt the hell out," he warns. "I just wanted to let you know that she's seeking help, that you don't need to worry so much."

My eyes fill with instant tears. "Thank you," I choke. "I feel so fucking helpless."

"That's what friends are for. You're not helpless, Daniel. You did help your sister. Remember that. Just because it isn't direct help doesn't mean that you didn't do it."

I shake my head in response. "I want to kill the bastard."

"Let's just get her safe, alright? After that . . ." he trails off. "The main focus right now is Tasha."

"Clayton and I are having her followed. I want a name," I growl.

"Don't do anything stupid, Daniel. Promise me that," Alec says, looking worried. I turn away in a huff. "Daniel, there are ways to deal with this, but I need your head in the game. Promise me you won't be irrational. Think of Tasha. She needs you."

"Fine, but only if you tell me what the hell happened to you," I agree.

Alec stares at me for the longest time. "There are only two people I've ever told that full story to, Daniel. Only a handful of trusted others know half of it."

"She's my sister," I argue.

He closes his eyes. "She's not one of them."

"And when she talks about it, what the hell am I supposed to say?" I ask, frowning. "I'm a fucking hypocrite."

"The truth will suffice," he snaps. "There's a difference, Daniel, punishment is not abuse. I wasn't punished, I was tortured. You have a choice Daniel, trust, respect, limits, safe words, I didn't have the privilege of any of that."

"What are you talking about?" I ask in shock. I know Clayton said Alec had been a slave to a collar, but I didn't realize he meant he was an *actual* slave. I just assumed he meant Alec had an abusive Master. I swallow vomit,

I can't fathom not having rights to what does and does not happen to my body.

"I was a slave Daniel." Alec frowns, confirming my thoughts.

"How did you . . . ?" I stop, unsure how to ask the question.

"Become a victim?" Alec asks, with a shrug, drumming the table nervously.

"I'm sorry. It's not my business," I whisper, casting my eyes down uncomfortably.

"I walked out of my house the day I turned fifteen, when my parents realized 'the devil was in me.'" he snorts in disgust. "I wasn't old enough to get a job. Life on the streets wasn't exactly the best scenario. I got odd jobs that paid cash so I could eat, but I had no place to sleep. Then I met him." He swallows hard. "He took me in, gave me clothes, food, a bed to sleep in. He seemed to support the fact that I was gay, and he introduced me to a glamorous life. He explained the rules and whatnot of BDSM but never pressured me. He only asked that I attend night school for my GED, clean his house, cook our meals, and give him oral sex in exchange for everything. I was happy to oblige." He stops, looking down at his hands. "He gained my trust for two years, all the while taking in subs, and encouraging me to watch if I wanted. I did a few times. I found it fascinating. But those subs were lucky. He never once did to them what he did to me."

"I realized the day I got my GED that I could leave him, and that was my goal. He also realized that, and he manipulated me so much that he made it appear to be a gift that I wear his collar." Alec's hands start to shake, and he drops them back under the table. "If I had known, I would have ran, but I trusted him. I accepted his collar with pride. It was the worst mistake of my life." Tears start to streak down his face. "I was a true slave, Daniel. Everything he had given me, he took away unless I somehow earned it or he needed it for appearances. I was constantly bound one way or another so I could never escape, but those were the moments I craved. The worst was when he just wanted to torture me, and he was good at it. He would leave me tied up for hours, while I tried to balance my weight on my toes to avoid electric shocks to my nuts, and when I slipped, not only did it hurt like hell, but you can't control yourself, and then I would be punished for that."

"How did you break away?" I ask, in tears from the small window Alec was revealing to me.

"I outgrew him. Apparently, my body matured too much for his interest," he answers in disgust. "He sold me to one of his friends with the condition that I attend college," he visibly shakes at the memories. "I don't think my new Sir realized how horrible I was treated until he made me tell him. He called the cops and had that ass arrested for abuse. Then he rented me an apartment of my own and made me get a job to pay the rent like a normal person, all the while requiring me to attend classes and keep my grades perfect. I was still his, though. I didn't have the right to say no, nor did I have an opportunity to run. Besides testifying put a price on my head and there were worse things out there than him. He was never really cruel. Once I graduated and he was satisfied I could support myself, he freed me, assuring me I was safe if I followed some basic concepts. Though I am truly grateful to him for giving me an opportunity at life, I've never want to see him again. It is a chapter in my life that I want to close forever, and I have."

"Why are you still in this lifestyle?" I ask confused.

"Like I said, it fascinated me." He shrugs. "I will never bow to another, and I will never treat my subs with anything other than respect. Bobby is truly the first man that I have ever loved and trusted enough to even try to take care of me."

"You're one of the most respected Doms this side of the Mississippi. That's why I went to you." I smile. "You have truly earned a lot of respect, Alec, respect you deserve."

"Comments like that make me wonder if I should have kept you for myself all those years ago." He smiles. "You have no idea how close you were."

"Why didn't you?" I ask with a raised eyebrow.

"You reminded me too much of Clayton." He shrugs. "Besides, I don't think you're complaining. I knew he'd pick you. I was just afraid you wouldn't pick him when he threw in that stupid multi-sub thing. I've always been curious. You were so adamant with a one-sub Dom. Why did you stay?"

I give a small smile. "I couldn't resist. Besides, it was a good challenge. Sometimes the sure thing is so dull."

"You fell for him, even then." Alec smiles. "So why do you fight it now, I wonder."

"I'm not ready."

"You told me how you felt. Why not him?"

"We're both not ready for that." I laugh. "You realize we haven't even been on a date. What's the rush?"

"Who hurt you?" he asks.

"Somebody who wanted power, not me." I answer, taking a final drink of my coffee.

"Now your choice in sub makes even more sense to me. I always thought it was your career, but your old money has to do with it too."

"Something like that. Now stop shrinking me." I laugh, checking my watch. "I need to go."

"This will stay between us, yes?"

"I might tell him that you are doing okay and about Tasha, but yes, for the most part, this will stay between us."

"Thank you, Daniel." He smiles. "It's nice to get along with my friend's boyfriend for once."

"Give me some time to get along with your boyfriend," I respond timidly.

"You'll like him when you get to know him. Promise." He assures me. "Take all the time you need. We'll be here."

Ridding myself of my empty cup, I drive straight to Clayton's and pull into his house at seven twenty. I take my time going in, deciding to remove my shoes before I enter the playroom. When I open the doors, he is in position, a puddle on the floor tells me all I need to know. I don't say a word, nor do I practice normal protocol to start. Instead, I go to the cabinet, grab the necessary supplies, and then approach him.

"This isn't how I was hoping our next session would go," I start, "but I will not be lied to." I walk around him slowly. "I will not punish you for things that you can not tell me. You should respect my choice in that. We've had a lesson on respect, Clayton. Do you forget so soon?"

"No, Master."

"Then why did you lie?"

"I was desperate for punishment."

I frown. "I will not play this game, Clayton. I will not punish you because you want me to."

"Yes, Master."

"If you ever lie to me with this intention again, then this will end. I want you to be aware of that."

He closes his eyes and his whole body shakes. "Yes, Master."

"Stand," I command, disapproval strong in my voice. He does as I instruct, getting to his feet. I walk over to the cabinet and flip the switch to lower the hook, attaching a spreader bar to it. "Lift your arms," I instruct, attaching his wrists to both leather cuffs, lined with sheep's wool on either side of the bar. Then I walk back over to the cabinet and flip the switch, raising his posture until he is straining to stay on his feet. "Do not use your arms to maintain your weight or your heels. Use your toes," I command. When he is in my desired position, I walk back over to him. "Spread your legs." He does so with effort, and I attach his ankles the same way I did his wrists. All the while, he struggles to keep his balance on his toes. I stand there for a good three minutes staring at his feet to make sure he doesn't rock back on his heels or take relief on his wrists.

"Comfortable?"

"No, Master."

"This is what you wanted, isn't it? Punishment?" I growl, walking around him. "Do you want me to leave you like this, Clayton?" I ask, watching him sway on his toes, face masked in pain.

"The right is yours to do as you wish, Master," he grunts out.

"Is it now?" I ask, standing in front of him. "I thought you were the one calling the shots. Aren't you?"

He gasps for air, but he doesn't speak while he continues to strain for balance. I personally know that having one's arms in this position for too long is stressful enough on the ribs and lungs, but to add to this strain by staying on one's toes, well, it's really overbearing.

"ANSWER ME!" I yell, losing patience.

"No, Master. You are the one who determines pleasure and punishment," he gasps. "I am yours to do as you wish."

I walk up to him, dropping my lips to his ear. "It's best to remember that, Clayton. *Never* force my hand like this again. Understood?"

"Yes, Master," he gasps.

I walk over to the switch. "On your knees," I command lowering him from the ceiling. He follows the command with grace, allowing his weight to follow the hook. I keep it as such a height that his arms are still slightly strained from his body, displaying his rib cage beautifully. I know that this too is an uncomfortable position, but it's a fucking cakewalk compared to where he was. Walking over to him I pull out the metal nipple clamps I had put in my pocket. I tease his sensitive skin with moistened thumbs before I clamp them both. Then I step back.

"You are my sub, Clayton. Your purpose is to serve me."

"Yes, Master."

"I want you to think about that for a while," I say, stepping out of his line of sight toward the doors. I walk completely up to them, despite the fact he's facing away, and open and close the doors, but I do not leave, even though we are both aware we have a sound system installed in case a master does choose to exit the room. All I'd have to do is flip a switch next to the lights to turn it on. I stand next to the wall and wait. Watching as he tries to adjust into a more comfortable position, thinking I left; the minutes pass by, and as his arms start to become painful from the strain, his breathing soon tells me that he has begun to cry. The moment I am sure he is, I slowly and quietly walk up to him. He jumps when he feels my fingers lace in his soft hair. "Shh . . . relax . . ." I whisper, dragging my hands from his hair slowly down his back. Then I kneel, rubbing his legs and slowly release his ankles from the spreader bar, placing my lips on his neck. Once his legs are free, I remove the bar and close his legs. Then I stand back up and place my fingers in his hair again. "I was hoping the next time we were in this particular position we would both be enjoying ourselves," I frown, disappointment clear in my tone; I really wasn't faking it.

"I'm sorry, Master," he whispers, causing me to tug on his hair. I had not given him permission to speak. Sighing, I release my grip, then I release his wrists one at a time. His hands drop behind his back, and I grab the bar off the hook taking the time to put both of them back. Hoping this session is enough for him to snap out of his mood, I walk up to him. "Stand, Clayton." He follows flawlessly. "Look at me." His eyes meet mine for the first time tonight. "Have I made myself clear enough?"

"Yes, Master."

"Good. Touch yourself, Clayton. Use whichever rhythm is comfortable."

I watch him grab his limp dick, and I walk behind him, breathing warmly in his ear. "I wanted a session where your soft lips were wrapped around my cock after you begged me eagerly for the pleasure. I wanted to drive you insane with just my feather-light touch." His breath starts to hitch. "I was going to use the crop, slapping your ass and listen to your delicious sounds as the sting of each blow warms your sensitive skin. I was going to follow it with a flogger until you were screaming. Then give you the enjoyment of having my fingers in your tight hole as I rubbed against your prostate while your ass was stuck high in the air, pushing eagerly against my hand." I look down and notice his dick is dripping as he strokes himself. I begin nibbling his ear dragging my hands down his defined 'V'. I glide my hand over his tight nuts, knowing that he is close. "You would have really enjoyed yourself at the mercy of my touch," I continue, pushing his hand away, taking over stroking him. His breathing changes again, and I know that he's fighting back his pleasure. At that moment, I growl my angry sentence in his ear while squeezing his cock tightly, cutting off circulation with one hand and yanking the nipple clamps off with the other. "But you had other plans as you tried once again to control me!" Clayton lets out a scream of pain. I step back from him and stalk to the doors. Opening them, I turn to him. "Red."

I wait for him on his living room couch, surfing the channels before I come across a decent enough movie to keep in the background. Not much later, he is sitting next to me in a pair of sweatpants and a T-shirt. "Are you hungry?" I ask.

"Not really," he answers with a shrug. "I have leftover Chinese in the fridge if you're interested."

"I've been worried about you." I frown pulling him into my lap. "I know it must be hard for you to have a strain with Alec."

"I've been worried about you," he retorts with a sad smile. "How is your sister?"

I shrug. "She's shut me out for the most part, but a good friend of ours has told me that she hasn't shut out help completely."

"You talked to Alec?" he asks in surprise.

I give him a small smile. "He says hi and he's doing well. Even Bobby said hello."

He sits up from my lap so quickly he falls off the couch; I catch him before he can hit his head on his nice oak coffee table. "You spoke to Bobby?"

"No. He spoke to me," I clarify.

He looks at me completely clueless and freaked out.

"I'm fine." I smile, pressing my lips to his worried wrinkles just between his eyes. "Don't worry, no one is pushing any boundaries here."

"You said *our* friend," he catches on.

"Yes." I smile, dropping my lips to his shoulder.

"You consider Alec a friend?"

"Yes," I answer, kissing his neck. "I really want us to be something, Clayton. That means making friends with each other's friends."

"When can I meet Tim? Or Fin? Or what's his name? The one who thinks I'm a fuck buddy turned boyfriend."

I chuckle. "You mean Amber's new boyfriend, Ben?"

"No, no, no, no," he complains. "She's such a bitch. I really don't want to make a bad impression on your friends."

"You're my fuck buddy turned boyfriend. How much worse of an impression can you get?" I smile, pressing my forehead to his.

"Your friends really have no idea, do they?" he asks astonished.

"No, and it's going to stay that way," I answer, pulling away.

"Hey," he says lightly, turning my face back to his. "Your secrets are safe with me, Daniel." He interlocks our fingers together. "I would never hurt you like that."

My breath hitches in my lungs as our eyes meet, the words I so want to express to him are at the tip of my tongue, and before I can say them, I collide my lips to his until both of us lose coherent thought.

"Stay with me tonight," he pleads, breaking away with a heavy gasp.

I moan in response, wrapping my arms around him, hitching him over my waist, finding the remote and turning off the TV. I stand up with his body wrapped around me while we continue to kiss. I find the light switch and make my way to the bedroom. Grateful that I know this house well. Then I lay him down softly on the bed, hitting the switch to his lamp. "Clayton."

"Yes," he says, pulling my shirt over my head.

I lick my lips, pulling him to me, pressing my lips next to his ear. "This means a lot more than last time."

I could swear his heart stops. He pulls back gently, searching my eyes for the answers to his unspoken questions. It's the closest I've come to telling him how I feel, but I know he knows. "Take me tonight, Daniel," he whispers.

"I won't hurt you, Clayton," I worry, running my fingers through his hair. "You've admitted it's been a long while. I think we should start with plugs first."

"If that's what you want to do in there before you fuck me, I don't have a fucking say one way or the other," he snaps, "but here, now, as your equal, I am asking that we take a step forward, letting me feel the meaning behind this as you fill me."

"No promises," I concede. I have no desire to argue; I want to. "You better be honest with me."

He nods his head, kissing the base of my neck. "Thank you, Daniel." I tug at the string of his sweatpants in response, listening to him moan as I release his hard cock, *fucking commando*. Our lips collide and I squeeze his muscular ass between my other hand. He growls in impatience, fumbling with my jeans. I pull back, stepping out of my clothes, and he does the same, throwing them aside so that we are naked for each other.

I search his nightstand, grabbing the lube before I climb into bed with him. Our lips meet, kissing and dry humping each other for what feels like hours before I feel that he's relaxed enough to try this. I lube my right hand liberally, and he spreads his legs for me. Our eyes meet when I enter one finger into his warmth, and we both gasp. He is so fucking tight I can barely get my finger in halfway. I pull back and trace his puckered hole in slow circles, kissing down his neck. "Relax, baby," I whisper, trying again with more success, able to push in completely. I start with slow steady strokes, with no bending or twisting, just in and out, until he starts to buck his hips. Then I add the bends and twists but not the second finger.

"Daniel, please, I'm ready for another," he begs. I give him a look of caution pulling away for a moment to add lube to the second finger, re-wetting my first. I enter one at a time slowly, taking my time until he is whimpering beneath me. Only then do I start to stretch him carefully, kissing on his skin. "*Please,*" he gasps, and I pull back, adding lube to my third finger before slowly entering it into him while I kiss my way down to his stomach, wrapping my lips around his cock. He gasps in surprise, his fingers finding purchase in my long hair. My tongue starts to distract him perfectly because I know his dick better than my own. All the while, my fingers pump and stretch inside of him. Soon, he is bucking his ass against my hand, moaning desperately.

"Daniel, I'm going to fucking cum," he cries. I look up through my lashes, not wanting him to hold back. "DAN-IEL!" he screams as his hot seed coats the back of my willing throat while my fingers stretch him wider. I slow my pace while he comes down from his orgasm and I lick him clean. His body is limp beneath me.

"Do you want to continue?" I ask, pressing my lips to his chest.

"Yes. Please fill me," he begs. I can't deny him. Slowly I pull out of him, and he whimpers at the loss while I lube my dick. When I am satisfied, I adjust myself in between his legs, making eye contact with him while I press pass his tight ring. I moan from the sensation of his warmth. It has been way too fucking long since I have been with a man this way. I force myself to keep a slow pace, inching in carefully, allowing him to adjust around me until his body relaxes enough for me to bury myself deep inside of him.

"Are you okay?"

"More than fucking okay," he whispers lustfully, bucking his hips in impatience.

Fuck. "You keep that up and I am not going to last long." I warn.

He smiles kissing my lips. "It's alright. I don't mind."

"I do," I growl, adjusting him beneath me until his eyes widen. *Sweet spot.* Only then do I move.

"Fuck me, Daniel!" he gasps, wrapping his legs and arms around me.

"Working on it, baby." I moan pulling in and out of him.

"Harder," he cries, I pick up my pace a little, listening to his continuous pleading for more speed, more pounding on his sweet spot. "Damn it, Daniel, I'm going to cum!" he gasps after a what feels like hours, and the words are music to my ears because I can't last much longer.

"Fucking cum!" I scream, and in that moment his tight ass spasms around me, all I can see is white. *Fuck me.* The power of my orgasm is so strong my arms give out, and I collapse onto him moaning as our naked, sweaty bodies collide, a sensation I have craved in my fantasies for many years.

"Fuck," he gasps, dropping his grip from me at last. "That was . . ."

"Yeah," I agree.

"You wanna go again?" he asks with a wide smile, flipping us over.

"Fuck, yes."

We devour each other, and by 3:00 a.m. Clayton's promising me he's taking a day off. Breaking away from my numb lips he gasps. "I can't get enough of you."

"I know, but we need to sleep, and our lips have lost feeling hours ago." I moan, truly exhausted from our consumption of each other.

"Are you sure tomorrow is okay? I'm not being needy by wanting to skip work and be with you?"

"You mean today?" I laugh, pulling him impossibly tighter. "I'm sure. Now get some sleep, baby. We have a date later today."

"Good night, Daniel," he whispers in the darkness. "I love you."

"Good night, Clayton." I smile. "I'm almost there."

16
Angels of Justice

Clayton's Point of View

Last night was incredible, and if every night was like that for the rest of my life, I would be a very happy man. As the morning light shines down on me, I open my eyes and roll over, muffling a groan from my soreness. *Fuck.* I reach for my phone and call work.

"Good morning, boss." my assistant answers, with a strained voice.

"What's wrong, Mike?"

"Nothing, boss," he lies, which just pisses me off.

"Lie one more time, Mike," I warn.

"Cassandra's here to see you," he replies in a pleasant voice.

Fuck. "Yeah, alright. I'll be there in twenty," I say, hanging up the phone, moaning.

"Everything alright?" Daniel asks in a sleepy voice, pulling me into his warm skin.

"No," I answer in my pillow. "I have to go to work," I explain with a frown. "I won't stay long, I promise."

"Want me to drive you?" he asks with a wink.

"No, stay here. Get some sleep. I'll be back before you know it." I smile, kissing him lightly on the lips, before dragging my sore, tired ass out of bed and throwing on some clothes. Then I brush my teeth, fix my hair, and go straight to work, avoiding my personal entrance, knowing Cassandra is probably waiting for me. The moment I see Mike, I think he's going to be sick.

"What's going on?" I ask, annoyed.

"She's tossing your office," he answers in a panic, raising his hands in a dramatic motion. "I tried to stop her. I even called security!"

That's when I notice it. I walk up to him and push his sleeves up his arms, one at a time. Both wrists are black with bruises. My eyes widen in shock and disbelief as he tries to pull away from me with little success.

"How long, Mike?" I ask evenly.

"It's nothing," he whispers.

"How long has your master been mistreating you, Michael?" I growl. His eyes light up in panic.

"I don't know what you're talking about," he denies. "Boss, I'd rather keep my personal and professional life separate."

"Too late," I spit in disgust, "besides, you think I don't do thorough background checks? You think I don't know your personal interests?" He blushes in embarrassment. "It's not something to be ashamed of Mike. If I had a beef with it, you wouldn't be working for me." He shakes his head nervously. "How long?" I frown.

"About six weeks," he answers in a whisper.

"Is he a new master?" I frown, not liking how recent it is, but it does explain a lot about his recent behavior. Damn it, how did I miss this for so long?

"Yes, well sort of. I've been his for over three months now," he answers, not meeting my eyes.

I frown at him. "Let me take care of Cassandra, then you and I are going to talk."

"Boss, I don't feel comfortable . . ." he stops, trying to take deep breaths.

"This!" I answer, grabbing his forearm and raising his wrists to his eye level. "This is abuse, Mike, not punishment. There's a difference." He looks at me for a moment shaking, then nods his head, fighting back his emotions. I frown. He's going to fucking run the moment I leave him. "I can help you, Mike. I can make this stop. I can introduce you to someone who will give you the respect you deserve."

"You talk as if you are an 'Angel' or some shit," he scoffs. My eyes flash, meeting his with my silent answer. "I'm sorry. I didn't mean any disrespect, boss," he rushes the moment he realizes.

"Come with me." I smile, keeping him at my side so he doesn't run.

He swallows heavily and follows me into my office after I use my damn key. I roll my eyes as I watch a very pleased Cassandra. "You honestly believe I keep all of my copies in my office? What kind of fool do you take me for, Cassandra?" Her eyes widen. "Finish the damn tour or you're ruined. End of story." Her eyes narrow as she stands up, assessing me for a moment before she takes all the copies she could find and leaves my office. I manage to keep from groaning as I look around. The place is a fucking mess.

"I will clean this up for you," Mike offers weakly.

"No," I answer, shaking my head. "You're not a slave, Mike. You're an assistant."

"I'd prefer executive assistant," he challenges.

My eyes flash for a moment. "You realize if I promote you to that than not only would you be assisting me with my schedule and clients but I would expect you to fill my shoes in my absence."

"I can handle it, if you give me a chance." He shrugs. "Besides boss, you desperately need one and I'm the best candidate."

"I can't respect those who don't respect themselves," I argue. "Let me help you personally, Mike. Then we'll talk about a promotion."

"I can't leave him," he answers in a panic.

"Yes, you can," I answer sternly. "Come on," I order, standing. "Seriously, we're leaving." Mike shakes his head no. "Give me one damn good reason why the hell not."

He lifts up his ankle to reveal a GPS tracking bracelet. "I can't call the cops. He'll kill me." My stomach is swirling, and I'm close to vomit. "He has a bug on my cell and both our work phones. He said that if I failed to disguise my punishment, then he would know about it."

"Is my office bugged?"

"Not that I'm aware of."

"My cell phone?"

"You never take it out of your pocket," he complains. Making me sick with the thought that he's been tortured for that. "Please, if you call the cops, he *will* know."

"He's a cop." I frown in realization. "Explains the equipment." Frustrated, I do the only thing I can think of. I call Bobby.

"Hello," he answers.

"Black." *Translation: I'm in trouble.*

"Really? You think I should wear black tonight?" Bobby asks in a panic. *Translation: Confirm.*

"Blue is always nice." *Translation: Not immediate danger, but I need help. Now.*

"How about I take you to lunch and we can talk about it?" He laughs.

"Sure, but I need to bring along a client," I answer. "We had a mix of communication and now my schedule is all scrambled. Can you meet me at my office?" *Translation: I need to scramble a signal.*

"Not a problem. I'll see you soon," he assures me.

"Bobby."

"Yeah?"

"Can you tell Alec that Daniel needs help with fixing the shelf in my garage?" *Translation: Get Daniel out of my house.*

"Will do."

I hang up the phone and start to clean up my damn office. Mike is shaking, but he starts to straighten some tossed files, keeping himself busy. About twenty minutes and a clean office later, Bobby walks through the door. He hands me a scrambler, and I turn to Mike. "Let's go to lunch." Mike nods and follows me through my personal exit, climbing in the waiting SUV with Alec and Daniel.

"How bad?" Alec asks the moment the doors close.

"He's a cop and has a fucking GPS anklet on him," I growl.

Alec nods, taking in Mike's panicked expression from a rearview mirror while he drives out of the parking garage.

"Where are you taking me?" Mike frowns, as he continues to shake.

"Some place safe," Alec assures him. "How long has this been going on?"

Mike doesn't answer, falling further into panic mode. I wrap my arm around him, pulling him to me. "It's alright. We're not going to let him hurt you again," I assure him, looking up to Daniel, who is also showing signs of shock and concern. Then I turn to Alec.

"He's been with him for three months. The abuse started about six weeks ago. I should have caught it sooner. He's been a fucking mess lately." I growl, annoyed with myself. Alec looks at me through the rearview mirror but doesn't say anything. We drive for a while until we are at the safe house.

"She's expecting us," Alec turns, facing us for the first time.

"Holy fuck, Alec?!" Mike says astonished, waking from his daze and realizing he knows everyone but Daniel. "If he's a . . . then that makes you the Grand Master," Mike stutters.

Daniel shows his confusion, but I ignore it, helping Mike out of the SUV. "You're reputation precedes you, Alec."

Alec rolls his eyes. "Stop it. You've known me for years, man. Get a hold of yourself. It's still me," he assures Mike. "Now we're going to get that damn anklet off. Then, you are going to give me a name."

"What's going to happen to me? I can't disappear. I have a family, a job," Mike frowns.

"Don't worry," I assure him. "You'll stay on my payroll. We'll contact your family and give them false information about covering a tour or some shit."

"Why are you doing this?" he asks. "No offense, boss, but you haven't been the easiest man to work for."

I laugh heartily at that. "Don't expect *that* to change."

"Doesn't answer my question," he shrugs.

"Because there's an understanding in our culture. There are rules you don't break," Alec answers for me. "Rachel will take good care of you here. Please don't run. Don't contact him." Alec squeezes Mike's shoulder. "We can only help so much. The rest is up to you." Mike nods. "Good," Alec says, taking Mike's hand, turning to us. "Wait here."

The moment they have clear the door, I turn to Daniel. "How are you doing?"

He frowns. "This kind of thing happen often?"

I take a deep breath. "Not normally, no, but enough that we have a code."

"He just happens to work for you?" Daniel asks.

"Actually, yes," I reply with a smile. "I knew about his past before I hired him but didn't really care. I hadn't met Alec yet, but I figured he was perfect." Daniel raises his eyebrows. "You know as well as I that keeping things out of the press is a bitch." I shrug. "I have less risk of extortion if my closest employees have secrets. I didn't realize he took on a new master. Had I known, I would have paid more attention."

"Clayton is our backup. Most of the time, it's us asking for his help," Bobby adds. "We enjoy the public scene. There's more than one reason why Alec has a reputation. Jerks like that love to broadcast what they believe they own, and Alec has a personal vendetta. We put a stop to this kind of shit often."

Daniel absorbs the information quietly. Not much later, Alec comes out alone.

"You get a name?" Bobby asks.

Alec turns to him and then to Daniel and me.

"I trust him, Alec," I snap.

"That's not what I'm worried about."

"I don't need to be protected," Daniel adds.

Alec stares at him for the longest time, then he nods. "Yeah, I got a name."

"What's next?" Bobby asks, almost bored, walking back to the SUV.

"We are dropping Clayton and Daniel off at our place, and then you and I will take care of it." Alec answers climbing in and starting the engine.

"He's my employee, Alec," I argue.

"I said I'll take care of it," he growls. "You're too close Clayton, not to mention Daniel's not ready for this."

"I can be the judge of that," Daniel answers defensively.

"No, darlin', Alec's right. The less you know the better."

"Clayton."

"No, Daniel, Not this time." I respond firmly.

"This time?" he repeats. "What about next time?"

"Never, if I could help it," I snap. "But I have a feeling it's going to get personal, Daniel. And when it does, I know I won't be able to keep you from it then."

His eyes narrow and then flash in understanding. "Tasha." I nod and turn away from him. He grabs my hand and squeezes it gently, not saying anything to anyone. The rest of the ride back to Alec's is silent.

When we get there, Alec cuts the engine and starts to ramble. "Don't go home, either of you," he warns.

"I know." I frown. "How long?"

"I don't know. I'll call you." He sighs. "Virgin Islands sounds nice right about now. You two are going to need a solid alibi."

I look to Daniel. "Can you swing that?"

"I'd need a few things from my place, but sure, I can swing it." He smiles. "Can you?"

"If I can borrow Amber." I smile causing him to cringe. "I'm sorry Daniel but the office doesn't run itself and I don't have Mike."

"I know," he groans, "and it's a part of our contract with you but the timing sucks with me gone too." He smiles at me, "Don't worry, I'll deal with Ben's wrath if it means uninterrupted alone time with you."

"Gagging here." Bobby laughs.

"What do you need, Daniel?" Alec asks.

"Three boxes in my office," he answers, handing Alec his house key. "And some clothes."

Alec laughs. "It's a private island, right? I'll pack light for both of you. I'm not risking going back to your place, Clayton."

"Alright." I agree, opening the door. "We'll make the arrangements."

About two hours later, Daniel and I are at the airport, on our way to the Virgin Islands. We haven't said much to each other since this whole thing started, but we haven't really had the chance. I know I will have questions waiting for me when I get to the island, but in the meantime, I let Daniel snuggle up in my arms, and pray this flight ends quickly and safely, distracting myself with the euphoria of last night. Damn balancing universe. Why can't I have all the good without all the drama?

17
No Such thing as Paradise

Daniel's Point of View

After we get off the plane, we go to the chartered boat that I demanded the airline pay for, and verify that the fridge has been stocked with food, with my good mate and caretaker, Vladimir. He was surprised to see that I had brought someone with me and continued to ask me questions in his native tongue as Clayton sat obliviously exhausted next to me. It didn't help the man had a fear of flying and was a ball of nerves, refusing to hold still the entire flight. He does light up when the island comes into view and is even more surprised when we dock.

"A golf cart?" he asks.

I laugh. "You don't want us to carry our luggage three miles inland, do you?"

He gives me a shocked expression while helping Vladimir load the cart. I pay him double my usual tip with a wink, warning him to call first if he wanted to avoid seeing anything he could live without. He gives me a hearty laugh, then takes one last appraisal of Clayton before going back to sea.

"What was that about?" he asks with a raised eyebrow.

"Just giving him fair warning about a dick show." I smile. "Don't worry. He'll call first if he needs to take care of anything."

When we get to the hut house my grandfather built by hand, I take the time to make us some sandwiches and pop open two beers. I had called Tasha at the airport telling her that I was going to be out of touch for a few days and if she needed anything than to call Mom or anyone she trusted.

That implied Alec without me actually saying it. I knew she trusted him. That's when she reminded me our parents are out of town but promised she'd call someone if she needed anything. Ben was agitated with the sudden demand for Amber, but I told him to put a sock in it because it's a part of her contract with us. The rest of my life could balance as was; I travel often, although usually expected, so nothing major was going to fall out of place with this trip.

"If you need to pay a bill or whatnot, we do have internet access." I smile, handing him his plate. "This place may seem third world but my dad had it modernized after my graddaddy passed; who would roll in his grave if he knew. He built this place to get away from the world, not to bring it with him. 'Stress isn't allowed in paradise.'" I give a small chuckle at the memory. "Anyway, we left in a small hurry, so I don't know how much that throws you out of whack."

"It's a nice place. Very cozy." He smiles. "My life will balance alright there's nothing pressing that Amber can't handle. Besides, she and Cassandra get along better."

"Cassandra?"

"The lead singer in *Gone a Blur*." He smiles. "She wants to quit, so who knows how much longer they will last."

"Why doesn't she?" I ask, taking a bite.

"I won't let her. She signed a legal binding contract and it's stone. Plus, I have incriminating evidence against her. That's why I went to work this morning. She knows about it and was looking for all my copies."

"What evidence would that be?"

"She's a sex addict. Likes to take three guys at once, cums, and takes three more all within an hour."

"How do you have pictures of that? How do you know it's her?" I ask, rather disgusted and intrigued all at the same time.

"Like I said, I have a rather good PI." He smiles. "The only reason he hasn't gotten a name yet is because the fucker hurting your sister has been out of town."

I give him a small frown but Tasha isn't my only worry right now. "How deep are you in shit, Clayton?"

He bites his lower lip. "Very."

"Can we talk about it?" I've been anxious about this the moment Mike called Alec 'Grand Master.' Have I really found the Angels of Justice after all this time? It would make sense why my PI came up dry, Clayton would have paid him off and I know that ain't cheap. Have I been submitting to an 'Angel' for the past three years and not know it? Dating one?

"Tomorrow morning. I promise. I will tell you everything, but right now, we both need sleep," he yawns.

I give a small chuckle, trying to hide my anxiety. "Yeah, after last night and today, my ass is thoroughly kicked."

We finish our sandwiches, and go straight to bed. The house doesn't have air-conditioning, so we have netting around our bed to keep the bugs out. Clayton wakes up tangled up in it twice with a panic attack, startling the shit out of me, both times it took a little thinking to get him out of it. The second time, I threaten to tie him to the bed so he'd stop waking us both up. He laughs, telling me he wouldn't mind. When the morning light breaks through the windows I give up on trying to fall back asleep. I leave him snoring softly, going for a run before I come back and make us breakfast.

"You spoil me." He smiles, coming into the kitchen with a yawn.

"I like to cook." I smile, kissing him tenderly before I bring my attention back to the sausage.

"Careful, I can get used to this," he warns, causing me to laugh.

We eat breakfast in friendly banter, and then we take separate showers and dress casually in shorts and sun block, which I was mildly surprised to find, but Clayton just laughs, saying that's Alec being Alec; always the caretaker. Then we head down to the beach, watching the waves crash into the shore.

"We're known as the Angels of Justice," Clayton starts, turning to me after a long moment of silence. I didn't bring it up, but we both knew that it was lying heavily on my mind. I manage to show shock disguising the fact I figured it out, but at the same time letting him realize I've at least hear of them. Which I'm sure he already knows with my snooping. "Alec started it not long after he became a Dom. He started as a solo act, but it soon blew up into an underground organization. I didn't know that he was abused until a victim's life was in danger and I accidently managed to get tangled up in it. After that I was helping him with his cause."

"What do you mean by help exactly?" I ask cautiously. The 'Angels' were known for their secrets, no one really knows their methods. We just

— 175 —

know they manage to get abusive masters out of the community and usually behind bars.

He frowns at that. "Usually, we give them a taste of their own medicine then call the cops on their ass."

"You torture them?"

"Yes, but nothing as nearly as horrendous as what they have done to their victims," he defends, digging in the sand with a stray piece of driftwood. We are quiet for some time before he turns to me. "We don't always get there in time. We can't always help. It's a risk if the victim goes back because they are not ready to leave them, if they do, nine times out of ten they wind up dead. That's why we have Rachel. She's a grief counselor by day and usually can get through to them, keeping them safe."

"Was Mike ready?"

He shrugs. "He told me about it after a few short direct questions. He was more ashamed that I knew he was a part of the culture than the fact that he was a victim. I'm pretty sure we got to him in time, before too much irreversible damage was done."

"And Tasha's boyfriend?" I ask in disgust.

He frowns tossing the stick into the ocean. "That's up to you. We don't normally deal with domestic violence. It's out of purview, but there are exceptions. We're not going to step on your toes, Daniel, but we can offer some not-so-legal justice before we hand him over to the cops."

"So why did you agree to skip town with me now?"

He keeps his attention to the ocean. "As Alec said, I'm too close to participate without getting the cops down my neck. It doesn't help that the guy is a cop." He turns to me again. "I'm not asking you to be a part of this, Daniel. I'd really rather you stay out of it, but that isn't my choice. It's yours. What we do is illegal, dangerous, and hard to stomach at times. But we do it to keep our culture safe, and it is safe because there are people like us who care."

"Do you always torture?"

"In abusive cases, yes. Others, it depends on the situation," he answers refusing eye contact.

"Such as?"

"Perverts taking advantage of young kids who are just figuring out their sexuality, sex trafficking, slavery."

"Are there others like you?"

"A few."

"Do the cops know?"

"Yes and no. We always leave our calling card, so to speak, they never really come looking for us because we leave a list of wrongs the victim has confessed to on tape. They hit the grapevine now and again, looking for cooperation on big issues, we help when we can."

"This guy being a cop makes it more dangerous." I conclude. "Do you think they will go after you, if they find out you did it?"

"The less of us involved the better." Clayton frowns. "Mike knows us so if he goes back, well, Alec and Bobby could be in trouble legally. If he doesn't, we shouldn't have any issues. We have loyalties in the force, it should protect us."

"Are you worried?"

"I'm always worried when we do this. But it doesn't stop me."

We are quiet again for a while. "You have my support, Clayton. I can see why you do it."

"Please tell me you don't want to join us." He pleads.

"I won't make that promise." I frown, looking to the ocean. He has no idea how much I need to. Ever since I heard of them I knew they were my answer to pay for past sins.

"I want to protect you from it." He laughs humorlessly. "I want you to continue to trust this culture, understand that if the rules are played right, then it's such a pleasurable release that should never cause shame. I want you to know that I'm there for you and not worry about all of this ugliness and how it may affect us directly or indirectly."

"You're talking about a fantasy world, Clayton." I frown, pulling him to me. "But here, now, we can have that world, if only for a little while. Just you and me," I whisper. He snuggles up to me, taking in the comfort of my arms around him. I lose track of time as we sit together, watching the ocean. The sun is high in the sky when he finally straightens and stretches.

"We should go back for lunch." I smile. "Then we can do whatever the hell we want."

He gives me a sad smile as he stands, whipping the sand off his ass, reaching out to help me up. "I plan on fucking you on every inch of this island," he growls, kissing me gently before he pulls back. I run my fingers through his hair, letting him know that I understand that he's too worried for anything like that.

"We have cell service too, you know."

He smiles. "What kind of vacation would that be? Amber would be calling me every five fucking minutes."

I cringe. "She's that annoying?"

"Yep."

"Fuck, Ben's going to kill me," I complain as we start walking.

Clayton gives me a sympathetic laugh, squeezing my hand. "Don't worry, darlin', I'll take the heat."

When we get back, Clayton takes me up on the offer of using the Wi-Fi and sends a few work e-mails. He seems to relax when Amber tells him that his assistant called in sick with a broken leg and would be out of the office for a while.

"Broken leg," he relaxes, falling back into his chair.

"Is that code for something?" I ask, more than grateful to see him so free since he's been here.

"Yeah, he's still at Rachel's." He smiles. "Maybe we did get to him in time."

I feel a small ping of jealousy realizing that Mike seems to mean more to Clayton than just an employee. "Any other messages?" I ask ignoring it.

"No, but that's a good thing." He smiles, looking up at the thick straw roof. "So tell me, what does this quaint place have to offer? Besides my sexy ass boyfriend, that is?"

I give a hearty laugh. "Oh, you know, the usual, hiking, zip-lining, surfing, snorkeling, scuba-diving—but only if you can prove to me you are trained or willing to learn, rock climbing, paint ball, you name it. Indoors we have fencing, a library, and an entertainment room with every game console and movie you can imagine. Pretty much everything my sister has asked my parents for. Which translates into everything, the spoiled brat."

"This is going to be so much fun." He grins.

We eat lunch, then pack a backpack with a small snack, taking a light hike, seeing as we don't have hiking boots. Then we do a little zip-lining, which is a total blast! I have to admit, I'm impressed on how well Clayton knows the equipment and doesn't need any assistance with his harness. I make a small comment about it, and he just winks. *Tease.* We decide to hold off on rock climbing because of lack of proper footwear, but Clayton makes me promise to bring him back here so we can explore the island together. We get back early, so we decide on some fencing to pass the time and then crashed in front of the TV, exhausted. I must have fallen asleep because I find myself waking to the smell of roast lingering in the air. Stretching, I find Clayton in the kitchen, hunting around for his desired tools.

"Need help?" I ask.

"No thanks." He smiles, showing off his sexy ass dimples. "I need to start pulling my weight around here."

"I really don't mind."

"I do," he insists, rummaging through the fridge for a beer for both of us. "Dinner will be ready soon."

"Thank you." I smile shyly.

"I have an ulterior motive," he admits.

"Which is?" I ask cautiously.

"You know more about me than most." He shrugs, taking a drink. "I'm curious about you."

"What do you want to know exactly?" I ask yawning.

"Everything," he answers, staring me in the eyes.

I swallow nervously. "You already know a lot about me, Clayton."

"Correction, I know a lot about your body. You, you are still a mystery, you surprise me a lot. I'd like to know how your head works and would love to know about your past."

"You want to know why I haven't run from you." I decrypt, peeling at the label of my beer.

"It's a part of it," he admits. "And why you haven't thrown a boyfriend tetra-tantrum about my choice in friends."

"That's easy. The day you dropped me off at your house from the airport, Alec basically told me that he wasn't going anywhere one way or the other. And you never really tolerated the jealous type. You just kept Alec out of the limelight. I didn't want that with us. I knew that if I was going to love you, I was going to have to accept your friends." I bite my lower lip for a moment. "You haven't exactly made that easy, mind you, but at the end of the day, I trust you, simple as that."

"So you're sacrificing?" he asks cautiously.

I shrug. "That's how it started, yes, but not now. I like Alec, and given time, I might be able to get along with Bobby as well."

"I'd still like to know more about you." He smiles.

"Not much of a story there. Look around. I was born with a silver spoon. By the time I went to high school, I knew who I was and rebelled against my parents and upbringing, like a normal teenager. My dad had the hardest time with my sexuality, but we've come to an understanding. My mom was the most supportive. She taught me how to love and how to treat people in general. All she really wants is for me to be happy. Tasha had a harder time with it, but I think it was more of what people thought than anything. We've collided more than once on things, but she still comes to me as her big brother. I graduated from Harvard to make my dad happy. I pursued directing because it was a challenge that you need an eye for, not something that money can buy."

"Friends? Boyfriends?" he asks, turning to the oven.

"Ben's my closest friend," I answer. "We met in college and he's basically my confidant."

"Does he know about Tasha?" Clayton frowns before he pulls the roast out.

"No." I shake my head. "We're not that close. He's from old money too. We're raised to keep private family matters private."

"Any other friends?" he asks, and I make note of the relief on his face.

"More of acquaintances," I answer. "Like you, I don't trust easily. I don't go as far as you do with employee background checks, but I'm not in the spotlight as much as you are. Or were I should say. Why did you go private?"

"You should think about changing that." He frowns. "It almost got me killed. It did kill the idiot trying to take my picture." He shakes his head changing the subject, "At least you don't have to worry about your assistant."

"Amber?" I ask confused.

"She's a madam." Clayton shrugs. "But she wasn't who I wasn't referring to."

"No!" I answer in surprised shock. "Oh, Clayton . . . Ben!"

Clayton laughs as he pulls out plates from the cupboards. "News flash, Daniel. If Ben wasn't into it, then Amber wouldn't still be dating him." My face turns beet red at the thought. "Guess you two have more in common than you think."

"Does she know who you are?" I ask, clearing my dry throat.

"Of course." He shrugs like it's no big deal.

"Will she tell him?" I ask terrified.

He turns to me, searching my face for a long moment. "I can see to it that she doesn't if she hasn't already."

"I'd appreciate that," I answer quietly. "I think it's a conversation between friends, you know."

Clayton nods, turning off the oven, and goes back to our room. When he comes out, he has his phone in hand.

"I don't want to hear it, Amber, really. This number is for emergencies, and that is not an emergency," I hear him say. "Yes, I have a damn good reason for calling." He grips into the phone, rolling his eyes. "Look, I just want to know if you told Ben who I was exactly." My palms start to sweat as I wait. "No, not publicly, the closed-door policy," he specifies. "I figured that, but it matters, so did you or did you not tell him?" Clayton looks at me shaking his head no, and my lungs deflate, *Thank fuck.* "Be sure that you don't. I know it might come up. Just deal with it . . . No, I'm not asking you to lie forever . . . Look, I'll pay you a pretty penny to keep your mouth shut, alright? . . . Thank you! Don't call me, Amber. Unless somebody lost a limb, I don't want to know about it." He hangs up the phone, with shaking hands.

"I thought you liked her?" I frown, walking up to him.

"I do, but she's a bitch, and Cassandra is really pissing me off," he grumbles.

"Thank you for calling. I'll pay for her cooperation." I smile, kissing his neck. "I'll tell Ben soon, so she won't hang it over your head, baby."

"You keep this teasing up, and our dinner is going to get cold," he warns.

"What teasing?" I ask, rubbing my hands down his back, resting them on his hips.

"Daniel," he laughs, stepping away. "I'm starving."

I give a small pout, but I sit down at the counter in the kitchen. He puts the meat and potatoes on some plates passing one to me. Then he sits down next to me.

"Besides, you haven't answered the boyfriend question," he points out.

"Neither have you," I retort.

His eyes narrow slightly. "We were talking about you."

"Fine." I grumble. "I didn't start dating until college, but none of it went really far. I mainly found out what I don't like. After college, I had one serious relationship and one semi-serious relationship. Liam, the serious relationship ended badly, very badly. The other, Brad, well, I had to get a restraining order on his ass." I laugh as Clayton chokes on his food. "I told you I hate needy."

"Holy shit, you're serious." He coughs, wiping his eyes.

"Yeah, it started out innocent enough, care packages, rides to and from the airport. Then you had the phone calls, flowers, chocolates, jealous tendencies, and possessiveness. It drove Ben mad. I have to admit, I wasn't far behind him."

"Why did you keep him around if you hated it?"

"He was wet clay in bed. I got what I wanted every time." I shrug. "Then I got bored. That's when I decided to seek out Alec. Having that much control in both my professional and personal life was so draining, and I couldn't get any satisfaction out of it."

"So you left him closely before you met me?" he asks. "That explains why your phone kept going off during our sessions in the beginning."

I narrow my eyes. "I always turn it off."

He smiles. "It just makes me curious, so I turn it on silent and turn it back off before we're done. Explains the 'Do Not Answer' screen name."

"I can't believe you do that," I mutter, stabbing my food.

He shrugs. "Shouldn't bring it in the playroom if you don't want it to be fair game." I give him a glare. "You pissed?"

"No. It's not like you ever call anyone with it or question me about it. You have a point. If I want privacy, I shouldn't give you the opportunity."

"So after Brad?" he asks casually.

"You," I answer, making eye contact. "No one else. Don't get me wrong. Ben tried, but I . . . it was you." He swallows hard before breaking eye contact. We finish our meal in silence, following it up with the chore of dishes.

He has his back to me when I hear him speak. His voice is soft and low, but I can hear him struggle with his words. "There hasn't been anyone since you became my solo sub. I tried justifying it by thinking I was just sick of dating, but I was lying to myself. You're the only sub I have ever gone bareback with. The only man who can make me feel things that terrify and excite me all at the same time. I know you're not ready to hear all of this, but I want you to know that I'm scared too."

I dry my hands before wrapping my arms around him. "It's not forbidden anymore, Clayton. We are together, willingly. We're giving this a chance, baby. Neither one of us knows where this is going to go, but we both hope that we wind up together."

"I need you so much it frightens the hell out of me," he whispers. "Never has a man made me feel so vulnerable, so lost, and yet all I want to do is protect you, love you, give every part of my being to you." He turns around in my arms. "I ran the last time I felt something like this. I'm not running Daniel, but I'm afraid you might if I keep fuckin' up."

"I'm not going anywhere, Clayton," I whisper on his lips. "I'm right here, baby."

"But I suck at being your sub," he protests, pulling away. I grab him by the waist, pulling him back to me, not letting let him get far. "I constantly disrespect you, I hurt you, and you can't tell me that it doesn't seep through, Daniel. We're not machines. We're human."

I give him a sad smile. "You warned me that you were going to have a hard time, Clayton. I was expecting this."

"I wasn't," he cries, "unsure with being restrained, sure, but disrespect? How can I do that to the man I love?"

"Shh . . ." I comfort. "We'll get there, Clayton, and if we don't, we don't."

"No, Daniel, you don't understand. I want to get there with you. I won't back down. You have to be the one to end it, and I don't want you to. I want to give myself to you the way you have given yourself to me. I want us to work in every way. Please," he begs in desperation.

"Okay." I smile. "We'll continue to work on it. We'll continue to take it slow. It doesn't help that we are developing a relationship while we're developing this. Mistakes are going to happen, Clayton. We're comfortable with me as a sub. The rest is new. This is just growing pains."

"I'm comfortable with you as my boyfriend," he adds timidly. "Are you?"

"Of course." I smile, tightening my grip around him. "It's just the blending that drives me crazy. I want to keep it separate. If we can manage that, then I believe we will be happy in every aspect of our relationship."

"Do you love me, Daniel?" he whispers so quietly I know I wasn't meant to hear it. I pull back a little lifting his chin until our eyes meet. Hoping he can see my unspoken yes. Then I kiss him tenderly before I pull away and rest my forehead on his, closing my eyes as I fight my internal demons. *Why can't I just say it?* "I'm sorry," he apologizes, kissing my lips as he rests his hands on my cheeks.

"Don't be." I smile. "But I think I need to tell you about Liam." Stepping out of his reach I continue, "he was the closest thing that even resembled love, and at the time, I truly believed I did love him."

"What happened?"

I give a dark laugh. "The one thing that my dad warned me against a long time ago. I hated that the old man was right, that I could be so damn naive."

"He loved your name and everything that goes with it, not you," Clayton translates.

"Such an old story." I smirk still feeling anger after all these years. "I gave him so much of who I was. I was so blind. Hell, we almost married, but I insisted on a pre-nup, and that is when it all came to light. He told me that if I loved and trusted him enough, I would never ask for such a thing. It struck me as odd, so I asked my mother about it. Three days later, my dad sits me down and reveals all of Liam's gambling debts, his desire to run for office, and his mistress. To say I was hurt is an understatement. I was frustrated with my dad for doing it, but I thanked him anyway. It was a lesson I needed to learn. I asked him for his contacts so I could do it myself from then on. I prefer the privacy." I look over to Clayton, noticing his eyes are full of unspoken questions, "When I confronted Liam, he went ballistic, and we ended up in a fistfight. He got a broken nose, a rich wife and elected governor. I got a hard lesson and learned to be skeptical of everyone and everything."

"You knew I was the owner of Blackboard Entertainment," he concludes. "Assuming your guy is good. Most in that culture think my last name is Lake, if they are ever brave enough to look me up."

"Yes and no." I shrug. "I researched Alec. I gave him a list of musts. Success and non-greed were two priorities. I never researched you. I didn't want to know that side of you. I only knew you were a successful business owner. I did know Lake was an aliases though you usually use Justin not Clayton. I believed it until I heard you answer your phone with your last name once."

"I slipped." He frowns. "You always did manage to get under my guard. Did you know about Angels of Justice?"

"I've heard of you guys, but you're good at covering your tracks. Even my PI couldn't come up with names," I assure him, relieved he asked instead of confronting. I just hope he doesn't ask why I was looking, my past demons don't need to taint us.

He nods his head and then meets my eyes. "I would never hurt you like that, Daniel. I'm not after your name, and I sure the hell won't have a mistress or cheat on you in any other way."

"I know." I frown. "I'm curious, Clayton. Paranoid as you are, why didn't you know who I was? What I did?"

"Alec asked me not to." He shrugs. "He never really explained it, but I think he knew that we would end up here eventually, that it would make you uncomfortable. I agreed on the condition that he screened you instead. I trust him."

"Remind me to thank him for that." I smile hoping it hides my stomach flip, does Alec know about my past? He couldn't, there is no way he would have put Clayton and I together if he did.

"So, off the wall question here, how do you feel about marriage? Kids?" he asks, moving to sit on the couch.

"Marriage." I repeat, chewing the word. "I'm not against it really. Obviously, I've seen myself that way before, but now, I just don't know."

"Even if with a pre-nup?" he asks with a shrug and then smiles. "You don't have to answer that. I'm not proposing or anything. I'm just curious as to where you stand."

"It's something that we'd have to talk a lot about, when we're there," I reply, sitting next to him.

"Yeah, I know. I'm five steps ahead here," he chuckles.

"More like two." I smile, causing his face to fall into awe. "Kids," I say in distraction, "never wanted kids really. You?"

"No, I would suck as a father." He laughs. "Besides, hiding half myself is not something I ever want to do with the people I love."

"Dogs?" I ask, trying to lighten the mood, avoiding his eyes.

He laughs. "That's something we'd have to talk a lot about, when we're there."

"Oh, come on. You have to admit it would be nice to have something to order around and give you respect at all times." I laugh.

"Why, darlin', when I want that, I have you," he teases, causing me to choke on my beer. When he's sure I've recovered, he turns serious, "How are you doing, Daniel? With Tasha, this sudden trip? Everything? Do you need me?"

"Yes, but not here." I smile. "You are helping me, Clayton. It's enough for now."

"Good to know." He smiles, readjusting himself on the couch so that he's facing me. "I know that this part of us will never be enough for either of us, but I'm glad that we're strong enough for challenges like this, that I can be enough for now." He runs his fingers through my hair, his voice turning lustful. "And you have no idea how glad I am that we can find everything we desire in each other."

He presses his lips gently to mine, and I pull his legs down, allowing him to lie flat on the couch as I lie on top of him. He grips my ass from under my shorts and thrusts his hips into me, causing our dicks to press together. I moan in his mouth from the sensation while my hand glides down his bare chest, finding his nipple and I begin teasing. He breaks away with a moan fumbling with the button of my shorts, freeing me from them, and pushing all my clothing to my knees. I lift up kicking off my clothes while yanking his off and tossing them to the side. Then I kiss down his stomach, making my way to his cock.

"Wait," he gasps.

I stop only to see him smirk while he pulls me up and flips me over, slamming my back onto the couch. "I want to do that," he growls, kissing down my stomach and swallowing my hard cock whole.

"Fuck!" I curse, the sensation of a hot mouth still so new after all this time. He hums around me in response relaxing his throat, taking me deeper while keeping eye contact with me through his lashes. Then he starts swirling his tongue all around, I find myself whimpering and trying not to fuck his mouth, but it feels so fucking good. "Clayton . . . baby . . . oh fuck . . . cum," I manage, and he sucks harder accepting my seed down his awaiting throat. When I stop pulsing, he drops my softening member and licks me clean.

"Don't move," he whispers, climbing off me and disappearing down the hall, only to come back with a huge ass bottle of lube. I can only smirk. *Fucking Alec.*

He climbs back onto the couch. "Now where was I?" he questions, dropping his tongue back to my dick. I jump a little from sensitivity, he meets my eyes with humor in them. Then he drops down and brings my balls into his mouth, rolling them with his tongue. "God! Fucking hell!" I gasp. He smirks, dropping them.

"It's Clayton, darlin'," he mocks, tracing my entrance with lubed fingers. *When the hell?* I lose all track of thought the moment he slides two fingers in and violently begins to twist and curl. My hips leave the couch involuntarily.

"I'm sorry, Mas . . ." I stop myself. "No, I'm not, Clayton. Fuck, that's fucking good," I moan.

He gives me a throaty laugh as he inserts a third finger. "I'm going to fuck the hell out of you, Daniel, but just remember, I'm Clayton." I whimper in response because he withdraws his fingers leaving me empty. I distract myself from it by watching him lube his beautiful dripping cock. I lick my lips knowing his taste so intimately, smiling when he resettles himself between me. He lifts up one of my legs and then lines himself up. "You ready, darlin'?"

"Fuck, yes," I gasp feeling him shove his way inside then pulling almost all the way out, violently. My leg is in such a position that my prostate is hit dead on. I start to touch him everywhere, moaning and gasping, enjoying this new experience of being with him this way. Despite my earlier orgasm, I'm fucking close to another while he continues to fuck me hard. "Fuck, Clayton, please," I beg, trying to hold out for him.

"Close," he grunts, picking up even more speed. I clinch my ass around him desperately, causing him to gasp while his warm fluids burst inside of me. I cum with him, shooting my spunk all over our chests and stomachs. He collapses on top of me. "Fuck."

"Yeah."

"Shower."

"Yeah."

We take a shower together and then climb into bed. I tell Clayton that I am serious about tying him up if he gets attacked by our netting tonight, he laughs pulling me closer to him, telling me he wouldn't mind as long as I took advantage of the situation and had my wicked way with him. The feeling of being in his arms is incredible, and I am so happy that I don't have to leave this up to my imagination anymore. I fall asleep almost instantly feeling safe and secure.

The next day, we wake up lazily in each other's arms. We share a quick breakfast of cereal and fruit, then walk on the beach, which turns into a sex fest. We both end up with sand in not-so-friendly places, so we had a swim in the ocean, where he tries to keep the fire going, but I am too chicken shit with all the salt. Hell no! That would burn like a motherfucker. He settles with the hot tub.

By early evening, Clayton gets a text message from a burn phone Alec had given us. *It's done.* He explains that once it is confirmed, we could go home, but it would cause unnecessary suspicion to confirm tonight and leave tomorrow. So we agreed on confirming tomorrow and leaving in three days. I don't mind; I am enjoying the freedom that is allowing our relationship to blossom. I do however, decide to work a little to help avoid Ben's wrath when I got back. Clayton shots off a few e-mails here and there but mainly stays away from his job saying he just can't get in the mood with weather like this. I can't help smiling at that, granddaddy would be so proud. Despite Clayton's anti-work philosophy he respects my discipline of working and manages to keep himself busy with various things, including making fun of the books in the library.

"Vampire books?" he questions.

"Tasha has a weird fascination. My father humors her," I explain, sifting through my boxes.

"Seriously, she enjoys books where people live off blood for survival. Yeah, and she would think you're weird if she ever knew." he laughs.

"Don't worry. She won't. She did look you up though, to prove a point or some shit that she knows how to take care of herself. She didn't find anything other than what you want people to find," I assure him.

"So her boyfriend doesn't have a history of violence." he concludes, not looking the least bit surprised about a background check being done; making me assume I wasn't the first to tell him about it.

"That was the point of her exercise, yes." I frown, sifting through the last box.

"Looking for something particular?"

"My sister sent me a script from a friend of hers in college. I promised her I'd look at it," I explain finding it. "I told her not to let her friend get their hopes up. It's about vampires." I wink at him.

"What's the title?" he asks with an eye roll.

"*Darkness* by Travis Ash-ton." I stare at the name in disbelief and the room starts to spin.

"Daniel?" Clayton questions in concern, but I can't think enough to respond. "Daniel, talk to me." Clayton says, falling to his knees in front of me. "DAN-IEL!" Clayton screams, snapping his fingers in front of my face. I blink. "Breathe," he instructs, taking the manuscript from me. I try to do as he says, but my lungs aren't cooperating. "Daniel." Clayton frowns, taking me by the arms, helping me off the chair and laying me down on the floor. He scoots himself above me, placing my head between his knees and starts to rub my temples. I know that this means I'm having a panic attack, which I haven't had in a long time. Usually, they are only triggered when we try something new, and I am pushed to my limits. I panic, safe word, and Clayton is there to bring me back down. But there are no safe word to use. There is no easy way out of this nightmare. Clayton moves his attention to the pressure points in my palms, and I can see the concern in his eyes as he tries to bring me down from my fear. "I'm here, Daniel. I'm right here. Whatever it is, I'm with you one hundred percent. You just need to breathe for me, darlin'," he says over and over. His touch and words are the only thing I can hold onto, and I cling to them for dear life.

"It's him," I whisper. "He's the one hurting her."

Clayton frowns at that, squeezing my shoulders. "May I ask what makes you think that?"

"He's rich, Clayton." I frown, struggling for words as my lungs grab shallow breaths. "He's never had a criminal record because he's paid to keep it clean. There was nothing to find with a simple PI check. Tasha should have dug deeper." I close my eyes, praying for calm. "She's been known to be sloppy in the past on this, but it's never really hurt anything. I always double check, always." I stop, trying desperately to catch my breath, "But I didn't even know she was dating him. That's why she wouldn't tell you or Alec either. She knew I would know him." My lungs are burning at this point as panic comes anew.

"Shh . . ." he encourages. "Relax for me, darlin'," he whispers.

"No, Clayton, you don't understand. I never told her why I didn't approve of the Ashton's, I told our parents but not her. I was trying to protect her."

"From what?" he asks as worry lines crease on his face.

"His girlfriend Seanna disappeared last year. He had a solid alibi, but we were friends." I swallow as I fight for control. "We got piss poor drunk one night and he admitted to killing her." Tears streak down my face. "I couldn't prove it. He didn't give details. I told the police, but they couldn't prove anything either."

"Give me your phone," he says, panic momentarily crossing his features before he can mask it. I fish through my shorts and hand it to him, still struggling to breathe.

"Alec, it's Clayton . . . I know, but we have a problem . . . It's Tasha. We need to get her out of there, *now* . . . I know that, Alec, but you don't understand. She's dating a guy named Travis Ashton . . . Daniel seems confident . . . Regardless, Alec, he's a murderer . . . Yes, I'm sure about that . . . Fine, you do that, but call me back in an hour."

"What'd he say?" I ask, unhappy with the way it sounded.

"He thinks it's too soon to move on anyone, and I have to agree." He frowns. "He wants us to stick to the original plan of staying here but has promised to talk to Tasha."

"She's going to hate me," I moan as breathing becomes a little easier.

"She'll get over it," Clayton assures me. "Alec is going to call you in an hour. Tell him what you know."

"What is he going to do in that hour?"

"He wants to make sure she's safe, invite her to dinner with them or something," Clayton explains, obviously foggy on the details. "He just wants to be able to reassure you when he talks to you."

"I'll never forgive myself. I should have told her. She would have wanted me to testify. Our families would have been under a microscope. It would have been all over the news. Oh fuck . . ." I trail off, realizing hiding my secrets have managed to get others hurt.

"Don't!" he yells. "No worse case scenarios, Daniel. You have held your secret close. The only real risk is Mike, and even he didn't recognize you."

"But the nine others, from when I met you . . ." I argue, my mind rushing past the fact I'm into BDSM into another more devastating secret that could destroy the Kingsley name.

"No, it's in the contract all of you signed, they wouldn't be able to play in Chloe's house where you were trained as an Untouchable, or any other respectable house, if they broke it. And if Alec had his way they would never play anywhere in the State of Texas. None of that shit is going anywhere," he assures me.

I don't say anything as I concentrate on breathing, while Clayton continues to try to relax me with his touch and reassurances. Eventually, my breathing evens out and the spinning stops, but I'm still on edge, waiting for my phone to ring. Relief hits me in waves when it does. I stand up to answer it, trying to feel normal.

"Hello."

"She wants to talk to you," Alec informs me. "She's ticked."

"Figured she would be. Go ahead, put her on."

"Daniel?" she asks, and I know immediately she's scared.

"It's alright, Tasha," I assure her.

"What's our mother's maiden name?"

"Young." I smile. It was one of our safe word questions.

"Where are you?" she snaps.

"The island." I frown. "I can't get a flight back for a few more days."

"They are saying that you sent them. Is that true?"

"Their names are Alec, whom you met, and Bobby. I trust them, Tasha."

"Tell me how you know his name," she asks in a whisper.

"The manuscript."

"You mean you finally took the time out of your precious schedule to read it?" she snaps again.

"Is that why he hurt you, Tasha? Because I haven't looked at it?" Her silence is all I need for a conformation. "I won't let him hurt you again, Tasha."

"You can't promise that, Daniel. Why did you never tell me you suspect him of murder? I know you were friends at one point in your lives."

"I was trying to protect you," I almost growl. "I was hoping that you respected our family enough not to go against our wishes like this."

"Oh, like you've never rebelled," she spits back with acid.

"You're not safe, Tasha. Can you do me a huge favor and go with Alec and Bobby until I get home?" I ask, not wanting to argue with her.

"When will that be again?" she asks, her fear coming back in her voice.

"In a few days," I repeat. "They won't harm you, Tasha. I promise you're safe with them."

"Can't I just stay here?"

"You live alone, Tasha," I remind kindly, "and Mom and Dad are in Europe. Please do this for me."

"How do you know them?"

"They're good friends of Clayton's, and I trust Clayton. Stop stalling, Tasha. I know you've trusted Alec in the past. We want to protect your life here. Please." I plead, rubbing my forehead against the instant headache, as I start to pace.

"How long have you known Clayton? Where did you two meet?"

"Three years, on a set. He was trying to get a feel for a music scene and asked to watch it in person. We started out as friends and it's just grown." *Damn! There's a lie if I ever had one.*

"Do you love him?"

"I trust him, Tasha," I snap. "Now please stop being difficult."

"Fine, but only for a few days."

"Thank you. I love you, Tasha."

"I love you," she replies. "Alec wants to talk to you."

"You okay?" he asks.

"Far from it," I answer defeated. "She's stalling, probably expecting friends over or something. Tell her to go shopping for clothes and get her out of there. She's going to be a pain in the ass, Alec. Just keep an eye on her, and if she tries to leave, lock her in a room or something. I don't care."

"Daniel?"

"I trust you, Alec. I don't trust Travis. Tasha is skeptical on all of this. She's young. I wouldn't put it past her to try and contact him."

"Thanks for the warning. I'll keep in touch."

"Thank you."

I hang up the phone and fall to my knees, trying to gain some control of my shaking body. Clayton's next to me immediately. "What can I do?"

"You're doing it," I reply, grabbing onto him for dear life. "I have to read that," I moan, looking at the manuscript. "I have to get inside his head."

"Daniel." Clayton frowns pulling back. "I know you said you didn't want to do this here, but circumstances have changed. Would it help if we had a session?"

I look at him in shock then I smile. He really does know me better than I know myself. I need to clear my mind, let go, just be for a while, he's offering that to me. "More than you know," I whisper, kissing him on the lips.

He returns a quick smile before his voice changes. "Red." He gives me a moment to cast my eyes down. "Go to our room and get into position on the floor next to the bed."

I follow his instructions and strip naked, waiting for him. When he comes into the room, he walks behind me running his fingers through my long hair. I break position, leaning into him for a moment before I fall back in line.

"This is going to have to be softer than usual, seeing as we don't have the equipment." He starts, "But I will make do. Walk over to the wall, brace your body with your hands, spread your legs apart and outward, displaying your ass."

I display my body for him and he comes behind me, touching my ass caringly. "Pick a number," he instructs, I know better than to pick low.

"Seventy-three," I moan, pressing myself into his hand.

He smacks me in warning. "Don't be an eager whore." I quickly put myself back in place. "Fifty-eight," he decides. "This is going to cause me some discomfort, Daniel. I suggest you thank me for the pleasure. Now count," he growls, slapping my ass hard against both cheeks with his bare hand.

"One, thank you, Master." By the time he gets to forty, my ass is hot with sheer pain. I'm grunting trying to fight back the orgasm that is dripping from my dick while I continue to count. When he gets to fifty-eight, he steps away from me, letting my body absorb the hot fire and sting. I take the time willing my body to calm, staving off orgasm. It causes me to go into a deep level of submissive state, which I could not be more grateful for. That's when I feel his warm hand pumping my cock and his hot breath in my ear. "Don't you fucking cum," he warns, pressing his hardness into my sensitive cheeks. I gasp out a moan, trying to follow his command. He drops his hand, only to use it to spread my sore cheeks wide so he can put his dick in my crack. Then his hand is back on around my cock and he starts to thrust his hips into me. "I know you want to cum, you fucking cum whore," he growls breathily in my ear, I moan at his dirty talk. I love it when he does this.

"Not without permission, Master," I answer, squeezing my eyes shut, knowing better than to beg. If I beg, he will not allow me any release. He smacks my sore ass. I let out a small scream. "You do not have permission to speak you naughty whore!" He pulls back and throws me halfway onto the bed. "Pick a number," he growls.

"Fifty-eight." I gasp, needing more, craving the pain.

"You want to start over like the eager whore you are?" he asks. I don't answer as I lie there with my hands positioned behind my back as though they were tied behind me. "Hmm . . . I think I will decide that. Count," he demands, hitting me harder than before with this new angle. The pain is pleasuring, and I am a whimpering mess when we get to thirty-three. He stops. I am unsure how much time passes, but I do not hear him move, and the sting in my ass has subsided substantially. When he continues, I start with thirty-four. He stops again at eighty-eight. At this point, my ass is burning like it would from a good flogger session, not a bare hand session. I whimper when I feel him spread my cheeks again. He rubs his smooth cock between them until his breathing hitches. Then he pulls back. "On your knees." I fall to my knees, facing him. "Open." He pumps himself a few times and then aims his cumning cock at my face and mouth. When he is finished pulsing, he instructs me to swallow. He leaves me there with his cum dripping off my face and comes back with a towel. He does not use it to clean me, however, instead he spreads it out on the bed and orders me to lie on it. I do so willingly, ignoring his quickly drying cum on my face.

"Hump the bed until you cum," he instructs, stepping to the side, watching me. It takes an embarrassingly short amount of time before I am cumming. When I am done, he walks behind me and slaps my ass ten times. "Clean up this fucking mess, you cum whore." I roll off the bed, fold up the towel and discard it. He smiles, checking that my face still has his dried spunk on it. "Good. You will be rewarded for that in the future." He smiles. Then he walks out of my sight to the door. "Red."

The next two days pass by slowly, and Clayton does his best to keep me distracted while we wait for the hours to pass. I have to admit, I love his distracting techniques and the fact that we haven't worn clothes since the library. Alec checks in periodically, giving Clayton and myself trouble about how difficult Kingsley's can be. He and Bobby end up taking shifts just to keep an eye on her. She is being childish and as predicted tries to call Travis, but they are able to put a stop to it before she does any real damage. We have a lot of phone fights, with the main argument being that she wants me, not some strangers. It is breaking my heart to be away from her like this. I promise her I will be home soon begging her for patience and understanding. The calls always leave me drained, and Clayton is always there to pick up the pieces.

We fall into an uncomfortable pattern. I know Clayton is becoming just as exhausted as I am. Reading through the manuscript doesn't help, nor does fact that it constantly causes my stomach to lose its contents. I want to go home and hold my sister. And I want my vengeance on Travis. Not just for Tasha, but Seanna. Travis is going to face justice.

I had just gotten back to bed after brushing my teeth, thus ending the fifth cycle of phone calls, reading, and panic attacks. Clayton is next to me instantly, trying to distract me with kisses of love all over my body. I pull him up by his armpits and roll us over.

"I want to kill him."

"I won't let you."

"Then let me hurt him."

He searches my eyes for the longest time. "Okay, but not enough to destroy who you are."

"Clayton . . ."

"There's three of us, Daniel. Let us help you."

"Alright," I agree then frown. "It doesn't frighten you? The way I feel? What we're agreeing to?"

"I'm not happy about it," he admits, running his fingers through my long hair. "I understand it, but I was truly hoping that you would never want to be a part of this. Don't you see, darlin', after knowing what he is capable of, who he's hurting, seeing you like this . . . justice is going to happen with or without you."

"She's my sister!"

"And I could argue that you're too close! Just as I was with Mike," he snaps. "Think about this, Daniel. Once you cross this bridge, there is no going back. Whether you decide to participate again or not, this choice will always haunt you one way or the other. The question you have to ask yourself is which decision can you live with?"

In that moment, I realize that the man lying beneath me really does love me. It's not just words; he truly means it. My lips crash into his, and I kiss him past his surprise until he is breathless. When I break for air, I kiss up his right jaw to his ear and whisper the three words I haven't shared with anyone the way I am sharing them in this moment. "I love you."

He gasps, pushing me away from him to search my eyes before crashing his lips back into me. Then he breaks away, kissing my neck. He doesn't say it back. Instead, he whispers, "Please show me." I smile in response, my lips meeting his again while my hands roam his body, realizing this is the first time in my life that I have ever truly made love.

18
Denial

Daniel's Point of View

The moment I walk into the airport, I am slammed by my sister's slim figure.

"Don't ever do this to me again," she cries, pulling me tightly.

"I'm sorry," I whisper, holding her just as tight. "I was so worried. I'm so scared."

"I want to go home," she cries.

"How about we talk about that over lunch or something?" I frown. I really don't want her to go back to her apartment alone.

"I'm not a prisoner, Daniel," she huffs, pulling away.

"I don't want you to feel like that, Tasha. Just let me take care of a few things first, alright?"

"Take care of a few things?" she says snidely. "Like what?"

I stare at her for a moment, feeling Clayton place his hand in mine and giving it a small squeeze. "A restraining order to start, I don't want him near you, Tasha."

"I can take care of myself, Daniel."

"I didn't say you couldn't. I just want the law on our side in case he is stupid enough to come near you again."

"I love him," she snaps and my eyes widen. "He said he was sorry. He was drunk."

Clayton moves his hand to wrap around my waist, knowing that my knees will probably betray me at this point.

"Tasha," Clayton frowns, looking around, "this isn't the place for such a delicate conversation. Let us get our luggage, and we will all go to lunch or something."

"You think I'm going to eat with you and my brother and your thug friends so I can't run away?"

"You are your own person, Tasha. We are trying to help you, nothing else." Clayton frowns with a shake of his head.

"I want to go home," she repeats.

"Fine." I concede. "We'll go to your place then." She crosses her arms, yanks her chin up and stomps past all of us. I follow behind her frowning, with Clayton still holding me and Alec and Bobby following on our heels. "These mood swings happen often?"

"Ever since we brought her back to our place," Alec answers. "She doesn't believe that he is capable of murder."

I turn to him with dead eyes. "Neither did I."

We get our luggage and climb into Alec's SUV. Tension is strong as Tasha glares at me the entire time, causing exhaustion to take a hold of me again while I mimic her stance, crossing my arms around my chest and glaring back. This was a regular occurrence with us, and I notice Clayton frowning as he watches us.

"How was the island?" Bobby asks, trying to make small talk.

"It was beautiful." Clayton smiles, lighting up. "Maybe if you two are lucky, you might get to come next time."

Alec checks the rearview mirror, and I take a glance to see his eyes light up, but my attention is brought back to Tasha as she huffs with an eye roll.

"What's the matter, Tasha? My friends not rich enough for you?"

"I don't have a problem with your *boyfriend*," she clarifies. "Except for the company he keeps," she mutters. Bobby lets out a hard laugh.

"You are only angry because they wouldn't let you have your way. They are good people, Tasha. Stop judging the damn cover," I snap, annoyed and embarrassed at her shallowness.

"What would Dad think, you hanging out with this riffraff?" she snarls.

"What would Dad think?" I ask astonished. "You're serious? I know, Tasha. How about I *call* him and tell him who we have been hanging out with lately and who each of us are dating. Then let's see who he will side with."

"I LOVE HIM!" she screams. "He didn't do what you said he did!"

"Seanna was your friend, Tasha! Where is your loyalty there?"

"You're wrong," she argues. "She disappeared like that just to give him heat because he cheated on her, and he only did that because he didn't love her!"

"HE CONFESSED!" I scream back, uncrossing my arms in anger, causing her to flinch away from me. The move is so shocking that I freeze. *I'm going to kill him.* "Tasha," I whisper. "What kind of man hits the women he loves? Look at you. You're flinching away from me, and you know the only thing I want to do is protect you."

"YOU HATE ME!" she screams in angry tears. The blood drains from my face as my breath catches in my throat. "Don't deny it, Daniel. You have always hated me!"

"No, Tasha," I manage in a strained whisper. "You're young. We grew up with different friends, different mindsets. Does it annoy me that you judge people by their checkbook? Hell yes, because you are missing out on so much of the world around you. But that doesn't mean I hate you, Tasha. You're my sister. No matter how much we bicker and disagree on the world, I love you. Please, Tasha, don't ever think otherwise."

"You're wrong about Travis," she snubs but her eyes are showing that she at least trusts my feelings about her.

"Am I wrong about the fact that he hits you?" I whisper.

"He said he was sorry. We are working through it. I'm not going to stop seeing him," she says stubbornly, stomping her foot and turning to the window. "The only reason I didn't run away from your boyfriend's thug friends is because I wanted to talk to you in person. You can't decide who I can and cannot date, Daniel. I will not allow you to go to these extremes again, otherwise I will disown you."

"Tasha."

"NO!" she screams, facing me. "This is *my* life, Daniel. No one is going to tell me how to live it. And you will *never* snatch me out of it like this again! Next time, I will call the cops for attempted kidnapping! I can't believe I agreed to it in the first place! But Travis and I were fighting, and you sounded so scared and I am a fucking idiot! Just because you two had a falling out doesn't mean that I can't love him. Get over yourself, Daniel!"

I know at this point it's worthless to argue; she has her mind made up and there is no changing it; she's not ready no matter how much I want her to be. "Promise me something," I whisper. "Please."

"What?" she asks with a huff.

"Promise me you won't mention Seanna to him again," I ask, meeting her eyes.

"Only if you can promise to take a good hard look at his script," she negotiates.

"I've read it."

"And?" she asks, lighting up.

"And I'll promise to pass it along to Ben *if* you promise me Seanna," I counter.

"Fine," she snaps like a five-year-old.

"Fine," I snap back while Alec pulls into her apartment complex.

She jumps out of the car and I grab her by the arm. She turns in surprise, fear washing over her when she realizes that she can't get out of my grip. "I'll let you live your life the way you want, Tasha, but if he lays one more hurtful finger on you, I cannot promise you that he won't end up in the hospital for it. Feel free to pass that along to him." I let her go, and she lets out a frustrated growl, slams the door, and stomps off. *Fuck.*

When I divert my attention back to Clayton, he is on the phone. "Yeah, keep a very close eye on her. If there is any hint that he will hurt her, then break your cover. I want continuous updates and her phones tapped." Hanging up his phone he turns to me with a whisper, "I'm so sorry."

"If he hurts her . . ."

"We will take care of it, Daniel," Alec assures me. "She's not ready, but the moment she changes her mind, we will be there."

"How do you know it won't be too late?"

"My guy is good, Daniel. He'll protect her," Clayton promises, grabbing my hand.

"She's going to hate me for this." I sigh, pulling out my cell phone. "But I love her too damn much to care."

Clayton gives me a quizzical look, taking my cell from me. "Who do you want to call, darlin'?"

"Our parents," I answer surprised.

"Not a good idea." Alec warns, putting the car in drive. "The less people who know about this, the better. Keep them in the dark, Daniel. You will thank us for it later."

Alec takes us back to his place, where we gather in the living room while I try to keep my hands from shaking. Bobby takes off his coat, and that's when I notice the nail marks all the way down his right arm.

"Tell me that wasn't my sister."

"She was trying to call Travis," he explains. "I didn't hurt her. I just grabbed the phone. This is the thanks I got."

I moan dropping my head down. "I'm sorry, Bobby." I lift my head up meeting his eyes. "How long before you realized that she called him do you think?"

He huffs, "I'm not sure, but I know she had no idea where she was. Why?"

"It was long enough for him to brainwash her." I frown. "I'm not accusing anyone, but it explains the turnaround and her attitude back there. Travis and I didn't have a falling out. I kicked the shit out of the guy. As far as snatching her out of her life . . . she was terrified and willing until she fucking talked to him."

"She wasn't ready to leave." Alec frowns. "I've seen this happen before. Give it time, Daniel. We've planted the seed of doubt that she needs. Now it needs to grow."

"I know you are right, but I still hate it."

"He will regret hurting her, Daniel. That I promise you," Alec says sternly.

"I want to kill him," I admit again, "but I won't. His face and my fists are going to meet before anyone lays a fucking hand on him, though. He's going to know *exactly* what it feels like to be helpless and alone."

"I'll agree to that *if* we can be with you to make sure it doesn't get out of hand." Alec nods.

I shake my head in response, standing up from the ottoman I was sitting on. "Fine, but if I can't go any further, I know for a fact I want to watch." He turns his attention directly to Clayton, and they share a silent moment of communication before Clayton comes up behind me and wraps his arms around me.

"Nothing needs to be decided tonight, darlin'," he whispers.

"Hey. It's six. Anyone up for watching the game?" Bobby asks, thus breaking the seriousness in the room and allowing us guys to do what we do best, just be guys. We end up hanging out with them at their place for a few more hours. Alec makes us all an early dinner and we watch a game while we get to know each other over a friendly game of truth or dare. Bobby and I ended up talking to each other, and I swallow my damn pride, telling him that the whole friendship thing could probably work, given time. Clayton is so ecstatic when he overhears this, he pins me to the wall and kisses me breathless.

After the game ends, we call a cab and go back to my place, where I call Ben to make sure everything is still alright, and Clayton calls Amber to letting her know he would be at work the next day.

The dark cloud of Travis Ashton is hanging over everyone's head, and the only thing we could do is wait for him to make his next move. The thought has me on edge like a snake waiting to strike. Clayton does his best to distract me, asking to meet Ben and possibly my parents. That leds to a long conversation of his parents and whatnot, who I discover live not so far away on a ranch at the edge of town. At the end of the night, my worry gets the best of me. All I can do is lie down and cry while Clayton holds me in his arms, assuring me that everything is going to be alright. But I know his words are meaningless until I get the opportunity to break Travis's face. Nobody fucks with my family and gets away with it.

19
Lessons

Clayton's Point of View

It's been two weeks since we've come back from the island and both of us have gone back to work. Daniel has been in pieces most every night. When he falls apart, I do the only thing I can think of and give him his release, taking him to subspace by being his master. When he is there, he is free, but the high never lasts as long as it should, and he just falls back into his shell of depression and lies to me, saying everything is fine. I have had enough.

My first instinct is to go to Tasha's apartment, rip her a new one and drag her kicking and screaming while Alec and Bobby take care of the worthless piece of shit that is hurting both her and the man that I love. I hate that my hands are tied, as my PI hasn't been able to stop the fucker who only seems to attack when they are behind closed windows and doors. But I have been an 'Angel' too long; I know that stepping in is useless and would result in terrible consequences. So instead, I decide to try something new, something daring, something I could only pray could help.

I get home from work and put my plan into action. I had decided not to ask for this outright, because if Daniel knew it was planned, then it would fail to meet maximum potential. No, he needed this to be his idea, and I was going to do everything in my power to make it happen. I text him an invite for dinner, telling him stir fried rice would be ready by seven. Then I go and sit on the couch for a while. At six-thirty, I go to the kitchen with the full intent of ordering takeout. I search my cabinets for empty grocery bags and some stray ingredients to put into them. Then I pull out the pots, pans and cooking utensils. Once this is accomplished, I put a pan on a burner, turning the burner on high. Then, I sloppily cut up the chicken, smiling as I watch it smoke in the all-too-hot pan, not bothering to turn it over. I want it to burn. I repeat this with a pot of water that I plan to forget about. Right around seven, I start cutting some vegetables, and when Daniel comes in, I slice my finger on purpose. *Small price to pay.*

"Fuck!" I scream, throwing the knife down, running to the sink. It's not long before his arms are wrapped around me, and it takes all the strength I have not to lean into him. "I'm fine." I sigh dramatically. "It's just been a tough day. I thought I had everything. I had to go to the store and fuck!" I curse, running over to the stove to pull the boiled over water off the burner, slamming it on the counter, causing hot water to slosh everywhere; luckily I didn't burn myself. I turn my attention to the burners, turning them both off and curse some more.

"It's fucking ruined!" I cry, slamming plates and throwing dishtowels. "Why can't I fucking do anything nice for you?" I continue in frustration, trying not to smile as I watch him take in my little hissy fit. Not too much later, he is gripping my elbows with his strong hands, holding me in place.

"Clayton!" he calls, trying to get my attention. I look at him in fake shock. "Breathe." He smiles.

I take a few slow breaths, faking some tears for dramatic effect but I don't spill them. "I just wanted this to be nice is all," I add, cracking my voice, turning away.

Obviously worried, he checks to make sure that the oven and stove is off and then guides me to the couch. "Talk to me, Clayton."

I look down at my hands, purposely avoiding eye contact. "I was just trying to make us dinner."

"Trying being the key word," he mutters. "What has you so distracted, baby?"

"It's nothing I want to bore you with," I answer, shaking my head. *God, he's eating out of my hand here!*

"I can't help you if you shut me out, Clayton," he retorts annoyed.

"It's just, well, with Mike gone, work has become more stressful." *At least, that's true.* "And now I have to deal with Cassandra more." *Again true.* "I'm just exhausted is all." *Again true.* This time, my frown isn't faked as I ideally wonder if in fact I would have burned dinner had I actually tried to make it.

"Anything else?" he asks, running his fingers through my hair.

"I'm worried about you," I answer. This time, the tears fall. I quickly turn from him, taking deep breaths, trying to control my sudden emotions. *Fuck, I'm not a girl.* He notices the two that escaped my eyes and brushes them off my cheeks. Then he nuzzles into the crook of my neck before his breath is on my ear.

"Right now, Clayton, I'm worried about you." I find the palm of his hand pressed against my lips gently to avoid any potential argument I might have. "You have been incredible to me, baby. I know that all I have been doing lately is taking. I love you, Clayton, and tonight, I'm going to take care of you." He pulls back, kissing down my neck, sucking and licking as he drops his hand from my mouth, moving his lips up the other side of my neck to my ear whispering, "Red." *Well, at least it worked.*

I drop my eyes down immediately and whisper, "Thank you, Master."

"Careful, Clayton," he warns in a stern tone, pulling away. I nod in understanding, I did not have permission to speak. "Get into position," he orders. I stand and make my way to the play room, finding myself fighting back my instincts of protection. It takes everything I have not to embrace him, kiss him, be there for him, as his boyfriend, as his Dom, but I know that he needs this more than I do, and I am determined not to mess up this time. I love him and I am going to show him that I respect him. I will not disappoint him for a third time. With this mindset, I remove my clothes and kneel in the center of our room, waiting patiently for him with my hands clasped behind my back. He has been through so much. I know he feels that life is spinning out of control. Tonight I will show him that he does have control, respect, love.

When he walks into the room, I take a calming breath. I can do this, for him, for us. He walks behind me, placing his hands in my hair, I lean into his touch just for a moment before I fall back into position.

"Hmmm. What shall we do with you today, Clayton?" he muses, roughing up my hair a little before he lets go. I try not to be annoyed by that, my hair may look messy but I style it perfectly thank you very much. "I think we will start with something simple, to test your control." *I will make him proud; I will succeed.* He walks in front of me, releasing his hardened cock. It's the first time I've had the opportunity to just admire it in its beauty, seeing as I don't have any distractions. I lick my lips in anticipation, causing him to give a soft chuckle. "Eager?" he asks, gripping the back of my neck. I want him so badly, but I will not break position to take him. He wants me to remain still. So be it. He takes his free hand to stimulate himself, causing pre-cum to seep out. Once he is satisfied with his results, he traces his tip over my wanting lips, coating them with his delicious juice. I want to taste him, but I resist. "Go ahead," he allows pulling back, immediately my tongue escapes my mouth, licking every drop he gave me. I let a small moan escape from me as I do it. He puts his tip back onto my lips once more. "Lick it clean," he orders. I eagerly comply, forcing myself to hold still except for my tongue and lips. "Swallow it." I open my mouth to take him and lean in just slightly only to have him pull himself back, gripping my shoulders tightly. I let out a small huff in frustration at my failure. "I take it that means you understand your error," he notes. "Now swallow it." This time, I open my mouth and wait for him to slide inside my mouth. I open my throat to him eagerly, and once he is in, I moan his name around him, my hands breaking free just for a moment until I remind myself of my purpose. He notices and steps away from me. "Stillness doesn't seem to be your strength," he muses, walking over to the cabinet. "In time, that will change, but for tonight, I think you might be more comfortable in these." He comes back to me, showing me a familiar pair of leather cuffs. "Would you prefer to be bound and suck me off Clayton? Or would you rather try something different where we continue to practice stillness?"

"The decision is yours, Master."

"So it is," he agrees, "but my question stands on your preference."

"I don't want to disappoint you, Master," I answer in almost a whisper.

"And how would either decision do that, Clayton?" he asks. My breathing hitches as I ponder my answer. How do I tell him that I can't fail him again? That this is important to me? That failure isn't an option? "I'm waiting, Clayton."

Suddenly I feel caged, closed in, I can't think, breathing becomes difficult. "Seed." I gasp, falling out of position as I try to gain control of myself.

Daniel is next to me at once. "Clayton, please talk to me."

"I just," I try, shaking my head, trying to steady my hands. "I can't fail."

"Fail?" he asks confused.

"You deserve so much," I answer, unable to look at him, "and I've proven to be so horrible."

"Shh," he says, pulling me into him. "I don't see it like that, Clayton. You just needed to understand your place. You have just proven to me that you do." He pulls back. "I don't consider the need for bondage failure. It just shows that we have a long way to go. You may have been a perfect sub in the past, but life has changed things for you. A sub role isn't an easy undertaking. It's not like riding a bike, Clayton. This is going to take time."

"I can do this," I assure him, but I think that I am talking more to myself.

"I know." He smiles sweetly.

"I think I will take the cuffs. We can work into the complete stillness thing," I decide.

"Are you sure?" he asks, raising an eyebrow. "You've mentioned that bondage is a difficult part of the transition."

That was before you said you loved me. "Yes, Master, I'm sure," I reply, taking my position once again.

He is silent for a moment, and I can feel his skeptical gaze, but I refuse to look up to confirm it. "Stand," he orders. I rise to my feet so he can capture my wrists into the restraints. "Now kneel." I carefully lower myself down to my knees once more. Although I am staring at the floor, I can see that he is re-hardening his cock for me. I internally scold myself for my disappointment; for I was unable to pleasure him like a sub is supposed to. Once again, he places his tip on my lips. I remain still, waiting for him. "Make me cum," he orders. I open my mouth, sucking him inside, relaxing my throat once more, swallowing him down, while taking my tongue and swirling it around his base before opening further to lick his balls. My gag reflux kicks in, and I'm forced to back up just a little to avoid choking, but other than that, I do not move while I work to pleasure him with just my mouth. It doesn't take long for him to fist my hair and fuck my face. Not much after, he gasps, "Swallow." And his delicious juice is squirting down my throat. When he is finished, I lick him clean before closing my mouth, awaiting his next command, praying that he doesn't stop because of my earlier weakness.

To my surprise and relief, I am ordered once again to stand. He releases my wrists from my bondage, only to have them recaptured as I lie stretched over our spanking bench. The feel of the crop on my ass causes me to jump in surprise, and I am grateful that I am restrained so that I cannot disappoint him again. By the time he switches to the flogger, I am moaning with each strike, the sting of the straps bringing the most pleasurable rush of blood to my body. My cock is hard, dripping and trapped between my stomach and the bench, soon I am struggling to split my attention from stillness and delayed gratification. When he is satisfied with his results, he drops the flogger and removes my restraints. "Hold still," he orders, I stay where I am, enjoying the heat of my flesh. Not long after, I am feeling cool lubricant dripping down my crack, I involuntarily jump at the shiver, but I force myself to relax and stay where I am. I feel his finger push inside of me, twisting and bending. I let out a moan, but stay still. By the time he adds a second, my breathing is hitched, because he has found my prostate and is relentlessly pressing into it. After countless strokes, he presses his body against mine, his warm breath in my ear. "You are doing so well, Clayton. I know I am driving you mad, and yet you are still for me. Your efforts will be rewarded." Then he plunges his tongue in my ear, and I force myself not to cum from the sensation. I moan and whimper when he pulls back and nipples my earlobe. "Cum for me, Clayton," he whispers. Instantly, my body pulses in orgasm while he continues to brush against my inner parts with his fingertips. When I am done shaking and fall limp he gives a deep sigh, "See what happens when you let go and stop pressuring yourself to perform for me. Now do me a favor and never go to such extremes as burning a fake dinner just so we can do this."

I swallow hard, "Master?"

"Don't ruin this by lying, Clayton," he warns, his voice stern as he yanks his hands out of me.

"I'm sorry, Master. I wasn't aware that you could see through me so easily," I whisper.

"You said you went grocery shopping, and yet the receipt in the bag was dated last month." He chuckles, standing up. I blush in embarrassment. "Why didn't you just tell me, Clayton?"

"Permission to speak freely?"

"As long as you stay still." He approves, sitting next to the top of my head.

"I wanted it to be your idea. I wasn't aware how much I needed it, but I knew you did. Being a sub usually allows you to stay high for more than two days before you need it again. It wasn't working. I was hoping this would help."

He doesn't say anything for the longest time, but eventually, he squeezes my hand, "Thank you, Clayton, but I'm not sure if anything will work while Tasha is with him."

I don't know what to say to that, so I just stay still, letting him have the final ounce of control while he disappears into his head. After what feels like hours, he stands up and walks out of my sight. "I'm going to order takeout. Go and clean yourself up." Right before the doors close, he adds, "Red."

That night did seem to help, and since then, we have been alternating every other time, just to try and relieve the pressure, which we have been doing for about six weeks now. But sitting here in my office chair completely frustrated at the fact that Daniel is off on some shoot ten thousand miles away, which forces us to have phone sex that doesn't quite cut it, I decide on another drastic move.

I tell my temporary assistant to hold all my calls and to cancel all my appointments. Then I sneak out my private exit and make my way to Tasha's apartment. To say she is surprised is an understatement.

"You're not changing my mind, so you might as well leave," she snaps, trying to close the door the moment she sees me.

I stop it with my foot, forcing my way inside while pushing her to the ground. She gasps in surprise trying to futilely run from me. I grab her by the ankle, pulling her to me. "What's the matter, Tasha?" I ask, grabbing her arm and twisting it behind her back as I raise her to her feet. "I've heard you are into this kind of thing."

"Stop it!" she cries, struggling fruitlessly.

"No," I growl. "Not until you learn to fight back!" I let her arm go at that statement and pin her against a wall. "You want to date an abusive murderer, that's your business. But you are my boyfriend's sister, and I am sick of watching him fall apart every night while you make the biggest mistake of your life. Now I am not leaving here until you learn how to defend yourself against your sorry excuse for a lay when he gets drunk and loses his temper."

Her eyes flash as she studies my expression. "He can't find out," she whispers. "When I tried to sign up for a self-defense class, I was bruised for three weeks."

"Why are you with him?" I growl in frustration, letting her go.

"That's my business," she spits back.

That's when it dawns on me. "Oh hell no," I gasp in pure shock. *No, no, no, please no!* "Do not tell me you are trying to get proof that he killed Seanna."

"Like I said, it's my business," she answers, crossing her arms stubbornly.

"How long have you known?" I ask, my eyes meeting hers. She doesn't answer me, so I grab her wrist and twist. "How long, Tasha?"

"Since before I started dating him," she whines and I release her.

"You're going to get yourself killed!" I growl. "Let Daniel and me take care of this."

"NO!" she screams. "She was my best friend. I owe her this!"

"You don't understand, Tasha. I have connections. I can get him to confess on tape, and you don't have to go through all of this," I argue.

"No, you don't understand," she retorts. "It should have been me, not Seanna. She started dating Travis to prove something to me. She knew I was into him at the time, but I just wasn't able to catch his attention. I think Daniel got some weird vibe or something and threatened him. I don't know, but the guy wouldn't date me. Instead, he dated her and it got her killed."

"Why didn't you take self-defense *before* you started to date him?" I moan.

"I didn't realize that he was abusive too. Seanna didn't tell me."

"I don't like this one bit, and you are going to tell Daniel your stupid suicidal plan. After that, you are going to swallow your damn pride and allow us to help you. Then and only then will I teach you how to defend yourself." I frown at her stubborn expression. "It's not optional, Tasha. I'll fucking kidnap you if I have to. So either this ends now, or you start doing things my way."

"Fine," she snaps crossing her arms like a child. Resisting an eye roll, I pull out my cell phone and call Daniel.

"This is a bad time, Clayton," he answers.

"Make time. It's about Tasha," I retort quickly adding, "she's safe, and I'm with her, so don't panic."

"Hold on," he groans, and I can hear him excuse himself to Ben, explaining it's a family emergency.

"This better be important," he growls. "Because if you are with her and she didn't come to you, then you have crossed a damn line, Clayton."

"I'll let her explain." I hand my phone to his sister. She's timid at first, but as the conversation gets going, so do both of their tempers. By the end, I am picking my phone off the floor wondering if it's broken. "Daniel?" I ask rolling my eyes when I hear a door slam.

"I'm here." He answers in exhaustion.

"I'm sorry I crossed a line, but something needed to be done. I just wanted to teach her self-defense so you would stop worrying so much. I had no idea she was crazy."

"We'll talk about it later, believe me when I tell you, I'm pissed. But right now, I need you to get Alec and Bobby involved. I will be home in a few days. Since you started this, promise me you will teach her how to stand up to the guy. I'd make her give this up, but she's in too deep. I'm afraid that if she leaves now, he might do something deadly."

I swallow vomit. "Don't worry, darlin'. I have it under control."

"Thank you, Clayton. I love you."

"I love you too, Daniel. Now if you'll excuse me, I have to take the hinges off the bathroom door."

"Good luck and don't say I didn't warn you. She's a fucking bitch."

20
Stress

Clayton's Point of View

    I end up spending about three hours with Tasha before I have to leave to avoid running into Travis. We set up a schedule on times for me to stop by and help. She has a long way to go, and teaching her upper body strength is going to be difficult because Travis discourages any and all things that could help her defend herself. The one thing we have going for us, though, is that she refuses to move in with the guy, so we can hide barbells and such in the ceiling. Overall, I teach her more about dodging and faking worse injuries to avoid getting the shit kicked out of her, reminding her that most of the time, he is drunk and incoherent. "If he knocks you down, struggle, but stay down," I explain.

    By the time I get home, I am completely exhausted, but I know that I have a long ass night in store for me. The first call I make is to my PI guy explaining the newest development. He's pissed, of course, but promises to help out and keep her safe as much as he can. I thought about calling Daniel next, but I chose to avoid him. He's pissed and I'm tired, not exactly a good combination. Instead, I break down and call my best friend.

    "Hello," Alec answers with laughter in his voice.

    "Hey, I know that we aren't in the best place right now, but I could really use a friend," I reply back in a weak voice.

    "What's wrong, Clayton?" he asks, his voice steeling immediately.

    "Can you come over? I'll order takeout or something," I answer in a dead voice.

I hear him sigh. "Alright."

"Alec?"

"Yeah."

"Bring Bobby."

"You really got me worried Clayton. We'll be there soon."

Hanging up the phone, I dig out my extra beer and put it in the fridge then call for pizza. As I'm waiting, my phone rings. It's Daniel. I think about letting it go to voicemail, but I don't want him to get even more pissed, so I answer.

"Hey."

"Are you alone?" he asks coldly.

"For about five minutes."

He's quiet for a moment. "Did you talk to Alec and Bobby?"

"Working on it," I answer. "They are on their way over now."

"I'm sure it doesn't take a rocket scientist for you to figure out I'm still pissed," he mutters. "Grateful, but pissed."

"I know. But it was eating you alive, and you and Tasha sure the hell weren't talking, so I had to do something. It's not like I know her friends and have them as a route to talk to her. And I knew if I asked you to try, you wouldn't." I argue defensively.

"So what? You decide to play hero and go behind my back?" he snaps. "I spoke with Tasha, Clayton. I know *exactly* how you got her to talk to you."

I cringe. "I didn't hurt her. I scared her, but I didn't hurt her. I would never hurt her, Daniel."

"You *ever* touch her like that again, and it's over. Am I making myself clear?"

I swallow hard, forcing my vocal cords to work. "Crystal."

"I need a few days, Clayton. I'm not ending this. I just need some space, alright?"

I take a few deep calming breaths. "I understand."

"I'll call you when I'm ready," he promises, before I can reply, the line is dead. *Fuck me.*

I sit down on the couch and stare at nothing. I honestly don't register Alec and Bobby coming into my house or even Alec pulling me into his arms. I can only register numbness and darkness while I force my lungs to breathe. I know deep down I did the right thing and Daniel does too. I probably didn't go around it the best of ways, but hey, I never think past the moment. He knows that. *I'm an idiot.* I break out of my trance and sit up, groaning as I pull on the ends of my hair.

"Are you ready to talk about it?" Alec frowns.

I look over at him in surprise, registering his presence for the first time. "No."

"Is it why we are here?" he asks, narrowing his eyes a little, appraising me.

"Inadvertently," I mutter.

"The beginning's always nice," Bobby comments.

"He's been a fucking mess," I bitch, fighting back tears of exhaustion. "Nothing was helping and I mean nothing. Not me, not sub, not Dom . . . absolutely nothing. It's like a never-ending subdrop. He needs me, and I give and give and give, but fuck, it's killing me. He's depressed and worried, trying to hide in work and me, and it just got to be too much. I had to do something."

"Tell me you left Tasha alone," Alec whispers, closing his eyes in hope to avoid the destruction he knows is about to be revealed to him.

"Yeah, no." I frown. "I confronted the bitch."

"You what?" Bobby growls. "Come on, Clayton. You know better than that!"

"It's not what you think," I defend myself. "She isn't with him because she loves him. She wants him to tell her what he did to Seanna. She's trying to get evidence against him."

Alec turns white and Bobby groans. This is the worst possible scenario for Tasha to be in, and all three of us know it.

"Bobby's right. Beginning is nice," Alec finally comments.

"I went to her place, pushed her around a little, not enough to hurt her, just enough to freak her out. I figured if she wanted to be with him, then there was nothing we could do, but she could at least learn to defend herself. I about choked when she agreed wholeheartedly to my help in under two minutes. I wasn't expecting her to confess to some fucked up hair-brained plan. She and Daniel got into it, but shit, when don't they? He wants her pulled out but agreed to her terms because if we pull her now, it could get her killed. We don't have a choice but to run with this."

"So what happened next?" Alec frowns.

"I taught her self-defense and called you guys for help," I mutter, turning away from him.

"And?" Alec pushes.

"And Daniel's pissed," I mutter. "He asked for a few days to himself. He stressed that he's not ending it but that I crossed a line, more than one really."

"You mean you didn't talk to him first?" Alec asks, annoyed.

"He would have stopped me."

"So you went behind his back." Alec snips. "Nice," he adds sarcastically.

"I know alright! Go ahead and side with him, but it doesn't matter now. We need to work on helping Tasha."

"Agreed, but one question first," Alec says, taking my hand in his. "You obviously aren't thinking clearly, Clayton. This has got you stressed too. So I want an honest answer. Are *you* alright?"

I run my hands through my hair a few more times. "No, not really," I answer. "I'll admit it, Alec. Life has been hard without you. I understand your need for a break and I respect it. I've been trying like hell not to call you, but I had to with Tasha, and hell, with Mike, for that matter. I wasn't trying to be disrespectful to your needs or anything. Daniel and I are okay for the most part. It's just I wasn't expecting him to ask for time too." Breathing suddenly starts to become difficult. *God, they both want a break from me.*

"Clayton?" Alec says, but his voice is more of an echo, I'm starting to panic. *I can't lose them both. No, please no.* "Clayton?" Alec says again, shaking me gently as he kneels in front of me. I blink. "Slow, deep breaths," he encourages, and I nod my head in understanding as I force my lungs to take in air.

Ding, dong. Saved by the fucking bell has never been more appropriate in my life then in this moment, I so need a distraction to keep myself from spinning. Relieved, I jump off the couch and generously tip the pizza guy. "Thanks, umm, Jeremy." I smile, reading his name tag. "You have no idea what great timing you have."

He gives me a Cheshire cat grin. "Thanks, Mr. Reynolds. Are you eating alone tonight?"

I give a heartily laugh at his wink. "Sorry, man, you got the right vibe, but I'm happily taken."

He bites his lower lip. "Well, if you change your mind and want a real man . . ." he winks again, writing his number on the box, "give me a call."

I roll my eyes, taking the boxes from him. When he starts to walk away, I holler, "Don't hold your breath. I think he's a keeper."

I watch in shock as he turns to me with a death glare, and I know all he is seeing is red. "What the fuck did you just say?" he asks, stomping back to me. I drop the pizzas to the ground, ready for a fight.

"I said I'm not interested."

"Who did you say your boyfriend was again?" he asks, through clenched teeth, his hands balling into fists.

"I didn't," I answer firmly, highly confused, running the name Jeremy through my head. *Oh, hell to the no!* I close my eyes and curse the universe. "You're Jeremy Richards." The moment the words escape from my lips, I find myself flying through my living room and landing hard at the back of the couch. Bobby is on him like white on rice, pulling him into my house and pinning him to my wall while Alec helps me to my feet. I shake it off, knowing I should just let Bobby take care of it, but fuck me if this guy was going to fuck with me like that and get away with it.

"So you're into G-strings," I laugh, walking up to him. "I take it your pissed my man got you fired from *Mile High*. Guess what? You're about to be fired from this job too," I growl, signaling Bobby to let him go. Fucker got a sucker punch the first time, but it didn't take me long to kick his ass, thoroughly. The adrenaline rush was fucking delicious, and Jeremy's face proved to be a great stress reliever. I think the guy would have wound up in the hospital had Alec not pulled me off him telling Bobby to call the cops. Jeremy ended up charged with assault; I ended up with free pizza for a year. In the end, it all worked out.

"I don't even know where to start!" Alec frowns, throwing me some frozen peas for my blackening eye.

"That was the flight attendant that tried to come between Daniel and me!" I defend pissed. "You know the story. Plus, I wanted to prove to his sorry ass that he doesn't fucking mess with Clayton Reynolds. I have an image to uphold. You have to admit I look better than he does."

"Nothing wrong with a good old fight every now and again," Bobby laughs, high-fiving me but sobers instantly when he sees Alec's glare.

Alec turns to me, studying me for a while. "As much as I hate violence, I can almost see your justification in that *childish* display of testosterone. I think it would have been more civil to judge dick sizes with a ruler, but that's just me." He sits down next to me rubbing his face before he continues, "You're taking on the weight of the world, Clayton. You were bound to snap, and I don't like it. Find a fucking hobby to relieve some damn stress, and back off with Daniel for a while, if need be. Maybe this break will do you both some fucking good."

I huff, bending my swollen knuckles. "Is it helping you?" It had been nearly three months since he's asked for space.

Again he is silent, studying me. "I didn't do it for just me, Clayton," he finally answers. "You needed to stand on your own two feet for a while." I nod, accepting his logic, fighting back hurt. "That being said, I think you may need my guidance if you want any relationship to last, more or less yours and Daniel's." he smiles mockingly and my eyes shoot to his hopeful. Then his eyes harden, "Seriously, what would he have thought if he was here tonight?"

"He hit me first!"

"And you're not five!"

"I'm sorry." I frown, opening a box of our second set of delivered pizza, seeing as the first set got cold with the whole ordeal.

"Well, at least you kept Bobby entertained," he mutters, and I knew that meant I was forgiven.

"We good?" I ask, biting my lip timidly. "Break over?"

"Yeah, we're good. Break's over." He smiles.

The grin on my face spreads from ear to ear, and I toss him a beer from the bucket on my coffee table that Bobby was insisting upon, saying that when it was empty, I could put my fists into it—he had a point, so Alec agreed, even though we all knew Bobby was just too damn lazy to get up and get himself a new beer every time he ran dry. The rest of the night passes by quickly while we catch up with things. I learn that Daniel and I weren't the only ones to go on a vacation, and as I watch them throughout the night, I can tell that they have grown even closer. Seeing Alec this happy helps lighten my mood, it's all I've ever wanted for him. Daniel ends up calling me while we are in the middle of the game, but for once, I don't answer it, letting it go to voicemail. He asked for space and I am giving it to him. Eventually, the guys call it a night. Right before they leave, I pull Alec aside and give him a strong embrace. "I'm so happy to see you happy," I whisper in his ear.

He pulls away with a small blush. "Thanks, Clayton. It means a lot."

When my head finally hits the pillow, I am out like a fucking light.

Sometime in the early morning hours, I'm awakened in a state of panic from the feel of someone touching me and I come up swinging.

"Clayton! It's me, Daniel!" he calls, gripping my wrist and pinning me to the bed.

"Daniel?" I ask through my sleepy confusion. "You're gone," I mutter, trying to break free.

"I took the red eye," he explains, holding me down. "I wanted to talk to you, but you weren't answering your phone."

"So you flew ten thousand miles?" I ask, glaring against the sunlight, only to wince in pain from the fucking swelling of my left eye.

"You were avoiding me," he huffs.

"How did you get in?" I ask, struggling again.

"Your door was unlocked," he answers, keeping me pinned. "Now tell me how you got the black eye. If it was Travis, I swear I am going to kick his fucking ass right now."

"Travis?" I ask and then moan. "No, this is from the fucking pizza guy."

"You got in a fight with the pizza guy?" he asks, with disapproval clear in his voice.

"Actually, he's the one who sucker-punched me across my living room. Then I beat the shit out of him," I scuff back, giving him my best glare, considering.

"And what did you do to provoke him?"

"I'm dating you," I moan. "Apparently, he was some smart ass flight attendant for *Mile High* before he started delivering pizzas."

Daniel stares at me for a moment. "You're serious, aren't you?" He asks letting me go.

"Got the shiner to prove it." I smile and we both start laughing. Once our laughter subsides, he is lying next to me in bed. "Still pissed?" I muse.

"Yes."

"Anything I can do?" I ask, rising up on my elbow to look at him.

"Give me time to get over it." He turns his head to me. "I warned you about needy."

"You did, but wanting to make you feel better after two months of depression didn't seem to fit that description. I just wanted to teach her how to defend herself, Daniel, so you could stop worrying so much."

"I'm not disagreeing that your heart was in the right place, Clayton, but you went behind my back."

"The only thing I can do about it now is apologize and give you time." I check my clock, turn off my alarm and get out of bed. "Is that seriously why you flew all the way here?"

"No," he admits, "I came to see Tasha."

"How did that go?" I ask, heading for my toothbrush and toothpaste.

"I think she likes you better than she likes me." He laughs.

"That's because I haven't told her what I think of her to her face," I point out. "You were an ass to her when she came to the airport, Daniel, something along the lines of judging people by their checkbook."

"It's the fucking truth," he defends himself. "She's seven years younger than me and has so much to learn about life and the real world. There is more to life than shoes."

"And solving your best friend's murder," I add, coming out of the bathroom minty fresh.

"Are you seriously siding with my sister?" he asks, almost in shock.

"I just think that you are being a little quick to judge her and that she may be above the maturity level you have her pegged at, but she's too stubborn to correct your ass."

"What makes you say that?" he asks, pulling his eyebrows together.

"She's a Kingsley." I smile with a laugh. "You are a stubborn ass, Daniel, and your sister learns from the best, but she has something you don't."

"What would that be?"

"Estrogen." I laugh. "She's a fucking bitch."

"That she is," he agrees, sitting up. "You work everything out with Alec and Bobby?"

"Yep, and I got my best friend back in the process." I smile. "Break's over, thank fuck."

"Glad to hear it." Daniel smiles. "Speaking of friends . . . how would you feel about meeting Ben when this shoot is over?"

"Well, I will have to check my schedule," I tease.

He rolls his eyes, "So tell me what exactly happened once you pounded Jeremy to a pulp anyway?"

"He got arrested and I got a year's worth of free pizza." I smile. "Hungry?"

"No, my flight leaves in less than an hour. I just want to see you in person to make sure you know we are okay even though I'm upset."

"Thank you," I whisper. "I won't do it again, promise." He crawls up on to the edge of the bed on his knees, pulling me to him. Not really in the mood for anything physical I distract him with a change of topic. "You talk to Ben about Amber?"

He moans, dropping his hands. "I've tried, but it just hasn't come up."

"You want help on our double date?" I ask with a knowing smile.

"You know me too well." He smiles back, resting his forehead on mine. "Are you getting Mike back anytime soon baby?"

"His ribs are almost completely healed now, and Rachel says that a light workload might be a good change for him." I smile. "I don't want to push him too much. I have big plans for him, but I want to take it slow."

"You need to bring him back, Clayton," he worries, holding my swollen hands out. "You are way too stressed. Between me and work, you are not getting any relief, except for Jeremy's face apparently."

"You've been talking to Alec," I accuse.

"Yes, just a few text messages," he admits. "And I want to apologize for being so damn self-absorbed lately."

"Don't," I snap, putting my finger under his chin. "I want to be there for you."

"You have to be there for yourself first, Clayton. And this is a two-way relationship, remember."

I stare at him for the longest time before I sigh. "You're right. I'm sorry."

"You're forgiven." He smiles. "Not for the Tasha thing yet, but for that."

"Would you like a ride to the airport before you miss your flight?"

"Thought you'd never ask." He laughs. "When you pick me up, I'll introduce you to Ben, and we'll go out not long after, alright?"

"Alright, just text me your flight numbers," I agree, running around for a pair of jeans and a shirt.

"Clayton."

"Yeah?" I yawn, pulling my shirt over my head, only to be surprised at how close he is.

He drops his lips to mine and traces my bottom lip. I open to him hesitantly at first, but the kiss slowly deepens. When he breaks it he places his forehead on mine. "I love you."

I give a small smile. "I love you too." Then I hesitate for a moment. "Daniel?"

"Yeah."

"I never questioned the way we felt for each other. I'll admit that taking a break really freaks me out, but I know that you are just needing to let off some steam or whatever. I know that you still love me and I still love you."

"I just need a few days."

"And I'm happy to give them to you." I smile, stepping away from him.

"That's why you didn't answer your phone, isn't it?"

I walk to the kitchen, grabbing my keys and my spare set. "Mixed signals, Daniel, sometimes you make me so damn dizzy. Case in point," I mutter, looking him from head to toe.

"Sorry." He frowns giving me a quizzical look as I hand him a house key.

"My front door usually isn't unlocked when I sleep, neither is my alarm off." I note, frowning at myself for being so sloppy; at least I live in a gated community that you need a passcode to get into. "I'll send you a text with an assigned alarm code later today. I'd rather you not lay on my doorbell when you randomly hop a fucking red eye."

He smiles taking the key, putting it on his key chain. "I'd give you mine, but I don't have a copy on me."

I shrug and head for the door. "You're going to miss your flight."

I drive him to the airport and drop him off, knowing that I wouldn't speak to him for at least three days but also knowing that I had nothing to worry about; well at least when it comes to our relationship. Tasha, on the other hand, well, there was plenty to worry about there.

= 221 =

21
Truth Be Told

Daniel's Point of View

Sitting on the plane, I stare at the key that Clayton just gave me like it was the most natural thing in the world. It wasn't. Well, at least it never has been in the past. This was a huge milestone, and yet for the first time, I'm not terrified. Trying not to overanalyze, I stuff my keys back into my pocket and turn my seat lights down. While the flight drags on, my conversation with Tasha replays in my head.

"Daniel? It's two in the damn morning! What the hell are you doing here?"

"What? I can't come by and check on my little sister?" I ask, in a harsh tone.

"Your boyfriend put you up to this?" she snarls.

"Come on, Tasha, I'm sorry it's late, I took the red eye. Please let me in," I mutter in a friendlier tone.

She studies me for a moment before she opens her door further, allowing me entry. "You're not changing my mind about Travis, so save your breathe."

"That's not why I'm here," I answer, turning to her and gently taking her wrist in my hand, pushing up the sleeve of her robe, forcing my breathing to stay calm when I see bruises. "Clayton do this?" I ask in a gravel tone.

"No," she answers, jerking her arm out of my grasp. "Give him some credit, Daniel. He wouldn't hurt you like that."

"You said he pushed you, twisted your arm, your wrist," I counter, trying to keep my angry voice calm.

"He did, but he didn't leave any marks. He came here to help me."

"I didn't send him, Tasha. You asked to live your life the way you wanted. I was letting you," I explain, avoiding her eyes.

"And I appreciate that. But I also appreciate Clayton's help."

"He went behind my back, Tasha."

"That's between you two. But his help is going to prevent this," she points out, holding up both of her wrists. She quickly drops them when she realizes her robe sleeves dropped revealing the extent of the damage. My eyes widen in shock, that piece of shit had her pinned!

"I'm going to kill him," I shout, taking both of her arms to study them.

"Stop, Daniel, please. I'm close," she begs.

"He's forcing himself on you, Tasha," I growl. "You expect me to stand by and let that happen?"

"Please, Daniel," she begs, tears falling down her cheeks. "I'm sorry, please! Just don't take Clayton away from me. This won't happen again I promise."

"This shouldn't happen at all!" I scream. "I hate this, Tasha. You should just let me take care of it."

"No!" she screams. "Please, just let me get what I need, and then you can do whatever you want. I swear I won't try to stop you, unless you try to kill him. Don't sink to his level, please."

"Damn it, Tasha. I love you and he is hurting you. Please, I can get this information. You don't need to do this." I beg, almost to the point of tears myself.

"Yes Daniel I do. I know you don't understand it but Seanna and I were practically sisters. I *need* to do this. I need to be the one that brings her killer to justice, me. One more month, please. If you really love me, please," she begs.

"You're killing me, Tasha," I cry, but I know her too well. She won't take no for an answer, and she will hate me if I step in. I don't have a choice.

"I'm so sorry, Daniel. I love you but please. I need this," she cries, dropping her head on my shoulder. I pull her to me and we both cry.

We moved to the couch and I held her while she continued to cry. When she fell asleep I moved out from underneath her, covered her with a nearby blanket and left for the airport, but my car detoured itself to Clayton's. I knew I shouldn't go in, and I knew that I shouldn't call again. I had asked for a break, but after seeing Tasha I needed him. I walked up to his door, hesitant to try the bell, so I tried the knob, believing that it was some sign that it was unlocked. Just the feel of his touch was enough to calm my inner demons.

Turbulence shakes me out of my thoughts and back into the present. I didn't really tell him why I was there. And truth of the matter is I'm angry. But I think it is more at myself than at Clayton. How can I let my sister continue on this destructive path? What the hell is wrong with me?

I must have fallen asleep with my destructive internal monologue because the next thing I know, the plane's landed and I am on my way back to the shoot. The moment I arrive, I'm grateful that I slept, because Ben looks like hell. The minute he sees me, he grabs me by the arm, all but dragging me to a private area.

"I'm sick of being ditched like this, man. I know you do this from time to time. I expect it. But damn it Daniel this is a complicated shoot, and yesterday, when I really needed you, you were just gone," he bitches.

"I had a family emergency."

"Well, tell your boyfriend to get off his rag. You have a job to do!" he growls.

"It was Tasha," I snap, pissed.

He steps back a moment, staring at me. "She alright?"

"No." I frown. "Far from it."

"She been in some sort of accident or something?" he asks, and I know that he is feeling like an ass at this point.

"Or something," I mutter. "Look, Ben, I get it. I disappear a lot. You had no idea that this was really important, although I wouldn't leave you hanging like that if it wasn't."

"She the reason why your brain has been half turned off the last few months, or is your boyfriend bringing you down?" he asks, stuffing his hands in his pockets. "Friends talk to each other Daniel."

I take a calming breath. "Ever hear of Travis Ashton?"

"You mean the guy who wrote that fucked-up script you gave me?" he asks, raising an eyebrow.

"Did you burn it like I advised or did you read it?"

"I tried to read it, but, dude, it was dark." He shudders.

"You ever hear of him socially?"

"Kind of, he dated a friend of mine once but I know *of* the Ashton's more than I know any one in particular. What does this have to do with Tasha?"

"She's dating him."

Ben's eyes gleam in understanding. "It's fiction, Daniel, don't let that script mess with your head. Seriously, my friend's family adore the guy." He assures me.

"No, Ben, not all of it," I counter, "and I can't seem to get through to her."

"You mean he's hurting her?" I give him a deadpan look. "I'm going to kick his ass," he roars, his temper boiling up again.

"Get in line," I laugh humorlessly.

"I'm serious."

"So am I!" I snap. "Look, I'm happy that you are on my side here, but you can't just look him up and give him a beat down. It could put Tasha in more danger, and I won't have that, Ben."

He kicks the ground a few times before he looks up at me, putting his index finger in my chest. "When you get through to that stubborn ass bitch of a sister and get her out of there, you better be fucking calling me or I will never forgive you."

Before I can respond to that, I see Amber turn the corner. "Everything alright, boys?"

"Good as they're going to get," I snarl, walking back toward our actors, avoiding making any promises. "Let's get this done so we can go home."

Forcing myself to only concentrate on work and avoid any part of my personal life like a plague; I find that the next three days go by fairly quickly. By the time we wrap up, I am satisfied with the results, and Ben and I are on good terms. I had asked him about meeting Clayton when we got back, and he just laughed before Amber had her claws in him, sucking his face for the entire flight.

The moment I step into the Texas airport and see Clayton's smiling face, I feel so much lighter. I walk up to him, giving him a death-grip hug. "I've missed you so much," I whisper in his ear.

"Can't breathe," he manages, and I pull back a little, keeping him trapped. He leans his upper body away so that he could meet my eyes. "You okay?"

"No," I answer with a frown. He searches my eyes for a moment, but before I could explain, Ben is grabbing my shoulder.

"You must be the fuck buddy gone boyfriend." Ben laughs extending his hand.

"You must be my boyfriend's personal bitch." Clayton laughs back, giving him a firm handshake.

"I like him," Ben says to me. "I'm Ben."

"Clayton." He smiles, breaking his handshake. Then he turns to Amber, lifting her hand to his lips. "It's good to see you, darlin'."

She blushes a little at his Southern charm. "If only you were straight."

"Hey now." Ben laughs, pulling her to him by her waist.

I just roll my eyes but I catch Amber and Clayton exchanging a wink that Ben doesn't seem to notice. I raise an eyebrow at him, and he just squeezes my hand reassuringly. "I hear we have a date later this week."

"Yeah, Daniel mentioned a winery or something." Ben smiles. "We're all in, if you guys are."

Again with the winking. "Yeah, maybe y'all should stop at my place, and we'll take one car. I don't practically care for wine, so I'll be the designated driver."

"If you're cool with that," Ben shrugs.

"Sounds like a date then." I smile. "I hate to cut this short guys, but Tasha's expecting me."

Ben's eyes flash to mine, and I can see the anger in them. I nod my head, steering Clayton away, hoping he didn't notice.

"What's up with the winking?" I ask after we reach the parking garage.

"What's up with Ben's temper at the mention of Tasha's name?" Clayton counters. "Please tell me you didn't tell him."

"Not everything."

"Damn it, Daniel, what part of the less who knows the better?" he bitches.

I look around, opening the passenger's car door. "Not here."

We don't say another word to each other on the drive to my place. When he pulls into the driveway, he turns to me. "Amber is getting overwhelmed by Ben and his 'we', constantly agreeing to plans without consulting her. His jealousy isn't helping his case either."

"So she wants you to intervene."

"Something along those lines, yes. Her request is a little, what's the word . . . dramatic maybe? Anyway, I told her I'd think about it."

"Think about what exactly?" I ask, pulling my hair at the image of a train wreck.

"Nothing for you to worry about." He shrugs. "Now, tell me, what on earth possessed you to tell Ben?"

"Travis," I answer, swallowing back vomit, "he's not just hitting her, Clayton. That's why I went to your place after seeing her. I needed to calm the fuck down before I did something stupid."

"What do you *mean* he's not just hitting her?" Clayton asks in almost a growl. I can't bring myself to say it. Instead I just look at him, and I can hear his breath intake as he says the word "No."

"She asked for one more month. I begged her to change her mind, but she wouldn't," I cry.

Clayton's jaw flexes for a while before he gets out of the car, walks to my side, pulls me out and into his strong arms. "I'm so sorry," he whispers. "We're going to fix this. He's going to pay."

"I'm sorry I was angry," I cry into his shoulder. "I feel so damn helpless, and she's letting you help and not me."

"No, don't," he says, pulling me tighter. "I crossed a line, Daniel. I'm sorry. I'm just glad you didn't end this."

I pull back a little, our lips find each other, timidly at first, until we are drawn into the kiss. A car drives by and honks, causing us to break away. "Want to come inside?"

"Yes, but I don't want to push you," he answers. "Besides, you are supposed to meet Tasha."

"Tasha and I have a lunch date tomorrow." I smile guiltily. "I just wanted to get you alone. You're not pushing me, baby," I assure him. "I know you didn't hurt her. I forgive you."

He wraps his arms around me tightly, and I can hear his breathing hitch, so I pull away, taking his hand firmly, leading him inside my house. Once we clear the entryway, I'm attacking his lips and lifting him up on his buttock until his feet are off the ground and he's wrapping his legs around my waist. I moan when my hardening cock gets trapped. Slowly I make my way to my bedroom while we explore every inch of each other's mouth. "I've missed you," I whisper when I break free to breathe.

"Me too," he whispers as I lay him down gently on the bed. He captures my face in his hands for a moment, searching for something before he crashes his lips to mine again. He tries to deepen the kiss roughly, but I pull back.

"Not tonight, Clayton," I whisper kissing gently down his neck. "Tonight I want to be wrapped up in your heat," I moan as I lick his sweet salty skin. "And I want to take all night to do it."

He moans in response, and my hands find the edge of his shirt, I glide one hand underneath, relishing the feel of his muscular torso against my fingertips. The moment my fingers find his aroused nipple, I nibble on his neck just a little, causing a gasp as he withers beneath me. I chuckle a little, and make my way to his earlobe. "Close your eyes baby," I whisper, watching as he meets my lustful gaze one last time before obeying my request. I shift my weight to my knees, slowly raking my hands up his shirt and over his head, discarding it somewhere out of my way. Then I sit back on my heels and ever so softly, ghost my hands over his upper body, causing goose bumps and shaky breathing. Next, I lean down, dragging my tongue slowly up his body from his navel to his neck. He gasps, bringing his hands to my sides. I lift up to check that his eyes are closed. I continue my torture with my touch and tongue, causing him to whimper and moan every time I find a new sensitive spot and take advantage of it. After a very long while, I travel further south, stripping his lower body of his jeans and smirk to find that yet again he is going commando. I take the time to strip off my clothes as well. Then I reposition myself back over him. My hands begin to explore, starting at his 'V', working my way down slowly.

"Daniel, *please,* you're driving me crazy," Clayton gasps when my lips find his inner knee. I reach for his hard, dripping dick in response, squeezing it as I rub my thumb over the tip, resulting in a deep throat moan. I smirk on his knee and continue to attend to his throbbing cock while I kiss his legs. "Dan-iel!" he cries, trying to lie still. I lean upward and swallow his steel rod down my throat with no warning, causing a string of beautiful curses to fall from his lips. I begin humming around him as my tongue swirls. I know I have him at the brink and my suspicions are confirmed when he tugs on my hair. "Fuck, darlin', I'm gonna cum," he gasps and his cock pulses, releasing his hot seed down my throat. I suck the last bit of juice before I release him.

Sitting back on my heels, I reach for the nightstand drawer, and find the lube, lathering my fingers lavishly, slowly sliding one inside of him. He moans in approval and starts begging me, I feel him slowly open up to me and eventually I add a second finger, until he is absolutely mad with pleasure. Finally, I add a third, and when he is relaxed and whimpering, I pull out to slick my dick, putting my tip next to his waiting hole, capturing his lips and kissing him breathless. I drop my lips back down to his ear. "Open your eyes, baby," I whisper, lifting up to peer into his ever so dark blue eyes. I push into him, and he moans, wrapping his arms around me, not breaking eye contact. I start a slow steady rhythm, enjoying the bliss of his warmth engulfed around me, but I don't let myself get too distracted by it. That's not the point. "I love you, Clayton," I whisper. He moans, rolling his eyes in the back of his head bringing our bodies closer.

"Always, Daniel, I love you so much." His words are my undoing. I cry out as the sudden, unexpected orgasm explodes out of me and I feel wet warmth between us. I can't help but collapse on top of him, trying to catch my breath.

"Wow."

"Yeah."

"Bath?"

"Yeah."

We sit in the warm water, holding each other until it cools, then we make our way back to my bed falling fast asleep, tangled up in each other, completely content.

22
Jealousy

Daniel's Point of View

It's Friday night and I'm running late for this weird, messed-up double date with Ben and Amber. I think my nerves are partly because Clayton has refused to tell me what he and Amber are up to and partly because Ben is about to discover exactly who I am. I've been debating if telling him was a good idea or not. This was either going to make or break not only our friendship, but our partnership. I've talked to Clayton about it a few times, who is supporting me either way; but has offered up the fact that he and Alec are so close because there are no lies between them. I want that, so I'm going to take the risk and find out if I'm flying solo or with a wingman.

When I get to Clayton's place, I do my best to appear composed, although I am reeling. Taking a calming breath, I walk in only to realize that I'm the last one there. Ben beats Clayton to me, approaching with fire in his eyes, "Can I talk to you? Alone."

My eyes shoot to Clayton, who just shrugs and Amber looks furious. Holding back a groan, I take Ben by the hand and lead him out to Clayton's deck. "What's wrong?"

"Your man is what's wrong," he snaps.

Fuck. "What happened, Ben?"

"When we got here, he was all over Amber," he accuses.

"Define 'all over'."

"You don't believe me?"

"He's gay, Ben. I doubt he was tonguing her. Now please define 'all over.'" I frown, trying to stay calm.

"He kissed her on the cheek," he mutters, "both of them."

"Where is this jealousy coming from, Ben? This is so not like you."

"Your man comes on to my lady and *I'm* the bad guy?!" he asks, pissed.

"Ben, seriously, do you not see what you are doing?" I frown. "Even at the airport, you were possessive of her. Did you even ask her about the winery or just assume?"

"Let me guess, he got to you before me," he answers defensively, dropping down in a patio chair.

"If you don't stop acting like a child, you are going to lose her," I warn with a frown. "Don't you see that's the point of the exercise? You're driving her crazy."

"She told you this?"

Here goes, fuck! "She doesn't have to, Ben. She's a madam. She's used to being in control and hates the jealous type." Ben's eyes widen in shock while he turns bright red. He attempts to speak a few times, but nothing coherent comes out. "I didn't know," I add. "Well, not right away, at least. But I have a feeling that's why you're so possessive. You're addicted. Dating your madam isn't easy, Ben. It's a fine line."

He's silent for the longest time, studying me, looking for any judgment. When he doesn't find any, his voice is just above a whisper and thick with disbelief. "You act like you know what you're talking about." Not sure what else to do, I give him an evil grin. "No!" he gasps, standing up. "No *fucking* way!"

I shrug at his response. "Now you know why I haven't been dating for the past three years. That's how Clayton and I started, but now, damn Ben, I think he might be the one."

"You're serious?" he asks, even more shocked, and I shake my head. "Wow, man, that's . . . that's wow."

"Yeah, tell me about it. Just keep that between us for now, alright?" He shakes his head in agreement. "Do yourself a favor, Ben. If you really are into Amber and not just the idea of Amber, stop the jealousy crap. She's close to walking away."

He turns to look at her through the glass door then back at me. "Thanks, man."

We walk back into the house, and I approach Amber, kissing her hand. "Good evening, madam."

She smiles up at me, and I blush, dropping her hand, to grab Clayton's. "So he knows then?" she smirks.

"Yep," I answer, hiding my face over Clayton's shoulder.

"We could have some fun with this," she muses.

"NO!" all three of us answer at once.

"D-a-n-g!" she drawls out. "It was just a suggestion. A girl can dream, after all. Hey, can I at least see the room?"

I didn't think that my blush could get any deeper, but I notice Ben perk up in curiosity, so I look to Clayton.

He shrugs. "It's up to you, darlin'."

"Well, it's not like others haven't seen it," I muse with a shrug.

"Okay, now I'm jealous." Amber laughs. "Come on, Master Clay, I want to see your goodies."

Clayton lets out a hearty laugh. "I'm not the only master in this relationship."

Amber's eyes grow wide. "No fuckin' way! You switch?"

"In every way," I add, getting bolder.

Ben blushes at that, but Amber isn't deterred. "How in the world does that work? Seriously, that has to be confusing as hell. Not to mention there is no way in fucking way I would ever do that."

Clayton shrugs, heading towards our room. "I actually enjoy it. I think it makes our relationship stronger. It's not without kinks, of course, but we're working through them." He turns to me. "You sure?" I nod my head and Clayton opens the doors.

Amber rushes past us and scoffs, "Padded floors, you're too soft." Clayton rolls his eyes, watching her inspect each item, one by one. Ben sticks next to us as he looks around, unsure what to do with himself. "Clayton Reynolds, you did not!" Amber giggles when she gets to the coffee table. "Oh this is just too much." Clayton smiles walking over to her, showing her how to turn it into a spanking bench. "I want to try it," she announces. Clayton gives her a firm 'no'. She gives a small pout before making a beeline for our cabinet. The moment she opens it, she gasps, her eyes flashing to Clayton's.

Ben gets curious from her newest reaction and starts his approach. "On your knees," she spits acid, and Ben falls to his knees, immediately casting his eyes down. I try not to react to the sight. Clayton squeezes my hand with an apologetic smile. She takes a final examination of our tools, closes the cabinet doors and gives us both a death glare. I look to Clayton for help when she takes our hands and exits the room, leaving Ben where he dropped; he shrugs helpless himself while she closes the doors and drags us both to the couch. "You *engraved* them?" she accuses, staring at Clayton like he had three heads.

"Calm down, Amber," he laughs, watching her pace.

"You're crazy," she says, looking me up and down. "How could you make such a commitment like that?"

"We love each other," Clayton answers like it's no big deal. But I know it *is* a big deal. It's a very big deal. What Clayton did for me all those years ago was unheard-of in our culture. Always desired, but unheard-of.

"I had no idea you two were that serious, Clay."

"Really?" he asks with a dark laugh. "You think I would just call you up to hunt down my boyfriend in Death Valley for the hell of it?" She stops and turns to him. "You are so naïve, Amber. It took an engraved whip for you to understand us."

"I don't know what to say really, except wow, this is *big* for you Clay." she says in awe, looking at him in disbelief. "I'm happy for you, jealous of course, but happy."

He gives her a smile and stands up to give her a small squeeze. "Thanks, that means a lot."

She laughs. "Don't you dare tell Ben."

"Speaking of Ben," Clayton says, nodding toward the doors to our room. She smiles sweetly, heading back into the room. "Be good, Amber. I am not ashamed of walking in on you," he warns.

The moment the doors close behind her, he turns to me. "You okay?"

"Yeah." I smile. "I feel a hundred pounds lighter actually."

He gives a small chuckle. "I'm going to have to reel Amber in a little. When she's with people accepting of our culture, she tends to be pretty public about it. I'm not sure if either of us really wants to be a part of that."

I stand up and hug him. "Thanks, baby. It's one thing for him to be accepting, but watching it is not really all that ideal."

"Come on, let's go get them before she has him naked," he chuckles, trying to keep the mood light as I flush red again. This is so new to me. Ben and I have always had more of an arm's-length relationship. When we walk into the room, Amber produces the cutest little pout before releasing Ben from his unexpected session.

Ben blushes the moment he registers Clayton and me and I give a small shrug. "Beer?"

"Yeah," he says, almost running out of the room. Clayton and I exchange a look before I follow Ben to the fridge. He takes a few long pulls on his beer before he has the guts to say anything at all, and I almost choke on my beer when he finally does speak. "Awk-ward."

"Yeah," I agree. "We're cool right?"

He stares at me for a moment. "You did this after Brad?"

"Like I said, it wasn't all it was cracked up to be."

"I get it." He smiles. "Had you told me before Amber, well, honestly I don't think our friendship would have survived. But now, now I get it."

"It stays between us, Ben," I assure him.

"Yeah, no kidding." He laughs. "I have to admit, though, I'm glad you know. Of everyone who could, glad it's you man."

I give him a short nod in understanding. "Yeah, me too. Now knock it off. You're starting to sound like a woman."

He chokes on the remainder of his beer, glaring at me before walking away to put his arms around Amber, who just walked in the room with Clayton. "If you don't want to go to the winery I'm sure we can think of something else to do."

Amber's eyes widen, and she turns to me with this huge grin that Ben can't see, mouthing the words, 'Thank you,' to me. I nod, wrapping my arms around Clayton.

"Actually," Amber smiles letting Ben go. "There is this band, *The Road to Life*, I really want to check out. They're debuting tonight. I think that we all might have some fun."

Clayton tenses in my arms. "They wouldn't happen to be friends of yours, would they, Amber?"

"Oh, come on, Clay, what's the harm? We're just going to be hanging out. It's not like you're working. *Please,*" she begs, pulling out this way-too-cute of a pout.

Clayton moans, throwing his head on my shoulder. "What do you think? Do you want to go watch a band with some beer?"

"Not if you find it more work than leisure," I answer, pulling him closer to me.

"If they suck, it won't be work." He smiles.

"And if they don't?" I ask, raising an eyebrow.

"I promise not to ditch you," he grins so wide his dimples show. I can tell he wants to say yes but I'm not sure if it's just the opportunity to hear a live band or because of Amber.

"What do you think, Ben?" I ask, not breaking eye contact with Clayton.

"I'm up for it. Nothing wrong with beer and a band, just as long as there isn't any karaoke. I'm good."

"Well then, I guess it's up to you, *Clay,*" I answer with a smile. He cringes with an eye roll at the use of Amber's nickname. Then he looks back to Amber.

"Fine, but if they suck, we are going elsewhere," he agrees. She lets out this shrill that makes me temporarily deaf as she plows into Clayton, causing both of us to stagger. Then she pecks him on the lips and hugs him before egging us to hurry before they start.

"We'll meet you in Clayton's car," I call, trying to keep my temper in check.

She meets my eyes for a moment and then Clayton's before mouthing, 'Sorry,' pulling Ben out the front door.

"I thought you said she was a bitch."

"She is," he answers, running his fingers through his hair nervously after unlocking his car remotely.

"How close are you two, *Clay?* I mean she's kissing you on the lips for fucks sake!"

"Please, don't get jealous. It's not like that," he rushes, grabbing my upper arms, giving them a slight squeeze. "That's just her personality. She does it to all her friends, guys and girls alike. Why do you think Ben's jealous side came out to start with?"

"I don't like it, Clayton. Tell her to keep her goddamn lips to herself," I growl, knowing I'm being hypocritical having just lectured Ben over this exact shit but Clayton was kissing her cheeks not her lips.

"You know you're hot when you're jealous," he smirks.

"I'm serious," I snap, my eyes flaring in fury.

"I know, darlin'," he smiles, pressing his lips to mine. "I'll talk to her, promise."

"Tonight," I insist, pulling him to me.

"You know you're the only one for me, right?" Clayton questions, pressing his forehead on my shoulder.

"I'm sorry if you feel that I'm overreacting here, Clayton, but Liam had a gal friend like that once." I sigh. "Now she's his wife."

"I'm not Liam," he scolds, meeting my eyes. "I'm not Brad, and I'm not any other man who has hurt you. It would kill me to hurt you like that, Daniel, please."

"I know," I whisper, "I know you're different. I'm just scared, Clayton. You have my heart."

Before he can give me a response, his horn is honking. "We should go before she turns into the devil's daughter," Clayton warns. "Believe me, you don't want to see that."

"Wait," I say, pulling on his arm as he walks away from me. "We good?" I ask, pulling him back into me.

"Yeah," he smiles, "and I will talk to her. I'm sure Ben would appreciate it just as much as you."

I smile at him before I press my lips to his, tracing his lower lip, that's when his car horn goes berserk. He pulls away with a moan. "Come on," he insists, pulling me out of his house and barely taking the time to set the alarm and locking the door before he runs to his car.

"'Bout damn time!" Amber seethes from the backseat.

"Sorry," Clayton apologizes, turning the key.

We make it to the bar and it's packed. Clayton asks to talk to the manager, passing his business card to the bouncer. A few moments later, we were sitting in the VIP section with free food and half-price drinks for the rest of the night. I feel kind of bad about it, considering we're technically there to have fun, not to judge the band, per se. But Clayton assures me it's fine, promising a huge tip to the waitress. Amber's too giddy, which is causing Ben to be happy, so I reluctantly give in.

The band turns out to be pretty good, and Clayton is true to his word. He doesn't ditch me. Instead, he excuses both of us and introduces himself to the band during their break.

"Clayton Reynolds, Blackboard Entertainment." He smiles with an extended hand. The lead singer turns a little pale for a moment but gives him a firm handshake. "You're pretty good up there."

"Thanks," he says, turning another shade paler.

"Despite his reputation, he doesn't bite . . . hard." I laugh, extending my hand. "Daniel Kingsley."

"The movie director?" he asks in shock, grasping my hand quickly before dropping it in confusion. "You two want us in a film or something?"

The rest of the band approaches us at this point, and I'm flashing Clayton a Cheshire cat grin. His eyes light up in understanding. I step back toward the table to call Ben and Amber over.

"What's up?" Ben asks with a smile moments later, extending his hand to the lead singer.

"The kid is brilliant." I smile. "What would you think about a film with them?"

Ben studies me for a moment. "I have the perfect fucking script."

"That is, if you don't get stage fright." I laugh, turning to a very quiet band.

"No, we're cool," the guitarist assures me, nudging their drummer.

"Yeah, cool," he mumbles.

Amber pipes up, passing her business card to them, "Here, call me on Monday, and we will work out a potential contract. It's your lucky day, boys. Welcome to fame." They all chuckle a little, still shell shocked. "Now don't fuck it up by sucking the rest of the night," she snaps in a one-eighty.

"Told you she was a bitch," Clayton whispers in my ear, walking us back to the table.

I let out a loud laugh, pulling him to me. "So you're good with working together?"

"Are you kidding?" he asks smiling. "I'm fucking thrilled! Besides, it makes sense. You have my choreographer, after all."

The rest of the night passes by without a hitch, as we all just hang out. I am impressed with the band's performance after our visit. They pretty much sound the same but seem to avoid looking in our direction the rest of the night; although, they were smiling more.

True to his word, Clayton doesn't touch a drop of alcohol and takes us all back to his place, where Ben and Amber end up crashing on his pull-out couch. I did catch Clayton pulling Amber to the side when she tried to kiss him again after he saved her from face-planting into the pavement. I'm not sure how much she retained from it, considering how plastered she was, but at least he kept his promise.

When we are finally alone, Clayton tries to make a move on me, "Not tonight, baby, please," I beg.

"Why not?" he whispers in my ear.

"Because I don't want to offend you by passing out." I moan. "I fucking drank a lot."

"You were nervous." He smiles lying down next to me, pulling me into his arms. "Sweet dreams, darlin'."

The next morning, I am awakened with a glass of water and aspirin, which I take gratefully. Not long after, I am dragging my hung-over ass out of bed and helping Clayton cook breakfast. The smell eventually wakes Amber and Ben, and they stumble in, squinting from the bright lights in the kitchen. I give Ben a sympathetic smile, passing him the aspirin. "Morning," I whisper.

He moans in response. "You didn't have to go to all this trouble."

"No trouble." Clayton smiles. "You lost most of your dinner in the parking lot last night. I figured you'd be starving."

"Thanks," Ben mutters, dropping down in a kitchen chair. "Mom."

Clayton chuckles, passing Ben some water. "That's Master to you." I just laugh and start cutting up some fresh fruit.

"You wish," Ben smirks and Amber laughs, causing Ben and I both to cringe a little in pain.

"So, hey, it's been forever since we sat down and talked, I forgot to ask you, Clay, how's Al?" Amber ponders, stealing some bacon from the frying pan.

"*Alec* is fine," Clayton corrects.

She rolls her eyes at him. "I know he was with Bobby there for a while, are they still dating or has he met someone else? God knows he deserves to be happy."

"Yeah, him and Bobby are still together," Clayton smiles, "can't say I've ever seen him happier actually."

"Really?" she asks smiling. "Since when did the 'Angel' boys get so damn soft anyway?"

I cut my finger at the mention of Angels of Justice, dropping the knife in a loud clatter. "Shit!" I curse, sucking on it, making my way to the sink.

Clayton's behind me in an instant, turning on the water and bringing my finger underneath it. "She knows because we saved her." He whispers in my ear. I nod in understanding, trying to force calm, even breaths.

"Am I missing something?" Ben asks, raising an eyebrow. "What are the 'Angel' boys? Some band or something?"

I swallow hard at his question. Telling him about my personal life is one thing, but this; this has the potential of putting him in danger and possibly discovering things about my past I'd rather keep buried.

"No," Amber starts, "They're a—"

"AMBER!" I growl, cutting her off. "A word." I stalk over to her and grab her by the hand, dragging her to the bathroom down the hall. "What the hell do you think you're doing?"

"What?" she asks, crossing her arms.

"What?" I ask. "It's bad enough you are all over Clayton, but then you go on about the Angels of Justice. Are you serious?"

"I'm not interested in Clay," she spits in annoyance. "If you haven't noticed, I'm into your best friend."

"Angels of Justice," I growl.

"I don't want to keep secrets from him."

"*Not* this," I spit through clenched teeth. "He doesn't need this, Amber. You don't know Ben. Not like I do. Trust me."

"He'll find out eventually," she says snidely.

"No," I answer firmly.

"Fine," she snaps, sticking her nose in the air, stomping back out to the kitchen. Clayton shifts his eyes from mine to hers and back, obviously picking up on the tension.

Frowning, I sit down next to Ben. "Sorry about that, man."

"So I am missing something," he confirms, falling back in his chair.

"I'd really rather you forget about it," I answer. "You're green, Ben. Let's just leave it at that."

"Are you in some kind of trouble, Daniel?"

I give a small laugh, rolling my eyes. "No, Ben, it's not like that."

"Liar," he accuses. "You only lie to protect me, and after last night, I don't see any other explanation."

Amber clears her throat, earning a death glare from Clayton.

"Fine, I'm trying to protect you," I answer with a shrug. "Now drop it."

"Daniel."

"No, Ben, don't," I demand. We stare each other down for a moment, knowing one of us is going to lose but unsure which one it's going to be.

"This better not have to do with Tasha," he warns.

"It doesn't," I snap.

"I don't like this." He frowns, crossing his arms.

"Ben sweetie, it's alright." Amber steps in, placing her hands on his shoulders. "They are good people," she reassures.

"What do they do, Amber?" he asks, causing her to frown.

"We help people who have a hard time helping themselves." Clayton sighs, sitting down. We exchange a hard look, but I can tell he's asking me to trust him, so I keep my mouth shut. "There are instances in our culture where madams and masters become abusive, and we step in and relocate their subs and get the police involved."

Ben studies him for a while. "That sounds dangerous, Clayton."

He shrugs. "It's not a walk in the park," he admits, "and secrecy is our number one priority. Amber slipped, which really fucking surprises me. You weren't supposed to know about this, Ben."

"Daniel knows." Amber frowns.

"That's different," Clayton snaps.

"Well, you trust Daniel, and Daniel trusts Ben," she reasons, "and I trust Ben. So there is nothing to worry about."

"Wait." Ben frowns. "If you are so secretive, then how does Amber know? Are you apart of it?" he asks her.

She stares at him for a long moment before she sits down, biting her lower lip. "I'm not one of them, no."

He looks confused for just a moment, and then disbelief, anger and pain come across his features. She throws herself into his arms. I stand up and walk away, letting them have their moment, and Clayton follows me outside to his deck.

"You lied to him."

"Not technically," I answer. "You really don't have anything to do with Tasha. It's not the purpose of your group."

"We can trust him right?" he asks, nervous. I know he only spoke up to keep Ben from digging.

"With our lives," I answer.

Clayton's eyes flash to mine, and he grabs me by the wrists. "You sound like you know that from experience."

I turn away from him. "Like I said, Liam really fucked me up. I was young and stupid. Ben got me to the hospital in time."

"Daniel?"

"Clayton, please," I whisper, grabbing his hips. "I'm good now. I have had life experiences, a great career, friends. I'm in a better place now. When I was with him, he was basically my life. I will never do that again."

"You can bet your ass you won't," he growls. "I won't let you."

I smile, kissing him gently. "I love you too."

He takes me into a strong embrace before he releases me at the sound of the sliding door.

"We're going to get taking off. How about we meet up tomorrow and go over the script I was thinking about for that band?" Ben proposes.

"Alright." I smile. "Don't do anything I wouldn't do."

He blushes for a moment before he laughs it off. "Right back at you."

"Ben!" I call after him. "If you need to talk . . ." I offer, knowing the rumors of his father's temper all too well.

"Thanks man." He nods keeping his face masked.

We walk them out and the moment the door closes, Clayton is asking if I really am sure about working together. I know I scared him, so I take the time to remind him that Ben and I will be worried about completely different things than he will be, pointing out we will probably not see each other all that much. He seems appeased by that, but I can tell he's not going to let it go, so I don't push him. Instead, I tell him I'm going to see Tasha and do some laundry. He seems happy about that, causing me to roll my eyes at him. Taking him in one last embrace, I do my best to reassure him, "I love you, Clayton, but I love myself more."

He pulls away from me, searching my eyes again before he smiles. "Thank you, darlin'. I feel the same."

"Good." I laugh, opening the front door. "I'll see you tomorrow."

"Be safe." He smiles, holding the door open.

"Always," I call behind my back, shaking my ass a little because I know he's watching. I hear him chuckle and I get into my car. Sitting there for a moment, I realize that he really is the one. And that thought makes me giddy and terrified all at the same fucking time.

23
Crazy

Clayton's Point of View

After Daniel leaves, I decide to go for a run to clear my head, trying to wrap my mind around the past twenty-four hours without freaking out. I make a mental note to call Alec and advise him of the most recent situation. He's going to be pissed, but I didn't do this, neither did Daniel. We did damage control. What else were we supposed to do? Leave Ben hanging so he can poke around? Yeah, that's not advised. We hate pokers, and we do our best to avoid them; there have been a few instances in the past where they came close, Daniel's PI being one of them, but we managed to get to him before it got too far. Yeah, I knew about that. I just didn't know for sure if our bribe had worked or not. Apparently, it did.

Then there is the whole issue of Daniel attempting suicide when he was younger. No fucking wonder he was so terrified to admit his feelings. Hell, I'd be scared to death too. Anger flashes over me thinking about how horrible this Liam guy treated him. I want to kick his ass, but I know that will never happen; instead, I have to pick up the jagged pieces and hope to not cut myself. Frustrated, I stop my run to catch my breath. I want to talk to him to know exactly what happened, but I'm not sure if it's wise to open those wounds.

Shaking my head at my internal monologue, I'm about to start my run again, when suddenly, I feel the wind getting knocked out of me, throwing me to the ground. *What the hell?* Trying to grasp the situation, I cry out in pain as another blow hits me in the ribs. "He's MINE!" an angry voice yells.

It's a fucking baseball bat, my mind registers as I turn sideways, looking for the source. My stomach gets hit while I struggle for the guy's legs, trying to knock him to the ground.

"Stop!" I try to scream, but it's muffled with another cry when the bat makes contact with my lower back. I stop struggling and I lie there in mind-numbing pain. The next moment, a hand is clenched around my throat. "You will leave him alone!"

"Who?" I grunt, confused.

"Danny!" he growls, throwing my head back hard into the pavement.

"Brad?" I ask, confused, which leads to a fist in the jaw. *Fuck me!*

"Leave him alone, or next time you won't be breathing when I walk away," he threatens, slamming my lower stomach with the bat once more, causing me to curl in on myself in excruciating pain. Everything is spinning, and I do my best to stay conscious, waiting for him to leave. When I can't hear him any longer I count to fifty then pull out my cell phone.

"Hello?"

"Alec," I moan. "Help . . . attacked . . . park." And with that, my world goes black.

When consciousness greets me I find myself staring at a very bright light. I squint, turning my head from it, only to moan at the motion and fight back nausea.

"Clayton?" a pained voice asks. I direct my eyes from the ceiling to see a very distraught Daniel on my right and a very worried Alec on my left.

"What happened?" I ask, closing my eyes, trying to ignore the pain.

"You were attacked." Alec frowns. "You've been in a coma. Three of your ribs are cracked and your kidneys took a beating, the doctors are doing their best to save them. They put you on some meds that cause nausea."

"Did you see the attacker?" Daniel asks.

I look at him for a long moment before turning to Alec. "Where's Bobby?"

Alec's eyes narrow at me. "Work."

"How long have I been out?" I wonder aloud.

"Three days," Daniel frowns. I can see the tiredness, he obviously hasn't shaven in three days.

"Tell me you've gone home." I frown at him. He just gives me this look that tells me that he's been here from the moment he found out. I turn from him. "What about the band?"

"We've scheduled a collaboration meeting for a couple of weeks. Amber will be your wingman. Ben and I will start on the film part of it for now, you can come in later." He shrugs obviously annoyed that I switched the topic to work.

"Have Mike help Amber." I tell him, licking my dry lips.

"Clayton, I know you took a hit to the head, but Mike? He's your assistant." Alec frowns and by the looks of him, he hasn't left my side either.

"No, he's my executive assistant, and he will be there when I can't be," I counter.

"Hey, it's your business." Alec shrugs. "We'll get in touch with him."

Daniel grabs my hand to get back on topic. "You didn't answer my question, baby. Did you see who did this?"

I look at him for another long moment and then back to Alec. "When will Bobby get here?"

"Stop that!" Daniel growls in frustration, releasing my hand and pulling on his hair. "You did, didn't you? Is that why Bobby's so important? Because he's an 'Angel' and I'm still on the sideline?"

I moan out loud because his voice is pounding in my head. "Daniel, I need you to calm the fuck down if you want me to answer your damn question." I meet Alec's eyes, which widen in understanding. He gives a small nod, stepping to the edge of the bed, bracing himself. I shift my eyes back to my boyfriend, taking a deep, painful breath. "I think it was Brad," I whisper.

Daniel stares at me for the longest moment dumbfounded. "Why?" he finally asks, his hands balling into fists.

I close my eyes, unable to look at him. "He said that you were his. That if I didn't leave you alone, then next time, I wouldn't be breathing when he left."

I hear something crash against the wall and watch Alec struggle with him. Damn it, why couldn't Bobby have been here. I know Bobby would win. Alec on the other hand; well, it's a tie really.

"Calm down!" Alec screams, and I feel my bed bounce. I lift up a little to see Daniel momentarily pinned to it.

"ENOUGH!" I scream, trying to help. "Red. Now calm the fuck down!"

Daniel stays where he is but makes eye contact with me, angry tears falling from his face. "It's been three and a half years," he cries, "Why now?"

"I'm the first boyfriend you've had since him," I guess, throwing myself back on the pillow.

"He's been following me for three and a half years?" Daniel cries, struggling out of Alec's grasp, running for the bathroom to get sick.

"Who the hell is Brad?" Alec snaps.

"Crazy ex." I frown. "Daniel got a restraining order on him. He thought that ended it."

"If he's been watching him for the past three and a half years, why is he after you now? He had to know that Daniel went to your place on more than one occasion."

I rub my face, trying to think of any weird signs. "I did get a few boxes full of maggots and roses. Then there's the death threats." I shrug. "Nothing out of the ordinary. I get crap like that all the time at work."

Daniel comes out looking rather green and sits down on my bed. "Are you calm?" I frown. He shakes his head, and I know that's he's freaking out on me. "Come here," I motion, scooting over to give him room to lie next to me. He's about to argue, but I raise my eyebrow at him, and he casts his eyes downward before he lies next to me. I gingerly pull him to me, ignoring the pain in my chest and put his head on my heart, running my fingers through his long hair.

"How do you want to handle this?" Alec asks.

"Legally." I answer sternly. "We're already taking a huge risk by going out of our purview with Tasha. We can't do both and expect to get away with it. I'd rather we deal with Travis and the law deal with Brad."

"If it doesn't work?" Alec frowns.

"It will." I smile. "Have faith in the system, Alec."

He snubs me but doesn't comment, knowing that I'm just saying it for Daniel's sake. "Fine, we'll try it your way, but if it doesn't work, you can go to hell if you think I am going to stand by and let anyone harm you, Clayton."

I can see his unshed tears, and I know that he's just as freaked out as Daniel. I have no choice but to be the calm, reasonable one. It is a weird role reversal with Alec, but I manage the strength to do it, patting the other side of the bed. He looks at me skeptically causing me to glare. Sighing, he sits down next to me, and I pull his upper body close. "You can't get rid of me that easily, Alec. I'm a pain in the ass, remember."

He gives a small chuckle and I just hold him. I can feel Daniel's tears soaking the blanket, and I nudge him closer, praying silently for all of us.

After I am sure he's calm and in a reasonable mind frame I order Daniel home to shower, shave and sleep, telling him when he wakes he's released. I know he wants to argue but doesn't safe word; which frustrates me to no end, he honestly should be. After he's gone Alec and I have another fight about doing things legally. Luckily for me, Bobby shows up and sides with me. It's simply too dangerous right now. Alec's clearly upset and warns us that if anything else happens he's not caring about the consequences. Bobby and I both frown, knowing there is no point in arguing that. All we can do is pray the law catches this guy before he gives Alec a reason to cross that line. They stay until visiting hours are over and a nurse comes in with a syringe. I'm grateful for the drugs, without them, sleep would never come.

My hospital stay lasts a full week, and though my kidneys are sore, they survived. The only other damage was a few cracked ribs and a bump on my head, but it wasn't anything I couldn't handle. Daniel tried to temporarily move in with me when I was released, but I wouldn't have it. After the third day, I kicked him out. I had filed a police report, given my statement, and had hired a bodyguard. I hate bodyguards. I always found them to be a pain in the ass, but I knew Daniel wouldn't leave if he didn't believe I was safe, so I bit the bullet, so to speak.

Mike came over about the fourth day after my release. He was thrilled that he had earned the promotion of executive assistant that we had discussed the day we saved him from a cruel master. I can tell he's nervous, but I know he has what it takes, which is why I hired him to start with. I had been waiting for him to grow the balls to ask for it, and I guess in a way, he did. My first order of business was to give any and all business of Cassandra to him. One less bitch in my life was a true blessing. The second order was to have him get *The Road to Life* into our studio and set up some demo tapes for me to listen to. He offered to coordinate between our company and Daniel's, taking care of all the small details. I took him up on it with the warning that I might step on his toes a little and communication between us is key.

Ben and Amber had also stopped by and talked about work, trying to iron out details. Amber was the most excited of course. That is when I discover the lead singer is her cousin's boyfriend. I knew I shouldn't have been surprised, but it annoyed me, and Ben for that matter, that she waited so long to divulge that information. I tell her to contact Mike and make sure all the extra disclosures are in order before they come back to our studio. I will not be sued over bullshit of a breakup or whatever. She understood and called Mike on the spot, Ben made a note to do the same. When she was thoroughly distracted, I took the opportunity to ask Ben not only about Brad, but Liam. In both cases, he was pretty tight-lipped, telling me that if Daniel wanted to share, he would. I frowned at that and pushed him a little by asking about Daniel's suicide attempt. Ben was shocked at the mention of it but closed up like a clam nonetheless. Even though I found it highly frustrating, it gave me a newfound respect for the guy. He really was a true friend to Daniel, and I thanked him for that. They left not much later, and Alec and Bobby were soon to follow.

"What does he have, some sort of schedule set up or some shit? I haven't been alone since he left!" I bitch when I find them at my front door. Bobby blushes. "Oh, hell no!" I gripe. "Leave *now*!"

"No," Alec answers firmly, walking past me with Bobby. "I happen to agree with him, Clayton."

I close the door, "I'm going to have to be alone sometime."

"True enough." Alec shrugs. "But hopefully not until after Brad is behind bars."

I moan making my way back to the couch. "Well, don't expect me to be a fucking host."

"What we expect is for you to get some damn sleep so we can make out on your couch," Bobby laughs.

Not really up for more entertaining today, I glare at him, standing up. "Fine, but if you fuck on it, you buy it."

Right before I fall asleep, I text Daniel.

This stops now, Daniel. You will be punished. Tomorrow morning, seven. M.C.

Not much later, I get a text back.

Yes, Master.

Followed by a second text.

Can I see you tonight, Clayton?

Frowning, I study the text message for a very long time before I make my decision.

Not tonight, Daniel. I really want to be alone. Call Alec and get him out of here already. Please.

I take my painkillers and lie down in bed, noticing another text.

I'm sorry if I upset you. I'm just worried. I understand you want to be alone. Please don't be ticked if you wake up in my arms in the morning. You said I could see you tomorrow.

Annoyed and touched all at the same time, I text back, *Fine, but not a damn minute before midnight.*

I fall asleep not much longer after that, startling slightly when I feel Daniel's warm body pressing against mine. "It's me, baby," he whispers. "I love you." His words are calming, and I press into him looking at the clock, 12:02 a.m. I smile to myself before passing out cold, feeling safe and warm, just how it should be. Hoping the whole damn time that these arms are the universe balancing itself out and not a tipping of some fucked-up scales that will make me pay once again for my happiness.

24
Safe Words

Daniel's Point of View

When I wake up, I find that I am alone, and there is a piece of paper on Clayton's pillow.

Good morning. Now quickly do your business and wait for me like a good sub. M.C.

Moaning, I roll onto my back as my morning wood twitches. *He must really be pissed*, I think to myself climbing out of bed and brushing my teeth while my dick calms down so I can take a morning leak. I knew that I would be in for a punishment session today, I just didn't realize that it would be the moment I woke up. Stretching, I make my way out of the bedroom, finding my master drinking coffee and reading the paper.

"Master?" I ask. "May I speak freely?"

He frowns over his cup before agreeing. "Make it quick, Daniel."

"It's just that, I trust you, but I'd like to resolve this with my boyfriend before I do my master."

He stares at me for a moment and then sighs, "Red."

"Thank you." I smile, and I can tell he's not happy about it. "I really am sorry I upset you with having your friends and I keep you company. I am just terrified this freak will take the opportunity to take you away from me," I stop as my tears catch in my throat and I can't form any words.

Clayton's at my side instantly. "Shh, it's alright. I know your heart is in the right place, darlin', I do. And I know you are putting unnecessary guilt on yourself for something that is out of your control. I've hired someone for my protection, someone you trust and recommended. That needs to be enough."

"I know. I'm sorry, but I'm going to be freaked until he's caught."

"He's crazy, Daniel. He'll make a mistake. Heck, he probably already has. They will find it and catch him, and this will be over. Until then, when I can't be with you, you have to trust our hired help and the occasional friend or two. Agreed?"

"Agreed." I answer reluctantly.

He kisses me gently before pulling away. "Red."

Accepting his transition, I make my way to our room, strip and wait patiently for him. The room is cooler than normal, causing my skin to react, creating goose bumps all over my naked body. He keeps me waiting longer than usual, and I know the cooler temperature is a part of my punishment. Ignoring it, I concentrate on breathing and take myself into subspace. My master surprises me with the feel of his fingers in my long hair.

"I've spoken with your boyfriend, Daniel," he starts, tugging a little as I lean my head back to see his annoyed yet lustful expression before I fall back into position. "He's a grown man, is he not?" he continues, dropping his hands from my hair. I shake my head in acknowledgment, for I did not have permission to speak. "And yet you felt he needed a *babysitter* even after he agreed to hire a bodyguard to pacify you?" Again I shake my head. "Explain yourself," he demands.

I swallow, trying to bring my voice above a whisper, "I'm worried."

My answer causes him to sigh and I feel his fingers running through my hair again, letting me know he understands. "You can't protect him 24/7, Daniel. You're going to have to trust him." I shake my head in acceptance, grateful he can't see the guilt in my eyes. I hate that he's in danger because of me. He steps away from me, and I can't tell where he is, which makes me believe he is wearing socks, to muffle his movements. He comes back, standing in front of me. That's when I notice he is not only wearing socks, he is completely clothed. "Stand," he orders. I slowly rise to my feet keeping my eyes cast downward, which allows me to watch as he produces our three-ring cock ring from his pocket. He traps my genitals into it, stiffening my cock with his warm hand to make sure it's secure. "When I order you to cum, you will be wise not to hesitate," he warns while he continues his fondling. "Tell me Daniel, when you are speaking to your master, do you normally make eye contact?" My breath hitches while my mind races, trying to think back to my error. "Speak!" he demands.

"No, Master, not without permission to speak freely."

"And in the hospital, did you follow this rule?" he asks, angrily.

I swallow hard. "I honestly don't remember, Master."

"I can guarantee that you did not," he seethes, his voice thick with venom. "What are your safe words, Daniel?"

"Rose, petal, thorn." I whisper.

"So you do know them," he muses, his disgust evident. He stops stroking my cock and starts to circle me. I nod in response. "Yet you didn't use it even when you knew you needed to escape Alec's grasp." I swallow hard as the memory comes back to me. He stops in front of me. "You were blending, Daniel. You yourself have expressed that you don't want that to happen. Therefore, you will be punished."

I close my eyes in understanding, though it is unexpected, it is appreciated. "Thank you, Master," I whisper, earning a hard slap on my ass for speaking out of turn.

"We'll see if you're so eager to thank me tomorrow." I swallow again. This is not going to be a light punishment. "Crawl to the X-frame," he orders. I dutifully lower my body to all fours, slowly making my way to the frame. I stay on my hands and knees awaiting his next order, gasping in surprise when I feel a cold, well-lubed plug being inserted in my ass. *F-u-c-k*. He doesn't comment on it. Instead, he orders me to my feet. I feel wool cuffs being attached to my wrists and give no resistance when he lifts my arms up one at a time, attaching the spring catch to the metal hooks of the X-frame. Once my arms are secure, I feel him attach my ankles in similar cuffs before attaching them to the base. Afterwards, I feel a cool piece of metal being dragged up my back. Then I feel him press his clothed body into me, while carefully turning my head so that he has clean access to my ear. I shiver when his warm breath falls onto it. "I plan on taking my time with you, Daniel," he barely whispers wrapping his hands around my body, working to arouse my nipple, following it with a metal nipple clamp. I moan when he nibbles my ear, only to pull back and turn my head, repeating his actions. "You are going to be mine all fucking day," he whispers, causing me to whimper as my other nipple is trapped in metal. I hear a slight click, and a new sensation overcomes me, causing me to gasp and throw my head back, breaking formation. *Fucking vibrating nipple clamps!* "What are your safe words, Daniel?" he demands, his disgust returning again while he steps away.

"Rose, petal, thorn," I answer, dropping my head back into position.

"And when do you say them?" he asks, walking further away.

"When I'm uncomfortable in any fashion or going to fail you, Master."

"What about when receiving punishment, Daniel?"

"When I reach my limit, Master." The room falls silent. I hear the air being cut by the whip before I feel it crash against my cold skin. I force my jaw closed while my body instinctively fights the restraints, but I do not scream. Then I feel his hand trace the sensitive skin, checking to make sure he didn't harm me. Very rarely did my master choose not to prepare my skin for punishment. I agree with him, though. Blending needs to be treated harshly. His hands leave my body, and I brace myself for a second blow. This time, the contact is concentrated on my ass, and though my toes curl, I'm able to absorb it without much resistance. The third and fourth blow go to my back, the fifth to my ass. By the time he reaches ten, tears are streaming down my cheeks, but I accept his punishment willingly. By fifteen, I'm in agony. When the sixteenth blow strikes, I can't stop myself from grunting out a scream. My master stops, his hands gliding gently down my sore back. "Do you have something to say, Daniel?" he asks, in a concerned voice.

"No, Master. Thank you, Master. May I please have another?" I respond with all the eagerness I can muster.

"Are you sure about that request, Daniel?" he asks, pressing his flat hands into my back.

I cringe in pain, but I manage to keep my voice steady. "Yes, Master."

He lets out a heavy sigh, stepping back and cracks the whip, harder than any other time today. I grind my teeth, but I don't cry out. "What are your safe words, Daniel?" he growls, his venom returning.

"Rose, petal, thorn" I answer with a stressed gasp.

"And why haven't you said any of them?" he demands angrily.

"I can take it, Master," I respond in a whisper.

"No, Daniel, you can't!" he snaps. I don't respond to that, and I feel him press his body into mine, dropping his lips to my ear, "I am your master, Daniel, not your masochist!" He pushes away from me and he becomes a ghost. Even when my breathing steadies I can't hear him at all. It's almost as if he's gone, leaving me to absorb his words. After some time passes, I feel him release my ankles, and he drops my arms from the frame but leaves the cuffs on my wrists. "Come," he demands, grabbing my upper arm, leading me to the bondage booth. "Sit," he orders. I mask the pain that the command causes, sitting on the bench. He latches my arms on each side of the wall, high above my head, then he attaches a spreader bar to my ankles, keeping my pose highly uncomfortable but endurable.

"This isn't the first time that you've shown weakness with your safe words, Daniel," he spits in disgust. "I can think of three instances in particular." Shame washes over me with the reminder of my failure. "Describe them. In detail," he demands, removing the nipple clamps with a rough pull. He leaves the cock ring, though, even though I am flaccid. I swallow hard, following my master's orders, painfully remembering my failures. When I'm done, my stomach is in knots, and tears have puddled on the floor. "Now describe the punishment that could have been avoided had you used your safe words in two of those instances and the other appropriately," he orders.

My breath hitches. This is not a memory I want to relive, *ever*. So instead of answering him, I whisper, "Thorn, Master."

"Good," he responds to my surprise. "I *can* get through that thick skull of yours after all. Truth be told, I was beginning to wonder." He drops to his knees in front of me. "Look at me," he demands. When our eyes meet, he asks, "Do you get punished for using your safe words, Daniel?"

"No, Master."

"That's right." He smiles. "You get rewarded." Suddenly, I'm surrounded by his hot mouth, and I feel his hands pinning my hips to the bench. I can't help the moan that escapes me, my cock hardening instantly in his wet mouth. I'm unsure how to react. My master has never once sucked my dick before now. Thankfully, he doesn't seem to mind the moaning as his talented tongue drives me into maddening pleasure. I find myself grateful for his hands holding me so I can't fuck his face. After a small while, I feel that familiar pit in my stomach, having no other choice but to fight it off with the damn cock ring, causing me to whimper and moan. My master starts moaning around me while he continues to work my overly aroused rod. Not much later, he has me pushed past the silicon barrier, and I know

I can cum at will. Groaning I fight it off, which only causes my master to work harder. Soon, sweat is dripping off my brow, and I know if he doesn't stop, I'm going to cum. I let out one last whimper, trying to avoid defeat, but it only causes him to suck and swallow me down his throat, and my eyes widen with the painful pleasure.

"Petal!" I gasp, and he releases me at once. I sit there taking calming breaths, fighting back my orgasm. When I am calm, he grips my hair and throws my head back, dominating my mouth until I am breathless and gasping for air. He doesn't stop his attention though. Breathing just makes him direct his attention to my neck while he strokes my sensitive cock until he decides to meet my lips again, demanding entry. All too soon, I'm pulling away in desperation. "Petal!" I cry, and again he leaves me be.

"It's important that you learn this, Daniel. There are things I want to do to you, limits I want to push you past, but I can't if I can't trust you. I'm not a mind-reader, Daniel. You have to tell me when."

I don't respond, my master has never once hurt me and I know he knows me intimately enough to understand my needs even if I don't speak my safe words. He seems to sense my defiance and soon he is sighing in frustration, releasing me completely, leaving only the ring and plug in place. "Get dressed and make us lunch," he snaps.

It clicks as to what he meant when he said he was going to take his time with me. I go to his kitchen and make us both a meal, calmly waiting for him to eat and finish before he gives me my plate. "When you are done, I expect the dishes to be washed." This command doesn't surprise me. I've been his complete sub before. I have to admit, it's not a role I appreciate. I find it borderline degrading. My master knows this, and after I completed my initial session, he promised to only do it as punishment. This is the third time in over three and a half years I will have to suffer through it.

While my mind processes these thoughts his stare bores into me, I can't help the tears of shame that streak down my face. I finish my food quickly, then I clean the dishes. His next instructions are for me to clean his house and do his laundry. All the while, he comes and goes as he pleases, ignoring me for the most part, except for the occasional command in which I dutifully comply. When he is satisfied, he directs me into his bathroom. I find a warm bath drawn and rose petals floating on top of the water. "Prepare yourself and get in," he instructs. I strip naked before him and slowly lower myself into his bathtub. He's not far behind me. When he enters, he pulls my body to him until my sore back is flush with his chest. His hand finds my flaccid cock, and he starts kissing and nibbling my neck. He doesn't relent these actions until once again I'm close to the point of no return, even with the damn cock ring. I moan out my safe word. He releases me immediately, giving me time to bring myself down again. When he's satisfied with my breathing, he turns me toward him. "Lace your fingers behind your back," when I comply he straddles me, moving his hand to play with my plug as he dominates my mouth until I'm breaking away again, gasping, "Petal." My master continues this cycle, only breaking it when our water gets cold. When it does, he drains the water and steps out dripping wet. *Fucking hot.* I follow him wordlessly, drying him and then myself.

Once he is dressed I follow him back to the playroom. "Lie down on your stomach," he instructs, patting our bondage table. I comply, internally grateful it's not my back. "Do you trust me, Daniel?" he asks, strapping me to the table.

"Always, Master," I answer, breaking protocol and meeting his eyes. He smacks me hard across the ass, and I drop my head back down.

"Good. Now I want you to lie here like a good sub and don't cum." His instruction confuses me momentarily until I feel the table vibrating. "And you thought this wasn't new," he muses in my ear adjusting me perfectly to verify my dick is getting friction. "No moaning." He smirks. "I have a meeting, and you will not distract me by letting me hear you pleasure." He starts to walk toward the doors.

Terrified, I let out a whimper, "Master, please, don't leave me. I will fail you."

He's next to the table in an instant, "Are you safe wording?"

I lick my lips. *I can do this.* "No, Master."

"I have the audio on, Daniel, rest assured you will not be punished for safe wording even if it interrupts me, understood?" he smiles, showing me his earpiece, letting me know he will be able to hear every sound I make. With that, he leaves me alone on the table, and I hear him lock the doors. *Fuck!* I groan, knowing better than to struggle because it will just make it worse in the end. Never mind it's pointless, I'm bound tight. Right when I know I can't hold off my building orgasm any longer, the vibrating stops. *Thank fuck.* I take calming breaths, trying to picture women naked, snail trails and bloody cunts to go flaccid, which works until the damn table starts to vibrate again. *Fuck me.* I'm forced to fall into a deep submissive state to endure this punishment and when I FINALLY hear the click of the lock to the doors, I let out a whimper of relief.

"How are you, Daniel?" he asks, approaching the table but not moving to shut it off. I lose all sense of dignity, crying out when the vibrations start again. "PETAL!" I scream and instantly the table stops moving.

"Talk to me, Daniel. Do you want to be free or can I leave you like this?"

"Please untie me, Master," I whisper, and instantly one arm is free followed by another. I sit up on my knees, rubbing my face. When my ankles are free, I turn to him again. "Rose, Master, I . . . I I'm done. I frown, removing the damn cock ring and plug.

"Daniel?" he asks, clearly upset with concern.

I raise my hand up to silence him. "Just, give me a few moments, Clayton," I answer, climbing off the table making my way to the playroom doors.

"Where are you going?" he asks, following me.

"I need to piss." I lie. "I'll be right back."

"Daniel I think you're dropping. Will you please sit down for a moment?" He worries grabbing my hand.

"NO!" I scream jerking away from him, bolting to the spare bathroom where I lock myself in. My heart is racing and the room starts to spin but I don't care, all I want is to be alone! "Leave me alone!" I cry out sinking to my knees and rocking back and forth. The world just needs to leave me alone.

Shortly after Clayton is trying the door. "Daniel? Daniel, please talk to me. Please, you shouldn't be alone right now. Damn it, Daniel, this is serious, you're dropping! You are at risk of being in real danger! Please, I pushed you. Let me be there to take you down," he cries on the other side of the door. *He pushed me!* Well, there's the understatement of the fucking year! I don't respond to his pleas, cradling my knees to my chest. "Daniel, please open the door. Would you like me to call Master Alec or someone to help? I can understand if you don't want me."

Moaning, I pull myself up off the floor, not wanting to get anyone else involved. I unlock the door to find a crying Clayton on his knees, his eyes almost black with fear. The sight of seeing him so terrified scares the hell out of me and I realize he's right, I've dropped. I sink back down to my knees, making eye contact. "You're right. I haven't been using my safe words like I should, and you needed to teach me that limits are not failures. They're just limits."

He studies my eyes for a moment then he crashes his lips into me, licking my tongue for just an instant before he kisses down my neck and stomach until he reaches my overly sensitive cock. The moment his mouth is around it, I moan, gripping at his hair and holding him there, fucking the hell out of his face until my cum is squirting down his throat. *Fucking finally.* I collapse on top of him. He stands us both up only to take my legs out from underneath me, taking me to his bed. "I'll be right back." He promises. When he returns, he hands me a bar of chocolate and a glass of milk. I don't argue, opening the wrapper and eating it as quickly as possible. He smiles at my compliance, lies down next to me and brings me into his warm body, where he holds me in his loving arms until I fall fast asleep.

25
Trust

Daniel's Point of View

When I awaken, I find Clayton is still holding me, and I can't help but melt into his touch. I know he is awake because when I start to stir, his hands find their way to my long hair, comforting me.

"You okay?" he whispers, pulling me closer.

"Yeah, I think so," I answer in a husky whisper.

"Can we please transition for a moment? You ended our session rather abruptly, and I have a few questions. I swear I just want to talk, but I don't want to be your boyfriend to do it," he asks with clarification.

"As long as it's just talking," I agree. I was really too emotional to go through any part of a real session again.

"Thank you," he whispers, kissing the back of my neck. Then he whispers. "Red." The room is quiet for a moment while he continues to hold me, but then his pained voice cuts through the silence, "Why did you let me get this far?"

The question, with such strong emotion, startles me. I turn abruptly, wanting to see his face, but I keep my eyes down and put fear in my voice, "Master?"

"Damn it, Daniel!" he moans, rolling onto his back, putting some space between us. "I want an honest answer, so please speak freely. You could have ended it anytime. *Anytime!* And don't tell me you didn't want to. I made you clean my damn house, for fuck sake!"

"You're upset with me," I whisper, causing him to turn to me.

"Look at me." I meet his eyes and I can see the pain and worry in them. "You scared the hell out of me, Daniel. I was waiting and waiting for you to end it, and you never did. You even resorted to begging me, but you didn't end it. Then . . ." he breaks off, his breathing hitched. "Then, when you finally did end it, you didn't let me be there for you. I knew you dropped the moment you used your safe word and instead of letting me be there, you ran away from me! You dropped Daniel! Dropped! You know the risks! It can kill you! Heart attack, strokes! Daniel, you needed someone, and you just ran and fucking hell, it could kill you! I wasn't trying to push you to your limits, more or less, past them. Why didn't you end it sooner? Why didn't you safe word?"

I continue to stare into his eyes as I contemplate my answer. Then I realize I don't really have one. "I don't know, Master." I answer in an honest whisper.

"You can't do this, Daniel. I know that I push you. It's my job. I know that you trust me, but you have to draw lines. Spoken lines Daniel, not body language. We are meant to pass your limits slowly, not so hard that you run from me." He swallows so hard I can hear it. "You broke the first and most revered rule of our contract; you abused your safe words by not using them. I have little choice but to end this part of our relationship with you."

"No Master *please* no." I beg, needing him in this way.

He laces his fingers in mine, squeezing them tightly. "Promise me, Daniel. Promise me I can trust you. That you take the dangers of this seriously."

"I promise, Master. I will start respecting myself more. I promise, please, please don't end this." I plead, my eyes beginning to tear again.

He stays silent for a long stretch before he speaks. "I need a choice from you, Daniel," he decides. "I know that you are in pain right now. I wasn't allowed to treat your skin the way it needed to be treated. I'd like to do that now, but if you would prefer your boyfriend do that, I'd understand."

"No, Master, I'd rather you do it," I answer, casting my eyes down from him, terrified of transiting without assurance we can be this way again.

"Stay here," he answers, and I feel the bed move as he once again leaves me alone. I close my eyes at the memory and decide to question him about it when he returns. He isn't gone long this time, coming back with the familiar lotion bottles. "You will need to take more vitamins than normal, Daniel. Your skin wasn't prepared, and I wasn't allowed to treat you afterward. Roll onto your stomach for me." I do as he says, and I feel him pull the sheets down, exposing my raw skin. The feel of the cool gel is pleasant, but I cringe nonetheless. My skin is fucking burning.

"Master, do I still have permission to speak freely?"

"Yes."

"You left me alone, bound and helpless." I close my eyes trying to keep my composure as the vulnerability of the memory overtakes me.

"Go on."

"What if I needed to use my safe words?"

Suddenly, I am being flipped onto my sore back, feeling my master's hand tighten in my hair. "You think I abandoned you?" his voice is laced with concern, anger and fear. My breathing hitches but I do not answer verbally. My tears do that for me instead. I feel him release his hold on my hair and the bed bounces from his weight shifting. "I am *not* a cruel master, Daniel," he snaps. "I asked you if you wanted to safe word before I started the exercise! And when you declined that, I showed you that I could hear you. Had you chosen to use your safe words, I would have known. You *know* this!" he says in anger. "It's not the first time I left you, Daniel. I realize it makes you apprehensive, but I have shown you that when I do this, you are not abandoned. I heard every whimper."

"You said you had a meeting, Master . . ." I clarify, knowing he's referring to his sound system.

"Were you under the impression I left the house?" he snaps.

"No, Master."

"So you were aware that I could hear you?"

"Yes, but you had a meeting," I respond timidly.

"Did you not trust that I would keep you safe?" he asks in a whisper.

"I always trust that."

"Then I don't understand, Daniel. Did you wait to safe word until I returned because you believed that I would ignore you or be upset that you interrupted me? Or did you wait for another reason?"

I close my eyes for a moment before I answer. "No, I know you put my safety above all else, Master. You do not get upset when I safe word, nor do I get punished for it. I chose to fall into a deep submissive state so that you could have your meeting and not be distracted by me making any unnecessary sounds. I wanted to make you proud."

"So what changed when I walked back in the room?" he asks, climbing back over me.

I frown. "I was expecting immediate relief, and you didn't give me that privilege. You were still pushing me. When I realized that the only way to end it for sure was not by having you next to me, choosing to end it yourself on your own terms in an unstated amount of time, but by me using my safe words, I used them."

"And you decided to come down from that without help, why?"

I close my eyes. "I was ashamed."

"Daniel?" he asks, his pained voice returning.

"I couldn't endure your punishment," I answer as tears fall from my unblinking eyes.

I hear him sigh as he lays his cheek on my bare chest. "The point was to push you until you ended it, Daniel. I was hoping you would with the house duties, but when you didn't, I knew that leaving you alone was another one of your low limits. That's why I did it. I wasn't expecting such a strong reaction or you locking yourself away from me."

"I'm sorry, Master," I cry. "Please forgive me, please don't end this."

"So am I," he answers. "Please forgive me, Daniel. Seriously, this could have ended badly." He combs his fingers through my hair for a long while, "If I decide to forgive you, you can't lock me out, literally, especially when you are coming down from a hard session. Had you not opened the door, I would have kicked it in. You seriously risk heart attack, stroke, even death." he repeats. The fear in his voice makes me meet his eyes. "God, Daniel, you are prone to panic attacks. You could have gone into shock. Even now, I'm going to make you eat more chocolate to help stave off any possible fits of depression. I'm serious, Daniel. This is fucking serious. You can't lock me out. Not ever."

I wipe a tear from his cheek, frowning. I've known about subdrop since I entered into this culture as an Untouchable. It was a lecture Master Alec gave every class . . . I've taken it seriously because he made it plain this game is a dangerous one. And I have had a few episodes in the past, mainly panic attacks, but nothing like this. "There's nothing to forgive, Master," I whisper, "I did it to myself. As you pointed out, I could have ended it at any time. I will respect myself more, and I did learn my lesson. Please, give me a second chance."

"I truly hope so." his face turns hard. "This is your one and only stern warning Daniel. I'm going to give you a second and final chance because I am partly to blame. At times, I have allowed you to communicate your limits through body language. Last night proved to me that you've become dependent on me and not yourself to keep your body and your mind safe. That ends. You must verbally utilize your safe words. I am dead serious, you break our contract like this again and I will end it, permanently."

"Yes Master, thank you Master. You're right to be upset. Subdrop is nothing to mess with." I frown, but grateful he's not ending it. "And honestly, I think that it wouldn't hurt to eat more chocolate, which has helped in the past."

"Are you feeling alright?" he asks, concerned again. I give a weak smile. "I'll get you more chocolate, but you are not leaving here until you talk with Master Alec." He demands. "I will not risk your mental health, and he is a board-certified therapist."

"Thank you, Master." I smile. "I would appreciate an amendment to our contract as well, no locked doors."

He nods. "No locked doors, by either of us." He smiles, running his hands through my hair. "I mentioned earlier that there is something I want to do with you, but I need to trust you, Daniel."

"May I ask what that is exactly, Master?" I frown, a little nervous.

"Do you remember the pulleys?"

"Yes, Master."

"They require you to work on one of your low limits. Do you know which one I'm referring to?" he asks, pulling up on his knees. "Roll back over," he instructs.

I turn, answering his question. "You want to leave me alone."

"Yes, Daniel, I do. As I said, my ultimate goal is to push you past your limits, but we will take it slow."

"That makes me anxious, Master," I answer as his lotioned hands meet my skin.

"What are your safe words, Daniel?"

"Rose, petal, thorn."

"And when do you say them?"

"When I've reached my limits or am uncomfortable.".

"Will you be punished for using your safe words, Daniel?"

"No, Master, I will be rewarded."

"Good," he says, and I can hear a smile in his voice. After he finishes treating my skin he adds, "Red."

He rolls off me and I meet his eyes. "I really do love you, you know."

He smiles. "I love you."

Our lips meet for just a moment, but before any passion could ignite, my phone rings. Debating on answering it, I check the caller ID and see that it is Tasha. Moaning, I break away from Clayton's lips bringing the phone to my ear.

"Hey, Tasha," I answer, smiling at Clayton.

But Tasha isn't the one to greet me. "If you ever want to see your sister again, I suggest you do *exactly* as I say."

26
Strike

Clayton's Point of View

Relief has begun to settle over me after Daniel and I talked. I got the answers I needed to hear and I believe he learned his lesson. As his master I should have ended it, but once again I have fallen victim to his pleading. I may be weak but I am not blind. I am still skeptical and plan on taking it very slowly. Demonstrating weakness in safe wording is detrimental and subdrop can be deadly. I'm angry with myself for letting it go on as long as I have. I will continue to test him with his safe words, this cannot happen again. Recognizing he's digressed, I fear the purchase of the pulleys is premature. Until I am comfortable that he can tolerate them, they are off limits.

I'm enjoying the feel of his soft lips on mine, and I try not to be annoyed that Daniel is breaking our kiss for a phone call. I smile when I hear him say Tasha's name, at least it isn't Ben. But all those comfy feelings slip away the moment fear crosses his features.

"What have you done with her, Travis?!" he screams, I tense immediately. *Travis? Done with her? Oh fuck.* "NO!" Daniel screams jolting upwards, causing me to fall off him onto the bed, I moan in pain from the sudden movement of my cracked ribs. "Not until I talk to my sister! I don't give a shit! Either I talk to her or you can go fuck yourself!" I grab Daniel's hand, squeezing it while shaking my head back and forth, letting him know I don't think it's a good idea to be pissing this guy off right now. "Tasha! What's our mother's maiden name?" he whispers, and he grows very still.

Suddenly Daniel is pissed again, and I know that Travis is back on the line. I wait and listen as Daniel starts breathing shallowly, eventually hanging up his phone.

"Daniel?" I ask, with wide eyes reaching for my cell phone.

"He used her phone. He swears he has her, that she's going to bury her next to Seanna." He cries.

Trying to stay calm I hit the speed dial on my phone and call my PI. "I need to know if Tasha is safe." Relief washes over me the moment I hear him say yes. I look up to Daniel, covering my mouthpiece. "She's safe, at a restaurant in the West End." He falls limp on the bed. "Break your cover, get her out of there now!"

"Tell him to tell her Beethoven," Daniel urges, shaking my arm.

"Tell her Beethoven, and bring her back to my place," I instruct him. "When you're safe have her call me."

Daniel and I quickly get dressed and soon my phone rings. I check the caller ID and hand it straight to Daniel, taking his to call Alec to tell him what's happening. He tells me he's going to call Rachel and have Tasha taken to a safe place while we finally come head to head with Travis. This shit ends tonight. Daniel is visibly shaking the entire time he's talking to his sister, and I can only thank the heavens we got to her in time.

"Tasha!" Daniel screams about twenty minutes later, as they collide in the middle of my living room. He takes her in a death grip, sweeping her off her feet. "I'm so glad you're safe," he gasps, and I can see tears streaking down his face. "I was so scared."

My PI walks up to me shaking my hand, but before we can talk my attention is diverted back to Tasha.

"I got it, Daniel. It's over. I got the proof I need on tape," she responds and my body goes rigid.

"Where is it, Tasha?" I ask, causing her to pull away from Daniel but doesn't let him go.

"Why?" she asks skeptically.

"Do you trust me?" I ask her, and she seems to grow a shade paler. "Give it to Daniel. The cops will have it by morning, I swear." She looks at me and then back to Daniel, who nods.

"What are you going to do?" she asks, fear strong in her voice.

"I'm going to kick his ass, and then I'm going to let the cops handle it," Daniel admits.

"You threatened to kill him, Daniel," she reminds him, taking a step back.

"I won't let him," I assure her, taking a small timid step forward.

She studies us for a minute. "Promise me he will be alive in the morning."

"Oh, he'll be alive." I smile evilly. "But he'll be wishing he was dead."

"That's risky," she accuses.

"And you getting a taped confession from a drunken, abusive, rapping murderer is a cinch?" Daniel snaps. "What's the matter, Tasha? Don't like the tables being turned?"

"You're my brother!" she cries. "I've already lost my best friend to this asshole. I don't want to lose you too!"

He grabs her gently by the arms. "I swear, Tasha, you won't."

My doorbell rings and I'm next to it in an instant, surprised to find Daniel behind me. "Do you know them?"

I turn to him with an eye roll. "It's Alec, Bobby, and Rachel." He nods and I let them in. Daniel smiles politely to them, taking my hand. "Excuse us for a moment," he mutters, dragging me back to my bedroom and locking the door.

When he turns to me, his eyes are wild. "Just because shit is going down with my sister does not mean that I have forgotten about Brad." My eyes widen in shock as I stare at him. He sighs and sits down on my bed. "I assumed the guy on the phone was Travis. The voice was masked. And it would be easy for Travis to take her phone. But the more I think about it, it could be either one really. Tasha hadn't confronted Travis yet, though I'm sure she was about to. He may or may not have known. Either way, I'm kicking his ass for abusing and raping her. But this could have been Brad just as easily, trying to get our guard down. It's easy to switch people's phones Clayton, all he'd have to do is set the same brand down next to hers. Think about it, if he's been stalking me for over three and a half years, he has probably been watching you and possibly her. He probably knows exactly what is going on and could be playing it to his advantage. We could be walking into a fucking trap."

I sit down next to him, taking his hand. "I hear you. I do."

"But?"

"But we can't take the risk this wasn't Travis." I argue. "We need to strike, Daniel. Then we'll figure out Brad."

"I know. I just want to put it out there, but I don't want to freak out Tasha more than I have to or have you drop your guard, alright?"

I shake my head, unlock the door and we exit the room. After some convincing and flat-out bribing, Tasha agrees to leave with Rachel. While she and Daniel were arguing, I sat down with my PI and had him give me the information I needed about Travis. I tell him to follow Tasha some more, briefing him about Daniel's theory, just in case. When those three finally leave, Daniel briefs all of us on the phone call and explains his theory to Alec and Bobby. When he's done, the room is silent.

"It doesn't matter," I finally argue. "We got the proof that we need to bring Travis down. Brad wouldn't be stupid enough to do something to all four of us at once."

"We could just give the tape to the cops and be done with it." Bobby shrugs.

"NO!" Daniel yells. "That fucker raped my sister. I'll be damned if he gets off that easy."

"So we strike." Alec nods. "Agreed?"

Frowning, I look at each face in the room. "Agreed," we all vote.

Once it's decided, Alec goes through the details as to what is going to happen and where. I give out the information that my PI provided on his observations of Travis over the past few months along with a list that Tasha and I had compiled once during one of her training sessions, pointing out his weaknesses, looking for an emotional component. After that is accomplished, I go outside and pay off my bodyguard to stay at the house to pretend I am there and promising a huge ass bonus for lying if anyone was ever to question him about it. When I make it back inside, Bobby is passing out masks and gloves. We are on our way to Alec's SUV when I grab both Alec and Daniel by the arms, keeping them from stepping outside.

"Daniel dropped," I inform Alec.

"What? When?" Alec asks, astonished and worried.

"Last night." I frown. "He's having issues with safe wording and we pushed too hard. He dropped."

"This isn't the time, Clayton," Daniel snaps at me.

"To hell it ain't," I growl back. "We need your head clear, damn it." He glares at me and I turn my attention back to Alec. "We were going to call you, and then his fucking phone rang."

"This timing sucks," Alec bitches at me.

"I know, but I am not going to allow this to happen with you driving blind," I agree, letting their arms go.

Alec looks at me. "Wait for us with Bobby." I nod my head, trusting Alec. I know talking Daniel out of this is impossible, but Alec will at least try. And if that won't work, Alec will make sure he's hyper-aware of Daniel just as I am going to be.

"What gives?" Bobby asks when I climb in.

"Suck ass timing," I growl. "Daniel dropped on me last night. I think I got him level headed, but that was before his fucking phone rang."

"You *think*?" Bobby asks in deep concern.

"It was the hardest drop he's ever had with me." I frown. "I honestly can't be sure."

"Hard as mine?"

"Not that bad, Bobby, but fucking close to it." My mind flashes to the memory of an emergency room with Bobby hooked to heart monitors. I shake head, willing the images to dissipate.

He turns back in his seat. "We won't be able to talk him out of this."

"I know." I frown. "But at least we all know his frame of mind."

"Thank you for telling us." Bobby nods. "We'll keep an eye out for both of you. A drop is hard on the Dom as well, Clayton."

"Thanks," I mutter.

The doors open and Alec climbs into the passenger seat while Daniel climbs in next to me. Alec frowns at me with a head shake and Daniel gives me a look that tells me he's alright. I grab his hand and whisper in his ear, "Do you remember what I told you right before you said I love you?"

His eyes flare. "Yes."

I squeeze him gently. "Before you throw that first punch tonight, *please* make sure this is the decision you want to live with."

"I promise." He smiles lightly, pecking my lips and putting on his seat belt.

It doesn't take us long to find Travis at the restaurant that Tasha had been at earlier. Alec and Bobby go in and warn us that he's drinking, hitting on every chick in sight, bitching about how his girl is going to pay for standing him up. When he finally decides to leave, it is past dark. Alec and Bobby follow him out. I drive the SUV up to his pathetic Porsche, pulling my mask on, and everyone follows suit. Right when Travis gets to his car, Daniel opens his door and jumps out, decking his sorry ass the moment he turns around. Travis falls flat on his back, scrambling backward on his hands and feet. Daniel grabs him by the shirt and throws him up against our vehicle. "That is for dating fucking Tasha, you arrogant prick." Daniel throws him through his door into Bobby's waiting punch. "And that is for fucking touching her," Daniel growls, climbing back in, slamming the door behind him.

"Please, man, I'm sorry," Travis sputters out.

Daniel lets out a dark laugh that makes the hairs on my neck stand up. "You are going to be, you sick motherfucker. We know all about you and your dirty secrets. Tonight, you will not only pay for Tasha, but you will pay for Seanna."

"No, please," Travis cries. I look into the rearview mirror as he tries to escape, but Bobby has him in a death grip. "I'll give you anything you want, please don't kill me," he stammers as pathetic tears fall down his face.

Daniel pulls at the roots of Travis's hair. "Is that what Seanna's last pleas sounded like?"

"Please," he begs.

The only answer Daniel gives him is another punch in the face, which is delivered with such force that Travis is knocked out cold. Daniel quickly sifts through his pockets and pulls out two cell phones. He takes his own out of his pocket and dials Tasha's number, relief washes over everyone when one of them rings. *Thank fuck it wasn't Brad.* Daniel quickly hangs up, turns all of them off and stuffs his and Tasha's into his pants pocket. Then he takes Travis's phone, pulls out the memory card and battery and tosses it out the window.

Alec takes the memory card from him and drops it into a half empty soda bottle, then he turns his attention to Bobby. "I've heard enough of this loser's voice."

Bobby nods grabbing one of two gym bags, producing a gag ball and a pair of handcuffs. While he's attending to Travis, I am driving to where we are going to do this. As the miles pass on, I continue to steal glances at Daniel, who I can tell, even through his mask, is beyond angry at this point, and I am getting worried. I don't want him to regret any part of this night, and if he doesn't calm down during this drive, I am going to have to intervene. *Fuck! I don't want to do that.*

Luckily, our drive isn't short, and Daniel is a whole hell of a lot calmer by the time we arrive. Once inside, Alec our grand master, orders Bobby, Daniel, and me to strip naked, except for our masks, and kneel before his clothed form. We all comply, expressing our individual loyalty to him then recite our safe words and when we should use them. Following this ritual he instructs us to our various tasks while he sets up the video equipment. Bobby tends to an unconscious Travis hanging him from the ceiling of a basement with a spreader bar, and I open both gym bags, preparing the contents in them. When I have completed my task I pull Daniel aside one last time. "Are you sure? There is no going back from this?"

"I'm sure, Clayton," he answers with confidence.

"Alright, but if it gets to be too much use your safe words, I mean it, Daniel. When you hit your limit, stop."

His eyes flash and he studies me for a moment. "I will respect myself, I promise."

"Thank you," I whisper, kissing him gently, only to turn from him when a muffled, panicked scream comes from Travis.

Daniel walks up to him slowly. "You have been a very bad boy, Travis. It's time for your punishment!"

27
Initiation

Daniel's Point of View

Breaking away from Clayton's lips, I walk away from my anchor, my love, toward a very terrified Travis.

"You've been a bad boy, Travis. It's time for your punishment." His eyes go wild as he struggles against his restraints hopelessly. He waits until I'm close before he tries to kick me, only to find that the spreader bar attached to his ankles is weighting him down, causing him to scream into his gag in panic. I smirk. "I think we'll start off with humiliation." With that comment, I start to unbutton his shirt, only to have my grand master hand me a pocketknife. I smile, shredding his fancy clothes until they drop to the floor. Bobby approaches his naked form and starts licking and twisting his nipples. When he's satisfied with Travis's bodily response, be it involuntarily, he pinches them into a cheap, quite painful nipple clamps. Travis lets out another muffled scream. I give a dark laugh, standing behind him and place my hands on his ass, "Shh, puppet, we're just getting started." Then I bring back my leather gloved hand and slap him hard across both cheeks before I step away.

Grand Master grabs my shoulder, directing me to a corner behind the camera. We're in Travis's line of sight, so he pulls me close, putting our chests together. He kisses my lips, before dropping down to my ear. "Forgive me, but as you know, Tasha said he's a homophobic. I think it would be safest in the end if we don't stick to our *traditional* parings." I moan in response, meeting Clayton's eyes. *Fucker knew this was coming. Why didn't he warn me?* Clayton gives a short nod, and Bobby approaches him. The way they kiss tells me this act is nothing new, but is just that, an act. Deciding to play my part, I pull back a little, rolling my eyes once at my grand master, before I surprise him by pushing him against the wall, dominating his mouth the moment he gasps. When I break away, he chuckles, "Yeah, very good thing I didn't keep you."

I smirk and push our aroused cocks together. "While this is fun, I really want to give Travis more than an upset stomach."

He lets out a small growl-like laugh before turning the tables on me, pinning me to the wall with his weight. Bobby and Clayton find this funny, and I roll my eyes again. Grand Master laces our fingers together, bringing our arms above our heads, pinning my hands to the wall.

"Watch!" I hear Clayton bark, slapping Travis with a leather paddle, causing him to scream again.

"I think Clayton might be enjoying this," Grand Master complains, before pushing his arousal into me and sucking my bottom lip into his mouth. I moan, opening for him, he dominates me until I'm fucking breathless; but fuck me, if it isn't fucking hot as hell. When he pulls away, his lips slowly kiss up my jawbone and up to my ear. "*That's* the way it will always be, Daniel. Never forget who the 'Grand Master' is."

I smile, leaning into him. "See, we would have never worked out, sexy."

He lets out a loud laugh before his face turns serious. "This bastard crossed a very wrong line, and I plan to give him our most severe punishment, though, in my opinion, sometimes it's just not enough. That being said," he moans, pushing into me again, "I'll let you start, because she's your sister, but I'm finishing this, Daniel." He can see the argument in my eyes, but before it can escape my lips, he cuts me off with another mind-blowing, dominating kiss, all the while pressing my hands harder into the wall. When he stops, his lips are on my ear again, "Remember, I'm the only master tonight, Daniel," he growls. He turns to face Clayton, indicating that he should approach. Clayton walks up to us, his eyes cast downward. "Kiss me," he demands. Clayton complies, opening his lips so our grand master can dominate him while his hands rest behind his back.

"Watch!" Bobby demands, slapping Travis with the leather paddle.

= 273 =

Grand Master breaks away from Clayton, studying me. "Are we clear?"

My eyes shift to Clayton, who looks up at me, giving another short nod, expressing his silent apology. Shifting back to our grand master's glare, I cast my eyes down. "Yes, Grand Master."

"Good," he says, pushing off me as he releases his grip.

Fuck it, might as well have fun with it, right? With this mindset, I put my lips to Clayton's ear, "I'm being very naughty, Master."

He turns to me with flashing eyes before he laughs and walks up to Travis. "Did you enjoy the show?" he asks, rolling Travis's balls in his gloved hands. "Don't worry, we haven't forgotten about you, and after tonight," he smirks, "well, you will never forget us. You see puppet, you won't ever be able to claim that a man has never gotten you off."

Bobby's behind him instantly. "Or that you never tasted another man's cum, because you're going to swallow a dick until you're choking on it." Travis tries to take deep, calming breaths, but none of us miss the tears streaking down his face.

Grand Master motions me to step behind Travis handing me a whip, whispering, "You'll notice the difference with the first strike." Clayton and Bobby move out of the way when I nod and grip the handle, making note the whip is shorter than ours. The first strike cuts the still air with a ghost of a whistle before snaking itself across Travis's unprepared flesh. The screams that shoot through his gag are gut-wrenching, but I find strength in them as my thoughts drift to Seanna. "Don't worry, puppet. Seanna's screams went unanswered too." I snarl, inching forward while drawing my hand further back, causing more contact and a hell of a lot more screaming. After the eighth blow, Clayton grabs my wrist, and we exchange a hard look. *He's worried about me.* Sighing, I accept his silent plea and hand him the whip. Before I let him start, I motion our grand master and Bobby to stand in front of him, which they do. When they start making out, I tug lightly on Travis's clamp chain and pull off my glove, wetting my finger and smile when the realization dawns on Travis of exactly where I plan on putting it, causing frantic screaming and squirming. "What's the matter, puppet? You don't want this?" I ask curiously, forcing my wet finger into his extremely tight hole. "Don't worry, I know you don't respect a woman when she tells you no." I bend and twist violently as he continues to freak out.

That's when I feel Clayton's lubed finger joining mine. I look over Travis's shoulder, meeting Clayton's eyes as we politely stretch Travis. We fall into a pattern of doing the opposite of each other, and we start to lick and suck on Travis's neck. "You'd be wise to watch them," I growl violently, when Travis closes his eyes. His eyes snap open and his body shudders.

"If you relax, puppet, you might find you enjoy this," Clayton coos, taking a thick tongue and licking him from the base of his neck to his ear.

At the same time, he hooks his finger in mine while still inside Travis's tight ass. I pull away from Travis's collarbone meeting Clayton's stare. He leans forward, and we start kissing, causing Travis to whimper while we grab his flaccid cock, stroking him until he's hard. Then we drop it and yank our connected fingers out of him. Bobby notices Travis's involuntary hard-on and breaks away from our grand master, walking to one of the gym bags. He comes back with a metal, three-ring cock ring and a very large plug that he shows to Travis. Travis starts struggling and screaming as tears spill from his eyes. Bobby lubes them both and hands the plug to our grand master. I hold Travis's hips steady from behind and Grand Master kneels down lightly scrapping my hard cock with his teeth before he turns his attention to Travis, inserting the plug into him rather roughly, while Bobby applies the rings. When they are done, I give the plug a tap and then step in front of him. I can't help the smile that comes to my face when Clayton pulls back the whip and connects it once more to Travis's back. Watching with increased pleasure, I try not to jump when I feel my cock being groped, my eyes widen on their own accord when I turn around and realize it's Bobby.

"My turn. Been wanting to do this since I laid eyes on you," he whispers, colliding our lips as he grabs my ass and pushes his obvious boner into my stomach. The man has a good three inches on my height. I count three more blows before he lets me pull away from him.

"Holy hell!" I gasp, and he drops his lips down to my ear.

"I know. I'm the best damn kisser here."

"You wish," I growl, causing him to grab his heart and pull out an imaginary knife.

"You two, enough!" Grand Master growls.

Bobby raises an eyebrow and walks up to him, kissing him breathless. I roll my eyes, and Clayton stops his motions, waiting for our grand master to decide if he should continue. When Grand Master breaks away from

Bobby, he clears his throat, "Twelve is enough." Clayton nods, moving to put the whip back in the bag only to pull out a cane. He lightly tosses it to me, and just the sight scares the shit out of Travis, causing him to have another panicked episode.

Bobby grins, approaching Travis's struggling form to reposition him. Bobby lowers Travis down by his arms, rearranging his position in such a way that his knees are on the concrete, with his ass up in the air and his arms above his head—*That can't be comfortable.* I walk behind Travis looking at Clayton in confusion, he smiles, understanding my question. He stands behind me, showing me how to swing the instrument properly, whispering seductively in my ear, "I'm glad you're not learning this one with me, darlin'." I give him a quick peck before taking my first swing and hear a series of high-pitched muffled wails vibrating out of Travis as the cane snaps back and hits him again.

"Don't be such a puss!" Grand Master snaps. "He's going easy on you."

My eyes snap to his, and I toss him the cane. "If you can do better, by all means."

"Come now, don't be sore." He frowns, walking up to me brushing his fingers down one cheek.

Annoyed, I grab his and Clayton's wrist, taking them back to the corner on the opposite side of the room behind the camera. "I'm not an idiot," I snap at both of them. "I know that you are both trying to shield me. Hell, even Bobby's in on it."

"What am I in on?" he asks, wrapping his arms around me from behind.

"Between the kissing and the challenging, you would think this is some weird orgy with a master power trip," I snap.

"You'd rather concentrate all your efforts on this scumbag and risk seriously hurting him?" Grand Master asks. I frown at that and he mimics me, gliding his fingers over my lips. "Don't you see, sexy? Tonight isn't just about avenging Tasha and Seanna. It's about you. This is your initiation, and if you can't take it or you feel uncomfortable with me as your 'Grand Master', then you can safe word, no hard feelings."

I turn to Clayton. "Is this why you didn't want me to be a part of this?"

He turns to our grand master, who nods, giving him permission to speak, then meets my eyes. "Not exactly, no," he says taking Bobby's place, holding me in his loving arms. "I don't want you to regret your choice darlin', because at the end of the night, Travis is going to be what you remember most. We distract ourselves like this to keep our sanity and our victims safe. Normally, we don't switch as much, but this is far from normal, especially so soon after a drop. I want you to stay you at the end of the night."

"So you're not getting jealous?" I ask, leaning into him.

"Subs can't get jealous of each other, Daniel," he whispers, "and your boyfriend trusts you."

"Are you still willing?" my grand master asks. "Think about that for a moment. I'm a little more demanding than your usual master."

I try not to scoff at that, "Yes, Grand Master, I'm still in this."

"Prove it . . ." he demands, but before he can finish his sentence, I surprise him and kiss Bobby, effectively silencing him, that is, until my hand is about to cup his boyfriend's dick. "Stop!" I turn to him, meeting his eyes which narrow into a glare. "Who's the *master* tonight?" he demands.

"You are," I whisper, casting my eyes down.

"Which means I call the shots," he growls.

"Yes, Grand Master."

"I was going to have you kiss me, but now . . ." he trails off, hooking Clayton's waist and pulling him flush into his body. Clayton shows no hesitation, allowing our grand master to dominate his mouth. *God, I hate multiple subs for this reason . . . jealousy.* When he finally breaks free of Clayton's lips he turns to me, studying me for a moment. "Now where was I?" He shrugs, walking back to Travis, with my wrist in tow.

"You two," he snaps at Bobby and Clayton, "give our guest here a little show, and I want more than kissing." I keep my eyes down, trying to ignore that Clayton and Bobby are giving each other hand jobs. "Watch my wrist," Grand Master whispers, licking my ear. I turn to him but falter slightly when I hear Clayton moan. I hear a sigh come from my grand master before he is dominating my mouth and groping me. When he finally breaks away, he growls in my ear, "I need your undivided attention." I nod, watching his wrist as he swipes the cane against Travis's ass, causing a very loud hyena scream, which everyone basically ignores. He delivers another blow and then another, after which, he turns to me, passing the cane back. "That's four.

I want twelve." Travis starts adding squirming to his screaming, making it a lot worse than it should be, but I don't bother advising him to hold still. By the ninth blow, I feel confident with the instrument but stop as I watch white ropes of cum being shot out onto the floor.

"Clean it up!" Grand Master growls. Bobby drops his head in shame and goes to grab the gym bag. Grand Master takes the cane from me. "You know better," he snarls.

"Yes, Grand Master," Bobby whispers, keeping his gaze down.

"Prepare," he demands. Bobby drops to all fours, exposing his naked ass to our grand master, taking the caning without so much as a grunt, even with five separate strokes. "Use the bleach," Grand Master says dryly tossing the cane back to me. "Finish!" he demands. My eyes flash to Clayton, who is still kneeling in front of Travis, stimulating himself. The sight is fucking erotic, and I use that as my stimulation to finish delivering the last three blows. "Good. Now suck him off until he cums," Grand Master instructs. I turn to him with a questioning raised eyebrow, until he points to Clayton. I nod and lower my eyes, choosing to crawl over to my lover and suck his dick into my mouth with a beautiful pop, causing Clayton to gasp.

"Watch!" Grand Master demands, and we hear Travis whimper next to us. I turn slightly to check and make sure his eyes are on me. Then I stick my tongue out and lick Clayton's balls. He bends over me with shaky breathing. I grab his ass and start tracing his entrance causing him to moan. By the tone of it, I know he's going to cum and I prepare my throat for his delicious juice. After swallowing, I lick him clean. When I sit up from Clayton's limp form, Grand Master motions me over to reposition Travis back to his original position.

"Rape and murder are hideous acts, puppet," Grand Master growls in disgust. Bobby and Clayton start to grab various wires and a strange-looking box out of the second gym bag. "It's time to test your endurance." Confused, I watch them set up and attach two small clamps to Travis's nut sack and a wire to the chain of Travis's nipple clamps. The first set of wires, attached to his nut sack, are connected to the box and the second, attached to the nipple clamps, are connected to a pulley system that seems to lift a piece of small metal from another piece of metal on the box. Once the setup is complete, Grand Master flips a switch, and Travis starts screaming instantly. When he stops, Grand Master snaps, "If you don't want that to happen again, I suggest you keep the live wire disconnected. Lean back." Travis complies and separates the two pieces of metal. This position isn't exactly comfortable because it puts strain on his nipples to do it. Grand Master continues his explanation. "Every time you lean forward, you will get electric pulses straight to your balls. You have a choice of thirty seconds of pulsing followed by twenty seconds of rest and the cycle starts over, or you could correct your position and turn off the circuit. Simple, right?" he asks as a devilish grin washes over his face. Travis's eyes go wide in panic. "On your toes!" Grand Master demands. Bobby and Clayton lift him on his toes, placing two break-like pedals under his heels. "I suggest you stay that way unless you want to up the voltage." Grand Master warns. Bobby hands him a flogger, and our grand master smacks Travis' legs with it, causing him to yelp and lose his balance, which takes a good three minutes for him to correct. "I will only do that again if you are not watching us." Grand Master chuckles, tossing the flogger between his hands when Travis finally stills.

Then he directs his attention to us. "You two, on your hands and knees." Clayton and Bobby drop to their hands and knees, while Grand Master tosses me a packet of lube then proceeds to unzip his pants, positioning himself behind Bobby. Catching on, I mimic him, position myself behind Clayton. Travis starts to scream again as he accidentally leans forward, we all ignore him. Grand Master and I start preparing our mates intimately. "Kiss," Grand Master orders. Clayton and Bobby begin kissing while Grand Master and I press our very hard cocks into them. *Fucking hell! The one and only hot perk of multiple subs.* I follow our grand master's lead, starting out slowly then pounding into my mate. Soon, I'm close but I know better.

"Grand Master, please!" I beg, wanting so badly to cum.

"NO!" he screams, pulsing into Bobby. I slow my pace with Clayton, but I do not stop. When Grand Master is satisfied, he pulls out of Bobby, zips himself back up and slowly walks behind me. "Begging will get you nowhere," he whispers, pressing a lubed finger in my ass. I take controlled breaths, accepting the fact that I am not going to fucking cum tonight. After a few moments of teasing, he falls out of me. "I'll forgive you just this once, but *never* beg me again," he growls. "Cum," he demands. Instantly I am spilling my essence into Clayton's warmth. *Fuck me.*

"Good," he smiles, nodding to Bobby. "It's time." Travis's eyes go wide in panic again while he tries to hold still. I look over and watch as Bobby produces a huge ass dildo and a normal size one, passing them both to our grand master, who shows them to Travis. "If you can't suck a damn good cock, then this is going up your ass tonight. If you can manage to get one of my subs off, well then I will allow this." Grand Master shrugs. "Don't worry. You have time to think about it. Say an hour or two." Travis panics losing his concentration and connects the wires. Grand Master orders us all to follow him upstairs, leaving Travis alone with the torture device.

When we get upstairs, I collapse into Clayton's strong arms. "I know, darlin'," he whispers, taking off our masks and begins running his fingers through my hair. "It's almost over. You don't have to go back down there," he whispers.

"Why didn't you tell me it was like this?" I frown, pulling away from him.

"Besides the fact it's forbidden to really talk about it outside of our meetings?" he asks. "Some things are better left to the moment."

"You're probably right," I answer with a small smile. "There is no way in hell I would have been able to develop a friendship with these two had I known. But since I do have a friendship, though young, I know that this isn't personal. It's an act. A really hot act, but an act just the same."

"Did I mention I like him?" Grand Master smiles at Clayton.

"He's got my vote," Bobby agrees.

"You hear that, darlin'? Congrats. You're officially an 'Angel,' if you want to be." Clayton forces a smile, kissing me gently on the lips.

"Do you want to go back down there?" Grand Master asks.

"Yes," I answer confidently causing Clayton to frown. "I can handle it."

Grand Master raises an eyebrow. "You know we aren't going to use the dildos, right?"

"The bastard deserves it!"

"Can't deny." Grand Master shrugs. "But it's not who we are and what we are about. It's over, Daniel. We've scared the hell out of him. He'll willingly talk to our camera, the police will have a case, and we will get the location of Seanna's grave so her parents will have the peace they have been looking for."

Muffled screams come up from the basement, and we all know that Travis has lost his balance. "I get it." I tell him, trying to hide my disappointment. "Thanks for going after him to start with. Seriously, it means a lot."

Grand Master smiles. "Welcome to the team, Daniel, but know this. You will not be treated so close to my equal in the future. Tonight was an exception, not the rule."

"Yes, Grand Master, thank you for the honor and letting me avenge my sister." I answer, casting my eyes down.

"You're welcome." He smiles, tucking my hair behind my right ear. "Now let's eat before we finish this."

We eat dinner in silence, which is periodically broken by Travis's muffled screams that go ignored. It's not enough. He deserves so much more; he deserves what happened to my sister at least, if not what he did to Seanna. That piece of shit doesn't deserve the air in his lungs.

When Grand Master decides it's time, I shake my head no. "Rose. I'm sorry, Grand Master, but I have to safe word. This isn't enough. If I go back down there, I will kill him."

Grand Master runs his fingers through my hair. "Safe wording has no shame, Daniel. I'm proud you know your limits. Bobby, stay with him. Clayton and I will finish this. And put your masks back on." I drop my head into my hands, gathering myself.

"You're doing great, man, especially so close to a drop," Bobby encourages me.

"Guess my punishment with Clayton was a breeze compared to what you have been involved with." I laugh humorlessly.

He gives a small smile. "Considering the circumstances, that was actually one of the more intense things I've witnessed."

"I'd say I regret it, but I don't. If I hadn't gone through it, who knows if Clayton and I would be together."

"He's happy, you know." Bobby smiles. "I've never seen him so messed up over a man before. I know that he's been making a lot of dumb errors, but if you ask me, I think it's because he's never felt this way before. He's crazy about you, psycho ex and all."

"Yeah, not to mention a fucked-up, bratty, spoiled rotten sister," I grumble. "Seriously, with all this shit, I am surprised he hasn't ditched me."

Bobby shakes his head. "The only way that will happen is if you either royally fuck up or if you ditch him."

Before I can respond, we hear a pleading scream escape Travis's lips, "Stop! No! Please don't! God plesase, kill me! I'll do anything! Please just leave me alone!"

"It's almost over," Bobby assures me, putting his mask back on. I follow suit unsure when Travis will make an appearance. "Just a taped confession for evidence and we're done."

"So how about them Rangers?" I ask, distracting myself. For about an hour, Bobby and I exchange small talk, getting to know each other. Our conversation only ends when Travis's naked and beaten body is being dragged up the stairs by Grand Master and Clayton. While Grand Master looks after a tied up Travis, the three of us go downstairs to get dress, clean up Travis's fluids, and gather our tools. When we are done Grand Master releases us and we go to the SUV.

"Where to?" I ask.

"To the pigs." Alec smirks, driving us to the police station. The drive is quiet, just like last time, except for the fact that Travis is conscious and weeping. When we get to the precinct, Bobby gets out, dropping both confessions off in the night box, and Clayton and I dump Travis in the alley. To ensure that he doesn't go anywhere before the cops find him, I cold cock his ass one last time. When I get back in the SUV, I remove my mask and fall into Clayton's welcoming embrace.

"Glad you didn't kill him?" he asks, running his fingers through my hair.

"Yes, baby. Thank you," I whisper. "I can live with this."

"I know, darlin'. You're welcome," he whispers back with a sad smile.

After some instance on my part, we get dropped off at Clayton's place. Once we pass the threshold, I all but collapse. Clayton sweeps me off my feet, walking to his bedroom, where he strips us of our clothes before carrying me to a warm bath. He washes my hair for me then my body, all the while whispering words of love and affection. When the water cools he drains the tub, dries us off, and takes me to his bed.

"I love you, Daniel," he whispers.

"Clayton?" I ask, very close to sleep.

"Hmm?" he asks, pulling me to him.

"If I were to propose, would you say yes?" Unfortunately, sleep takes over me in that moment, and I don't hear his answer.

28
Monster

Daniel's Point of View

When I wake in the morning, it is to an empty bed. I close my eyes, only to discover Travis's terrified face seems to be burned into the back of my lids and I open them quickly. *Holy fuck!* Moaning, I roll over while last night's events come crashing back at me causing my stomach to flip. Disgusted and creeped the fuck out, I run to the bathroom and lose my stomach contents.

"Daniel?" Clayton asks in concern, barging through the door.

"I'm fine," I moan, resting my head on my forearm while I lean into the bowl.

"No, you're not," Clayton argues, sitting next to me.

"What the hell did we do?" I cry, getting sick again.

"We got a murderer and rapist to confess and gave the cops evidence they need to make him pay for his crimes. We served parents peace and the ability to finally bury their daughter. And helped a brother deliver his vengeance for his sister. We gave justice."

"It was a mistake." I frown into the toilet.

"Which part?"

Pale, I slowly lift my head up to him. "I don't know, the whole thing," I gasp, before losing more stomach contents. "We tortured him. Purposely tortured him. Fuck, Clayton, what happened when you went back downstairs?"

"Not much, Daniel."

"Not much my ass," I scuff in a dead laugh. "I distinctly remember him pleading you to stop, begging for death! What did you do? Who did it?"

Clayton's eyes go wide for a moment before he closes them, keeping his temper in check. "You honestly think either of us is capable of anything that you are implying?" I give him a blank stare and he turns to me. "We're not! Have you forgotten that Alec *is* a rape victim?"

"No, you're right. You weren't the bad guys. I was. I could have killed him. I wanted to. If I wouldn't have safe worded . . ." My stomach betrays me again.

"You DID safe word. You DID stop yourself. You kept your promise to me, to Tasha. It's over, Daniel. You did the right thing!" he reassures me.

"The right thing?" I ask disgusted. *How the hell can willfully torturing someone and wanting to kill them be the right thing? Holy shit, I'm a monster.* "Clayton, I—" but I can't finish the sentence.

"Have you come back to me, darlin'?" he asks, shaking.

"What happened after you brought me upstairs?" I ask again.

"We hit him with the cane some more. When we took off his gag he begged us to stop and confessed everything on tape."

"That's it?" I ask in relief.

"That's it," he confirms. "No rape, no murder either. We always copy the tape if you want to see it for yourself . . ." He offers reaching for my hand. "You scared me to death last night, Daniel. I was terrified that I lost you forever."

"I'm right here."

He watches me skeptically. "I want you to talk to Rachel." Surprise washes over me, and I stare at him dumbfounded. "I know you trust Alec, but he's too close and she specializes in grief. And come on, Daniel, look around for a moment. Your sister was in a highly dangerous and abusive relationship. She was raped and dating a guy capable of murder, never mind the fact the guy *did* murder your friend. Not to mention that you've been stalked for over three and a half years and your first boyfriend gets attacked by the psycho. Damn it, Daniel, it's no wonder you were close to losing it. Thank you for safe wording. I honestly believe it saved your mental health, if not your life." He stops and takes a breath, "Darlin', I can only do so much for you, give you so much release. It's not enough. Last night proved that to me. You need to talk to someone."

"And if I don't?"

"Then it's over between us."

"Ouch." I sigh, leaning back on my ass away from the toilet.

"It's not negotiable, Daniel. Think about it." He frowns, standing and reaching his hand out to me. When I stand up, his sad eyes are boring into mine. "I really do love you and I want to be there for you, but I can't do this without help."

"I hear you." I assure him. "I should go."

"Yeah," he agrees. Not a word is spoken while I collect my clothes and grab my things. When I get to his front door, he calls out to me. "Daniel! I truly hope to hear from you again."

I look at him with sadness. "No promises, baby, but either way, I will always love you." I can see his breathing falter, but he doesn't move or respond. I grab the door and force my way out of it for what I know is the last time. Honestly, how the hell can I face him again after I turned into such a monster?

29
Broken

Daniel's Point of View

Fuck my life! I'm lying here in some no-name hotel room wishing that I had at least one picture of my ex. Just one. One that showed those beautiful deep blue eyes, his sexy ass dimples, and his lovely laugh lines. *God, I miss him.*

The past seven months have been hell as I have unsuccessfully tried to move past him. I tried to bury myself in work but found that even that was tainted with Clayton. Amber and Ben are engaged to be married, and my friendship with him almost ended when he realized that Travis had been arrested for murder, his mug shot giving away the fact that I got to him first. Ben wanted to be there. I explained to him that he should be glad he wasn't, he was still pissed. I, on the other hand, could not be more grateful. At least I had someone who didn't know what I was capable of. Ironic that I thought Angels of Justice was my answer for my past sins. It only made me more of a monster than I already was.

Travis stars in my nightmares almost every night since it happened. But when I look at Tasha, seeing her smiling and laughing with her girlfriends and kissing her new, shy boyfriend, I'm happy to carry these demons. She's worth it. She and I have grown closer because of it really. We're kindred spirits, willing to go to the extremes for the ones that we love. We have dinner together at least once a week, and I know our mom is suspicious, but she's so happy that we are finally getting along that she doesn't push for an explanation. I have been trying to influence Tasha not to be so quick to judge people, and she has been working on changing my misconceptions of others.

I haven't spoken to Clayton or anyone in Angels of Justice since I left. I can't bring myself to face them. Though I could never be more grateful that they were willing to go to such extremes to make sure I could live with my choice, I still hate myself. I should have listened to Clayton. I should have stayed the fuck away and let them deal with it. But I made a choice, the wrong choice, and I have to live with that for the rest of my life. *Without Clayton.*

I'm not saying they haven't tried to contact me; Alec in particular, so much so, that he showed up to one of our shoots to confront me, considering I was ignoring everyone's calls and text messages. Like the coward I am, I had Ben explain that I just wasn't in the best place. Alec was upset and begged for five minutes, but Ben refused, threatening security if he didn't leave. Clayton resorted to snail mail, but all his letters lay on my counter, unopened, unread, unanswered.

Ben and Amber took over *The Road to Life* project where we were working directly with Blackboard Entertainment. I've snuck in to view the final cuts and left notes for Ben, but I've avoided Clayton completely. He hasn't made that easy, according to Amber, he has made this his pet project and refuses to let anyone near it, hoping he will run into me.

Ben has tried to pull me aside on more than one occasion, asking me if I've made the right choice. I know he's worried, but I assure him that I have. I know he doesn't believe me. Hell, I don't believe me, but I can't go back, not after coming so close to being everything that I hate. Between my past and this, it's a surprise I can stomach the image in the mirror.

I did take Clayton's advice. I got help. I found a psychologist with an impeccable background and paid a heavy sum of money, although I am using an alias, to keep his damn mouth shut. I never told Ben I was in therapy, no one knows, not even Tasha.

Trying to fall asleep, I think back to the very end of that night, where Clayton gave me everything he had to make sure I made it through. I could not appreciate him more for that. But the more I look back on it, the more it feels like a master helping a sub come down from a really hard session, instead of a boyfriend taking care of a boyfriend. Hell, I practically proposed to him that night, and I have no idea what his answer was. Today, I am grateful for that fact; I'd rather not know.

In my imagination, he said yes. In my imagination, he is here with me tonight, holding me in his arms. In my imagination, I am loved. Desperately, I hang on to the only thing that I have, the memory of him, treasuring it for all it's worth, knowing when sleep overtakes me, my nightmares await me.

The next day, I am on my way home, and in the airport is where I see him. He's standing there waiting for someone. *Me? Dare I hope?* The moment our eyes meet, my defenses crumble, but before I could run into his arms, another man greets him with a hug. My heart shatters into a million painful pieces. It takes every bit of strength I have not to fall apart. I turn away from them willing myself not to run as my feet make their way to the long-term parking. When I get to my car, I sit there trying to catch my breath. *He's moved on.* The pain that washes over me is absolutely unbearable. I can't help but weep over the devastation that I made to my own heart.

When I'm finally coherent enough to drive, I slowly make my way home. Once there, I sit and wonder what the hell the point of life is anymore. Without Clayton, it's meaningless. *What the fuck, Kingsley?*

I believe in therapy this is what is called a breakthrough. I promised myself I would never do this again, that I would never let a man control my life in such a way that without him, I would not see the point of living. Freaked, I call the only person who is willing to deal with me right now.

"Hey, Daniel, forget something?" he asks with a small laugh. "I got your suitcase, seeing as you walked away from it. Abandoning luggage in an airport, what the hell are you thinking?"

"I'm not." I admit, clearing my throat. "Ben, I'm fucking scaring myself. Can you get here? Now."

"Hey, what's wrong?" he asks, his voice filled with concern.

"He moved on," I whisper, staring at a bottle of sleeping pills.

"Daniel?" Ben says cautiously. "Where are you?"

"Home."

"Go outside in your front yard and wait for me, alright? Don't touch anything. Just go outside and wait for me," Ben orders.

"Alright." I frown, forcing my feet to move me outside and away from the pills. Ben takes about twenty minutes to get there, refusing to hang up the phone. He screeches into my driveway, not bothering to close his car door, and runs up to me. Quickly, he checks my body for any potential danger before he sighs and drags me into his car.

"Where are we going?"

"Somewhere you needed to go a hell of a long time ago." Ben frowns, pulling out of my driveway.

"I can't see him, Ben," I whisper.

"I know, man," he says, grabbing my hand and squeezing it. "Don't worry. That's not where I am going."

True to his word, Ben does not take me to Clayton's. Instead, he takes me to Alec's. The moment I realize it, my breathing hitches. "Ben . . ."

"Shut up, Kingsley," he growls, putting the car in park and all but dragging me to Alec's front door.

When it opens, Alec seems shocked for just a moment until his face relaxes. "Can I help you?"

"God, I hope so." Ben moans, dragging me past Alec and into the house without so much as an invitation. Bobby's on the couch and turns toward us, when he registers who we are he jumps to his feet.

"Why are you here?" Alec asks, staring at me.

"Don't look at me. I didn't drive," I snap.

"How close were you, Daniel?" Ben asks, ignoring Alec. "How close were you to killing yourself tonight?"

My eyes widen. I can feel the blood drain from my face as I stare at the one man in this world I thought would never betray me. I thought wrong.

"Daniel?" Alec whispers, trying to approach me, but I take a step back.

"He's not Liam. He's not Liam," I chant to myself. "I ended it, me. This isn't the same."

"Daniel?" Alec frowns, taking another step closer.

"He has the right to move on. I ended it, me. I made a bad choice. I have to live with it. I love her. She's the reason. She matters, not me. She deserves happiness. I love her."

"Daniel," Alec says, smacking me across the face. *When did he get so close?* I blink, looking up at him. "Look at me." He pulls his eyebrows together. "Tell me you are seeing someone."

"Not since Clayton."

"No, not like that. A professional," Alec clarifies.

I nod my head. "Yeah, for about seven months now."

"Thank fuck." Ben mutters, flopping down on the couch.

"I'd love to sit down and talk to you, if you can handle it." Alec frowns, offering his hand to me. "We weren't exactly expecting you to snap like this. Hell, I should have tied you up and not let you go, to start with. You were still in recovery from a subdrop and then you add this. No wonder you had such a hard time. I've tried to come to you, to help, but you are a stubborn ass Kingsley."

I stare at the floor for a very long moment before turning my attention to Ben, who just shrugs at me. Nodding at him, I turn to meet Alec's pleading eyes. "Alone," I whisper. He nods, and I carefully wrap my fingers around his. He gives me a small smile, taking me outside on his deck.

"Tell me Daniel, how did you go from proposing to walking away from him?" Alec frowns, offering me a patio seat.

I let out an exhausted sigh. "I didn't propose." He frowns, thinking I don't remember. "I asked him what his answer would be *if* I proposed. Hell, I didn't even hear his response."

Alec's eyes flash at this information. "Then what happened?"

"I woke up, freaking the fuck out." I frown, yanking on my hair and dropping my head to my hands. "I seriously could have killed him, without even blinking." Tears start to streak down my face.

"You didn't. You safe worded when it got too much." Alec responds unmoving.

"Had I not . . . I could have killed him. I won't deny it, Alec. If it wasn't for you guys, I probably would have." My breath shakes. "How do I deserve to be loved by anyone when I have the capability of doing something so horrible? Clayton deserves better."

"So that's what's been playing round and round in your head for over half a year now? The could-have-beens? Daniel, stop for just a moment. Look at it for what it was. You beat down that demon inside of you. You wouldn't let him out. You had the man who raped and beat your sister, who murdered your friend, in your grasp, and you let him live."

"But—"

"No buts, damn it!" he growls. "We are all capable of murder, Daniel. But you stopped yourself. You safe worded. You said no. You are a better man than Travis Ashton, and you brought justice. You deserve the title of 'Angel' because you know your limits as a human being, and you embrace them. When you had enough, when you knew that you could harm him, you stepped aside. Tell me, Daniel, how the hell does that make you a monster?"

Tears streak down my face as Alec continues. "Look, that night wasn't easy on any of us, including Clayton. He's not perfect, Daniel. He can't solve all with a hug or a whip. He was right to ask for help, and you just walked out on him. There were four of us, Daniel. You were not alone. I know the hate in your eyes scared the shit out of him, but he should have never been so hard on you directly after that and a subdrop. Believe me when I tell you he regrets it. He's since tried to apologize, but you haven't exactly been cooperative in that department. Forcing an ultimatum on you at that moment was one of the worst ideas he's had." Alec groans, putting his face in his hands. "He always fucked up so royally with you. He was so terrified of losing you that he kept making mistake after mistake. He gave you an ultimatum because he was scared for you. Rightfully so, he knew you pushed yourself too hard, that you would have guilt he wouldn't be able to manage, mainly because he feels he caused it. He wasn't wrong in his request, Daniel, just his timing, which you apparently agree. You have sought out help."

"She's my sister," I whisper. "I would have hated you all if I didn't do it."

"I know, and you gave a part of yourself to protect her honor." Alec smiles, taking my hands in his. "She has herself a very loving brother."

"You know, that's the only good thing that's come out of this whole fucking mess." I smile back. "We've grown closer and actually talk instead of fight."

Alec laughs. "You mean you stopped calling her a bitch?"

I laugh too and it feels so fucking good. "No, she's still a bitch. But I love her anyway."

"Will you talk to him?" he asks gently.

I shake my head. "I can't."

"Why?" Alec asks, squeezing my hands.

"He's with another. I'm not going to get in the way of that."

"You mean he's having a relationship with his cousin?"

"How did you?"

"He called me the moment you all but ran out of there. It's not too late Daniel, if you're willing." Alec shrugs, leaning back. "But I won't deny that you're cutting it close."

"I wouldn't know how to start, Alec." I frown, not liking his caution. "Besides I don't want to mess anything up."

"Hello, is always nice." He smiles. "If you love him, now's the time to fight Daniel. Or let him go, start dating. Ben's been worried sick."

"I don't think a phone call is a good idea." I mutter, unsure what to do.

"Who said anything about a phone call?" he asks, twisting his wrist a little to look at his watch. "He will be here in about ten minutes."

I close my eyes at that, concentrating on breathing. "I'm right here, Daniel."

"No." I frown. "I need Ben. Clayton needs you."

"I realize that our friendship is well . . . rocky at best," he frowns, "but I'd really like to work on it, maybe talk some more sometime, when you're ready. No pressure."

"How about one 'Angel' at a time."

He gives a small laugh, stepping inside. I take the time to collect my thoughts, deciding on at least talking to Clayton. It should be his choice if he wants me or whomever he's with. Ben comes out about three minutes later.

"We can go," he offers. "I didn't know Clayton was coming. I didn't answer when Alec tried to call me because I was on the line with you."

"No, it's alright Ben." I frown. "Running isn't doing any damn good, I love him."

"You contemplated suicide," Ben snaps.

"Yes, but only for a moment, because of what *I* did. And I wised up and called your ass to help me."

"But he set you off," Ben points out.

"The thought of him moving on did, yes." I admit. "Look, I'm not saying it's healthy. I promise to talk to my therapist about it. But if I can fix this, if we could be together and I can stop being so damn miserable . . . I need him, Ben. He's the other half of me."

"You're the other half of me," Clayton interrupts from behind, standing on the side lawn. Our eyes meet, and I intake my breath, but neither of us move.

"On that note," Ben stands, making a hasty exit to leave us alone.

"I'm a fucking idiot." I frown, barely registering Ben's absence.

"So am I."

"So now what?" I ask, unsure what to do.

"I don't know," he whispers, "but this living-without-you shit sucks ass. Please, Daniel, come back to me, darlin'."

My eyes well up with tears as I spring from my chair and all but knock him over, attacking him where he stands. I kiss his neck, breathing in his scent. "I'm so sorry. I'm getting help. I swear. I've just been ashamed to face you, scared you'd see me differently."

He pulls back just an inch, staring at me. "I thought, I thought you saw me differently, that you left because of what I did that night. I wasn't trying to lay it all on you like I was giving up, Daniel. I was just scared for you, and the words came out all wrong. I was afraid you might leave when you realized I was the reason you were able to get so close to him and meet the darkest part of yourself. I knew I couldn't help you alone."

"Shh, the only person I hate from this is myself. I should have listened to you, Clayton. I should have never done this. It was too personal. You were right. I needed help beyond us. Fuck, baby, I could have killed him. But I safe worded. I didn't let myself. Forgive me, please. I'm so sorry I broke us."

"I'm sorry too. I should have stopped you, but it didn't seem real. When it all came down on me, it was too late," he cries, pulling me tighter.

"It's not too late, Clayton. If you'll take me back, it's not too late," I cry. "I love you."

He pulls away from me, meeting my eyes. "I love you."

"Does this mean you will take me back?" I ask timidly, catching the cautiousness in his eyes.

He rubs the back of his neck. "I want to. But if I do, there is someone I need to explain myself to." I lose the breath in my lungs from the feeling of my heart being torn into two. *Is that a hickey? Fucking hell!* My eyes widen in shock and I look away quickly to hide the pain of him being marked by another.

"Alec implied I was cutting it close. Is he enough Clayton?" I ask needing to hear it from him. Hurt hitting me like a freight train, at the thought of truly letting him go, but I will if I must. I won't hurt him more than I already have. "If he is, I don't want to stand in the way of that."

"I think I could love him, if I'd let myself." He frowns, seeing me go green. "Don't look at me like that. This hasn't been easy, Daniel. To answer your question, yes, I'm settling and he and I both know that. But I won't end it with him unless I am fucking certain you want this."

I fight back my emotions, trying to absorb this. "I want you back in my life, Clayton. I want to be each other's again." He doesn't say anything to that, it's obvious he's not a hundred percent convinced. I can see the question in his eyes, *Is our love enough?* Unsure how to answer that, knowing his and Alec's wasn't and praying his and this new guys isn't, I deflect, "Can I ask you something?"

"Of course."

"Am I enough?" I swear my heart stops beating, waiting for his reply.

"I want you to be." He smiles nervously. "I'm willing to give this another shot, okay? Let's start here."

"Okay," I answer in relief, he's willing to give us another chance, this new guy isn't enough. I can't blame him for his cautiousness, but I hate myself for doing this to us.

"Kiss me," he whispers and our lips collide. God, I've missed his taste.

"So does this mean you two are finally back together?" Bobby calls and we break away, grabbing each other's hands which I hold up to display.

"'Bout fucking damn time!" Bobby bitches. "Come on, pizza's getting cold."

"You're right." I agree, walking up Alec's deck. "We need to go slow." Catching another glimpse of his mark I add, "Besides, you have someone to talk to first."

"Slow doesn't mean frozen, Daniel," he reminds me. "Just give me time, alright?"

"I won't hurt you again." I promise, placing my hand on his heart. "You can trust me."

His eyes speak volumes, and I know we have a long road to go. "Rome wasn't built in a day, Daniel." He smiles, opening the door and walking into the house, effectively shelving the conversation. God, please let us be able to fix this.

30
Starting Over

Daniel's Point of View

When we go inside, the atmosphere is awkward at best. Initially we spend the time catching up on the things that have gone on in our lives in the past seven months. That's when I discover that Alec and Bobby are really close friends with Amber and Ben, which is how he knew where he lived. I also find out that Ben has joined the Angels of Justice, which doesn't sit well with me at all. We exchange a look about it, and he nods, knowing he has some explaining to do later when we are alone. Clayton is in light spirits telling me that he finally let Cassandra quit the band, and he could not be happier. The group is currently scouting for a new singer, and they have some decent prospects. I also find out the *The Road to Life* has hit the top ten in the charts for six consecutive weeks.

After dinner, we all move to the living room and Clayton pulls me into him. "I'm not trying to put you on the spot, darlin', but what's this shit about you contemplating suicide?" My body goes rigid in his arms, causing him to hold me tighter, "We're all worried, darlin'. I think it would be best if you only had to explain yourself once."

"How much of that did you hear outside?"

"Enough," Clayton says, kissing my hair.

I look around the room, noticing that everyone is waiting patiently for my answer. Frowning, I lean back into Clayton's chest and idly play with his hand, putting my thoughts in order. Tracing his scar I realize I still don't know the story behind it but I'm certain it has to do with Alec. I hold back the hurt that he's allowed two separate men to mark him, yet I never have. Needing to distract my thoughts away from this selfish pain, I force my voice above a whisper, avoiding eye contact with absolutely everyone.

"I was twenty-four when I attempted suicide," I stop, biting my lower lip. "It was about a month after Liam and I had the fistfight that ended it. I was reading the Sunday paper and came across their wedding announcement. I was devastated. Up to that point, I thought . . ." *Don't you fucking cry over him, Kingsley.* "I thought he'd come back to me. I was an idiot."

"I thought I couldn't live without him. That life was meaningless. I had nothing to fall back on. He *was* my life, and I hadn't moved past him. And at the time, I didn't see how I could. So I went upstairs and started searching for the best way to end it. I considered slitting my wrists in the bathtub, but I didn't want my mom to see that. So I took a two bottles of painkillers and the sleeping pills that I was prescribed. It's a wonder I didn't fucking die."

"When did you call Ben?" Clayton asks, running his fingers through my hair. I didn't have to look up at him to know he was crying.

"I called him when I found the announcement. He must have detected something in my voice. I don't know, but whatever it was, he dropped everything and raced to my house. I remember him barging in my room and then waking up in the hospital but that's about it."

"I called 911," Ben frowned, "but the ambulances were on the opposite side of town, so I raced to your father's den and begged him for help. We carried you to my car and raced you to the nearest ER. They pumped your stomach, and you were in a coma for two days."

"My dad knows?" I ask in shock.

"Yes, but to this day, your mother and sister don't. I'm sorry, Daniel, but I couldn't carry you."

"Don't be. You saved my life. That's what matters," I answer, giving him a stern look. "Explains a lot though, doesn't it? Guess I know why we got that internship two weeks later."

"I promised your old man I would keep an eye on you. I also told him you needed a distraction and film is what you loved, so just go with it."

"So you're the reason why my dad did a one-eighty." I smile. "I always thought it was the success of getting the internship, but it was you, my best friend."

Ben shrugs. "Don't sweat it, man. I was so going to sit down with your dad either way. Or have my dad sit down with him. We were meant to do this, so we are."

We fall silent and the room gets tense again. I know what the next question is going to be. I'm just not sure how to answer it, mainly because the answer scares the shit out of me. "It was such a fleeting thought this afternoon. The moment it crossed my mind, I berated myself. I have a life, a good one. I have my family, my friend, my career. I don't need you to breathe. I prefer it, but I don't need it. Without you, I feel empty somehow, but I never thought about ending it. Not until he hugged you, but it was just pain. I knew to call for help. I knew to step away from my sleeping pills and wait for Ben."

"Your shrink put you on sleeping pills?" Clayton scolds. "Did you tell them about your past?"

"No, my shrink is a psychologist, not a psychiatrist, the difference being that my shrink, as you call him, doesn't have the ability to prescribe me medication. I thought it would be safer that way."

"But you have sleeping pills?" Clayton frowns.

"I only take them when my insomnia kicks in for more than two days," I admit. "I had my normal doctor prescribe them."

"You have insomnia?"

"Most my life really," I admit, ghosting over his ring finger. "Until I met you, until you gave me something no one else ever could."

He grips his fingers around mine in understanding, pulling me impossibly closer. "Throw them out, darlin', you won't need them anymore."

Tears seep down my cheeks and I bury my face in Clayton's chest. "You have more than one friend you know," Bobby chimes in. "Just because you refuse to talk to them doesn't mean we've given up on you."

"He's right, Daniel. They call me every fucking day checking up on you." Ben smiles and I turn my face to him. "They won't tell me exactly what the fuck happened, but I know it shook you to the core. I was beyond pissed at all of them, but Amber convinced me to watch a session. After hearing the shit that guy confessed to, I asked to join the cause."

"I still don't like it, Ben."

"There's a reason why we don't normally let those who are too close to the situation interact with the punishment." Alec frowns. "I'll never make that mistake again. You held your temper for the most part, except that last punch. When I found out you put the guy in a coma for almost a week, I knew I let you go too far."

I give a dead laugh. "You mean the one thing that I don't regret is what hurt that prick the most."

"He deserved it!" Ben snaps. "Damn it, Daniel, Tasha's basically my sister! And Seanna, I told you I knew her but I didn't tell you we dated before I met you!" *Damn small, rich circle of friends.* "She's how I knew Ashton's name to start with! Fuck. She broke up with me to date him." He fights back tears. "I'd give anything to kill that son of a bitch."

My eyes widen in shock. "Then it's a damn good thing you weren't there! That shit changes you, Ben. Believe me!"

"You think I haven't witnessed that in the past seven months!?" Ben fires back.

"ENOUGH!" Alec growls, jumping to his feet.

Ignoring him, I continue to shout at Ben, jumping to my feet and getting into his face. "Then why the *hell* are you a part of it?!" But Ben doesn't answer me. That's when I realize that his eyes are cast down. I look around the room, *all* of them are, except for Grand Master Alec.

He flares his nostrils the moment our eyes meet. "Are you going to continue to challenge me, Daniel?" he asks in a low, seething voice. I know it's a loaded question. He's asking me if I really want out. And of all of them, I'm glad it's him that's asking, especially grateful that it isn't Clayton.

"I don't know . . . Grand Master," I answer, slowly lowering myself to my knees, casting my eyes to the ground. "The jury is still out."

"Maybe if you witnessed a normal punishment?" my grand master ponders, walking around me. "I'm curious. That night you had the *balls* to challenge me in a way no other man has. You know my past, Daniel. You know that I'm the dominate one. That even *your* master kneels before me, yet you tried to take control nonetheless." He sighs. "That should have been my red flag. I should have had you brought upstairs in that moment, but I found it . . . erotic. I've never experienced a power struggle like that. I take just as much blame, if not more, for all of this fallout. I'm sorry I failed you, Daniel."

"I'm the only failure, Master." I argue. *God, I missed this role.*

"And there it is again," Grand Master says snidely, stopping in front of me. "You challenging me, except this time it's not nearly as glamorous. It's insulting. Tell me, Daniel, do you normally treat Master Clayton this way? Or would you appreciate *your* sub treating you this way?"

"I'm not sure if I have a sub, Master." I frown in admission. "I'm not sure if I trust myself for that."

He steps behind me, tugging my hair. I close my eyes to avoid eye contact while he forces my face upward. "Strip him, Clayton," our grand master instructs. Moments later, I feel Clayton's hands on me, removing my clothes.

"Part of the problem is the fact that you and I have never had a one-on-one session," Grand Master explains. "I can't honestly expect someone to bow to me if they never have before. I let my personal emotions get in the way of that. Considering you were who you were and dating who you were dating, I assumed that if Clayton respected me, then you would too. Obviously, I was wrong."

"I respect you, Alec," I retort, opening my eyes, meeting his.

His eyes narrow in anger. "You have a *very* poor way of showing it."

Realizing my mistake immediately, I close my eyes. "My apologies, Grand Master. It's been so long."

"Seven months has made you forget the basics of respect?" Grand Master growls, releasing my hair. "Then I guess it's time to remind you. Come," he demands, grabbing my left arm and taking me down the hallway. I don't argue nor do I look back at Clayton, though I want to. Grand Master has me kneel in the middle of the floor, leaving me there only to return with a clothed Bobby, Ben, and Clayton, who are instructed to kneel next to the wall.

Grand Master orders me to his horse, telling me to grab the bars where the restraints are normally attached, warning me not to move. As I stand there bent over for all of them to see, I force myself into a submissive state, trying not to flinch at Grand Master's touch. *Damn it, it has been too long, I'm an expert at stillness.* When he moves to insert a gag ball, I hesitate but decide to just go with it. It's Clayton who decides to argue, breaking his position. "No, Grand Master! . . . Lightening!"

Grand Master stops short, staring at him in confusion, "Why are you using your hard limit safe word Clayton? Am I not aware of some injury that prevents you from kneeling?"

"Please, Grand Master. I'll take twice Daniel's punishment, just don't gag him," Clayton begs, falling back to his knees.

He stares at Clayton in disbelief then back at me, displaying the ball for me to see. "Does this make you uncomfortable?"

"Extremely, Grand Master," I admit, grateful that Clayton stood up for me.

"Why didn't you use your hard limit safe word, Daniel?" he asks gently.

I don't answer him. After a very long silence, Clayton speaks out of turn again, "He pushes himself too hard, too fast. As you know, we were working on it. It's why he dropped in our last session. Please Grand Master, he's been my sub for years. I can read his body language when he's uncomfortable. That's how I kept from hurting him when he pushed himself. I understand his body's safe words just as much as his verbal usage of them."

"You realize that you are in trouble, yes?" Grand Master snaps.

"Yes, Grand Master, but he's worth it."

"So we have a style issue here?" Grand Master muses, running his fingers down my spine, before walking up to Clayton. "You really did grow quite comfortable with him, didn't you, Clayton? I didn't have much of a transition issue with Bobby. I'll admit I have a strong distaste for it Clayton, verbal safe words are essential."

"I love him, Grand Master."

"I know." He sighs, stripping Clayton of his T-shirt. "On your hands and knees, display your back horizontally for Daniel to see."

Clayton follows his instructions to the letter. Grand Master goes to his cabinet retrieving a crop, a flogger, and a whip. He takes his time preparing Clayton's back. When it is red hot, he drops the pleasure tools and prepares the whip. "Count Daniel," he instructs taking the short whip and snapping it over Clayton's skin. *Fuck.* After ten lashes, Grand Master approaches me.

"Did you see that, Daniel? He's taken punishment for *you* not using *your* safe word. If you don't want that to happen again, I suggest you speak up when you are uncomfortable. I don't read body language."

My eyes meet Clayton's for a moment, giving him a silent thank-you before dropping my gaze. "Yes, Grand Master."

Testing me, he picks up the gag ball.

"Thorn."

"Good." He smiles, tossing it aside. "Now for your lesson on respect." The sting of the flogger on my ass is beyond welcoming. Fuck I've missed this. Trying to stay silent I bite my lower lip to the point of bleeding holding back my moans. All too soon, the flogger is replaced with the whip, and damn it if that fucker didn't have a sting to it. My muscles flex with the first blow to my ass, but I do not move or scream out. "Impressive," Grand Master notes. "Most men cry out for their mothers when they first feel this whip." I don't respond, taking the rest of my ten blows in much the same way, managing not to break formation though my legs are shaking uncontrollably. After the last lash he steps away but has me remain in position. It all gets overwhelming and I find myself screaming out, "Rose, Grand Master, please!" I collapse, feeling Grand Master's strong arms catch me while my body shakes from head to toe.

"Daniel!" Clayton screams, breaking formation to come to me.

"Stop!" Grand Master growls. Clayton freezes, fear clear in his eyes. Grand Master snaps his eyes to Ben, who has also broken formation. "You two will be dealt with." He snaps. "Bobby prepare them." Bobby nods while Grand Master picks me up and takes me to a very large hall bathroom, having me sit on the toilet while he moves around, preparing things. "When we are in here, Daniel, you can speak freely unless I instruct otherwise, but don't forget I'm your master." He tests the temperature of the shower spray one last time with his hand, "Get in."

"Thank you," I smile, stepping in. "For everything."

"You know I have never once had a sub react the way you did. It fucked with my head and having Clayton in pieces . . . if it wasn't for Bobby and some trusted others, I'd have lost my fucking mind."

"I'm sorry you felt guilty, Grand Master. It wasn't my intention."

"Pushing you tonight was not mine. But if you are going to fall apart so damn easily, I'm glad it's with me and not him. You two have been through enough."

"Why are you doing this?" I ask, turning off the spray.

"Doing what exactly?"

"Taking me back under your wing like I never hurt you? Supporting us getting back together?" I frown in guilt. "I hurt your best friend, and you are welcoming me with open arms. Aren't you pissed? Or do you just hate whoever he's dating?"

"Careful, Daniel, you're blending." He warns, handing me a towel. "But to answer your question as friend to friend, it's because I love him. I've never seen that man happier or more unstable than I have when he was with you. He ate so much shoe leather I had a sinking feeling that something like this was going to happen eventually. I just wasn't expecting it to last seven damn months or involve Angels of Justice, for that matter. And yes, I was pissed. Until he walked into my back door holding your hand and giving me this look that told me he was whole again."

"Hands on the sink," he instructs. I follow his order and he starts to put familiar lotions on my ass. When he is done, he squeezes my tender cheeks tightly and his voice comes out low and threatening. "If you ever break his heart like this again, I swear I will break your fucking face." I do my best to hold back a grimace, failing miserably while I nod my understanding. "Don't jump into this blind, Daniel." Grand Master warns stepping away from me. "Talk to him. There are some things that you are not going to like but need to hear. *Then* decide if you want him. Not a moment before."

I swallow hard. "Yes, Grand Master."

"Good. Now get dressed and wait for us in the living room, when we come out you are released," he orders, leaving the room.

After about half an hour of enduring my internal monologue of a pity party and running through worst-case scenarios, trying to prepare myself for the hard truths of Clayton's dating life, everyone comes in to join me.

"Would you like a ride home?" Ben asks.

"It's alright, Ben. I'm already going to get a royal ass-chewing from Amber for keeping you so long. I really don't want to get bitch-slapped too."

"You sure, man?"

"Yeah, I'm good." I smile, standing up and stretching.

"Alright, I'll see you tomorrow. No excuses." He laughs, giving me a quick shoulder squeeze. "You have one life man, live happy."

This isn't the first time he's given me this advice. "With friends like you, how could I not?"

He drops his arm. "Tomorrow," he warns, heading for the door.

"You going to call a cab, darlin'?" Clayton smiles, knowing full well I'm stranded without his help.

"Actually, I was hoping my boyfriend would offer to drive me home."

"You're boyfriend's here?" he teases, smiling but I can see the cautiousness in his eyes.

"He is," I smile, my voice strong but my confidence timid at best.

"Well, if you're referring to me, I have no plans on takin' you home tonight."

I cringe. "I have too. Otherwise, Jeremy is going to tear the place apart after four solid hours of being alone."

His eyes go wide. "Jeremy?"

I shrug. "My black lab. It seemed fitting."

Bobby and Alec bust up laughing, and as the words sink in, Clayton joins them. "You got a dog?"

"Yep, bitch is spayed and everything."

"Holy fuck! You named a female dog Jeremy." Bobby laughs, catching it.

"No, I named a *bitch Jeremy*," I correct, and with that, I lose it, and we all start laughing.

"How does that work with all your traveling?" Clayton asks catching his breath.

"Hired help." I shrug. "I just needed something to come home to. My therapist suggested it. I thought about it, went down to the shelter and rescued her. She's had a tough life but has taken to me, her dog walker, and the maid, so all is well. Except she can't stand Tasha. Haven't figured that one out, except maybe she feels threatened with another bitch getting all the attention."

"Daniel," Alec scolds, trying not to laugh.

"What? Tasha knows I still think that."

"So you two are still cats and dogs?" Clayton frowns.

"On the contrary, we're really close." I smile. His shocked expression isn't a surprise to me, so I shrug it off.

He catches my vibe that the topic is off limits for now. "Do you think Jeremy will like me?"

I give a half smile. "Probably not at first, but you'll grow on her when she realizes you are not going anywhere. But don't call her Jeremy. Her name is Bitchy. And after you two get friendly, you can call her BJ."

"When?" he asks biting his lower lip. I frown at his continued cautiousness, and correct myself.

"If."

He can see the sadness in my eyes, and closes the distance between us, pulling me into him. "Healing takes time, darlin'. We'll get there."

"I hate this," I moan, putting my forehead on his shoulder. "We were so close to having it all and now we're starting over."

"Not from the beginning," he assures me, kissing my neck. "I'm sorry I panicked Daniel, I'm sorry I brought us here."

I gently pull back. "Don't. I am in the wrong here too, and we don't need to play this game, alright? We both fucked up. We're both sorry. We want this to work, end of story."

He drops his forehead on mine and asks in a whisper, "Can I stay tonight?"

"What about your family? From my understanding, your cousin is in town."

He lifts his head up and shrugs. "It's Thursday. I told Ma'ma I couldn't visit 'til Saturday."

"I see." I smile sadly, running my fingers through his soft hair.

"Would you like to come?" he asks and sees my hesitation. "I'm sorry. Too fast."

"No, that's not it," I rush. "It's just, well, Saturdays are Tasha's. Let me talk to her, see if I can reschedule for Sunday."

He gives me a small smile before he kisses me gently on the lips. Our eyes meet, and rather quickly after that, we have deepened the kiss while our hands start exploring frantically, only to stop short when Alec clears his throat. We both look up blushing, and Bobby rolls his eyes. "Sorry," I whisper.

Alec shakes his head, walking away. "Don't let the door hit your asses on the way out."

I blush deeper. Clayton waves to Bobby and we make it outside to his car. The ride is eerily quiet. I can tell that Clayton is nervous because he won't stop tapping the steering wheel with his thumbs. By the time we make it back to my place, the tension is so thick you could cut it with a knife.

"You want to talk about it?" I ask.

"About what exactly?" he asks, turning to me after shutting his car off in my driveway.

"What's bothering you?" I clarify. "I realize it's been seven months, Clayton, but I can still read you."

He frowns, throwing his head against his seat. "I don't want to fuck this up, Daniel, but this is going to hurt . . . a lot."

I close my eyes in painful understanding. *Fuck he didn't just date.* "How many have had the honor of calling you master?" I ask, my voice cracking while instant tears stream down my face.

"Six." He answers simply.

I swallow hard. "And your dating life? Just the one?"

He shakes his head. "Not exactly, I had three one-night stands," he shrugs, "they didn't help."

"Does he?" I ask, wiping my face.

He turns from me. "Yeah." He's quite for a while then adds. "I wasn't expecting him to and at first he didn't. We were fuck buddies but somewhere along the way things changed . . . and he did."

More tears streak down my face. I feel like he just stabbed my heart and twisted the knife. "Are you sure you want to pick me?" I ask, brushing my thumb against the mark on his neck.

"Yes." He answers, turning to me. I turn away from him, not wanting to see the conflict reflecting in his eyes.

Fuck. After a long moment, he asks, "Did you?"

"The only masters I have ever known are you and Alec," I answer firmly. "You being my one and only sub."

"Others?" he asks, his voice cracking.

"I didn't give myself the pleasure." I admit. "I came close one night, with an extra, but every time I closed my eyes, I saw you. It wasn't fair to him, so I apologized and left." Frowning, I realize how sticky this situation really could be. "Are you still a master to any of those six?"

"Yes," he answers quietly. I'm beginning to feel ill. I know I did this, me, this is my fault but it fucking hurts! *What did you expect, Kingsley? Him to put his entire life on hold for you? It's been seven months, over half a year, he moved on.* I've never wanted to drown my voice of reason more than I have in this moment. Fuck I need a drink.

"You're right, it hurts," I whisper. "I understand, I do," I assure him, squeezing his hand while falling into uncontrollable sobs. "But it fucking hurts." He doesn't say anything as he pulls me into him, letting me soak his shirt. *You had to walk out on him, didn't you?* I cry until there is nothing left in me, and when my body starts to shudder I pull back, drying my face with my hands. "So where does this leave us?"

"Besides being brutally honest with each other?" he asks. "My subs are meaningless, Daniel. As far as . . . I'll end all of it with all of them if I know that you've come back to stay."

There it was again, "If?"

"If," he responds, meeting my eyes.

"There's no 'if,' Clayton." I assure him. "Just," I take a deep breath, "were you careful?"

"Yes," he answers in a whisper.

"There's no 'if,'" I repeat.

He frowns. "I won't hold you to that quite yet." He takes a deep breath. "His name is Mike, you've met, he's my executive assistant."

Ouch! Motherfucker! Fuck! And damn, he's hot too. "Are you done with the land mines?" I snap.

"No." He frowns. "One of the one-nights was a chick." He shrugs. "Like I said, one night stands didn't help." Then he turns to me. "I know you tried to hide your pain in a liquor bottle, Daniel. Ben's been worried sick about you. Why didn't you tell him you were seeing a therapist?"

"Hell, I didn't even tell Tasha." I frown, my anger deflating a little. Then I cringe. "Mike?"

"He's a great fuck. Like I said, it just happened. Neither of us planned it, more or less what it turned into."

"He one of your subs?"

"No," he answers sternly. "I don't mix that shit, Daniel. You being the exception."

"Since you're choosing me Clayton, can you end it with all of them tomorrow?"

"It's going to take time to severe some connections, Daniel. *If* you are really in this."

He doesn't trust me. Hell, why should he? Trying to change the subject if only for a moment, I deflect, "Has Brad ever?" I ask, uncertain how to ask the question.

"No, no contact." He frowns. "Cops haven't contacted me about it either."

"I want a blood test, Clayton."

"I can respect that."

"Six in seven months?" I ask, trying to wrap my head around it.

"Multiples." He shrugs. "Two at a time."

"You hate multiples," I answer, rolling my eyes.

"I couldn't go solo, Daniel. It just felt . . . wrong."

"You burned through three pairs in seven months?" I ask, still shocked.

"I don't have patience with cum whores," he growls. "You should know that."

"Alec was giving them to you untrained." I smile, making a mental note to thank him. "He wanted you to burn through them." Clayton's eyes snap to mine. I give him a knowing look. "He loves you and knows that we were really happy together. You can't hate the guy for trying to make sure that we get back together."

"Why does it feel like you know him better than I do sometimes?" he asks. "I didn't see it that quickly, but I did see it. After the first two sets, I confronted him, threatened to go elsewhere if he kept it up."

"You were too close." I point out, looking out my passengers window. "So these last two work for you?"

"Not really," he admits then turns to me with questioning eyes. "Is Alec's optimism justified?"

"You tell me." I frown. "Is our love strong enough to survive me walking out on you? And the repercussions of that?"

"I want it to be."

"Yeah, me too."

"This won't be easy. I have to be honest, Daniel. My trust in you . . . it's damaged."

"I know. If I could take it back, Clayton, I would. But I can't."

"Can I ask you something?" He asks, taking my hand in his.

"You can ask."

He bites his lower lip. "Can you quit the liquor bottle on your own, or do you think you might need help?"

I take a deep breath and exhale slowly. "I don't know. To be honest I could really use a drink right about now." I shake my head, feeling him rub circles on my hand with his thumb, "I'd like to try the solo approach first, if you'll support me. If it doesn't work, I promise to enroll in AA."

"I will always support you Daniel. We can try the solo approach but if it gets to be too much I will ask for help." He agrees cautiously. "Is the therapy helping?"

"Yeah, I think so. I didn't hate myself enough to go through with it today. That has to mean something, right?"

"You won't stop?"

"No, Clayton. I won't stop my therapy sessions," I promise.

"Can we hold each other tonight?" he asks, tears spilling down his cheeks.

"Thought you'd never ask." I smile. He goes to open his door. "Clayton, wait." He turns to me with concern. "There's nothing else, no more land mines. Everything's out?"

He thinks about that for a moment. "Angels of Justice has changed some," he finally answers. "But you've seen how. We used to never really have meetings like that, but now Alec requires them at least once a month. He doesn't want a repeat of being challenged in front of a victim."

"So he's our grand master." I smile in relief, honestly grateful I didn't lose this connection to redeeming my past.

"Our?" he asks, carefully turning toward me.

"For now, yes. Our."

"That scares the hell out of me," he whispers.

"It won't come between us again. I promise," I answer, pulling him toward me.

"I can't lose you twice, Daniel."

"You won't," I assure him. He looks me in the eyes, searching with his pleading ones. "I swear if I get near my limits, I'm out forever. At the end of the day, I want to support this, Clayton, but I'm a selfish man. I'd rather have my heart, my soul, you." When he relaxes at my words, I smile. "Come on, let's get inside and start over."

He kisses me gently. "Not from the beginning."

"Not from the beginning." I agree.

"Alright, I guess it's time to meet the bitch of the house." He smiles.

I bust up laughing, taking his hand and stepping inside to be greeted by a very anxious BJ. Quickly, I let her outside to do her business. While I am feeding her, Clayton notices all of his letters. "Would you mind if I took these back? There are some things that I think are better left unsaid."

"Thought we were being brutally honest with each other." I frown, dropping the food in the bowl.

"Anger isn't honesty, Daniel," he replies, pocketing them inside of his coat and draping it over a kitchen chair.

"How can I make this up to you?" I ask, letting BJ back in.

"Time," he answers, hugging me. BJ lets out a friendly growl, sniffs Clayton for a moment, then heads to her food.

"Don't worry. She doesn't sleep with me or anything." I laugh watching her stare Clayton down while she chews.

"Creepy," Clayton shutters before laughing it off and kissing me, causing BJ to bark.

"Heel!" I order, causing her to whine as she sits down and stares at us, tilting her head a little when we kiss again. Breaking away, I smile. "Good, Bitchy," I encourage, throwing her a rawhide. She jumps to catch it and I grab Clayton's hand pulling him back to my bedroom and closing the door. BJ groans throwing her weight into the door; when she realizes she's shut out she lies down next to it and begins chewing her rawhide. "Don't trip on her when you wake in the morning. She's there for the rest of the night."

He smiles. "That's alright, as long as you're in my arms for the rest of the night."

We start kissing at that, but it doesn't go any further. Neither of us wants that, considering he technically isn't mine, at least not yet, and soon we are both drifting into sleep. It's the first night since I can remember where I can sleep so easily and my dreams are actually peaceful.

31
Destruction

Clayton's Point of View

~Seven Months Ago~

"It's not negotiable, Daniel. Think about it," I hear myself saying watching him frown. I stand, reaching my hand out to him. When he's on his feet, his sad eyes are boring into mine, breaking my heart. "I really do love you, and I want to be there for you, but I can't do this without help."

"I hear you," he assures me. "I should go."

"Yeah," I agree, numb. *Stand your ground, Reynolds. This is important.* But as I watch his face while he dresses, panic starts to wash over me. No, he wouldn't choose to end it. He proposed. Our love is stronger than this. But he gives no reassuring words while he walks to my front door, so I call out to him. "Daniel! I truly hope to hear from you again."

He looks at me with sadness and my heart breaks. *Oh my fucking fuck! He's ending it.* "No promises, baby," he replies in a shaky voice, "but either way, I will always love you." I'm frozen trying to gasp for air, drowning in sorrow. It's over; we ended it. And with that terrifying thought, he grabs the door and walks out of my life. *Fuck me.*

~Three Days Later~

"Clayton!" Alec calls, using his key and alarm code to get in. I hear him walk through my living room, but I don't move. I'd rather lie here and smell Daniel's scent that is still lingering on my sheets. "Clayton!" Alec calls again, walking into my room. When he turns on the light, I moan, rolling over. "What the hell happened to you? Mike says you haven't been in the office in three damn days."

"Has it really been that long?"

"Clayton? Are you alright?" Alec asks, kicking off his shoes and climbing into my bed, pulling me close to him.

"No," I answer as a fresh set of tears spill out of my eyes. "It's over."

"What's over?" Alec asks, wiping them away.

"Daniel and I, he left," I cry uncontrollably.

"Oh, Clayton," Alec whispers, holding me tighter. "What happened?"

"I'm and idiot." I sniff, "He proposed and then . . ." I fall into a hard sob, "and then I stuck my foot in my mouth and he walked out."

"Put your foot in your mouth?" Alec asks, running his fingers through my hair.

"I gave him an ultimatum: he starts therapy or it's over," I cry, picking at the sheet.

"Clayton." Alec frowns.

"I'm aware I fucked up, Alec," I snap. "He won't answer his phone or his texts. He's just gone."

"Have you thought about going over there?"

"He's not home. I know him. He's drowning in work."

"You could talk to Tasha," Alec offers.

"She's been through enough, don't you think?" I growl.

"When's the last time you ate? Drank?" Alec asks worried. My silence is the only answer he needs. Moaning, he rolls over and pulls out his phone. "Hey, love, I'm going to have to cancel. I know. I'm sorry. Yes, I'm aware of that, Bobby. It's not that simple. Daniel left. As in they broke up. Yeah. Love you too."

He hangs up the phone and climbs out of the bed. I hear the bathwater running and I moan when I feel my socks being ripped off my feet. "You can either strip yourself or I will do it for you." Alec snaps, taking his shirt off. I'd be lying if I said my dick didn't respond to his tan, muscular torso. Beautiful.

"Go away," I mutter, rolling over onto my stomach. "I don't need a mother."

"Yes, Clayton, you do."

"Out, Alec," I yell, pointing to my bedroom door. I feel my arm being twisted roughly but caringly behind my back and the other one being drawn into it. "That's not the way to talk to your master, Clayton," he growls. "Now take your damn clothes off and kneel."

I could argue that I didn't want a master, that mine abandoned me, but I couldn't reject him, not Alec. Frowning, I lift my eyes up to see the concern in his and I sigh, casting my eyes downward. Realizing that I'm accepting, he releases my wrists so I can begin stripping my clothes off. He walks away from me to attend to the bathwater. "You need to take care of yourself, Clayton." Master tells me. "Come," he orders, taking me into my bathroom. "Get in." I slowly climb into the tub. He kneels down next to it, still in his jeans, and starts to wash me. "You will live your life, Clayton. You will go to work, you will eat, and you will stay in touch with your friends."

"Yes, Master."

"You will call me every day, and we will talk." He continues.

"Yes, Master," I respond, tears spilling from my eyes. "It hurts, Master. It hurts so much." I break down in sobs, and he pulls me to his bare chest, letting me sob.

"I know. I'm so sorry. I'm here. Forgive me," he repeats over and over.

After all the tears have racked my body into painful cramps, I ask, "Master, why would you need forgiveness?"

"I pushed him too hard. I should have never let him go." Master explains, his voice telling me he's clearly upset. "Especially directly after a drop."

"He would have hated us all if you didn't. This is my fault, Alec, no one else's."

"It's Master," he growls, but that's the only response he gives me, blatantly ignoring the fact that I've been talking out of turn since we transitioned. I frown, knowing that he's not taking my reassurances to heart. He blames himself. Perfect. After he cleans my body, he gives me a shoulder massage then pulls the plug, instructing me to get out. I do, and he takes care of drying me off before ordering me in clothes. He takes me to my couch and holds me as I cry some more. Bobby ends up coming over with dinner.

After we watch a movie I realize they are not going to leave, so I open the pull out couch and call it a night.

The next day, I go to work where Mike is relieved to see me. I end up calling him into my office to tell him that I am pulling him completely from *The Road to Life* assignment, explaining that it's officially become my pet project. He's insulted by this until I assure him it has nothing to do with him and he will be needed with the everyday operations of the office.

"Does this have anything to do with your disappearance, boss?" he asks, looking me in the eye.

"Stay out of my personal life, Mike," I snap.

"I saw him yesterday. He looks like hell. Almost as bad as you do." he bites his lower lip. "If you need a friend or whatever, let me know."

"Thanks, Mike. It's appreciated."

~Three Weeks Later~

"Get dressed. We have a plane to catch," Alec growls, snapping my bedroom door open at four o'clock in the damn morning. *You have got to be kidding me.*

"Go away," I moan into my pillow.

"No, I'm on a mission to get your man back, and since he won't fly home, we're going to fly and see him," Alec growls, yanking the covers off my naked body. "Jesus," he complains when he realizes my morning wood.

I smirk. "Jealous?"

He rolls his eyes while throwing me my pants. "You have thirty minutes."

I hate flying but luckily I'm exhausted and I sleep almost the entire flight. When we get to our destination, Alec walks right up to the set, while I sit in my car stealing glimpses of my man. *He's not yours, Clayton.* This is abundantly clear when Daniel notices Alec, and walks away with some guy wrapping his arm around Daniel's waist. Ben approaches Alec and they talk for a few moments. Alec looks back at the car and Ben shakes his head. Frowning, Alec comes back empty handed.

"I'm so sorry," he whispers after he climbs in.

"Nothing to be sorry about. You didn't end it. We did. He's obviously moved on. It's time for me to," I growl in anger as jealousy takes hold.

"Clayton."

"Just go, Alec," I snap.

We still have three damn hours before our return flight, so we stop off to get some lunch. The waiter is fucking hot and is not wearing a name badge, but it doesn't matter. I need an ending, something that I can't go back from. So I excuse myself to the restroom, and on the way, I grab his hips from behind. "You know you want the ride of your life gorgeous," I exhale in his ear, tracing the shell with my tongue. I pull back shrugging, giving him a wink, and showing off my dimples while I walk backwards into the bathroom.

Not a full sixty seconds later, he's placing a sign on the door stating 'closed for cleaning' and locking us in. "What about your man outside?"

"Not mine. You clean?" I answer as he approaches me. He pulls out his wallet, grabbing his blood test results and an extra lubed condom.

"You?" Luckily I tested last week for the possibility of new subs. I don't answer verbally, handing him my results. When the formalities are finished, we crash into each other's mouths while our hands move pesky clothes out of the way. "How do you want me?" he asks, when my lips bite down on the vein in his neck.

"Bent over the sink," I answer, turning him around and pushing his loosened pants to his knees. He kicks one leg out. I rip open the condom with my teeth and roll it down my hard as fuck shaft. I spread his cheeks, lick my finger generously and shove it up his ass. He moans, and I take that as an opening, so I shove a second up his ass and begin stretching him. When I think he's ready to handle it, I ask, "You ready to ride?" He lets out a deep throat growl. I pull my fingers out only to shove my dick in his ass, grateful for the lubed condom.

"Oh fucking Christ," he gasps.

"It's Clay, but Christ will do," I moan pulling almost all the way out before slamming back into him. He groans and I start pounding him hard. Instead of looking in the mirror in front of me, though, I close my eyes and pretend I'm in Daniel's heat.

"I'm close. Oh fuck, so big," he moans, then I feel his ass tighten around my dick. Fucking cum whore! Annoyed, I keep pounding until I cum, not saying a goddamn word. Fuck, I didn't even touch the bitch. When I'm done, I pull out of him and start cleaning myself up, tying off the condom and trashing it, then washing my dick in the sink before tucking it back up.

"Thanks for the fuck," he says, passing me a cigarette.

Taking it, I let him light me up. "Back at you." I inhale and hold the smoke, enjoying the damn burn.

"You from around here?" he muses, tucking in his shirt. *Fuck! Time to go.*

"Nope, just passing through," I answer, running water over the cigarette before throwing it in the trash.

"Too bad." He frowns. "Damn fine cock you got."

"So I hear." I smirk, unlocking the door and walking back to the table. "It's time to go," I say to Alec, who is content on sitting there glaring at me.

"So that's it, then. You've given up on him?"

"Pretty much," I answer, dropping a fifty on the table.

"You're making the biggest mistake of your existence," Alec warns, standing up.

"You don't have to watch," I snap.

"You see, Clayton, I do. Because I'm the one who's going to be picking up the damn pieces," he hisses.

"I don't need you, Alec," I growl as we make our way to the car.

"Yes, you do." He argues. "Don't worry, I'm not going anywhere no matter how much you try to push me away."

~Two Days Later~

"I want subs, Alec," I state over dinner.

"Subs?" he asks, pulling back.

"Two of them," I answer matter-of-factly. "And don't start with the not-a-good idea, not-the-right time bullshit. My mind is made up. Either you help me or you don't. Either way, I'm getting two willing subs."

He exchanges a look with Bobby and then shrugs. "Fine. Two subs it is. But I want fresh blood tests."

~One Week After That~

Alec had helped me pack up my playroom. No matter how much I wanted to move on, I just couldn't see using anything in there with anyone else. So it all went into storage, and the walls got a new coat of paint. Hell, even the floors got new padding. I pulled out some of my old equipment, including my horse, and made a new setting, then I purchased some new toys and went from there.

The two subs that Alec had given me were extremely untrained. The first session was just concentrated on stillness alone. I had a fleeting thought that Alec did this on purpose, but I refused to let it detour me. Everyone is trainable to some extent. By the third session, I was confident that we could have some fucking action.

I have one of them on all fours and the other kneeling behind him. Unwilling to fuck them myself, I wrap the kneeler in a condom and prep the other. When I'm satisfied, I tell him to enter him. I straddle myself over the taker and put my dick in front of the kneeler. "Suck it," I demand, when his mouth is wrapped around my cock, I add, "Now fuck him slowly." The taker starts to shake but is wise enough to keep his mouth shut. After a relatively short amount of time, my cock gets dropped from my sucker's mouth and he starts pleading to cum. The other screams his safe word and cums, causing the fucker to cum too. Pissed, I step away from them, and that's when I notice them exchange a look and wink. Motherfucker!

"Get out, you fucking cum whores," I growl. "I told you not to fall for each other. You broke the contract. It's over."

Neither one of them say a thing as they grab their clothes, dress quickly, and leave.

Frustrated, I kick the discarded play tools and step outside for a fucking smoke.

~Three Months Since Daniel~

Nothing is helping. The subs were a bad idea, fucking falling for each other. Damn it! I hate multiples. But I can't go solo; I just can't. Every time the thought crosses my mind, the joy in Daniel's face flashes before my eyes when I told him he was my solo sub, that he pleased me the most. I can't do that again. I can't ever risk falling in love with a sub again. No, multiples are my only option, a pain in the ass, but a better option.

Frustrated, I decide to try something new, and make my way to a gay club. Drowning myself in the beat of the music does seem to have a healing effect, but it's ruined the moment I feel hands glide down my chest. "I want you," a male voice growls in my ear.

I lean my head back. "The only way that will happen, hotty, is if you bend over." I smile, showing off my dimples.

He cups my instantly hard dick. "Hmm . . . I think I could enjoy that."

Moaning, I turn to him, dropping my lips to his ear "Follow me . . ." I take him to the back, flashing my V.I.P. badge to security, who nods and points to a room. The moment the door is shut, I throw him into it. "You clean?"

"Back pocket," he gasps. I pull out a paper that has valid blood test results.

"You're diabetic."

"You gonna fuck me or what?"

Not answering verbally, I drop his pants and drag him over to the couch. Then I drop my test results in front of him and pull an extra lube condom out of my wallet. What can I say, the first guy had a good idea. This guy is impatient, stripping his pants completely off and spreading his legs, waiting. I frown, sticking a wet finger in his ass.

"How old are you?" I groan, feeling his tight ass around my finger.

"Twenty-one," he moans.

"I'm not the fucking cops, kid. I just want to make sure you are legal," I snap, pulling my finger out of his ass.

"Nineteen."

Fuck me. "This your first time?"

"Third."

"You realize this is just a fuck?"

"We gonna do it or talk all damn night?"

Smirking, I put my finger back into him and smack his ass. He moans his approval, and like an eager whore, he sticks it out further, giving it a shake. I smile to myself, but I don't smack him until I replace my fingers with my thick cock. He hisses, and I hold his hips in place. "You need to stretch. Give it a minute," I whisper, pulling him upwards so I can kiss his shoulders while I reach around and grab his cock. He moans, throwing his head back on my shoulder. I take it nice and slow for a while, letting him melt. When I'm satisfied that I'm not going to hurt him, I whisper. "You ready to be fucked?"

He gasps, when I throw his weight back onto the couch, pounding into him hard and fast. The only sound in the room is flesh on flesh. While I'm riding him, Daniel's face floats through my closed eyelids and I start pounding harder, faster.

"Fuck, close," the guy beneath me gasps. I smack his ass telling him to cum and I join him in the bliss. When I come down from my high, I quickly pull off the condom, pocket it and tuck back up.

"You're going to be sore in the morning." I warn, tucking my shirt into my pants, and grabbing my tests results. "I suggest you skip the gym tomorrow." He blushes, fumbling with his belt. I put one of Alec's business cards in his pocket. "If you're interested in BDSM, he's the best and can find you a perfect fit."

"Do you trust him?" he asks, to my retreating form.

"With my life, kid. Seriously, it's a hell of a lot safer than picking up strangers in a club. He's also a good listener if you ever want to talk. Tell him Clay sent you."

"That your name?"

"Best you're gonna get." I smile, flashing my dimples, pulling the door open and make my way down the hall to the nearest exit. After lighting up a cigarette, I text Alec in warning, hoping Mr. John Doe does call him before he fucks his life up royally.

~The Next Day~

We are in the middle of watching a baseball game when I turn to Alec. "I want another set of subs."

"What happened to the first set?"

"Cum whores," I growl, rolling my eyes at his raised brow. "Regardless, they broke their fucking contract."

"I'll see what I can do." He mutters, turning back to the game. "By the way, the kid called. Nice save, Clayton. He was circling the drain."

~**One Week Later**~

The moment I meet these subs, I know they are going to disappoint. But I let them pass the initiation anyway. If Alec keeps this shit up, I'm going to have to find a new damn supplier. My thoughts are floating to Daniel while a wet limp mouth is attempting to suck my cock. I find myself desperately wishing for Daniel's talented tongue, desiring the way he gave just the right amount of suction. Craving the way he yanked up and down my shaft, teasing my slit with the tip of his tongue only to drop his lip down to my balls and suck one in while he licks it. I moan and attempt to grab this new guy's hair, but it's too short for my fingers and it kills my daydreams. Frowning, I suffer through and change the lesson to delayed gratification. This guy just was not doing it for me, nor was the other one. *F-U-C-K!*

~**Three Weeks Pass**~

"Boss, you have a delivery," Mike calls over the intercom.
"Well, sign for it and move on."
"I'm sorry, boss, she needs your personal signature."
"Seriously?" I frown. He doesn't answer. "Fine, let her in," I growl, disconnecting the phone.
Not much later, this beautiful fucking brunette walks through my door. "Special delivery for one Clayton Reynolds." She smiles.
"What is it?"
"A thank-you, I think." She smiles passing me black roses and walks around my office, admiring the different things. "Careful, that's not water," she whispers. "It's acid."
I pull my brows together, and immediately my mind snaps to Brad. "Why are you telling me?" I ask cautiously, knowing that it probably wasn't the plan.
"Because if that bitch let you go, then it's her own damn fault." She smiles, dropping her hand from my bookcase with a smile. "I'm Rose by the way."
Rose? Are you shittin' me? "Who sent these, Rose?"

"I think her name was Cassandra." She cringes, approaching me. "So does this mean you are single, handsome?"

My eyes narrow slightly. "Something like that."

She giggles a little, and one of her long ass legs comes out of the high-cut slit of her skirt. I give an apologetic smile. "I hate to disappoint you, but you're not exactly my type."

"And what type would that be?" she asks, tracing the waistband of my pants.

"The type with a dick," I answer dryly while her hands make their way to the small of my back.

She squeezes my ass cheeks. "See, I knew she was hiding something," she giggles. "Have you ever tried the other side, sexy?" she asks, nibbling on my neck. I moan while she pushes my surprising boner into her. "Obviously you are attracted," she notes. And the thing is, I am attracted to her. I have no idea why, but I have a strong feeling it's the fact that her name is Rose. Deciding not to question my body's response, I lower my head down and dominate her mouth, causing her nails to skim my neck. The taste of lipstick is a total turnoff, but she jumps me. *Fuck it, why not?* I clear my desk with one swipe of my arm and lay her down on it. She laughs as she rolls over. "I think you might be more comfortable like this, baby cakes. Don't even think about putting that rod where you normally do."

Laughing, I pull my wallet out and dig for a condom, then I undo my pants. My dick is starting to go limp, too limp for a condom so I stroke myself while I gently remove her underwear. My finger searches for her opening once I hike up her skirt. I am beginning to freak out, but at least I don't have to look at it.

"Ladies first," I moan, trying to buy time to re-harden. I bend and twist my fingers, looking for the woman's sweet spot, but completely uncertain what the fuck I'm doing. She doesn't seem to mind though, because she's panting and withering like a whore beneath me. When I'm self-stimulated enough to rubber, I put my condom on. That's when I notice Mike walk in and freeze in his tracks. I put my finger to my lips and motion him to stand in the corner that her head is turned away from, giving him a please-help-me look. Understanding my predicament, he quietly closes the door and doges out of sight, then he starts touching his nipples through his dress shirt and drops one hand down to his cock, fisting himself. The visual works surprisingly well, making me wonder what those pesky clothes are hiding. I plunge my way into this women's hot, wet tunnel, finding that if I close my eyes or stare at Mike, I can pretend this is normal. But every time I close my eyes, I see Daniel. Damn it! Will he ever stop haunting me? "Oh, yes! Right there baby cakes!" she screams beneath me, lifting her head up. Mike quickly dodges out of her line of sight and comes up behind me, resting his hands on my hips and pressing his clothed, hard cock into my naked ass while I pound this woman to oblivion. Suddenly, she freezes and then goes limp. I'm assuming she's cum, so I let myself think of Daniel and cum deep inside of her. Mike drops his hands and heads for the door, and I pull out of her removing the condom.

"So you a switch-hitter, after all?" she asks pulling her skirt down and stuffing her panties in her purse.

"Sorry. I prefer my tunnels a little tighter." I frown with a shrug. I can tell my comment hurt her, but she manages to somehow walk out of there with her head held high. If she only knew.

"So you switched to women?" Mike shrugs, entering my office while I'm still buttoning my pants.

"Stay out of my personal life, Mike," I growl. "Unless you want to be unemployed."

He comes up to me and roughly pushes me against a nearby wall, pressing his hard-on into me. "You want to self-destruct? Fine! But knock it off with the stranger's boss. Do you want to end up with some shit you can't get rid of that could kill you?"

"You offering?"

"Fuck, yes," he growls, capturing my lips. The kiss is hotter than I thought it would be, and the moment he shows weakness, I push his hands off me and grab him by the waist, spinning him around and bending him over my desk, where the fresh fuck was. I unbutton his pants and drag them down to his ankles. He kicks out of them handing me some lube and a condom. I dutifully attend to both of us quickly, and the next thing I know, I'm buried in his hot tight ass, thinking of Daniel.

"Fuck, boss, yes," Mike growls, standing on his toes for a different angle, knocking me out of my daydreams. I grip his ass cheeks and give a good squeeze, causing him to release a deep-throated moan. "Always knew you'd be a fucking great lay," he gasps. "Right there. Fuck yes. Tell me when." I smile at that. At least the damn man was trained. After a good fifteen minutes I reach the point of no return and smack his ass, ordering him to cum. We both ride out our orgasms for a good three minutes.

When I finally pull out of him, I collapse in a guest chair, and he mimics my actions.

"Holy shit!" he pants.

"Yeah."

"Fuck buddies?"

"Yeah."

~One Month Later~

These subs are on my last fucking nerve. Every damn session, they fuck up, and I've tried to be patient, I have. But I have had enough. And this evening proved the end of my patience when my calf was coated with cum from a really fucking pathetic blow job. Enough!

~One Week Later~

"I need new subs, Alec, and if you don't get me ones that can fucking suck a damn cock and control themselves, I'm going elsewhere," I growl over the phone.

"You know the trained ones are hard to find, Clayton."

"I'm serious, Alec. He's not coming back, so get over it, and get me some decent fucking subs."

This time he listens to me. I never thought I would be more happy when a sub shook in fear and apologized for cumming involuntarily. Yes, I can at least work with these two.

~Six Months Since Daniel~

It's been six months since he walked out on me, six months since I had any type of contact with him. I had tried everything I could think of, but all my reaching out did no good. He hated what I turned him into, end of story. I had caved a few times and called Tasha, just checking to make sure she was alright. She was always polite and begged me not to give up on her pigheaded brother, but I told her he's the one who gave up on me, which was evident when his cell phone number got disconnected. I had even tried to send letters but they were turning more and more angry, so I thought it best to stop. The emptiness in my chest is still there, but I've learned to live with it. Alec and I are drifting further apart, I'm sick of his guilt and optimism over the damn thing. I've talked to Bobby about it and he seems to understand how I feel and has kept us apart more and more. I've thanked him for it, and he just nodded, telling me that when the time is right, I will find someone. And when I do, Alec and I will work things out. I just smiled and agreed, but my voice was dead. I had found someone. Short as it may have been, he was the one.

Sitting here in my self-loathing, I curse when my damn doorbell rings. I need to stop giving people the code to my gate. I frown further when I find Mike on the other side.

"I have a few vacation days built up." He shrugs, bringing in two bags of groceries.

"Your point?"

"I'm aware of the date. I have a feeling we are going to be tuckered in for a while."

"You have the balls to ask for me here?"

He turns to me. "I'll sleep on the fucking couch and bend over it too. But you need to eat. I know you well enough by now that if it's not stuffed down your damn throat when you are in these moods, you won't."

"Alec put you up to this?"

"Alec doesn't approve of this," he reminds me, wagging his fingers between me and him. "He can go fuck himself, for all I care. I'm worried about you."

"Fuck buddies don't worry about each other."

"I'm more than that, Clay. I'm a friend, whether you like it or not." He shrugs. "Not saying I wouldn't drop your hot ass the moment something real comes along, but until then . . ."

"And had someone turned your head, would you be here?"

"Yes, but I wouldn't be planning on bending over for you."

"How many days of vacation?" I ask, walking up to him to undo his pants.

"Four plus the three-day weekend but I have other plans here and there," he moans, our lips meeting. The kiss becomes passionate quickly as we discard our clothes. He drops to his knees and begs before I shove my dick in his mouth. His talented tongue starts working my shaft while his hand reaches up and yanks my balls. I stifle a moan, throwing my head back while I just feel. I lace my fingers through his hair, wishing it was as long as Daniel's, while I begin to fuck his mouth, all too soon my stomach gets that familiar knot.

"Fuck, you can give head!" I curse, shoving my dick down his throat while he swallows my cum. He smirks and licks me clean.

"Thanks for the warning."

I roll my eyes and help him make dinner.

Three days later, we just finished up a movie, and our lips start to tease each other's skin. "This could be something, you know," he whispers, "if you want it to be."

I pull back and look at him shaking my head. "I'm sorry, Mike. I don't do relationships."

He sighs but doesn't stop kissing me. "Hopefully, I'll be here when you change your mind," he whispers, fisting my cock in his hand. I moan at the sensation, and suddenly the atmosphere is caught on fire. We quickly strip our clothes and open the pull out couch. He turns slightly and my eyes widen. "Michael!" I gasp in horror, staring at his bruised ass and back.

"Don't freak out!" he pleads. "I deserved this, and Alec recommended him. I'm fine."

"Define 'deserved.'"

"I didn't use my safe word and had a major panic attack that almost landed me in an urgent care." He explains. "I swear to you, Clay, it was just punishment. I'm not being abused."

"Can I meet your master? Or will you at least let Alec?"

He stares at me for a moment. "Alright. I'll arrange it."

"Good." I smile, grabbing his hands and pulling him to me. "Now come here and let me kiss it all better."

We kiss slowly, deeply, before I stretch him out on the bed kissing and licking his sore skin. "I'll be right back," I whisper in his ear, he whimpers softly but doesn't move. Being as careful as I can, when I return, I put my three favorite lotions on his skin. "This will help heal it faster," I explain, giving feather light kisses in the trail of my lotioned hands. After I am satisfied, I pop the lube cap, that I also got from the bathroom, and start to finger fuck him.

"Goddamn, Clay, you're fingers are fucking heaven," he moans, relaxing into my touch easily. I give a smirk to that, ripping a condom packet with my teeth, putting it on one-handed while I make him squirm beneath me. Eventually, I decide to stop my teasing and replace my fingers with the long thick cock pressing into him gently, keeping my weight off him, cautious of his bruises.

"Please Clay, fuck me," he begs after a few short strokes. Who am I to deny him? I pull out of him and count to ten before I slam into him and start riding him hard. A caveman-like growl escapes his throat as he lifts his ass to the perfect angle that has him fisting the sheets and calling to the heavens. He keeps saying my name over and over, and I keep hitting him harder and harder.

"Fuck Mike, cumming," I warn, grabbing his dick and stroking it until we are both cumming.

As I roll off him to catch my breath, the thought occurs to me. *This is the first time I didn't think about Daniel to get off.* Terrified, I roll off the bed deciding on a shower. Fuck, I'm officially over him.

~This Week~

Mike comes into my office for a meeting and winds up on his knees while I sit in my chair. My office phone rings and I growl, "I told you to hold all calls until after my three o'clock."

"It's your mother, sir," Mike's assistant explains.

Fuck! "But her through," I mutter hanging up. "Be good," I warn Mike before picking up the phone. Unfortunately, Mike doesn't take my warning to heart and continues to suck my dick as my mother starts rambling. I have to squeeze my eyes shut to concentrate and participate in this phone call.

"I understand, Ma'ma. I know he's coming on a Thursday, but I can't get down there 'til Saturday." I bite my lower lip, trying not to moan from Mike's motions on my steel rod. "I can't take off. I'm in the middle of a huge project." I feel myself in his throat, causing me to drop my head back trying not to gasp aloud. "No, it's not that we don't get along. We get along just fine," I answer, trying to stay coherent while he picks up his motions. "No, I'm not getting sick, Ma'ma. I'm just stressed." Fuck, Mike's going to pay for this. "I'll pick him up at the airport, I promise," I assure her, tugging on Mike's hair, trying to get him to stop. He just looks up at me through his lashes and smirks.

"Mr. Reynolds, your three o'clock is here to see you," Mike's assistant chimes in over the speaker phone. I look at the clock, they're early. Mike just pulls my chair closer to my desk and scoots himself further underneath. I try to argue, but his legs are wrapped around the wheels, and before I can respond properly, my door is opening. Fuck. "Ma'ma, I have to go. I love you too," I answer, motioning my new guests to take their seats. When I get off the phone, I write a note on a sticky and pretend to put in a drawer, but Mike takes it.

You will pay for this, so you better make it fucking worth it.

The next thing I know, I feel his nose buried in my balls, and his tongue is inside my entrance. I clear my throat, trying not to kick in surprise, I was expecting a blowjob not a rimming. This damn meeting is supposed to be an hour fucking long. I work on keeping a decent conversation and cough when Mike inserts a finger along with this tongue. To avoid the risk of groaning out loud, I lean forward, thus effectively cutting Mike's mouth off from my ass but accidently trapping his finger. I try to concentrate, while he sucks and rolls my balls with his mouth. Not much later, I am discreetly putting my hand under my desk to grip his hair, pulling him back up to my cock. The moment he swallows me down his throat, I cum. I don't know how the hell I maintained control or eye contact, but I did.

I make the mistake of thinking that since I came, he was finished with me, but he was far from it, my eyes involuntary widen when he wiggles his trapped finger in my ass and begins sucking my sensitive balls. For the next forty minutes, he continues to tease me, keeping me hard and on edge, only relenting to stave off orgasm just to tease me some more. Meanwhile, I'm trying not to whimper from my sensitivity and pleasure. I give him anal access again, just to relieve the pain, but his teasing tongue gets me so worked up, I am almost sweating while I'm attempting to bargain cost with our external marketing firm. Completely at wits end, I lean forward again and endure more of his mind-blowing blow job on my sensitive rod, but this time, when I'm on edge, instead of neglecting my needy cock to avoid orgasm, he fucking cock blocks me with his fucking tight grip around the base of my shaft. It takes everything I have not to scream. *Fucker's going to pay for that.* I can feel the smirk on my nuts as he starts to work me up again. When they finally leave, I pick up my phone. "No interruptions or you are fired," I warn his assistant. When I hang up, I clear my desk with one swipe and pull Mike up off the floor and bend him over my desk. Fucker is naked. "Stay," I order, walking to the door and locking it. Then I walk back up to him and slap his ass. "I told you to be good."

"But it was good, wasn't it?" Mike asks with a smirk.

I don't bother taking the time to stretch him one finger at a time. Instead, I start out with two and lift his ass so I can stroke his cock. When I'm sure he's holding back his pending orgasm, I stop everything and step away from him, sitting down in a guest chair, watching him lie there and suffer through blue balls. When he stops whimpering I lean forward and kiss him senseless. "Learn your lesson?" I ask, amused.

"Fucking fuck me already, Clay," he snaps. The authority in his tone is new, but I find that I like it and my dick twitches. I don't deny him his request, slamming my rubber wrapped dick into him hard and fast, reaching around to stroke him until white ropes of cum spill all over my desk. Then I wrap my arms around his broad chest and lift him to me, fucking him until my legs are about to give out as I cum deep within his heat. "MIC-HAEL!" *Fuck me.*

He turns to me, his eyes pleading. "Clayton, please make me yours," I freeze. He never calls me Clayton. I search his face and it's clear he didn't slip.

I hesitate for only a moment. Then I crash my lips into his and sit him on the edge of my sticky desk. "I'm out of condoms, Mike," I whimper, pressing my thumb into his ass.

"I trust you, Clayton," he moans, grabbing my overly sensitive cock. "Please, if you want this, show me." I know I care for him. Could I be his? He lifts his eyes to me. "I will never hurt you," he promises, and it's my undoing. I press my bareback cock into him and moan at the warmth of his heat. Something shifts in that moment, and we both give each other something we had been holding back. He places his palms at the edge of my desk using it for leverage, slamming his ass up and down my shaft as he truly lets go. I hold him by his ass with one hand and work his sexy cock with the other. We've fucked enough that I know his body well and I use my knowledge and work him into a frenzy. "Fuck, Clayton, so goddamn good," he moans, working his hips.

"God, Mike, you are so fucking sexy," I gasp. "Let go, darlin'. Let me watch you lose control." He lets out a deep growl and squeezes his ass around my hyper-sensitive dick. "That's it, darlin'," I encourage.

"CLAY-TON!" he gasps, pulling his weight onto me by my neck, slamming our lips together as he fights off his orgasm. "Tell me," he demands, breaking the kiss before kissing me again. "Tell me this means something to you."

I put my forehead on his and continue to rock as I make my way to a wall. "It means something, Michael," I whisper, pressing his back against the cool drywall. "If you'll have me, I'm yours."

"Fucking hell, Clayton," he moans, placing his wrists in my hands. I take his hint and pin them to each side on the wall, fucking the hell out of his ass until my sore cock painfully explodes into yet another orgasm. "Yours!" he gasps, when I shout out, seeing only white.

Slowly I bring us down to the floor. "Please Clayton, if you mean it, mark me, claim me." he begs, coming down from his high.

"I mean it." I smile, leaning in to kiss and nibble his neck before I find the perfect spot that will show above his collar. I suck his skin hard in between my teeth and grab his neck, holding him in place as I bite down, locking my jaw. His stubby nails dig into my back and he moans while I lick and suck his trapped skin until it is numb. I twist my mouth to a different angle causing him to gasp out and then I break away. Keeping his neck exposed to me I smack his fresh mark hard and smile at his yelp. Then I blow on his skin. "Now fuck off and get to work so we can go back to your place and fuck all night long." I smile pulling back.

"Not yet Clayton." He argues, holding me to him. Our eyes meet and I know he's challenging me. I lean into him, offering my neck while dropping my lips to his ear. "Make it visible darlin'. I want the world to see that I'm yours." He doesn't hesitate and sinks his teeth deep into my upper neck. I hiss, it's been so long since I've allowed anyone to mark me, I've forgotten how much it stings. I've also forgotten how much I like it.

"That's it darlin'." I encourage grabbing his dick. "Make it dark, don't stop until you cum." He moans on my neck and I feel his breathing falter while he works to breathe through clenched teeth. I stroke him with one hand while the other tangles in him hair. I'm his, he's mine. When I take him to the edge he grunts out, twisting my skin while he covers my hand in cum. He pulls back gasping and licks his mark before he slaps it.

"Okay, now I'm going." He whispers, his eyes falling to his mark. I kiss him gently before lifting him off me. He crosses my office and grabs my pants from under my desk, stuffs the pockets with tissues and tosses them to me. I quickly clean up and redress. He dresses quickly and comes back to help me with my tie. "Mine." He growls nibbling in my ear before leaving my office with a slight limp. I smirk, knowing that his ass is sore from my dick. I finish dressing myself and exit out my personal entrance. As I light up, I rub my neck and smile.

~Yesterday~

I'm waiting for my cousin in the airport, tapping my foot impatiently. Damn flight is delayed, and I'm officially late for a meeting. I had called Mike to tell him what's going on, and he assured me he would take care of it, telling me not to worry. That really annoyed me because I wanted to meet with these clients one on one myself, but shit I can do about it now.

Trying not to be frustrated, I search the faces of the latest passengers, and my heart stops. *Holy shit!* Our eyes meet, and I'm about to walk up to him, when my cousin fucking ruins everything and hugs me. Hugs me! Seriously, we're close but not that close. I can see Daniel swallow hard as pain crosses his features. He doesn't even grab his luggage. He just bolts.

"Daniel!" I call out, but if he did hear me, he doesn't answer.

"Clayton?" Ben asks, approaching.

"He forgot his luggage." I frown, turning away from him. I didn't need his worry today, not with my cousin here. "Come on. Ma'ma's going to get worried."

I all but drag him out of there, ignoring him completely as I dial Alec's number. "I saw him. Damn it, Alec."

"Did you talk to him, Clayton?"

"No, my fucking cousin had to hug me and . . . he ran," I cry into the phone, ignoring my cousin's stares.

"Do you want to talk to him, Clayton? You seem to be moving on from him."

"There is no moving on from him," I answer in a whisper.

"I'll see what I can do. No promises," Alec moans. "You better appreciate this. Amber is going to have my ass!"

"What are you going to do?"

"I'm going to figure out how to get Ben to bring him to my place. I suggest you figure out how to get here in a hurry if you don't want to miss him. I can't guarantee he won't run," Alec warns.

"Thank you." I smile into the phone, pulling out my wallet.

"What's going on?" my cousin asks when I push him into the taxi line, handing him a hundred.

"I have to go. Tell Ma'ma I'm really sorry. I just have to go," I respond, leaving him there dumbfounded as I race to my car. God, please don't let me be too late.

~Present Day~

I can't sleep. I'm lying here holding a man that I know I love and I can't fucking sleep. Frustrated, I find my jeans and throw them on quietly tiptoeing to the door. Before I walk out of the room, I notice the clock: 3:02 a.m. Sighing, I walk into the hallway.

"Yelp!"

"Fuck!" I curse, tripping over BJ.

"Clayton?" Daniel asks, bolting upright in bed.

Damn it. "Sorry, darlin'. I just need some fresh air," I whisper. "Go back to sleep." I don't wait for a response, making my way to my coat to pull out my pack of smokes and a lighter before stepping out onto his patio in the dark. Yawning, I sit down on the concrete half wall that separates the patio from the lawn and stretch my legs out in front of me. I light up and pull out my phone to check my text messages, finding three from Mike.

6:03 p.m. Meeting went great! Can we meet up for dinner tonight?
7:49 p.m. Hope your cousin is safe, text me alright, I'm worried.
10:17 p.m. Miss you Clayton. Yours, Mike

"You smoke?" Daniel asks, scaring the hell out of me, causing me to lose my balance and drop my phone. "Shit Clayton, I'm sorry."

Frowning, I grab my cell and pocket it quickly before I reposition myself back on the wall. Taking a long drag, I hold it in my lungs for a moment before slowly exhaling. "It's a habit I had kicked years ago."

His eyes look sad as he takes a seat in a patio chair. "I thought you were leaving."

My eyes narrow as I take another long pull. "Not unless you want me to."

"I don't," he answers, his eyes meeting mine in the bright moonlight.

I turn from him, unsure what to say, "I'm not the man you fell in love with, Daniel."

"Neither am I," he shrugs. "That night changed us both, forever."

"Yeah, that night and my stupid fucking mouth."

"I told you, don't. You were right to want me in therapy. I went."

"An ultimatum, Daniel? I fucking knew better," I argue, taking another drag of my cigarette. "I just wasn't sure that I could get through to you any other way, and I jumped to the conclusion that I couldn't. And here we are." I exhale.

"I'm the proud one."

I don't say anything for a moment while I continue to drag on my cigarette. "You know, I was with Alec the day he hunted you down on the shoot. I was waiting in the car," I admit, still not looking at him. "But you refused to even talk to him, and then that guy wrapped his arm around you, and you went with him willingly. That's when I knew it was over. That's the day I moved on." I look over at him, seeing the pain in his face. "Alec begged me not to. He told me that you just needed time. But when do I ever listen to good advice?"

"So why did you replace Mike with yourself on *The Road to Life* project?"

I wanted to torture myself and kick that no-name's ass. "I was hoping to see you, face-to-face. I knew that if I could just see you," I whisper. "But you avoided me like the fucking plague. You all but dropped out of the project the moment Mike left. That's when I started the subs. Then I met her . . . Rose." I smirk, putting my burned cigarette out and lighting another. "I'm sure you understand the attraction." I laugh humorlessly.

"Fucked her right there on my desk. Mike walked in on us but didn't make his presence known, well at least to her. When she left, he cornered me, telling me if I was going to self-destruct, then I should do it responsibly. Our argument got heated, and the next thing I know, I have him bent over with my dick up his ass listening to him moan my name. Believe me, I was shocked. He's so not my type."

"But you kept fucking him?" Daniel questions with a raised eyebrow.

"Yep, kept fucking," I answer, taking another long drag. "He was safe. I knew he was clean. I knew he knew it meant nothing. We both took what we needed and lived our separate lives. But as time went on we realized that we were more than just a causal fucks."

"How did you know your two other one-nights were safe?" he asks in a whisper.

I shrug. "They had updated blood test results. Like I said, it happened after you shut Alec out. I was so fucked-up I took a guy on a public bathroom sink on the way home and another in a back room at a club."

"Have you been tested since?" he asks, pain clear in his voice.

"Two weeks ago. Still clean." I assure him, "I wasn't an idiot, Daniel. I used a rubber every time, well until recently."

"Even with your subs?" he asks in a harsh tone.

I jump off the wall and sit in the chair next to him. My anger clear on my face as I toss my cigarette on the concrete. "I told you. You are the only one I've ever gone bareback with." He nods, looking down at his hands. Wanting to give him something I reluctantly admit, "I haven't fucked any of them." His eyes flash to mine. "Advantage of multiples, they can fuck each other. Not saying I haven't gotten plenty of head, if you can call it that, but that's a part of being a master."

BJ starts barking uncontrollably, but Daniel chalks it up to jealousy and tells her to heel. She whines a little more but eventually groans and lies down, looking nervous. Daniel turns his attention back to me.

"So three guys, one girl," he whispers, taking my hand. "And smoking."

"The smoking bothers you?"

"Not enough to give you an ultimatum, but I normally don't date smokers." His eyes meet mine as he laces our fingers. "I want to grow old with you, Clayton. Please don't cut your life expectancy with those things."

"Now look whose five steps ahead," I moan, throwing myself back in the chair, breaking our connection. "Why are you being so forgiving? I know this shit hurts. It's not something that I can just say. Well, it's the past. It happened. Let's move on."

"Just because I had a hard time moving past you, Clayton, doesn't mean I expected you to. I figured eventually you would find someone. And in the airport, when I thought . . ." he stops, trying to steady his breathing. "One-night stands are easy to move past, since you've tested clean. Mike hurts baby, he hurts bad, especially considering I know him. The subs hurt too, but I'm more jealous than anything. The only one who should please my master is me." He drops his head down and runs his fingers through his long hair. "You said yourself you are settling with Mike, and you're here, with me." He swallows hard, "I'm not in a relationship. We both seem miserable without each other, we both seem to want this to work. So what's left, Clayton? We dwell on the shit we did when we were apart? Or we forgive each other and ourselves and move on?"

"You're right, I am here, I want to choose you, but I have to be sure you're in this, really in this Daniel." I reiterate.

"I'm in this, Clayton, for life," he promises in a whisper.

I study him for a moment, seeing the sincerity of his statement in his eyes. I know he means it today, but tomorrow? The next? "It's late. We should try to sleep." I sigh, throwing myself into my chair. "Fuck, I don't want to go to work."

"Then don't." Daniel shrugs.

"I can't avoid him forever. Besides, when I pull that shit, he just shows up at my house. Well, either him or Alec. They tag team. It's so fucking annoying."

"You're dreading ending it with him?" he asks in a pained voice.

I chew on the inside of my cheek. Do I really want to end it with Mike? Can I trust Daniel won't run again? Is Daniel worth the risk? "The aftermath is going to suck," I admit not wanting to share my hesitation. "Having to see him daily. He's too damn good to let go, never mind the possible lawsuit and shit. I'm just dreading the awkwardness. But I still want him as a friend, if he'll agree to it."

"So another friend who's had feelings for you." He mutters. "Fuck, Clayton, of all people, it has to be the one guy you are closest to professionally."

"We are friends, Daniel. Accept that or move on now." I snap. I can see the hurt in his eyes, but I don't give a shit. He did this to us. He has to deal with the fucking fallout. He bites his lower lip, turning away from me. "Alec didn't approve," I admit. "Not the fuck buddy part, the Mike part. Looking at your face now, I can see why."

"You're in a serious relationship, Clayton. You let him mark you for fucksake!" He cries, tears streaking down his cheeks. "Am I too late?"

"No," I assure him, climbing on top of him. "Please, Daniel, I love *you*."

He gives me a sad smile as he runs his fingers through my hair. "Then end it with him," he whispers. Dropping his hand, he adds in a pained voice, "It's late, Clayton. You should go."

I take a few deep, calming breaths, clamping my legs around his waist. "I'm not going anywhere, darlin'. You are *not* going to shut me out again."

"I'm not shutting you out." He argues with a sad smile, ghosting his fingers over Mike's mark. "This just doesn't feel *right*, not yet. Forgive me, baby but let's respect your friendship with him."

"Daniel, I . . ."

I'm stopped with his finger on my lips. "You and your best friend are in love with each other. Hell, his partner is in love with you too. I just don't think you realize how easy it is to fall for you, Clayton." He sighs. "I've accepted both of them and given time, I will accept Mike too. But I won't be surprised if he has fallen in love. He was there for you when I abandoned you, and for that, I am forever indebted. I just don't want to start this off wrong. I want to go back to us with no commitments to anyone else as boyfriends or masters."

"I can't end it all in a day, Daniel." I moan. "And I really want you to meet my Ma'ma."

"There's always another day."

"No, there's not." I whisper, taking his hand. "She's not doing so well."

"Clayton?" he asks in a sad voice.

"It's alright," I respond. "She's been sick for years and she won't admit she's dying, being as stubborn as she is. But she's been asking to see all our family, making arrangements. I know she's saying goodbye. I can feel it in my bones." I lift my eyes to his. "I can end it with Mike later today. *Please* let that be enough for now. *Please.*"

He takes a deep breath, pulling me into him. "Only on the condition that I can talk to Mike."

"Thank you," I whisper, kissing his neck. I pull back a little, kissing his lips, but when I trace his bottom lip with my tongue, he denies me. Hurt, I pull away, searching his eyes.

"Not until you end it," he whispers. "Well, that, and you brush your teeth."

I give a small chuckle. "I'll buy some gum today too."

He wraps his arms around me, and we just hold each other until the sun comes up. "Promise me you won't change your mind," I whisper when I feel his arms fall to our sides.

"The choice isn't mine, Clayton. It's yours."

I pull back, searching his eyes for a long moment before I whisper so softly, "I love you."

"I love you."

"I'm going to go now. Will you call me, seeing as I don't have your number?" I frown.

He smiles, digging my forgotten cell phone out of my pants pocket and programs his number. "Just leave with your shirt on." He smiles, tapping my ass playfully. "What will the neighbors think?"

"Lunch?" I ask standing up. "Then a meeting with Mike?"

"Sounds like a plan." He smiles, walking back into the house. "I'll see you at one."

I take my phone and give him a quick text. *I miss you already.* He seems surprised to hear his phone alert but makes a beeline to his bedroom, I follow him to retrieve my shirt. When he reads it, he smiles with an eye roll. "One o'clock." He laughs. "I have to get moving. Otherwise, Ben is going to have my ass."

"It's my ass." I growl.

"It will be." He smiles.

Sighing, I grab the rest of my clothes and coat, dressing hurriedly before heading out his front door. That's when I notice my windshield. *Oh, hell no.* Careful so as to not disturb anything, I read the message that was written in shoe polish before it was smashed.

I told you to stay away from him bitch. He's mine!

32
Painful Endings, Delightful Beginning

Clayton's Point of View

I stare at my car and notice that not only is my windshield destroyed, all four tires are flat, so are Daniel's. *Bitch.* I look around for a moment before I make my way back into Daniel's house, trying to stay calm. I hear water running and assume Daniel is in the shower, so I call Alec.

"So how did it go?" Alec asks in a friendly voice.

"I need you to pick me up from Daniel's." My voice comes out in an unexpected whisper and I clear my throat, trying to get volume.

"What? Your car won't start? Call a mechanic. I'm about to start a meeting," Alec complains.

"No, Alec. It's Brad."

"Motherfucking hell! Not again!" Alec growls. "Are you alright?"

"He smashed my windshield and slashed my tires, Alec. I'm fine." I assure him. "Can you please come get me? Daniel's tires are flat too."

"Damn it, Clayton, this is the worst timing."

"You brought me around your kids before," I growl, annoyed that he's giving me the cold shoulder.

"True, but this is *the* kid." He sighs. "From the club."

"Of course it is," I growl. "What about Bobby?"

"Not an option today."

"Fuck! I'll call Mike."

"Clayton, is that wise?"

"Any better option?" I growl.

"Yeah, Ben and Amber."

I think about that for a moment. "No, I don't want Amber near this."

"That's not your choice, Clayton." Alec reminds me. "Call Ben. Don't leave Daniel alone."

"Alright, I'll call Ben."

"Call the cops, Clayton," Alec reminds me.

"Yeah, working on it." I grumble as Daniel makes his way into the living room, frowning when he realizes I'm still here.

"Do me a favor, Alec. Call Mike. Let him know I will be late, tell him . . . tell him I'm sorry about last night."

"Are you sure you're making the right choice Clayton?"

"I don't know." I answer honestly.

"Don't worry I got your back, I'll soften the blow." He assures me.

"Thanks." I sigh, guilt suddenly overtaking me. "I have to go."

"Be safe, Clayton." Alec worries and hangs up the phone. I take a deep breath and pocket it before I meet Daniel's worried stare.

"Why are you going to be late?" he asks, nervously.

"Would it be too much to ask that you sit down for a moment?" I frown. His breathing falters as he chooses the seat furthest away from me. "I'm not ending it, Daniel," I assure him.

He just nods his head. "But?"

Trying to stay strong, I approach him, gripping his hands in mine. "Don't freak, okay?"

"Not helping, Clayton," he complains.

"Brad's back," I respond and watch the blood drain from his face.

"No, that's not possible."

"My windshield says otherwise."

He takes a moment to register that, and before I can stop him, he's bolted out of his seat, through his front door, and to his driveway. I'm on his heels, and the moment he sees it, he loses his balance. I catch him. "It's okay. I'm here."

He turns to me, anger clear in his expression, and he attacks my face with his, grabbing me by the waist and throwing me against his garage. I'm surprised, to say the least, but I respond to him. When he pulls away, he growls, turning toward the street.

"Did you see that, bitch? I want him! Him! My husband!" he screams.

"Daniel." I frown, taking his hand cautiously. "Come on, darlin', let's go inside. Call the cops."

"I hate you!" he screams. "I love him!"

"Daniel," I try again, pulling him to me. "Inside."

He shakes his head no and tries to kiss me again. "Red," I growl. His eyes flash for a moment before he shakes his head in approval, dropping his eyes. "Inside," I command. He takes my hand, and we walk back into the house together. BJ senses the tension and starts whining while she licks our heels. "If you agree to stay inside, you can be comforted by her while I call the damn cops."

"Yes, Master," he whispers in a shaky voice. I squeeze his hand and let go. He drops down to his knees, petting his dog while I pull out my cell.

After the cops, I call Ben, and then I sit down on the couch, holding Daniel, who is holding BJ while we wait. I don't release him from my hold as his master, mainly because I'm spinning and I know that talking will do more harm than good, so instead, I run my fingers through his long hair. When the doorbell eventually rings, I whisper, "Red," and he squeezes my knee to get the door.

The cops are the first to arrive, followed shortly by Ben. We spend the next two hours answering questions, linking my previous attack with this and explaining our theory as to why now, after all this time. This just leads to the cops saying, "Uh huh," as they fill out the report that I have a sneaking suspension would have never gotten followed up on, had it not been for Daniel throwing around his family name. I call my insurance company while we wait for the tow trucks to take both our cars back to the evidence lab, which only happened because of Daniel's insistence. When everything is finally dealt with, I'm fucking exhausted and dreading the rest of the day with a passion.

While Ben plays taxi, I find myself avoiding Daniel's eyes. I know I will have to tell Mike almost immediately upon my arrival and my stomach's in knots because of it. *Am I making the right choice?* Ben pulls into my reserved parking space and I'm surprised when all three of us get out of his car. He shrugs at my corked eyebrow, I was expecting them to just drop me off.

That's when I get informed that they need to work out a few kinks with *The Road to Life* project and Amber was already here. *Perfect.* Daniel sees my hesitation, but I just shrug him off. Honestly, he can't expect me to be happy about having to talk to Mike after all of this, especially with them hovering.

After entering the code to my private entrance, I feel Daniel's hand on my shoulder. I take a few deep breaths and turn to Ben. "Give us a moment."

Ben nods, and I pull Daniel on the other side of the door. "I'm just exhausted, darlin', that's all. I haven't changed my mind."

"Do you love him?" Daniel asks, lacing his fingers in mine.

"Yes," I answer honestly, adding in a pained voice, "You were almost too late, Daniel. Him and I, we were working on something, and I didn't realize how significant it really was until the weight of having to tell him came crashing down on me."

"Are you sure I'm not?" he asks, tears streaking down his cheeks. He presses his forehead to mine and brushes his thumb over Mike's mark. "I'd understand, Clayton. I won't hate you for it. We can still be friends. If you want to choose Mike, choose Mike."

"Look at me," I whisper, and he reluctantly raises his sad eyes to mine. "I choose you, Daniel. Yes, I will admit this is a hard choice, but it's mine to make and I choose you. I love you. You are the one that makes me feel whole, complete. Mike is a shadow of our happiness. I would be settling with him and missing half of myself to do it. I want to be whole, Daniel. I want you."

"It would be easier with him," he argues. "No crazy ex's, no painful past, no trust issues."

"Since when the hell do I ever do anything easily?" I scuff. "I'm willing to fight for you, Daniel."

He pulls back and stares at me for a moment before he smiles. "Well, go on. Tell him so I can kiss your sexy ass to oblivion and not feel guilty about it."

Steeling myself, I close my eyes and open the door for Ben before we all make our way up the stairs to my office. Daniel is the first to walk through the door, and I grab Ben's shoulder, holding him back as the exit door closes, effectively giving us privacy. "Don't you leave him alone," I warn. "He's unstable enough, and with this damn bitch, I don't trust he can handle his own head right now."

Ben narrows his eyes at me and then relaxes. "I know he walked out, Clayton. And I know he kept you away, but there's some reason why he left. So don't think for a moment that I have forgiven you for that. I know how to take care of him a hell of a lot better than you do. If you fuck this up again, your face meets my fists. Are we clear?"

"Crystal," I growl, opening the door, masking my anger. I look to Ben, and he's doing the same.

"We should meet with Amber." Ben smiles, heading for my other door.

"Actually, I missed an important meeting with Mike. He and I will catch up with you," I shrug, flipping through the calendar on my desk. Ben looks at me skeptically and then at Daniel. Annoyed, I snap, "I have other clients, Ben." He thinks about that for a moment and nods, and they both leave.

Sighing, I drop into my chair and hit the conference button. "Mike, my office, now."

"Yes, boss," he answers in a dead voice. The moment he steps through, he locks the door.

"That's not necessary."

He shrugs and walks up to me. "Isn't it?"

"No," I answer dryly.

"Come on, Clayton. *He* just walked out of your office. You can't tell me that you don't want to forget," Mike cooes, sitting on my desk directly in front of me, displaying himself as he spreads his legs. "I can make you forget." I have to give him credit; at least he's fighting.

I scoot my chair back and stand up, meeting his eyes. "That's the problem, Mike. I don't want to forget. I love him." He closes his eyes at my words, turning away from me. I know they hurt. Fuck! Watching him suffer hurts, I walk away from him, unable to see the pain in his eyes. "I'm sorry, Mike, but this . . . well, it's over."

"Don't do this, Clayton. He hurt you." Mike jumps off the desk and walks up to me pressing his body into mine. "I've never hurt you. I will never hurt you. You've finally allowed yourself to move past him in just the past month. You swore this means something. Please." He begs, touching the mark he gave me and bringing my hand to his neck to touch the mark I made. "I'm yours Clayton, you're mine."

"It's not enough, Mike," I whisper.

"Bullshit!" he accuses, pushing me into the wall, pressing his lips to mine. He growls in frustration when I don't respond and grabs my hard cock. When I gasp in surprise, he takes advantage and starts dominating my mouth but pulls away quickly, looking me in the eyes. Then his lips are back on mine, and I'm kissing him with an equal amount of fury. *No! Damn it, Clayton! You love Daniel.* I break away from the kiss, turning my head. "I'm so sorry, Mike. I never let myself love you."

"I was breaking down those walls," he cries, dropping his forehead on my shoulder. "Please," he pleads. "I'm yours." I close my eyes to his pain, trying not to cry. "Fucking Kingsley and his goddamn timing! You're mine! We just need to build something stronger. We just need a little more time."

I drop my forehead on his shoulder in response, knowing he's right. If Daniel had waited just a little longer he would have been too late. "I know, darlin', but we're out of time."

"I'll take you back," he says stubbornly, lifting his head up. Accepting he's lost the battle, but determined not to lose the war. "When he hurts you again, I will take you back."

"Mike . . ." but I'm cut off with his lips press gently to mine. Sighing, I step away from him. "I'm giving you another promotion," I explain, my back to him. "Congrats, Mike. You made manager of operations. You can keep your assistant and hire any other staff you think you will need."

"What about you?"

"I'm going to be restructuring a little, have a new personal staff," I answer walking to the door.

"So you create a new position, and you're no longer my boss?" he asks. I can tell he finds it insulting.

"No, Mike, I'm still the boss. You just won't be working with me on a daily basis, I'll get the arrangements started and you will get your own office." I explain, unlocking the door. "Take fair warning Mike, if I ever catch you fucking in it, I will fire your ass in a heartbeat."

"Where does this leave us, Clayton?" he asks, swallowing hard while putting his hand on the door to keep me from opening it. "Besides work."

"I'd like to try the friendship thing, if you can handle it."

"Friends," he says snidely. "Fuck, Clay! We were so much more than that."

"It's the only thing I can offer, Mike." I frown. "But even that comes with strings."

"Strings?" he asks, dropping his hand.

"Daniel wants to talk with you," I explain, biting my lower lip, opening the door and walking through. "We're a package deal, Mike."

"Of course you are," he growls, catching up to me, we wait for the elevator in silence. When we step in he presses a button, "I have to think about it, Clay. I'm not sure if I can." He shakes his head. "Fuck! I fell for you. I knew this was a risk and I fell for you anyway. I need time."

"I can respect that."

"Just do me a favor, as a *friend*."

"What's that?"

"Keep your hands and lips off each other in front of me. I'm not ready for that shit." He winces.

"I'll keep all working relationships professional," I assure him. "But beyond that, no promises."

"I'm serious about taking you back, Clayton. The moment he hurts you, I'll be here," he swears.

"Don't, Mike. Live your life. Don't pass up happiness waiting for something that won't happen." I frown. He stares at me for a long moment, but he doesn't say anything. The doors open and he goes to step out. I realize we're on the ground floor and grab his shoulder, stopping him. I lean forward and press a different button, closing us back into the elevator. "We have a meeting with them, Mike." I sigh. "That part is mandatory, so don't argue. Your meeting with Daniel one-on-one is optional, but as a friend, I'd appreciate it."

He doesn't say anything and I work to keep my stomach in one piece. Hating myself for hurting him like this, hoping he can get past this easily. Praying for the sake of us all I made the right choice. When we get to the sound booth, Daniel meets my eyes and I give a small nod.

"So Mike's back on the project then?" Ben asks, confused.

"He's here for budgeting purposes mainly. He's the new manager of operations," I explain.

"So no longer your executive assistant then?" Ben asks, curious.

"Nope."

"What gives?" he demands, crossing his arms.

"Last time I looked, Ben, I was the co-founder and CEO of Blackboard Entertainment. I'm the fucking boss of this place, and I don't have to explain myself to you or anyone else when it comes to my staff. Understood?" I snap, causing Daniel to squeeze my hand. I give a small squeeze back and pull away, not looking at him.

"Are you two done with the pissing contest? I'd really like to work on this," Amber snaps, effectively ending the twenty questions and bringing us all back to work.

And work is what keeps us there until almost six o'clock in the damn evening. By the time I make it back to my damn office, I'm a walking zombie, and Mike and Daniel are at my heels. Ben and Amber had gone home, and Daniel and I were going to use the company vehicle, until I can switch it out for a rental my insurance company is paying for. Might as well, I can test drive the newest wheels on their dime.

"The conference room is three doors down to the right," I snap, when they both sit down in my guest chairs.

"It involves you too, Clayton." Daniel frowns.

I roll my eyes before leaning forward. "Here, how about I save everyone time? Mike, Daniel is going to tell you that he's aware that he hurt me and that he's not going to do it again. Then you are going to tell him it's only a matter of time and when he fucks up you will be waiting. Explaining that we needed just a little more time, and things would have been different. And Daniel's going to get pissed, saying that you had your chance and this is the way it worked out. Then I'm going to have to go in there and break it up, and you two will attempt to find middle ground for me. Am I missing anything?"

"Keeping professional relations professional," Mike mutters.

I give a small nod, looking at Daniel. "For all of us," I specify. "I promoted him because he deserved it. It's a perk that we won't be working together on a daily basis, not that I need to explain myself," I grumble. "It's going to take time for me to hire new staff. Until Mike has them trained, we are going to be working together as is, although your title and paychecks will reflect your new position on Monday." I stare at them staring at me. "It's the best I can do on such short notice, and this balancing act isn't exactly my favorite thing in the world," I snap, "especially because I'm blending my personal and professional lives."

"Boss . . ."

"Baby . . ."

I hold my hand up. "Not tonight, alright? I get it. Neither of you are happy about the situation, and news flash, guys, neither am I. But I'm the one who created it, so I have to live with that. I'm fucking tired, and I still have to hire my goddamn bodyguard back, so if there is nothing else, I will see you on Monday, Mike."

"Bodyguard?" Mike says. "Shit, Clay, no! Don't tell me that crazy bitch is back." I just look at him. He snaps his head to Daniel in anger.

Before he can open his mouth I warn him, "Don't you dare, Mike. He didn't do this. Leave now before you do something you will regret. Don't make me end our friendship too. Walk away right now."

His eyes flash to mine. "Fine, but don't be surprised if I call you this weekend, and if you don't answer, you can bet your ass I will be sitting on your front door until you prove to me you are safe."

"Package deal," I remind him.

He grunts as he stands up, towering over Daniel. "I'll play nice until you prove to me that you're not worth it," he growls, stomping out of my office.

When the door closes, I calmly stand, walk over to it, and lock it. Then I turn my back to it and slide down to my ass, putting my head in my knees, while wrapping my arms around my legs. Daniel is next to me shortly after, pulling me into him as I cry. "You shouldn't have to see this," I mutter in his chest.

"Shh . . ." he responds, running his fingers up and down my back. "I'm here for you, baby."

"I don't want to hurt you anymore, Daniel," I sob. "I'm so tired of hurting you."

"It's okay, baby. I can't expect you to end a happy chapter in your life so abruptly without a few tears. I know you feel a fresh start with us is worth it, so I will support you through this."

"Have I ever mentioned you're too forgiving?" I mutter. "I should have never started it to begin with."

"You had no idea we were going to be back together," he points out, running his fingers through my hair.

"I should have tried harder," I argue in his chest.

"I would have only pushed you away more. It would have hurt beyond repair."

"And this doesn't?" I snap, raising my head and drying my eyes.

"You're choosing me," he answers with a very sad smile. "That's the thought I need to get through this. Just promise me you won't cry over your subs and we will be fine."

I give a small laugh. "*That* won't be a problem." My eyes meet his. "I can't wait to have you like that again."

"One step at a time, Clayton." He moans looking at his watch, "I need to get back to BJ."

"Do you think she will mind staying at my house?" I ask timidly. "Gated community and all."

"I'm not ready for that, Clayton."

"I'm not leaving you alone," I growl.

"Then come back to my place," he negotiates. "The cops will be parked outside, we'll be fine."

"I'll work on changing it back to ours," I answer, understanding his reservations. "I have to borrow Bobby's truck and get things out of storage, so it will take a couple of days."

"You stored it?" he asks with a smile. "You didn't toss it."

"I never fully let you go, Daniel. I tried to, but I failed miserably."

He leans into me. "You will never have to try that again, Clayton. I love you and I'm not leaving." His lips brush against mine, and very quickly, the kiss gets heated. Soon I find myself on my office floor and start to have very uncomfortable flashbacks causing me to go soft. Daniel notices not long after and pulls away when he grabs my flaccid cock in surprise.

"Two things," I respond, rubbing my face so I don't have to look at him. "One. Not here, at least not until I remodel." He understands immediately and sits up. "Two. This could easily go past the point of no return, and I want to get tested before that happens."

He groans, "I hate this, Clayton. I just want to be with you and not have to worry about formalities. We were past this."

"I know, darlin'. I'm working on it, I promise." He just nods his head. "So, will you call Tasha and reschedule so you can meet my Ma'ma, or is it still too fast?"

He gives a sad smile, stands up, and offers me his hand. "I'll call her in the car."

We make our exit shortly after, heading back to his place, giving a small wave to the cops. Tasha had agreed to Sunday, and we talked a little more. We ended up eating pizza and winding down with a movie. Daniel smiles when BJ curls up on both of our laps and falls asleep. "You see that, baby? She knows you're my other half," he whispers, kissing me gently.

That was the first night, she was allowed in Daniel's bed due to all the whining when we shut her out of his room. It took her a few moments to get comfortable, but she was satisfied with lying on both of our feet and tucked in for the night. Daniel pulled me into him and held me close. "I love you, Clayton, always."

I let out a small moan and push my body closer, kissing his hand. "I love you too, Daniel. Good night."

33

Heart to Heart

Clayton's Point of View

"Mama!" I cry the moment I walk through the door, wrapping her in a gentle but strong embrace.

"Clay, what's wrong?" she asks, concern thick in her voice.

"Nothin', Mama, I just missed you," I assure her, not letting her go.

"You can't lie to your mama, Clay. Out with it," she snaps, pulling me back a little. "Oh," gasps noticing Daniel for the first time. "My apologies, son. Clay didn't tell me he was bringing someone."

"No need for apologies, ma'am. I didn't mean to intrude." Daniel blushes.

"Nonsense," Mama scolds. "I'm just surprised. Clay has never brought a man home before, well except for his best friends."

I clear my throat and look at my feet. My mama has always been accepting of who I am, but I've never flaunted my lifestyle in front of her. She knew about Ryan and Alec but we were always discreet. Besides, I never admitted to dating Alec, though she suspected. God help me if she ever knew *exactly* what I was into.

"Mama, this is Daniel. Daniel, my mama," I introduce.

"*The* Daniel?" Mama asks me quietly. I blush a little and nod. She smiles widely, turning her attention to him. "Well, you are somethin' special, Daniel." She takes him into a welcoming hug. "Do you happen to have any interest in computers?" she asks, pulling away.

"I dabble, ma'am."

"Good, it would be helpful if you could give Daddy a hand while my son and I have a little heart to heart." She smiles.

I give Daniel an apologetic smile and he just nods.

"Sure thing." He laughs.

"He's the second room on the left at the top of the stairs. We'll give a holler when dinner is ready."

"Yes, ma'am." He smiles. I grab his hand for just a moment, giving it a small squeeze as he walks past.

"Now, out with it, Clayton," Mama demands the moment he passes the kitchen door.

"I'm a horrible person, Mama," I cry, sitting down in the kitchen chair. "I love him and I messed up so bad."

"And yet he's here in my home, with you." She sighs, sitting down next to me, handing me a peeler and some potatoes. I get up to quickly wash my hands before I return to the table and start peeling them with her.

"We had a break, and well, I thought it was over." I explain, popping a raw potato peel in my mouth.

"And?" she asks, raising an eyebrow.

"*And* I didn't fight for him . . . *and* I gave up . . . *and* I'm horrible. I didn't wait for him, Mama," I answer in tears.

She looks at me extremely confused. "So you two broke up. You had relationship or whatever. Now you're back together, and you're regretting your choices while you were apart?"

"In a nutshell." I frown. "But it's more complicated than that."

"How long were you separated again?"

"Seven months."

"And you're supposed to do what? Lie around depressed and miserable while the world spun around you?"

"Mama!" I moan.

"Clay, life has no guarantees. You know that. You could not wait around forever hoping you'd get back together." She laughs at the absurdity. "Don't get me wrong. I'm glad you two did. You have to be happy if you brought him here."

"I hurt him so badly," I cry.

"Nonsense," she snaps, and I know she's holding her tongue about him hurting me. "Unless you're the reason you broke up?"

"I played my part," I admit.

"But you two are back together?" she reminds me, pointing her peeler in my direction.

"You keep sayin' that, Mama."

"Because it doesn't seem to be sinking in." She laughs and then frowns. "If you can't handle the fact that he's willing to accept you, flaws and all, then maybe you shouldn't be with him." My eyes flash to hers. "I don't sugar-coat, honey. You know that."

"Have you ever loved more than one person at once, Mama?"

"Is it the same intensity, Clay?"

"No, but they are both powerful in their own way."

"Are you happy with your choice?"

"I think so."

"Then why are you upset with yourself, sweetheart? You take one spin around this crazy world. Use it wisely. Happiness is important, love is a blessing, and making a difference is a must."

"Daddy always says that." I smile, finishing my potatoes.

"Your daddy is a wise man, Clay."

"Are you okay Mama?"

"Of course, Clay," she answers, gathering the potatoes and taking them to the stove.

"Mama, are you dying?" I ask in almost a whisper, feeling like a small child.

She turns to me with the saddest eyes. "Yes, Clayton. I am."

Tears build up quickly. It's all I can do not to scream out as we rush up and hug each other. "Damn it!" I curse, and for once, she doesn't scold me.

We break away when we hear a throat clear. "Sorry," my cousin apologizes.

"It's alright, Kenny. What do you need?" Mama asks.

"Well, it's just Uncle Charlie is cornering some guy in his office and telling him his war stories. I think the guy might be getting a little freaked out."

"Shit!" I curse, running past them to the stairs.

"Clayton William, that mouth!" Mama calls after me as I take the stairs two at a time.

"Sorry Mama!" I call down to her before stepping into Daddy's study finding a rather pale looking Daniel. "Daddy." I frown, taking Daniel's hand.

"No need for introductions, Clay. Daniel here explained that your mama wanted to talk to you."

"How bad is she, Daddy?" I ask in a small voice.

He takes a deep breath. "Doctor's say less than six months now."

More tears threaten, and I feel Daniel wrap his arms around me, whispering in my ear, "I'm so sorry."

Daddy watches the exchange, giving me a nod with a smile. It's the closest to an approval I'm going to get from him, so I just smile back as I shed some tears.

"Come on, boys. Let's eat." Daddy sighs, standing up and stretching. We both follow him down the stairs and help Mama with setting the table. During supper the conversation is a little forced at first, but as we get more comfortable, it begins to flow. Daniel is insistent on helping Mama with the dishes, which she gracefully accepts but kicks me out, wanting a heart-to-heart with him. I'd have argued, but considering everything, I just didn't have the heart.

"He seems like a good man," Daddy appraises.

"You only scratched the surface." I smile.

"You rarely bring a man here, except your friend Alec," Daddy comments. "And Ryan of course."

"Alec is just a friend, Daddy." I clarify for the umpteenth time. "Daniel, well, he's my other half."

"You two look like you've been through war together," Daddy notes, causing me to straighten upright and snap my eyes to his. "Thought so." He frowns. "It will change everything, Clay, but if you two can survive it, nothin' will ever break you apart."

"How did you survive it, Daddy?"

"Talking to someone you trust is always nice."

"You suggestin' a shrink?"

"I'm suggestin' a neutral third party, not necessarily a shrink."

Daniel walks back in and sits down next to me, placing his hand in mine. "Thanks, Daddy. I'll think about it."

"You do that, Clay," he answers sternly. "Now normally, we'd ask you to stay for pie, but your mama has pushed herself enough for one day."

"Alright," I agree. "I'm going to make it a point to come by more often." I promise. "I'm sorry I've been so distant lately. I won't do that again."

"You see to it that you keep that promise, Clay."

We say our goodbyes, and Mama stuffs the car with care packages, before allowing me to head back home. I ask Daniel to drive. I'm just too shaken to be behind a wheel. The drive is silent for the most part while the day comes crashing down on me. When it dawns on me that I don't have to be strong anymore, I lose it. Daniel ends up pulling over and taking me out of the car just to hold me while I weep. His words of love and endearment are welcome, and *he* is exactly what I need in this moment.

Eventually, we get back into the car, and he drives us back to my place. I pack a few things in a duffel bag, check my messages, and get my mail before heading to his place. After he attends to BJ, he turns to me with a sad smile.

"Would you like to invite Alec and Bobby over?"

"No. We're not all that close right now." I admit. "I'd prefer to just be with you."

"What do you mean you are not all that close?" Daniel asks in shock.

I shrug, pulling out my pack of smokes, heading for his patio. "We just grew apart. It happens."

"He's your best friend, Clayton," Daniel reminds me, following me outside with BJ at his heels.

I light up my cigarette and inhale. "I'm not sayin' we don't talk, Daniel. I'm just sayin' we're not close."

"Translation, you shut him out." Daniel accuses grabbing my wrist and tracing my scar with his fingers. "I've always been curious about this." He muses, "I know it has something to do with him, his scar is almost identical."

I pull my hand away and trace the scar myself. "We made a blood oath. To always be a part of each other's lives."

"Blood oaths are serious vows Clayton." He notes. "Something to be valued above all other promises."

"I'm aware, that's why I did it." I shrug, dropping my hand and drawing on my cigarette. "You know, for a guy who has seen the worst in people, he's way too much of a sucker for happily ever after and second chances." I bitch. "We don't see the world the same in that aspect. I'm grateful for his life's work, *he* makes a difference with that attitude. It's just not my way of thinking."

"His life's work?"

"You know, he's a therapist." I smile, "Did you know he has Youth-In-Need center here in town, catered to gay teens? His specialty is helping teens communicate with their parents or get assisted living if they turn out to be bigots." I take a short drag on my cigarette before I continue, "You met him as an Untouchable instructor, something he takes great pride in. But he doesn't keep the BDSM training to Madam Chloe's house. He also educates his kids, if they show interest, and on more than one occasion has kept them from making mistakes like going through the wrong channels. However, he refuses to let any of his kids enter into the lifestyle without a good six months to a year of counseling first."

Daniel gives a small chuckle. "You ever have to take his tests? Or watch him correct a master who tried to touch one of us before we graduated?"

I give a short laugh. "I can only imagine." I shrug, "With Alec, the glass is always half full."

"But not for you."

I take a long drag. "Life's too short for wishful thinking. Live the moment, live your dreams."

"So all of this has made you hard."

"I've always been hard, Daniel," I correct, shaking my head. "It's just I normally keep my damn thoughts to myself."

"The Clayton I knew wasn't this cold."

"The Clayton you knew was weak and pathetic, so damn terrified of losing the man that he loves he kept tripping over himself. Then my fears were realized, and guess what, I survived." He doesn't say anything to that while I finish my cigarette. "I'm not sayin' I'm not happy we are trying again. I'm just sayin' that you are going to see changes, Daniel, changes you may or may not like honestly. I'm not going to worry about being needy nor will I cling to your every word. I'm gonna speak my mind and if I think you're being an ass, you will know. Fuck the damn eggshells. If I want to take you to the damn airport, I'm going to. And if you can't handle this, tell me now."

He still doesn't give a verbal response, so I start throwing a stray ball with BJ. After a while, he joins us, and we play with her until she gets tired. Then he wraps his arms around me. "I hear you, and I understand. We'll probably fight more, but makeup sex is always hot."

Before I can respond to that, my phone rings. I check the caller ID and frown but decide to answer it. "I'm alive, Mike. Stop worrying." Daniel's arms tense, but he doesn't let me go.

"Did you still want to meet him?" Mike asks with a sad voice.

"Yes," I answer sternly. "We're friends, Mike, and I want to make it crystal clear to him that if he hurts you past punishment, he is answering to me."

"What does Daniel think about all of it?"

"Don't know. Don't care. This is about us."

"Is today good?"

"Tomorrow would be better," I offer, remembering that Daniel will be with Tasha.

"I'll arrange it. Have a nice day," he replies dryly.

"You too," I smile, hanging up the phone to find Daniel frowning at me.

"You told him Monday," Daniel snaps.

"I did," I answer evenly, putting my phone back into my pocket. "But this is important."

"Why?" he asks jealously.

"His back was black and blue. He swears that it was just punishment, but I don't like it."

"Can't Alec do it?" he asks, pulling on his hair like he always does when he's stressed.

"No," I answer simply. "You're going to have to trust me."

"It's not you I'm worried about," he snaps.

"You won't choose my friends, Daniel. That's a deal breaker, you know that," I snap back, walking away from him and into the house, where I wash my hands and proceed to brush my teeth. After a small while, he joins me.

"I'm sorry," he whispers, leaning against the sink. "You say nothing will happen. Then nothing will happen."

I look at him for a long moment with my toothbrush in my mouth. Eventually I spit and rinse, turning to him. "Thank you."

He takes me into his arms and kisses me until my knees get weak. When we break away, he starts sucking on my neck and unbuttoning my pants. Moaning, I grab his wrist. "No."

His eyes snap to mine. "It's okay, Clay. We'll use protection," he whispers, taking his free hand and squeezing my ass under my clothes while dropping his lips back down to my neck and starts to suck harder.

"No," I repeat, yanking away from his lips before he can leave a mark. "Please, Daniel, not like this."

"Like what?" he asks, pressing our hard cocks together.

I pull back and rest my palms on each side of his face, placing our foreheads together. "I want to give myself to you completely. No protection required," I whisper. "And because I want to, not because of a reaction to a phone call." His eyes narrow, I'm calling him out and he knows it. "My name is Clayton, Daniel. Don't call me Clay because he does."

His eyes close as he takes a step back. "Come on. Let's go."

"Go where exactly?" I ask cautiously.

"My clinic. We're both getting tested, and this shit will not get between us ever again," he snaps, grabbing my hand, dragging me out of his house. The next thing I know, I'm getting blood drawn next to Daniel, who is doing the same thing. He passes some cash to the tech when we get our cotton balls and tape. "We'll wait." I couldn't hide the shocked expression on my face and he just shrugs. Not sure what to say to him at this point, I try to keep myself busy by flipping through magazines, but it isn't working very well. Frowning, I drop the magazines and start fidgeting.

"Will you knock it off already?" he snaps.

"What?"

"You're nervous," he notes.

"Not about the results." I shrug. "The means of getting them so quickly is a little obscure."

"I told you my reasoning."

"I'm sorry."

"For what?"

"For not stopping you from leaving me."

"Clayton, we've been through this."

"No, Daniel, we haven't," I snap. "Every fuckin' time I try to apologize, you take the damn blame and tell me it's the past." He glares at me. "I'm sorry I hurt you. I'm sorry I freaked. I'm sorry I didn't get out of the car that day with Alec, even though you say it wouldn't have done any good. I'm sorry I took you home alone that night instead of staying at Alec's, who I haven't been avoiding just because he disapproves of Mike, but because the damn guilt in his eyes from believing he fucked up my happiness is so damn draining. But I'm not sorry that after seven months without you I started to attempt to move on. Maybe I started too early and gave up too easily when you refused any and all contact with me. Maybe I had enough when you changed your goddamn cell phone number, but damn it, I'm sick of feeling guilty for shit that I can't change and I honestly don't regret."

"Clayton!" Daniel growls. "Stop." He sighs. "I told you I get it. I meant it. I'm sorry it hurts, but I played a part in this too. I'm sorry I pushed you away and refused any contact. I'm sorry that I couldn't even think about moving on with sex, maybe then you wouldn't feel so damn guilty. Instead I was stuck on rewind. In the end, your reaction was probably healthier. Baby, what we have together is rare, but when we mess it all up the way *we* did, it's even rarer to take a second chance. So please stop apologizing, and after these results, let's move on."

I stare at my hands for a long moment. "Thank you for finally hearing me out," I mutter.

"You're welcome," he says with a sad smile.

Not much later than that, our test results come back and we are both clean. With that technicality out of the way we grab a quick bite to eat then go back to Daniel's. On the ride back I text Bobby, asking to borrow his truck. Then I text my subs and set up a meeting for tomorrow afternoon. When he pulls into his driveway, it's about nine o'clock at night, and we are nowhere near tired.

We head into the house with one goal in mind. The moment our lips meet, I know that this is the fresh start we were searching for. We don't take the time to make it to his room, instead we throw ourselves on the couch ignoring BJ's yelp when we almost land on her. We are about to remove our shirts when his doorbell rings.

"Ignore it," I moan.

"Plan to," he agrees.

"Police! Open up!" a voice says on the other side of the door, and we both freeze. *Brad.*

Moaning, Daniel stands up, straightens his clothes as he walks to his front door, opening it. "Daniel Kingsley?"

"Yes."

"I think it would be best if you came downtown with me. We have a few questions," the cop says.

I frown, walking up to him. "Badge?"

He hands it over. "This isn't a setup, Mr. Reynolds. We have a few questions about Travis Ashton."

I keep my eyes down, studying his badge, trying not to react to the name.

"You mean my sister's ex?" Daniel asks, his voice laced with anger.

"We can do this with or without bracelets, Mr. Kingsley." The cop shrugs.

Daniel turns to me. "Take care of BJ, I won't be gone long."

I nod and lean in for a kiss, whispering in his ear very softly, "They have no proof. Admit nothing."

He just wraps his arms around me and gives me a small squeeze before he pulls back. "I'll see you very soon, I'm sure. Wait here?"

"Yeah, sure thing." I smile.

Daniel gives me one last kiss and then goes with the cop. The moment I'm sure he's gone, I pull out my cell phone, and when the other side answers, I snap, "Alec, we have a huge fuckin' problem."

34

Cry for Help

Daniel's Point of View

I've been sitting in an interrogation room for almost twelve hours, knowing that they don't have solid evidence on me. Otherwise, I would be sitting in a jail cell. They are waiting for me to ask for a lawyer, but I know if I do that, then I will prove my guilt. So instead, I just sit here, tapping my feet and hands, playing the impatient part. I even request that I call my partner Ben so that he wouldn't worry about me missing work and report me missing or some shit. They allow it so I ask him to call Clayton just to keep him updated.

The man on the other side of the table just keeps watching me, not saying a damn word, until finally a coworker walks in with a file. He nods and the second person leaves the room. After a few moments of him reviewing the file, he slides it over to me. I stop it with my thumb before it falls to the floor.

"Angels of Justice ring a bell?"

"What if it does?" I answer with a shrug.

"I want names," he snaps.

I give out a hearty laugh. "Good luck with that one. I've tried, and believe me, my guys get paid a hell of a lot more than you do, and they came up dry."

"So you admit to being into BDSM," the cop answers, raising an eyebrow.

"It's not a crime, free country and all," I answer dismissively.

"That is," he snaps, stabbing the file in front of me. "Open it."

Frowning, I open the file and close it rather quickly. I didn't recognize him, but I had a sinking feeling it was Angels of Justice work. I slide the folder back to him. "Never seen him before."

"He was a fucking cop," the man growls. *Of course he was. Damn it! Mike's ex-master.*

"Was?" I point out. "What's the matter, Angels of Justice reveal his true colors?"

"Where were you on March nineteenth?"

Thank you, Alec. "I believe I was on my family's private island with my boyfriend. You can check with Mile High Airlines. They gave us the tickets free of charge after their idiot flight attendant insulted me."

"That was almost a year ago. You can remember the date so easily off the top of your head!"

I give a smile, leaning into him. "I remember that entire week very well. I was naked with my boyfriend almost the entire time. It's kind of *hard* to forget."

"What's your boyfriend's name?" he asks, reaching for his pen.

"Clayton Reynolds," I answer with an eye roll. "You met. Remember?"

He sits back in his chair for a little longer, and finally, I get annoyed. "Look, do you have a point in bringing me in here and keeping me up all damn night and most the morning?"

"Do you know Travis Ashton?"

"Yeah, we were friends until he confessed to killing Seanna Summers," I growl. He tenses, and I bite back my temper, "Check the damn file, Detective. I'm the fucking one who told your staff that he confessed to me. But no proof, no arrest. Then he had the balls to date my sister and . . ." I cut myself off. "Bastard will burn in hell for all of it one way or another."

"Did you realize he was dating your sister *before* he was arrested?"

I was waiting for this, and I preform perfectly. "NO!" I snap, jumping out of my chair. "I thought Tasha knew better! My father had forbidden it. She was stupid to cross him! Is that what this is about? My sister?"

He stares at me. "Where were you the night of June second?"

I knew the date all too damn well, but I choose to pretend I didn't, unsure if my sad eyes gave it away. "Why?"

= 359 =

"Travis Ashton was beaten and tortured by the Angels of Justice that night. *That* is what this is about."

"And you think I had something to do with it?" I ask defensively, crossing my arms.

"You don't seem all that upset," he muses, tossing another folder this time open and showing Travis's swollen face.

"That abusive garbage touched my sister, never mind the fact that Seanna was a family friend. I've known about his beating for a while. Tasha told me when he was in the hospital. If you ask me, he got what he deserved," I answer dismissively, praying for calm while I fix my chair and sit back down.

"I want names, Daniel," he says, leaning in.

"You're asking the wrong guy," I snap. "Look, you've got nothing to keep me here, and you're wasting my time, so if there is nothing else . . ." I stand to leave and right when I get to the door he speaks again.

"We need their help." He admits. "We'll give them immunity for everything."

I stop short, turning to him. "What did you say your name was, Detective?"

"I didn't," he answers, standing next to me. "Cole, Dale Cole."

I stare at him for a moment. This has to be a trap. If it's not, it's my destiny as I repent from my past sins. God what I would give . . . but this is fucking risky, too risky I can't hurt Clayton like that. Can I? "Why would you want their help?" I ask skeptically, but the look in his eyes tells me he's genuinely pleading with me.

He frowns. "They have the expertise we need to bring down a really bad target."

"So why don't you go through the appropriate channels?" I snarl.

"It takes too long. Besides, you're in. I just want a meeting."

"I'm into BDSM," I correct, admitting nothing. "But you're right. I can pull a few strings. Tell me, Detective Cole, why should I trust you?"

"You want a lawyer to put it in fucking writing?" he snaps.

I grin. "Sure do, and I want it signed by the fucking governor." That will be a cold day in hell, seeing as Liam is our governor. "Then and only then, will I *think* about helping you."

"Fine, but I can't guarantee you that if they slip up between now and then, that this deal will stick. That bastard cop may have been abusive, but he was still a cop. Loyalties are split," he warns.

"Why me?"

"Travis called you out the day he was arrested," Cole shrugs. "I'm sure you know by now we try to look the other way when we can. You're the only name we got, and we need your help, Daniel. Simple as that."

I glare at him for the longest time, thinking of how to get the hell out of this and protect the others. "I don't know their names," I lie. "I can contact them, but I have no fucking clue who they are."

"Did you contact them about Tasha?" he asks. "Or did they contact you? Perhaps it was Tasha?"

My jaw clenches, "Tasha has nothing to do with anything."

"Won't stop me from talking to her."

I laugh, trying to lighten the mood and smolder my temper. "You do that." Walking out, I turn to him. "Detective?"

"Yes, Mr. Kingsley," he answers, following me into the hallway.

"Just to warn you, she's a fucking bitch." I walk away and make it to the other end of the hall before I hear him holler at me.

"I'll keep that in mind. I got my eye on you, Kingsley."

That is the final straw, and now I'm just fucking pissed. I turn, stalking back up to him. "If you care so goddamn much, then why don't you hunt down my crazy ex-boyfriend, Brad Pazzo? *That* fucker beat the hell out of my boyfriend with a damn baseball bat in broad fucking daylight! And no one has produced anything on *that* case. As a matter of fact, if you keep breathing down my neck for shit that I have nothing to do with and you don't find and arrest Brad, I swear I will smear this entire force on the news. Then I will talk to my very rich friends and have your donations run dry. Understood?"

"I don't take to threats, Mr. Kingsley," he growls.

"It's not a threat, *Detective*." I shrug. "Brad Pazzo. P-A-Z-Z-O," I repeat with the spelling. Then I pat him on the back and walk out of there with my head held high.

When I get to the fucking street, my hands are shaking. I know I should call Clayton or Ben for a ride, but I'm too damn worked up to deal with either of them at the moment. Plus, I had a feeling Clayton called Alec, and knowing what I know, it would be a bad idea for all of us to be together without damn good reason. So, I decide to make a reason, walking until I find the nearest bar. Planning on having one or two drinks, I pull up a stool and flag down the bartender.

"What will it be?" he asks.

"Whiskey, straight."

He nods his head and starts to pour from a fresh bottle, no less. The moment it hits my throat, I feel relief. *Okay, maybe not such a good idea.* Swallowing the burn, I slam the glass down. "Leave the bottle."

"That will cost you," he answers with a raised eyebrow.

I pass him a hundred. "Keep the change."

He just looks at me for a moment, taking the money. "You okay, man?"

"Fan-fucking-tastic," I answer dryly.

"When you want to leave, tell me. I'll call a cab." He sighs, walking away.

As the time passes and the whiskey bottle begins to empty, my racing thoughts start to take hold. Clayton and Mike? Mike! Fuck. Why him? And how long has he been ogling his damn boss?

Let's not forget the slight detail that he fucked a woman. That is really the only thing that saved me from being absolutely pissed. He was spinning, pure and simple. *You can't be pissed. You were broken up. You left him.* The voice of reason echoes in my head. I quickly drown it out with another glass.

How fucking close are these two going to be anyway? I begin to wonder. Yeah, sure, Clayton gave the guy a promotion to keep away from him, but was that to please me or to avoid temptation? Then there's the phone call where he decided he was meeting Mike tomorrow whether I fucking liked it or not. I'm sure Mike got off on that and it pisses me off. And fuck that fucking hickey! I'm still astonished Clayton let Mike mark him like that! Fuck how long is that going to take to heal already? Never mind that when I tried to make my claim, Clayton fucking stopped me! And don't think I didn't miss the fucking mark Clayton left on Mike. *Do you have the right to be jealous? If he were jealous of Ben or something, how would you feel?* That's different. I argue dismissively taking another drink.

Then he tells me no more eggshells, and I'm pissed at my dick for responding to his dominating behavior. That's what it all was really. Clayton was taking control of his personal life, of *our* personal life. I can't resent him for that. It's part of the attraction.

But we don't really have all the control. Especially not with that damn bitch stalking me. Fuck! Why haven't the damn cops caught his ass? What the hell does he want from me? Why the fuck did I ever fuck him?

As I pour myself another glass, my thoughts go to Travis. Fucker recognized me. Shouldn't be surprised. We were friends at one time in our lives. But why now? What the fuck do the cops want?

"Are you numb yet, darlin'?" Clayton asks with concern written all over his features, pulling up a seat.

"Hoow'dd yyya findd mee?" I ask, slurring my words. I had planned on calling a cab.

"You're at the closest bar to the police station. It doesn't take a genius," he answers with a shrug.

"Justtt leavve mee aloooonnne," I slur.

"So how much of this is me? And how much is the cops?" he asks, pointing to an almost dry whiskey bottle.

"Moore yoou," I answer with a head shake, causing him to frown while he lights a cigarette.

"Figured as much." He sighs. "Let me guess. You're trying to drown, Mike."

"I doon't wanT to tal-K right, noow," I stammer.

He stares at me. "Probably for the best," he agrees before turning to the bartender. "He good?"

"As long as he ain't driving," the bartender answers.

"Don't worry about that, I got him." He assures the guy, putting my arm around his neck and helping me off the stool. "Come on, darlin'. Let's get you home."

I don't remember much from that point forward, except for Clayton putting me in his car and then being face down in bed while my shoes are being stripped off my feet. After that, the world goes black.

When I wake up, I hear voices, and my head is fucking pounding. The clock reads 6:28, but I have no idea if it is morning or night. Slowly, I rise up, trying to get my bearings. I notice that I'm still in my clothes, and Clayton is not in the room with me. Frowning, I head for the living room.

I have to admit that I was not shocked to see Angels of Justice in my living room, considering, but I really wasn't all that happy about it. Ben takes one look at me and crosses his arms, pissed. Alec and Bobby give me sad eyes, and Clayton, well, he just looks at me as though he was expecting it. He doesn't seem hurt or disappointed, just accepting. This reaction makes me the most uncomfortable.

"Umm, hey guys. Hope I didn't keep you." I frown, scratching my head.

"This isn't a casual get-together, Daniel," Alec snaps. "Clayton, go clean his ass up and give him some painkillers. We have a long night ahead of us."

"Yes, Grand Master," Clayton replies, standing up and taking my arm. He doesn't speak to me until he turns on the water to my shower, waiting for it to heat up. "Take off your clothes, darlin'," he tells me as he too begins to strip.

"I'm sorry, Clayton." I frown, biting my lower lip while I unbutton my jeans.

"It's not the time for that," he answers with a sad smile.

Once we are naked, we step into the warm shower, and he begins to clean me with a soapy sponge. "It's hard not to be jealous of Mike." I frown and his eyes flash to mine, but he doesn't falter his movements or speak. "I know you gave him a new position, so you are not working so closely together, but I'm not sure if you did that for me or to avoid temptation," I continue rambling. He's still silent as he begins to wash my feet. "Then you make plans with him when you specifically said Monday, and I was standing right there, Clayton. I heard what you said. You basically told him you didn't care about my opinion one way or the other." I frown. "Then you add the shit with Brad and Travis and well . . . here we are."

He hangs up the sponge and spins me around so fast that my arms slam against the tile wall of the shower. Then I feel him spread my legs, and his hot breath is in my ear while his hand wraps around my cock.

"Obviously, words aren't enough," he snaps. "I get that Mike is going to be hard for you, but trust is something you are going to have to deal with, Daniel." He rests his head on my shoulder and begins to stroke me, "The promotion was a convenient way for me to make all three of us comfortable, and I'll admit, it's a little premature, but considering the circumstances, it's for the best. He's my friend, Daniel, and I will not go behind your back and lie to you about meeting him. Which in my mind translates to you accepting the fact that we will meet up from time to time, and you will trust that nothing will happen." He takes his other hand and starts to trace my entrance. "As far as Brad, I'll be honest, Daniel. It scares the shit out of me. He could have killed me, and the fact that he's back . . . well fuck . . . but if I wanted to run, darlin', I would have done it already," he assures me, kissing my neck as he enters a wet finger into my hole. "Fuck tight," he whispers. "And the Travis thing is why everyone is here," he finishes, adding a second finger and begins to thrust but not stretch my hole while squeezing tighter on my dick, matching his motions. "I want you, Daniel. I choose you. But you have to trust me, darlin'," he whispers, picking up his movements both in my ass and on my dick.

"I do trust you," I gasp. "Damn it, Clayton, cumming," I moan softly as cum sprays the shower wall.

"Good. Now, just remember all of your orgasms belong to me," he growls, releasing me.

I grab him by the shoulders and throw him into the wall. "Same for you," I respond, kissing him, and just as the water begins to run cold, the bathroom door flies open.

"You two, out!" Our grand master snaps. We break away from each other, shut off the water and step onto the cold floor, dripping wet. "Hands on the sink, asses out," he orders, and that's when I realize he's holding a wooden paddle. "I told you to freshen him up, not have your way with him," he growls, slapping the paddle on Clayton's wet ass four times. "Did either of you cum?"

"Yes, Grand Master. I was pleased," I answer, causing six consecutive smacks on my wet ass.

"Now get in the living room and kneel," he demands, not giving us the privilege of drying off.

We walk into the living room and kneel our cold, wet naked bodies before Ben and Bobby. I feel my grand master's touch on my shoulders. "Tell me, Daniel. What did the cops want?"

"Our help, Grand Master."

It takes a very long moment before he speaks again. "Start from the beginning, Daniel," he orders, which I do, telling him the only name they have is mine because Travis ratted me out, but they let it go, then about Mike's ex-master, and finally end with immunity.

"This is so not good." He worries. "All of us here tonight, they're staking your house for Brad!"

"No, Grand Master, it's fine," I assure him. "Ben is my best friend, so that is easily explained. Clayton is my boyfriend again, easy. As for you two, you are close to Clayton and you are a therapist, so it fits."

His eyes narrow. "What fits?"

"I'm an alcoholic, Al . . . Grand Master." I frown. "I have been for some time now. I knew that Clayton would call a meeting. Now we can just claim it was an intervention."

"This was a setup?" Clayton asks in surprise, earning another slap from the paddle.

"Grand Master, may I?"

"Go ahead."

I turn to Clayton's down cast eyes. "At first blush, yes, but I wasn't supposed to drink that much, but well, my head just wouldn't shut up."

He nods his head in understanding, and I move back to my previous position.

"Tell your cop friend no," our grand master snaps.

"Grand Master, they could arrest him," Clayton pleads.

"It's a risk," he agrees, "but even if we do get immunity, then it ends us."

"May I talk to my lawyers, Grand Master?" I offer. "See if there is any possible way."

"You want to help them, Daniel?" he questions in surprise.

"That's the point of this, isn't it?" I ask, grateful that my eyes were cast down, I don't want him reading anything more than he needs to, my past demons are screaming at me, and no one here needs to know about that. "If they are coming to us, then there has to be a reason."

"You don't think it's a trap?" he asks skeptically.

"You didn't see his eyes, Grand Master. He was desperate."

"Clayton," Grand Master growls. "Get your PI to do some digging on this guy."

"Dale Cole," I fill in the blank, even though I am talking out of turn.

"See what he comes up with. Understood? The more information we have as to why they are seeking us out, the better."

"Yes, Grand Master," Clayton responds.

"Good. Now get dressed, Clayton." Our grand master orders. "Daniel, follow me."

I stand slowly, following him to my spare bedroom. "Sit on the bed, Daniel." I follow his instruction and he sits down next to me. "This drinking shit stops," he growls, "if you still want to be in this."

"I do, Grand Master," I answer softly.

"We're going after Brad," he informs me. "Just me and Bobby. The rest of you are too close."

"Aren't you too close?" I frown. "He's threatening your best friend. He almost killed him, Alec." I reach for his scarred hand, in effort to trace it.

He stands abruptly, taking a fistful of my wet hair. "What will it take for you to see me as your 'Grand Master', Daniel?"

"I went there, Alec. I almost didn't survive it. Please just think about it before you do something you can't take back," I plead, not giving a shit if I am going to be punished or not.

He releases his grip and goes to the door. "Clayton, in here now!"

Almost immediately, Clayton enters the room. "Wait here on your knees, both of you," Our grand master growls with a frown, leaving us alone. A few minutes later, he returns and drops down in front of Clayton, whispering in his ear. I can't resist the temptation of looking and watch shock and surprise filter into Clayton's face as he speaks. Clayton responds in the same fashion. They exchange a look before our grand master stands and approaches me. "Considering the circumstances, I felt it best to consult our partners before I went to this somewhat drastic measure," he explains. "Both are a little shy to the idea, but they understand the purpose behind it. If you are uncomfortable, I suggest you use your safe word now."

"Uncomfortable with what exactly?"

"What exactly . . . Grand Master," he growls in correction. "If you insist on speaking out of turn at least do it with respect! Eyes down."

"My apologies, Grand Master." I quickly cast my eyes back to the floor.

"It's necessary you to respect me as your 'Grand Master', Daniel; that is if you want to be an 'Angel'. I'm hoping if you and your master show me that said respect willingly than we can put an end to your constant insubordination. And as your 'Grand Master', I want to accomplish this by having you suck me off while Clayton finger-fucks you. You will not be allowed to cum."

"May I have a moment alone with Clayton, Grand Master? We are just starting fresh, and I don't want this to affect us."

"It won't," Clayton assures me.

"It's up to you, Daniel." Grand Master shrugs.

"And if I refuse, Grand Master?"

"To keep your 'Angel' status, whip or cane, your choice."

Not really wanting to deal with any bruises, I timidly raise my hands up to my grand master's jeans, undoing the first of five buttons, meeting his eyes. "Eyes down, Daniel," he reminds me. I correct myself again and quickly work on the rest, dropping his pants and boxers to his knees. That's when I feel Clayton behind me, rubbing his hands down my ass. I turn to him. "Are you sure we can keep this separate?"

"I can, darlin'. Can you?" I shake my head yes before swallowing our grand master's dick in my mouth; hearing Clayton fidget with a lube packet. He gasps, grabbing my wet hair at the back of my head while my tongue begins to work his shaft into a hard rock. I keep my hands to myself and begin to moan when I feel Clayton slip a lubed finger in my ass, submitting to both of them. *Holy hell! This is hot!* I begin sucking and pulling on my grand master's cock while my tongue teases his main vein, and both our dicks grow harder. Not much later, Grand Master starts to fuck my face. I force myself to stay still while Clayton presses against my prostate and rests his chin on my shoulder, watching us. Grand Master pulls out of my mouth and shifts. "Open," he demands. Clayton wraps his lips around our grand master's cock. The view is so fucking hot, and I can't stop the moan that escapes me. "You like that, Daniel?"

"Yes, Grand Master."

"Then why don't you pleasure me too?" he muses. I lean in to trap his balls in my mouth. "Lower Daniel, you're allowed to move for better access. Clayton can stop his ministrations on you."

Clayton's fingers fall out of me and I find myself crawling behind my grand master, spreading his sexy ass cheeks, to get access to his delicious crack. I lick it with my thick tongue twice before I plunge into him. It doesn't take but a few moments before our grand master needs to steady himself with Clayton's shoulders as we both hum and suck on his body. Shortly after that, he's cumming in Clayton's throat. I continue to pleasure him through his orgasm while Clayton licks him clean, only stopping when he steps away.

"Kiss," Grand Master demands. Clayton and I start to kiss, tasting our grand master between us. "Jack each other off. Clayton you may cum at will. When he does, you both may stop." he orders. Immediately Clayton's hand wraps around my cock and I start to fumble with his jeans before I can return the favor. My orgasm is close, but I hold off, aware I have lost the privilege to cum. I quickly work Clayton to orgasm to avoid safe wording, having relief wash over me in waves when I feel hot cum on my hands and stomach. We drop each other's dicks and wait for our grand master's next instruction.

"I know you could taste me on each other. Let that be a reminder that I am a master of both of you. Now get dressed," he orders, stepping out of the room.

I frown, standing up to realize I need to exit the room to follow his command. Shrugging, I open the door and head for my bedroom where my clothes are. I try not to smile when I notice Clayton is following me. He goes straight to his duffel bag and pulls out his toothbrush and toothpaste. I smirk, following him to the bathroom so I can do the same thing. When our mouths are rinsed and minty fresh, Clayton is attacking my face and kissing me breathless. "I love you," he whispers.

"I love you," I respond, combing my fingers through his damp hair. "Would it upset you to know I found that fucking hot?"

"No," he chuckles. "I did too." Then he cringes. "Just as long as we don't do threesomes outside of this, we should be fine."

"Agreed. Hey, why wasn't Bobby in there?"

"Grand Master was trying to make Ben comfortable."

"It's weird to have a straight guy in this." I shrug pulling, Clayton to me.

"It usually keeps it non sexual." Clayton muses, pressing his head to my naked chest.

"We need to get back before we piss him off again," I mutter.

"I know," Clayton says as he holds me tighter. "But I've missed this so much."

I give a small chuckle. "Let's get them out of here so I can have my wicked way with you."

He pulls back with a smile and runs to my closet changing quickly to half follow our grand master's original instruction, he throws me a pair of jeans and a T-shirt, which I quickly put on before heading down the hallway and back into the living room.

Grand Master walks up to Clayton with a frown. "I didn't say to change your clothes Clayton. You will wear boxers for a week as punishment."

Clayton holds back a grimace and nods.

"Clayton will get the research done before we do anything." Our grand master orders, addressing the group. "Agreed?"

"Yes, Grand Master," we agree in unison.

"Okay, then. Who's hungry?" he asks.

Clayton and I bust up laughing as we say, "Red."

"What's 'red?'" Alec asks.

"It's our transition word," I answer, walking to my fridge and pulling out a soda.

"Convenient," Alec notes.

"Where's BJ?" I frown.

"Outside, where she's stayin'," Bobby grumbles. "I hate it when bitches hump my leg."

That causes me to choke on my drink. Clayton comes to my aid, patting my back. "Fuck, Bobby, I missed you," I manage to gasp out, noticing Ben shuffling through my cabinets and pulling out all my liquor. Not much later, Alec joins him, and they start to pour it down the drain. "Thanks, guys." I frown, walking into the living room and leaving them to do their business.

The night seems to drag on slowly while we all talk and eat. Near the end Ben corners my ass. "I'm glad I finally got more help, Daniel. I can't do this by myself anymore. Talk to your damn therapist, go to AA meetings, or whatever, but knock this shit off already."

"I'm working on it Ben."

"You've been saying that for six damn months," he snaps. "If these guys can't snap you out of it, get professional help, Daniel. Don't let this shit come between you and Clayton, because I promise you, it will. I don't know if you could survive losing him twice."

"If it wasn't for my damn pride, I wouldn't have lost him to begin with."

"Just don't let your insecurities get in the way again. If you are thinking about doing something stupid, call me. It's obvious you two love each other, Daniel, but love will only go so far without trust, both in yourself and in him."

"I hear you, Ben. Honest." Wanting to change the subject I shrug. "Alec wants to go after Brad."

"What?" he snaps.

"Just him and Bobby."

"Oh, hell no! Am I the only one with a goddamn brain?" he growls, walking away and going straight to Alec. Their discussion gets heated instantly, and the next thing I know, three of us are going off on Alec and Bobby shouting over one another for a good five minutes.

"ENOUGH!" Alec eventually screams, and the room falls silent. "You want the damn cops to continue to have their thumbs up their asses, fine." He turns to Clayton in bewilderment, "But I swear, if he hurts you again, he's answering to me, and I don't give a shit what you think." He turns from him, fighting back his anger. "And that goes for you too Daniel."

"It will change you, Alec," I whisper. "And not in a good way."

"I get it, Daniel." He frowns. "I think we've had enough drama for one night."

"Yeah, Amber's going to start to text me off the damn hook if I stay too much later," Ben agrees.

We all end up saying our goodbyes and Ben rushes out the door. Clayton and Alec exchange a few more words before him and Bobby call it a night. Stressed, I let BJ inside and cuddle up with her on the couch for a few moments. "Do you think we got through to him?"

"For now, yes," he answers, pulling me and BJ into him. The feel of his arms around me helps me calm my nerves and I relax into him.

"So tomorrow is a busy day," I muse, grazing my fingers over his ring finger, thinking of the perfect way to state my claim.

"It seems to have turned out that way." Clayton frowns. "Are you going to have to leave soon?"

"I have a few more days."

"Is that going to be enough for you to trust me?"

I turn to him, meeting his eyes. "As I told you in the shower, I do trust you."

His arms tighten around me. "Can we move forward tonight?"

I smile, leaning my head back to kiss him. "Most definitely."

Our kiss gets heated, and BJ starts to whine. Ignoring her protests I pick her up and place her on the floor before I turn my body around and press my hard cock to Clayton's. He moans at the sensation and starts to raise my shirt, I do the same to him only breaking our connection to get them over our heads and toss them aside. We fumble with the rest of our clothes, and before I know it, Clayton is picking me up in his arms and walking me back to my bedroom.

"Is this alright, darlin'?" he asks. I just moan my approval on his skin, and he gently places me on the bed. Before he joins me, he pulls the lube out of my nightstand and places it on a pillow. We kiss until our lips are swollen and our hands get reacquainted with each other's bodies. "Daniel, please take me," Clayton moans. I hesitate for just a moment, my body involuntarily going rigid, fear crashing into my thoughts. He reads my mind and his breath is in my ear at once. "None of them, darlin', only you in so long." I relax, grabbing the lube, wetting my fingers before tracing his entrance. When I breach him, he moans and I gasp.

"Speaking of tight," I mutter working to stretch and tease him until he's whimpering beneath me. Smirking, I drop down and wrap my lips around him, causing a string of beautiful curses to escape his lips. I continue until he's shaking, warning me of his orgasm. I just look up through my lashes before I taste his cum on my tongue and in my throat. I lick him clean, rising up to his nipples while I slick my dick. When I'm sure he's ready, I push deep inside him. He moans loudly, wrapping his legs around my waist. My ministrations are purposely, maddeningly slow, our release nowhere in sight. I get lost in his deep blue eyes for the longest time. "Marry me,

Clayton." He pushes himself closer, causing me to get deeper as he studies my face.

"Okay."

Our lips meet, and I smile into the kiss. He is *mine* and the world will know it. Mike will know it and he will run away from *my* man just as he should. Breaking our kiss I move my lips down to Clayton's chest and mark him just over his heart. *Checkmate.*

35
Drama, Drama, Drama

Clayton's Point of View

I have never fucked so much in my life. My dick is fucking sore, and my ass isn't much better. The last damn thing in this world I want to do right now is get up out of this bed, but my bladder is screaming at me. Fuck! The moment I rise up, I have to stifle a whimper. Not being penetrated for seven damn months really takes a toll. Never mind the fact that Daniel is rather thick and long. I'm going to be sore for a damn week.

Slowly I make my way to the bathroom and do my business. Then I make my way to Daniel's coffee machine and let BJ out while I eat some pop tarts. Daniel is still sleeping, so I decide to use the guest bathroom to avoid waking him, taking a long hot a shower and following it up with a clean shave. All the while, my mind is on last night. *Shit, Reynolds! You're engaged.* I never thought something like this would happen after Ryan, until I met Daniel, and both times, he proposed perfectly. In the moment, no planning, no nerves, just him and me, right then.

"Clayton?"

"In here," I call back as I'm drying my shaven face. Daniel opens the door and stares at me, completely pale. *Fuck.* "Daniel, what's wrong?" I ask cautiously.

"You weren't there, just like last time . . . you weren't there when I woke up," he answers as his breathing becomes more and more shallow.

Understanding, I drop the towel in the sink and grab both his shoulders. "I love you, Daniel. I'm not going anywhere, and I don't want you to go anywhere. I'm sorry I startled you. You just looked too peaceful to wake up," I explain.

His breathing seems to calm a little. "So you're in this?"

"Yes."

He bites his lower lip. "This is the trust thing you were talking about, isn't it?"

"Yes."

"Okay," he says, nodding his head up and down. "I'm going to go take a shower now."

I smile and squeeze his shoulders. "Coffee's ready if you want some."

"Thanks, baby." He smiles, stepping away and out of the bathroom. I debate on following him, but I don't, figuring he may need a few moments to himself. After I finish getting ready, I sit down with the newspaper and wait for Daniel to join me. When he does, I can tell he's back to his confident self and I smile.

"Move in with me," I blurt out the moment he sits down.

"What's wrong with here?" he asks timidly.

"Hmm . . . not a gated community for one, you don't have a playroom for another. You gotta admit, I got the better bathrooms," I answer with a smirk.

He looks at his hands for the longest time. "Did you ever take Mike there?"

"Ahh, the ghost of Mike." I sigh, sipping on my coffee. "He has a key," I admit, "but I will get it back if it makes you uncomfortable. He's only been in my living room." I clarify, "He's never been to my bed, and he has never been in the playroom." I study Daniel for a while and then shake my head back and forth. "I'll toss the couch."

"Why don't we just both move?" he offers.

"It's not just Mike, is it?"

"No," he answers honestly.

"Fine, but we're hiring movers," I warn and then mutter, "the things I do for love."

He chuckles, taking my hand. "Thank you."

"You're welcome." I frown. "I have to go if I plan on getting my to-do list done today. Tell Tasha I love her."

"Can we have dinner tonight?"

"We can try, but no promises," I answer, pecking him on the lips. That's when I notice his eyes. "I'll stay the night, alright? I just can't promise a time, darlin'." He nods his head, and I sit down staring at him for a moment. "What can I say or do to get that look off your face?"

"If I answer that honestly, you are going to think I don't trust you."

"You want me to call you after Mike," I conclude, trying to hold back my annoyance.

"I can understand if you don't want to."

"Darlin', if it makes you more comfortable, I'm willing to bend. But I want to warn you. As your master, we are going to be starting where we left off. You and I need to build some stronger trust bonds. I think it will be helpful if we work on it on both sides of our relationship."

He gives a scuff. "We're talking about trust and we're engaged."

"Did you propose just so you can make a claim on me?"

"No," he answers, looking down at his hands. "I proposed because I love you."

"Which is why I accepted." I smile shyly at him. "We're still healing, Daniel. As you said, it's going to take time. When we're ready, we'll hop a plane to California and go from there."

"When we're ready," he agrees. "But we're house hunting now?"

"Yeah, adding a realtor to my list of to-do's as we speak." I wink. "I really have to go, darlin', but know that I will miss you only for a short while."

"Me too." He smiles giving me a quick kiss. I stand and head for his front door. "Clayton!"

"Yeah," I answer, turning around to find him walking to his kitchen. "In the meantime, you're going to need this," he says, handing me his house key. I give a rather large smile, then peck him on the lips. "Thanks, darlin'. I love you."

I make it to my car and head out to meet Mike, calling my PI while I drive, giving him my latest request, offering double to keep the questions to a minimal and my name out of it at all costs. Then I call by old bodyguard and explain I need his services, which leads to a bidding war, but I eventually win out. I'm drained by the time I get there. And knowing I still have a list a mile long isn't helping. My nerves are shot. *Mike's not going to be the first to know.* With that thought in mind, I call Alec.

"So have you called your PI?" he asks, not waiting for a hello.

"Yeah, he's on it, but that's not why I'm calling."

"What's wrong?"

"Nothing's wrong, Alec. For once, everything is right," I answer cheerfully.

"What do you mean?" he asks skeptically.

"He proposed again last night, and I accepted," I answer. The phone falls silent, and I know he's debating on a lecture of too far too fast; even if we hadn't broken up, we only really dated for about six months. "Please don't, Alec, not this time. I need you," I whisper.

"No Clayton, I know it's real." He whispers trying to disguise the fact his voice is shaking. "I'm just happy for you."

"Alec."

"I'm sorry. I was expecting this, honest. Maybe not so soon, but I figured it was coming," he answers in a slightly pained voice, that I can tell he's trying to hide. *Damn it.*

"Will you be my best man or is that too much to ask?" I whisper, drumming my thumb on the steering wheel.

"Of course I will, Clayton."

"Thanks, man." I smile. "Hey, I've gotta go."

"Let me know what your PI says."

"Will do." I sigh, hanging up. Yeah, glad I did that over the phone. I don't think I could have survived that in person.

Frowning, I get out of the car and make my way into the restaurant. I find Mike by himself waiting, and I realize I'm about five minutes early. *Might as well get it over with.*

"Hey." I smile, sitting next to him.

"Hey, yourself." He smiles back.

"Thanks for arranging this, Mike."

"Thanks for still caring."

"I'm serious about the friendship thing." I glare and then look down at my hands. "Mike, I've got something to tell you that's not going to sit right for a while. But I hope you can grow to accept it."

"Damn, Clay, you sound like you're getting married or some shit, lighten up." He laughs, trying to break the tension. Then he reads my facial expression, but before he can comment, another man sits down with us.

"Am I interrupting?" he asks.

"No," Mike answers in a really harsh tone. The man looks taken aback for a moment and then meets my eyes.

"So you're the concerned boyfriend."

"Concerned friend and confidant," I correct him.

"Nothing to worry about," he answers shortly.

"You see to it that there isn't," I snap.

H narrows his eyes, "Mike never mentioned your name."

"You won't get it from me." I shrug. "Just see to it that you stay on Master Alec's good graces. He and I are near and dear. And everyone knows he has a line to the Angels of Justice. Just ask Mike here what happened to the last master that crossed him."

"You threatening me?"

"Just stating facts."

"He had a panic attack, he didn't safe word, and risked subdropping," the man growls. "If you were a master, you'd understand."

I give a dark laugh. "Ain't no if about it." Then I lean in. "You need some training on after care and panic attacks period. If you don't take me up on this, then I suggest you walk away from Mike right now."

"Not from you," he growls.

I check my temper. "Fine, I'll have Master Alec contact you."

"Fine," he growls and turns to Mike. "Leave us for a moment." Mike doesn't even hesitate as he makes his way to the men's room. The man turns to me. "I do care about him. He just really freaked me out."

"Know the feeling." I sigh. "Safe words are meant to be used, not ignored."

"Thanks for worrying enough to contact me. I was skeptical, thinking you were a jealous boyfriend or whatever but you genuinely want to help me and I thank you for that."

"He's a dear friend. Don't think he won't tell me what's going on."

"I'm glad he's got you."

"Yeah, I just hope he feels the same way," I mutter, pulling out Alec's business card. "Tell him Mike sent you."

"Will do." He promises, standing up.

I snatch his hand. "If you don't call, I'll know."

He just nods and walks away.

Frowning, I walk back to the restrooms. When I realize we are alone, I pull his back into me. "He's gone."

"Yeah, so are you." Mike sniffs, shaking his head back and forth, looking at me through the mirror.

"Mike."

"Don't," he whispers, taking my hands in his. "You sure about this Clay?"

"Yes."

"We could have been so damn good together. If only you would have let yourself love me."

"Mike."

"I need some time, boss." He sighs. "A week or two, I have the vacation for it. My assistant can help with the transitions."

"Alright." I agree squeezing his hands tightly. "I want you in my life Michael. Promise me that."

He kisses my hand, meeting my eyes in the mirror with an all too serious look. "I'm not going anywhere Clay, promise." He turns in my arms suddenly causing his lips to be too close for comfort. I take a step back, turning away from him. "I really do hope he doesn't hurt you again, Clay," he sighs, dropping his head on the back of my shoulder. "I guess it's true. Sometimes love just isn't enough." He pulls back and walks away.

I stand there for a moment trying to gain my composure and deal with the tear in my heart. *God, how did he get to me?* I get my bearings, wash my face, and walk out of the restaurant to my car. When I get there, I pull out my cell phone and call Daniel.

"Hey, how did it go?" he asks without a hello.

I run my hands over my face. "His master is seeing things my way."

"Hey, you okay?"

I take a calming breath. "I will be."

"You told Mike, didn't you?" he guesses correctly.

"Yeah. He's taking some vacation." I frown. "Guess it went as well as can be expected."

"Do you need me?"

"Later, I still have some more shit to take care of." I fight back the emotional exhaustion, wishing I had Alec's shoulder. I really need a friend to talk to but Alec's not an option today. Maybe seeing Bobby will help.

"You don't have to do it all in one day, Clayton. I know this has to be draining," he replies in a small voice which tells me yes-I-do.

"I'm fine, darlin'. The rest of this shit is easy. Promise."

We say our goodbyes and I head to my house, taking care of a few things like paying bills, packing for a few days, and laundry while I wait for my subs to show up. When they arrive I let them wait for a few moments in my kitchen chairs until I go out there and end it, explaining that it wasn't their training. It was my real life that was getting in the way. I encourage them to look Alec back up and send them on their way. Bobby shows up not long after, and we spend the time packing up his truck with my current playroom equipment and driving it down to my storage locker, replacing it with mine and Daniel's equipment. We also hauled my perfectly good couch to Alec's Youth-In-Need center as a donation. *Might as well, right?*

"Need help setting up?" Bobby asks on the drive back to my place.

"No." I frown. "It needs a personal touch. You wouldn't happen to know a good realtor, would you?"

"Nope, sorry, dude." He shrugs. "You moving?"

"Yeah. Have you talked to Alec?"

"About getting hitched? Yeah, man. Congrats." He smiles.

"Daniel wants a neutral place," I explain. "That's why the couch had to go."

"What about your bed?" Bobby snorts.

"Not an issue. Never fucked on it," I answer with a shrug.

"So you never really let go." Bobby frowns. "Explains why you two are warp speed now, but that shit ain't healthy, Clayton. Had I known, I would have been down your damn throat."

"I moved on, I had Mike!" I growl defensively.

"Couldn't have meant much. The moment you saw Daniel you dropped Mike like yesterday's news." Bobby argues.

"It did, well it was starting to." I shake my head, "It doesn't matter now. I ended it." I frown, looking out of the passenger window.

"And there you are, Classic Clayton."

"What the fuck does that mean?"

"It means that you *always* end it. You never let anyone in, and the moment either side shows potential, you quit."

"That's not what happened with Daniel."

"I'm aware of that. He's the first man to ever get behind those walls, and stronger men have tried, Clayton. I don't know what makes him so special, but you two are co-dependent. He needs you right now, and I can tell you are stepping up, but you are going to need him too, and he needs to be strong enough for that."

"You're worried?"

"I care. Just because I'm the side line to Alec doesn't mean I don't care. It kills me to watch you sometimes, Clayton."

"Don't worry. I'm back to my old self."

"That's not reassuring," he mutters.

"Seriously stop. As you said, he got behind those walls. He's a stubborn man, Bobby. He's not going anywhere." I smile. We are silent for a while, and when he pulls up to my house, I wave at my bodyguard letting him know I plan on sticking around here for a while. We quickly unload his truck and I hand him a soda. "Thanks for your help today."

"Anytime."

"I lied to you." I frown, sitting down in a kitchen chair. "This Mike debacle matters." He sits down next to me. "Fuck Bobby he got through when I wasn't looking."

"You've known Mike longer than you've known Alec." Bobby points out. "The man has been there for you through a lot. You didn't recognize the friendship you had, which is why Alec was so against you two. He didn't want you to risk that."

"I'm so good at fucking shit up." I moan, dropping my head on the table.

"You tell him about your engagement?" Bobby asks.

"Yeah. Didn't sit well but he's promised to stick around." I sigh, sitting up in the chair.

"He's an honorable man Clayton. It might be bumpy for a while but you two will survive this." He smiles. "You got yourself a great friend there."

"I know I do." I smile squeezing his hand, letting him know I wasn't referring to Mike. "Go home to Alec. He needs you, Bobby."

"He was hoping you wouldn't pick up on that."

"Then tell him I didn't."

"He'll know that I'm lying."

"Probably, but I won't tell if you won't." I smile. "So when are you going to grow the balls and propose anyway?"

Bobby lets out a hearty laugh. "Alec is not the marrying kind."

"He is," I argue solemnly. "You have no idea how much you changed him, Bobby. You are the only man in this world he has ever dropped his defenses to. He'd marry you if you'd ask, but he will never ask you."

"You got past his defenses."

"No, I could have. There's a difference," I correct him. "Think about it."

When he leaves I call Amber and ask if she knows a good realtor, which of course she does, and the next thing I know, my inbox is flooded with houses for sale. As I filter through them, I call my mama and we chat for a good three hours about nothing in particular. I don't tell her that I'm engaged though. I want to do that in person, and I make a mental note to ask Daniel to go back down there tomorrow, before he has to leave again.

When I get off the phone, I make an off-handed decision and text him.

Six, kitchen chair, bring a can of your favorite color paint and equipment, no excuses –M.C.

I spend the rest of my time going over some work projects and e-mail Mike's assistant explaining that Mike's on vacation and what I will need from him in Mike's absence. I also work on wording the promotional e-mail and the new job post for our intranet. At 5:58, Daniel is walking through my door with a paint can and some painting supplies. Like a good sub, he doesn't say a word, waiting for instructions in the kitchen chair. When I'm ready, I close my laptop and walk behind him, running my fingers through his hair. "Our room is empty," I explain. "Well, not exactly empty, but nothing is set up." I shrug. "I thought we could do it together, considering the room is ours."

"I'd like that, Master."

"Careful." I warn. "What are your safe words?"

"Rose, petal, thorn."

"When do you say them?"

"When I've reached my limits or am uncomfortable."

"After seven months, will your limits be the same?"

"No, Master."

"Is it a sign of weakness to safe word?"

"No, Master."

"Do you trust me, Daniel?"

"With my life," he whispers.

"Strip," I command. He stands and quickly tosses his clothes to the floor.

"I'd offer you a seat on the couch, but I don't have one." I smile. "Follow me, bring the supplies."

He does as I command. I have him paint the entire room while I take the time to hang each tool carefully in its rightful place. Then I hunt down a fan and open the doors to alleviate any paint fumes, that's when I notice the can. The paint is environmentally safe. "Are you pregnant, Daniel?" I muse.

"No, Master."

"Then why spend so much on safe paint?"

"Less fumes for a windowless room, Master."

"So you were thinking," I chuckle. "Eager?"

"Yes, Master."

"You will be both rewarded and punished for that," I growl in his ear making my way to my kitchen for the perfect tool, leaving him to think of what I meant. I go to my refrigerator pulling out my homemade ginger plugs that I use for my own personal pleasure and place one in a small bowl. Then I go back to the room and debate on where I am going to tie him up for this. I can't use any wall fixtures because the paint has to dry. I could hang him from the ceiling. Or I could tie him to the spanking table. Hmm, decisions.

"Pick a number, ten your maximum," I command.

"Three," he answers immediately.

Should have guessed. That number does have significance to the day we met. Either way, vibrating table it is. When the walls are sufficiently covered in wet paint, I order him to lie on his stomach and I tie him down to all four corners, slapping his ass hard.

"Safe words."

"Rose, petal, thorn," he answers as I turn on the vibrator, putting friction on his cock. He moans at the sensation. I don't make a move to touch his body. Instead, I just stand back and wait. It takes about five minutes.

"Petal."

I turn off the vibrator and lightly graze my nails down his back. "Good. Now it's time for your pleasurable punishment." I put the bowl down in front of him and place the plug to his nose. "Smell," I demand.

"Ginger, Master?" he asks, and I slap his ass harder.

"I did not give you permission to speak," I growl. "Have you ever performed figging, Daniel?"

"No, Master."

"I find it rather enjoyable as a masturbation technique," I grin, wetting my finger and sliding it in his ass. "It just burns so fucking good. You are going to have to relax for this, Daniel. And remember that I would never experiment things like this with you without having done them myself. Are you comfortable?"

"Yes, Master."

I give a smile to myself, climbing up on the table. "First, a little moisture," I whisper, pushing my tongue into his hole. He jumps in surprise, and I smack his ass for not remaining still. Not long after, he is moaning deep in his throat. I pull back, taking the plug from my hand and begin to slowly insert it into him. He gasps in surprise, squeezing his eyes shut. I stop.

"Safe words."

"Rose, petal, thorn."

"Do you need to use them?"

"No, Master," he answers as sweat starts to bead up.

"I can see you are pushing yourself a little, Daniel. I will let you, but when it gets too much, you will do best to stop me, instead of me stopping you."

"Yes, Master," he moans while I push the plug completely in his ass, except for the thick large round end for a handle to pull it out later. Then I jump off the table and put the vibrator back on.

"Fuck!" he cries out, and I smirk, walking over to the cabinet and pulling out our crop. I smack him with it. "That's ten leather paddles for you," I snap. Then I start to twist the plug ever so slowly and a string of curses fall from his lips. This time, I smack him with my hands. "Make that thirty." He silences himself to a whimpering mess as I continue to twist and tug on the ginger plug, he even goes as far as fighting his restraints. *I should have used the spanking table.* "Count slowly, Daniel. I will stop when you get to two hundred." He starts counting and I continue my torturing, knowing he's enjoying the burn from the plug and fighting back his body's natural instincts.

"Seventy-three. Fuck, petal," he gasps, and I immediately pull the plug out and stop the vibrator.

"Are you alright?"

"Yes, Master. I just didn't want to cum," he explains. I give a small smile. "I think that's enough of this for one day."

I detach him from the table. "Get on the spanking table and prepare to be paddled," I instruct, going back to the cabinet for the leather paddle. When I approach him, he has his ass perfectly displayed for me. "I'm going to tie you up again, Daniel. It seems your stillness is out of practice," I explain. When he's sufficiently secure, I give him a dominating kiss and slip a cold, metal, lubed plug in his ass. He moans and I smirk. "Count and thank me," I demand, slapping his ass with the paddle. He takes it with pleasure and moans every time I hit the plug. *God, I've missed his sounds.* After his paddling, I slowly remove his plug and drip cool lube down his crack, causing him to shiver. I watch it ooze downward until it hits the bench while I pull my dick out of my pants and begin to coat myself. I give him absolutely no warning before I plunge into his ass. We both hiss a little from the aftermath of the ginger. "Burns so fucking good darlin'" I whisper in his ear. He nods. And I begin slow strokes.

"Please, Master, harder . . . the burning . . . from the ginger, please harder," Daniel cries, and I smack him on his cheeks for each word, but I understand his request and start slamming into him because I can feel the tingle burning too. It doesn't take Daniel long to start struggling against his restraints, and I'm right behind him. "Cum, Daniel," I command, and the moment the words escape my lips, his ass is pulsing around me while I lose my load. We ride the aftershocks together, and all too soon, I am breaking our connection.

"Stillness, Daniel," I snap, tucking my dick back up. "It's a skill, one that needs to be practiced." He doesn't try to comment or apologize as I undo his restraints, and he's smart enough not to move. "Follow me," I demand, leading him out of our room and into my living room. "Kneel," I order, pointing to where my couch used to be. He does so willingly, but I know he's going to be uncomfortable shortly due to the hardwood floors.

I leave him there in that position as I check my e-mails content on sifting through more houses. While I'm filtering I come across a file that my PI sent me. I read through it myself before I begin talking. "It appears Detective Cole's sister has been kidnapped into what they believe to be some sort of sex cult. They have a suspect of the leader but no proof, which explains why they need our help," I mutter opening the attachment labeled "Suspect." The moment my eyes fall on the picture, I freeze and the laptop falls to the floor.

"Red!" Daniel screams and runs up to me. "Clayton?"

"It's Cassandra," I manage, causing him to frown, looking at the computer screen.

"Oh, hell no!" he gasps in anger.

"Daniel?"

"That's Cassandra Lupa, Brad's cousin."

36
Panic

Clayton's Point of View

Everything comes rushing at me, the acid flowers, the insults, the drama. Cassandra has been a pain in my ass for years. I signed her two weeks after I started a Dom/sub relationship with Daniel. I just chalked it up to the universe balancing itself out. I had no damn clue that it was intentional until now. Goosebumps run up and down my spine at the thought of exactly how much Brad knows about both of us.

Daniel is staring at the computer screen and his hands are shaking. "Clayton, I need a drink," he whispers.

I drop to my knees in front of him, closing my laptop. "No," I whisper. He closes his eyes and starts to dry heave. Frowning, I lean into him and whisper, "Red." He doesn't argue with me. I frown, running my fingers through his hair. "Stay here," I command, leaving him for only a moment to grab our leather cuffs. When I get back, he's still in the same condition I left him. I gently pull his hands behind his back and trap his wrists. Then I kiss the back of his neck, grazing my nails over his muscular torso, trying my best to soothe him. His breathing eventually steadies for me, and I pull him into me while digging out my cell phone.

"We have a huge problem," I growl, not waiting for Alec to say hello.

"What's wrong now?" Alec asks concerned yet annoyed.

"We know what the cops want, and Brad has become a major issue."

"Can you and Daniel come to us?"

"No, I'm sorry, Alec. We can't. Daniel is in pieces."

"Are you at his place?"

"No, mine."

"We'll be there shortly," he promises.

I drop my phone to the floor, not bothering to check that the call disconnected. I figure it did when it rings, but I just let it go to voicemail. Nothing in my world is more important in this moment than my Daniel. About a half hour later, Alec and the rest of the 'Angels' walk in on me comforting Daniel, and Alec's eyes narrow. "Clayton."

"Alec."

"A moment," he demands.

Frowning, I lean Daniel forward a little, letting him balance on his own legs, whispering, "Stay here," before I get up and follow Alec to my bedroom.

"He's cuffed," Alec growls.

"I'm aware of that," I snap. "He needs order. It's the only thing keeping him stable."

"I don't appreciate walking in on one of your sessions," he growls. "You knew we were coming."

"You prefer him to drown in a bottle or contemplate suicide?" I snap, pointing to my living room. "Because that's your option, Angel!"

Alec's eyes flash, and I find my arm being twisted behind my back, gently but quickly. I immediately fall to my knees, bending my will to him. In that moment, he switches from my friend to my master. "Don't ever call me that again," he growls in my ear. "That's the past, Clayton. Leave it there."

"I'm sorry, Master," I gasp as reality sinks in around me. "I'm spinning. I don't know where that came from."

He releases my arm. "You're scared. That's where it came from."

"Extremely," I whisper.

"What's going on, Clayton?"

"Brad and Cassandra are cousins," I whisper. The next thing I know, I am being dragged back in the living room and ordered to kneel next to Daniel. Alec then kneels in front of both of us.

"Transition," he orders.

I close my eyes and whisper, "Red."

"Blue," our grand master smiles, leaning into Daniel. "I'm your master now. Understood?"

"Yes, Grand Master," Daniel answers firmly.

"Clayton," Grand Master growls, "start from the beginning."

I explain to the room how my second cousin first introduced me to Cassandra, his girlfriend at the time, which is why I tolerated her. I inform them about the drama she caused when she was in the band and how I kept her in a contract out of spite due to her attitude more than anything. I also mention the acid flowers and the fact that I have a ton of PI research on her but no direct proof of a sex ring.

"Daniel, call your Detective Cole. Tell him that we can't find proof on his suspect and we need more before we will act on anything like that. Make sure he knows that we have the upper hand," our grand master orders him.

"Yes, Grand Master."

"Did you talk to your lawyer about the rest?"

"It's plausible, Grand Master."

"What's the problem?"

"There's bad blood with the governor and the Kingsley's," Daniel mutters. "I can't keep my name out of it at this point. He might not sign off on it."

"He'll sign off," Grand Master retorts confidently.

"How the hell can you be so sure?" I snap, rising to my feet. "This is stupid!" I scream, getting in his face. "We need to just stay the fuck out of it. I get that it's this guy's sister, I do, but we are risking too much! It's too dangerous! If we're going to put our necks out, it should be for Brad."

He stares at me speechless for a moment. "I didn't realize it's up for a vote, Clayton," he growls. "At least not yet."

"Alec."

"I'm sorry. I didn't hear that," he snaps.

Frustrated, I correct myself. "Grand Master."

"Silence!" he bellows.

He takes a few calming breaths before walking behind me. The room is so quite that my ears begin to ring. I hear a door and I know that he has left us alone. Not much later, he returns. "Come, Clayton." He commands. I turn and approach him sitting on a kitchen chair, paddle in hand. I stop short of him, waiting for his embarrassing order. He notes my reluctant expression by touching my face. It's a silent moment between Dom and sub, letting me know he's aware that I'd prefer a cane or whip over this humiliation in front of the entire group, communicating that this is my punishment for going too far, on more than one account really. I close my eyes to his touch, refusing to let him see my complete shame. "Prepare," he demands. I slowly remove my clothes and lower myself so that I can drape my body over his lap. "Ben, I want you to count for him," our grand master instructs, and my body tenses. I know he notices because he shifts me but makes no effort to comfort. "Are you aware of the offenses?"

"Yes, Grand Master," I whisper.

The feel of the wooden paddle on my ass isn't even really painful. It's just the act of it happening that upsets me. Of all the days, it just has to be today, doesn't it? I know I shouldn't have snapped at him like that, but I needed a friend more than a master. Hell, I needed to control something, anything. Without control, there is chaos, and with chaos, there is my life. *Fuck.*

"Twenty-three," Ben counts and I feel the paddle continue.

I need to run, to escape. I safe word and bolt upright turning away from him in one quick movement. Not saying another word, I rush to my bedroom and close the door behind me. I consider locking it, but I remember how scared I was when Daniel did that to me, so I leave it and ball up in a corner. My mind is racing as I rock myself, trying to get today's events in perspective. It's just too much. I've had enough.

"Clayton," Grand Master's voice calls through the door after a few moments have passed, but I don't make a move to get it. I hear the door open directly after but I don't look at him. "Clayton, please," he pleads in a pained voice touching my arm. I don't react.

"Let me try, Alec," Daniel says.

"He needs me, I did this," he argues.

"You have no idea what kind of day he's been having. Please, Alec, let me love him."

"I'm not leaving with him in pieces." I can tell by his voice that my reaction has clearly upset him but I have no strength in me to even attempt to comfort him.

"Then stay," Daniel counters. "Just let me do this. Besides, Ben is white as a ghost. I don't think Amber or you have ever pushed him to his limits before. Has he ever seen a subdrop? Maybe you should explain to him what the hell is going on."

"Are you telling me how to play my part?"

"No." Daniel sighs. "You released us, Alec. I'm giving you advice as a friend."

"Just try to get him to talk to me, alright?"

"No promises," Daniel answers, and shortly after, I hear the door close.

"Baby, it's me. Just me," Daniel whispers reaching out to gently caress my back.

"I just need a second," I mutter.

The moment his arms are around me, I break down crying. "Shh . . . I'm here," he whispers. "I'm right here," he soothes, kissing my hair. I don't say anything, and he eventually picks me up and takes me to my bed, laying me down and pulling me to him.

I don't take note of the time or how much of it passes as my mind races through the most recent painful events, my humiliation being the least of my worries. My mind relives the painful memory of breaking Mike's heart and cracking mine followed by the painful notion that I added yet another crack in Alec's. Never mind the fact, I find out how obsessed my future-husband's ex really is.

"Cassandra sent Rose," I manage to sob out in Daniel's chest. "Shit, Daniel," I moan. "She's the only one I didn't ask."

"Didn't ask what, baby?" he asks, gliding his fingertips down my back.

"For test results," I answer. "Women don't normally carry them around," I mutter. "I used protection, I swear. But fuck, Daniel, Cassandra sent her," I cry.

His body tenses around me. "How long ago, baby?"

"Three months," I answer with a sniff.

"You've tested clean how many times since then?"

"Six."

"Sounds like the only thing you have to worry about is a child." Daniel smiles.

"That's not funny," I warn.

"True," he agrees with a chuckle. "But now, I definitely want a pre-nup. No redheaded stepchild is going to steal my family's fortune."

"Still not funny," I pout. "God, Daniel, she looked just like you. She could be your twin."

"Now that's not funny."

"I think it was the point."

"Yeah, but why?"

"I don't know," I answer, picking at his shirt.

"Clayton, out of curiosity, how protective are you of your identity?"

"You're asking Mr. Paranoid." I laugh. "Believe me, if they tried that, I would know."

"Both Lake and Reynolds?".

"Yes," I assure him.

"Then I have no idea what she wanted."

"Besides me to hurt you more?" I frown.

His eyes meet mine, but before he can answer, there's a knock on the door. He turns to it then back to me. "You are freaking him out, you know."

I just curl into him. "I know."

"Will you please talk to him?" Daniel asks kindly.

"I prefer this little bubble," I mutter.

"I know, baby, but he's terrified." Daniel sighs. "Remember when I ran away from you? How you felt?"

I lean back, meeting his eyes. "Fine, but we need to be alone."

"I know." He smiles, kissing my forehead before climbing out of bed and opening the door. "Eggshells," he warns stepping out of my room as Grand Master steps in.

"Hey," Grand Master says when the door clicks, passing me my clothes and two chocolate bars. "Here, eat these and get dressed. Talk to me Clayton."

"Thank you Grand Master," I acknowledge, taking my clothes and turning from him as I dress. When I am clothed I begin to chew on the chocolate.

"I'm sorry," he whispers climbing into my bed and pulling me to him. "You obviously needed a friend, and I couldn't . . . not after the angel slip. Forgive me."

"I'm the one that should be apologizing, Grand Master. I'm the one that disrespected you." I frown, taking another bite.

"That you did," he agrees. "Did you learn your lesson, Clayton?"

"Yes, Grand Master."

"Good," he says sternly. "Blue."

"I'm sorry I called you angel, Alec." I sigh, sitting up and pulling away from him. "I'm sure of all the damn days for me to slip that badly, today had to be the worst."

"It didn't sit well."

"You going to tell Bobby?"

"We don't have secrets."

"Don't," I warn. "He wouldn't understand, not that. Just leave it in the past, Alec. Like you said, it's where it belongs."

"I'll think about it."

"He really loves you," I note. "More than you realize." I smile, turning to him at last. "Don't push him away, Alec. He's close to a really solid wall around your heart. Just don't run when he starts taking it down."

"I don't plan on running from him," Alec answers, narrowing his eyes.

I lean into him. "I didn't plan on Daniel running from me."

"Clayton."

"Just call me, alright, if you think about running? Call me before you make the biggest mistake of your life," I beg, lacing my fingers in his. "I love you too much to let you experience the pain that I went through, Alec. And I'm sorry that my happiness hurts you."

"Clayton," he whispers with shaky breath.

"Shh . . ." I soothe, ghosting my lips to his, just for a moment, before dropping to his ear. "I'm not the one, angel. Bobby is. Trust him, love him. Give your soul to him."

He drops our laced fingers and grips me tightly, crying, "How did you know? How did you know I've been freaking out?"

"We're friends, Alec. I can read you just as easily as you can read me," I answer rubbing his back. "Don't run, promise me that."

"I promise," he cries.

Moments later, there is a knock on the door, and then Bobby sticks his head in. "Ya'll hungry?" he asks. "Oh, um sorry," he says, backing away.

"Bobby."

"Yeah?"

"He needs you." I smile, pulling away from Alec. "You're the one."

Bobby stares at me. I walk up to him and give him a hug, standing on my tiptoes to reach his ear. "Give it a few weeks. Then ask him."

He pulls away, looking at Alec and then me before he nods. I smile and step out, giving them their moment.

The rest of the night passes without confrontation, although Ben is still a little shaken by the whole thing. Even after assuring him that I am fine, he really won't completely understand subdrop until it happens to him, and it will happen. After dinner, I wound up in a huge lecture on safe words and why they are so important and signs of subdrop in case it happens when he's alone. Daniel winds up stepping in and rescuing the poor guy.

The next day is spent at Daniel's. We play with BJ and make a shit-load of phone calls, having papers couriered back and forth between the police station, the district attorneys' office, Daniel's lawyers, and his house. While we wait, we go through a few prospective houses that we would like to see in person and agree to sell Daniel's place first, then buy a new home before we put mine up for sale. Having a playroom is a seller's no-no, and we didn't want to go without.

That night as we lay down, Daniel is frowning. "What's wrong, darlin'?"

"I have to fly out tomorrow morning," he whispers.

"So soon?" I frown. "I was hoping we could go see Mama."

"When I get back, promise," he says, kissing the top of my head.

"Will you leave me your flight numbers?"

"Always," he chuckles. "We'll visit your parents and mine when I get home, okay?"

"Okay," I agree. "Daniel?"

"Hmm." He smiles.

"Will you take my bodyguard to the airport?"

"Will it make you feel better?"

"Yes."

"Then I will," he whispers, kissing me lightly.

"Thank you," I answer, pulling him closer. "Alec and Bobby are getting married."

"Oh?"

"Bobby hasn't asked yet, but I worked it out for them."

"Good for you, baby," he laughs. "What I would give to see Alec's face."

I start chuckling. "God, I know he will call me the moment it happens," I groan. "Then I will have to remind him to say yes to the poor guy."

"You really think he will?"

"Yeah, I do." I smile happily.

We end up talking each other to sleep, and the next day, I wake to an empty bed with a note listing Daniel's flight numbers. As I'm brushing my teeth, my cell goes off, it's Ben.

"Hey."

"Hey, were you two so involved that Daniel missed his flight or something?"

"What are you talking about?" I ask, panicked.

"He's not here," Ben answers.

Fuck me. "I'll call you back."

The first number I dial is my bodyguard's. When it goes to voice mail, I forget how to breathe listening to an evil laugh. *You have reached Brad Pazzo. I have both your loves, Clayton. If you want to save just one of their lives, then you will do exactly as I say. Check your mailbox for further instructions. See you soon.*

The phone falls from my hand, and everything around me goes black.

37

Kidnapped

Daniel's Point of View

Wow, headache. I go to rub my face but find that my arms are tied behind me. Panic sets in as I struggle without avail to break free, only to discover that my legs and chest are bound as well. I try to think of the last thing I remember. The memory flashes, it's of Clayton's bodyguard helping me into his car . . .

"Settle now," Brad's voice rings in my ear. "You're alright. I'm here," he whispers, releasing my blindfold. I blink at the light in the room.

Confused, I look up to I see Clayton's body guard staring at me. "Won't be needing this anymore." He smiles, peeling off his face to reveal his true identity, why didn't I think to ever have a conservation with this guy? His voice would have given it away immediately. I work to keep my fear from showing. He's been this close all this time? "There was a time there when I thought it wouldn't be necessary. Fuck Danny, it took forever for him to trust me with you."

Although I am not gagged, I choose not to respond. "Come now. The drugs have worn off. You should be fine in just a few moments." I start to look around the room and find the walls covered in pictures of me, when I study the backgrounds of a few I realize that Clayton or Ben should be with me but they've been cut out. I swallow back the bile in my throat and start to breathe deeply through my nose to keep from crying. "I missed you so much," he continues, placing his hand on my cheek. I violently turn my face away from him, earning a hard slap. "He doesn't love you!" he screams. "I'm the only one who ever has!"

"Has Clayton made contact yet?" Cassandra interrupts in a bored voice, coming from somewhere behind me.

"He will." Brad shrugs. "Ben just needs to realize that he is missing first."

"I need your help," Cassandra tells him, studying her nails.

"Now?" Brad snaps.

"Yes, now," she growls.

"But he just woke up." Brad whines.

She studies me for a moment. "I'll let you play with him in a little while. Right now, Mike needs to be disciplined."

"Mike?" I ask confused.

Brad turns to me with a frown. "Mike Walker, yes, Clayton's true love, he's here. You'll see."

"Here how?" I ask cautiously. "Against his will or working with you?" But Brad doesn't have to answer because at that moment, I can hear Mike's piercing screams. I do my best not to shudder.

"Let's go," Cassandra snaps, grabbing Brad's arm, dragging him out of the room. The moment I am left alone, I try again to struggle against my restraints only to find it's useless.

After a little while and some more horrid screaming, Brad returns and drops a video screen down from the ceiling. "Now, let me show you exactly who he loves," he smiles, turning on a projector that shows multiple pictures of Clayton and Mike, kissing, holding hands in public, laughing, fucking in his office. I do my best to hold back the hurt on my face, watching slide after slide, and just when I think I can't handle it for one more moment, the pictures change. They are of Brad and myself. I can't help it. My body reacts involuntarily and I vomit all over myself.

"*These* sicken you!" he screams, yanking my hair. "I think it's time that you realize who your master really is."

God help me.

38
Choice

Clayton's Point of View

Sitting in my car, I stare at a warehouse Brad has directed me to. I know Daniel is in there, and it's taking every ounce of strength that I have not to run in there and beat the guy to a pulp. I know this is a trap. I can feel it in my veins.

I have both of your loves, Clayton . . . Save one of their lives.

This guy's mental. And knowing Cassandra professionally, it doesn't surprise me that she is too. His instructions said to come alone warning that if I brought anyone into it, he would know and they would both die. I have no doubt that it's not an empty threat. Bracing for the worst and sending prayers up to all the heavens I could think of, I steel myself and step out of my car. As I approach the building, I am greeted with what could only be Brad.

"You come alone?" he snaps, closing the distance, searching me for wires that he will not find.

"Yes."

Satisfied, he grabs my upper arm and forces me inside. He takes me into the center of a main room, on each side of me is a gate. In front of me, I can clearly see Daniel and Mike being held up by some chains attached to their wrists, dangling from a hook in the ceiling. Both gagged. Both over a pool of water.

"I've always wondered what it would feel like to kill someone," Brad muses, stepping in front of me and showing me a switch that I presume is connected to the chains. "I just wanted to drown one of them, but Cassandra is a freak and thinks acid would be more fun."

"Why are you doing this?"

"Danny is MINE!" he growls. "And if he won't have me, than nobody will have him."

"If I choose to save Daniel?"

"You will be saving his *life*, Clayton. You will not get to keep him," Brad snaps.

"And by choosing Mike?" I ask, keeping my expression neutral.

"Then we both win." He shrugs. "You get to save your true love, and Danny chooses his fate for not choosing me."

"You're just going to let us walk out of here unharmed?"

"Killing either of them will leave you unharmed?"

I don't answer turning my attention to Cassandra. "Explain Rose," I snap. She gives an evil laugh and a projector starts in the wall in front of me showing Mike and me in various compromising positions in my office. "You couldn't have done that yourself?" I growl. "You were in my office a thousand times."

"True." She shrugs, swiping the controls from Brad and climbing up some wired stairs that are hanging from the ceiling. "But your *lover* has proven to be even more paranoid than you. Every time I left, he swept the office. Apparently, he didn't think Rose could do any harm, which of course, he was wrong."

"You know what, Cassandra? You're a fucking bitch." I laugh but stop abruptly when she flips the switch just for a moment, lowering both Mike and Daniel a little closer to the acid.

"You only have time to save one," Brad warns, when they stop moving.

"You run left, you save Mike. You run right, you save Danny. I wouldn't dwell on it too long, Clayton. Otherwise, you won't save either."

"There's no dwelling. I've already made my choice."

"You hear that, Mike? You're going to die!" Cassandra cackles.

"You sure?" Brad asks.

"Without a doubt," I answer confidently.

"Then start running." He laughs, giving Cassandra the cue to flip the switch back on.

My feet are like led, but I turn toward my choice, praying to all the gods in all the heavens and run *LEFT.*

39
Cost

Clayton's Point of View

~This Morning~

I wake up to my phone ringing over and over. Shaking, I squeeze my eyes shut, answering in a raspy voice, "Hello."

"Clayton? About damn time. I've been calling for twenty minutes. I'm almost there," Alec's relieved voice rings in my head. Alec, he's safe. "You had me fucking worried sick, I thought something happened. Ben said Daniel missed his flight and you never called him back. Did you two have a falling out? What's going on?"

"Who are you?" I ask, too scared to admit to myself that this could be a trap.

"It's Alec," he answers with concern.

"Prove it. Where did we first meet?"

"Outside your buddies bar,'" Alec answers with annoyance. "At an *Eyes of Seduction* concert."

"Are you safe, Alec? Really safe?"

"What the hell is up with the twenty questions, Clayton? Where's Daniel?" he snaps.

"Brad was my bodyguard," I groan.

"F-U-C-K."

~Present~

The scream of "NOOOOOOO!" is so loud that I think everyone in the building is going to go deaf. I glance over my shoulder to confirm Brad is running to save Daniel, knowing Cassandra is too twisted to stop. *Thank the heavens.*

"Mike!" I scream, making it to the pool of acid and watching in horror as he gets closer to it. "Swing for me, darlin'." He understands my request and starts to sway his body while I climb the ladder, careful not to get too close to the edge. Just as he gets the momentum, the unexpected happens. Everything goes black.

"NO!" Cassandra screams in the darkness, I hear her heals running on the metal and am pissed that I can't stop her. That's when I realize that it's not just the lights; all the power is out. I can't reach Mike, which means Brad can't reach Daniel. *Shit.*

I stay where I am on the ledge, holding my breath, waiting. It feels as though three lifetimes pass, listening to the clattering of Daniel's and Mike's chains while Brad continuously cries out to Daniel. "*I* love you! *I'm* here to save you. Just hold on, sweetheart. Your true love is here." I shudder at his catcalls, unsure exactly how to explain myself to Daniel. Before I can get too deep in thought, I see flashlights.

"We need power!" I scream, wincing as the light hits my face. "It's acid. Watch your back. Cassandra's here somewhere."

"Go," Alec's voice rings in the dark. I watch as a flashlight disappears, leaving just Alec standing there taking in the scene the best he can. He doesn't say a word while we wait.

"Keep swinging, darlin'," I encourage Mike. "You're almost safe." The power gets restored moments later, and Mike comes at me full force, knocking me off my feet and partially into the acid. "AHHHHH!" I scream, hanging onto him for dear life. I raise my feet instantly at the feel of the pain, searching for the landing. "It's okay. We're going to be alright," I chant as Mike starts screaming in his gag. As we fall lower, we are on the opposite end of the pool, away from the landing. Mike's unable to bend his legs, so I wrap one leg around them and twist, putting him at an angle to keep his feet from falling in as I sacrifice my other foot again while we swing back to the other side. I manage to hold back a scream, and wrap my throbbing foot around the ladder, stopping us.

"Stop him!" I scream, looking up to see Brad taking Daniel into his arms and start to run toward a different exit. Bobby is on him in an instant. One punch sends Brad to the ground as Bobby sweeps Daniel from his arms. "A little help." I frown as my wet foot starts to slip. Alec is at my side moments later. It takes a few clever moves, but we manage to get Mike unhooked without harm.

The first thing I do is remove his gag while Alec releases his hands. "Clay! Clayton! I knew you would pick Daniel. Why? Why did you save me?" he cries, falling onto my shoulder.

"Because I love you both, and I made a very dangerous gamble," I whisper.

"You?"

"Shh . . . I'm sorry, Mike. It's not enough," I interrupt.

"You saved your life too," Daniel adds from behind us. "He was going to kill you if you chose me."

Ignoring my burning skin, I jump off the platform and land at Daniel's feet. "I'm sorry. I just . . . If you would have lived and he . . . you would have suffered . . . Alec told me that Brad couldn't kill you . . . I couldn't choose . . . I gambled . . . fuck, if something would have happ . . ."

I'm cut off with Daniel's lips on mine. "I know, baby. I do," he assures me, taking me in an embrace. "We need to get you to a hospital."

"It'd be best to strip his socks and shoes, possibly his pants," Alec agrees, coming down with a very terrified Mike.

"Where's Cassandra?" I frown, following his advice carefully, using only my fingertips.

"Can't find her," Bobby calls. "Brad's a little tied up at the moment."

"Daniel," Alec frowns, taking in the sight of my very raw, red feet. "Detective Cole is waiting outside. Have him take all three of you to the hospital. Tell him to keep his phone on. We'll call him. Clayton needs to get that taken care of immediately, and you two are covered in bruises, go get medical attention."

"Alec." I frown.

"Damn it Clayton, I told you. If he harms either of you, he's mine," Alec snaps.

I grab his arm and meet his eyes. "Don't do anything you can't live with. And remember the cop's sister. We need Cassandra, and Brad is our only hope."

Alec gives me a weak smile, nodding. "Go. You need your feet."

I want to argue, to try to stop him, but I know it's useless; never mind the fact that I'm not on my feet much longer. "Daniel!" I protest, kicking at the knees.

"Oh, shut up, Clayton," he growls, wrapping Mike's arm around his neck, walking us outside to safety.

~Twelve Hours Later~

Alec knocks on the door of my hospital room, letting himself in. "I'm sorry Clayton I can't stay. I just came by to say hello. How bad is the damage?"

"I won't be running marathons anytime soon." I frown.

"He needs skin grafts." Daniel growls. "Tell me that fucker paid." Alec just looks at him, and Daniel visually relaxes. "Detective Cole turn you in?"

"No." Alec shrugs, flexing his bruised knuckles. "We lost Cassandra, and Brad's not talking. I promised cooperation when she turns up. We'll find her. That's where I'm going from here, to talk to our attorney's about immunity." Alec takes Daniel's hands. "How are you?"

"It was more mental than anything else," Daniel answers, stepping away from him. "Mike's the one that suffered. Doctors say he'll be here for a while."

"You plan on sticking with your therapist and away from alcohol?" Alec asks.

"Of course," Daniel answers. "I'm more worried about Clayton."

"Well, I'm worried about all three of you." Alec retorts. "Both physically and mentally."

"You're not our father, Alec," I answer in a shy smile. "But thank you, for everything."

He gives a short smile. "I'll be back the moment visiting hours allow tomorrow, promise."

"Alec!" I call out as he starts for the door. "It's okay to cry. Let Bobby love you." He just gives me a sad smile, nods, and leaves the room. "He's right to be worried about your mental welfare. How are you doing Daniel?"

"I'm fine," Daniel smiles, sitting down on my bed, "but I'm pretty sure Mike really hates me."

"Why do you say that?" I ask confused.

"I stole his boyfriend from him after I was stupid enough to throw him away in the first place." He sighs.

"I'm sure having intimate details thrown at you wasn't easy." I frown. "I don't know how or why he slipped through, but it doesn't change things, he's not enough, Daniel."

"Are you sure?" he asks. "Those pictures, Clayton. You were so happy."

"Not as happy as he is with you," Mike whispers. We both turn to the door to see him standing there holding his I-V cart. "That's what I saw in those pictures. I was the happiest. He still had a ghost in his eyes. He doesn't do that with you, Daniel. Even after everything, you are what he wants. He loves you."

"What are you doing out of bed?" I ask, rising up quickly.

"I wanted to see you."

"Heard of a wheelchair?" I snap with a glare before I turn to Daniel for help. Daniel takes Mike off his feet and gently sets him on the side of my bed. "You shouldn't be walking in your condition!"

"Yeah, because sitting isn't painful." He bitches, "Thanks for the worry, Clay. Really, but I'll live." Mike smiles. "Thanks to you."

"You're a great employee. I can't lose you."

"Ha, Ha." He smiles.

"Seriously Mike, what did the doctors say?" I ask upset.

"They think the thirty percent loss in my right leg is permanent. They want to do back surgery to see if they can fix some of the damage, but if the nerves are shot there's not much they can do. I'll start therapy after that. It's not good, but it could be a hell of a lot worse." He frowns.

I pull him into a hug. "I'm so sorry."

"I don't blame you Clay." He assures me pulling back with a sad smile. "I still want my vacation when I get out of here."

"Consider it done." I smile. "Good thing I pay for great medical benefits, huh?"

He gives a hearty laugh. "Yeah." Then his face turns solemn and he takes my hand in his, "Seriously, Clay, I came in here to give you my blessing. To let you know I understand. Maybe one day I'll find my other half eh?"

"He's out there, Mike," I assure him.

"I can only hope. In the meantime, I'm going to need a raise."

"Oh really?"

"Yeah, you see, my boss made me deal with this bitch that hates me so much she wants me dead. Seeing as though she's still out there, I need to hire some protection," he answers seriously.

"Talk to Detective Cole for good names. Then give them to me. We will run so many damn background checks we'll know the day he first spoke."

"Sounds good."

"Mr. Walker!" a nurse gasps. "What are you doing out of bed?!"

He cringes with a laugh. "Busted."

"I'll come visit, okay? And there are phones here, Mike." I smile.

He rolls his eyes as he stands up and puts his weight on the nurse. "See you around, Clay."

When the room is ours again, I turn to Daniel. "You still in this?"

"Yeah, you?"

"Hell yeah."

Epilogue
Surrender

Bobby's Point of View

"Alec?" I ask, watching him stare off into the distance again.

"Hmm?" he asks, turning to me but not looking me in the eyes.

"Are you alright?" I ask with concern.

"Yeah everyone's safe. Justice has been served." He shrugs turning back to the window.

"No Alec." I frown. "Are *you* alright?"

He gives a weak smile. "I'm fine."

"I'm sorry he's hurt you," I whisper, knowing where his mind is, to the Clayton-could-have-beens.

"He's hurt . . . ?" he asks lost, giving me his full attention for the first time. "Oh, Bobby. I'm so sorry. That's not, no . . ."

I know he's lying, but I don't call him out. I don't have the strength to hear the truth. If the man wants to be in denial, then I was going to let him be. "I love you, Alec," I whisper, taking his slender form in my arms, pressing my lips to his.

He kisses me deeply before pulling away, frowning. "He said something, about you, love. That's where my head has been."

"About me?" I ask, confused.

He gives a small blush, "I'm sorry, Bobby. It just scared me, that's all. I swear."

"Scared you how?" I ask trying to figure out what Clayton told him. I know it had nothing to do with proposing marriage. Clayton and I both knew if we attempted to introduce the idea, Alec would shut it down before I could get a chance to ask. I know Clayton wants Alec to be happy, and he knows that I can do that, given the chance. So I'm worried hearing that Alec's scared because it means he's scared of us.

"It's hard to put into words, love," he responds, lacing his fingers in mine. "I won't insult you and lead you to believe that Clayton's engagement doesn't hurt, because it does. I love him. We both know that, and it's been that way since you and I started." I close my eyes to the words, fighting back the emotions they cause. Alec would never say them to hurt me, so I know he has a point. I just have to be patient enough to let him get there. "But I love you too. And it's different." I open my eyes in concern, but his gaze is steady, reassuring. "I've never once allowed myself to compare. I never thought it to be fair. But with you, there's something I can't define. And that's what's scaring the hell out of me."

"Enough to end this?" I ask with a cracking voice.

"No," he answers, touching my face. "But I have a feeling I know what he wants for us. And I am begging you not to ask it." My eyes widen, but his stare is not one of fear, just love. "Would you have ever thought to ask if he hadn't planted it in your head?"

"No," I admit.

"Why?" he asks, stepping closer.

"Because it's not us," I answer confidently.

"Exactly," he whispers. "We don't need that to be happy, do we, love?"

"I need you."

"And I you." He smiles. "The only two people who should define us, is us." I do my best to keep the question from showing in my gaze, but I should know better, Alec has always been perceptive when it comes to my feelings. I hear the sigh as he gives a weak smile. "If you really needed it, Bobby, you know my answer."

"I don't. I just need you."

"I'm right here, love." He smiles before standing on his toes. Suddenly I know what he's afraid of. He's ready to take the final step. He's ready to surrender to me. I read his body language and close the gap between us, kissing him deeply. He starts to walk backward toward the bedroom, and I stop him halfway down the hallway, pinning him to the wall. He breaks the kiss in confusion, and I stop all movement, cautiously waiting for his okay, never daring to push him like this without his explicit permission.

His lips tentatively meet mine and I pull back. "I promise you'll enjoy this." I encourage, my eyes meeting his, letting him know I understand his fear. Assuring him he's safe, that I would die a thousand deaths before I ever hurt him.

"I trust you," he assures me, striping off my shirt, willfully surrendering. Not wanting to push I decide to take it slow, making sure he has plenty of time to change his mind. I close the distance between us again and press my hard-on into his stomach. I know he's with me at the moment because he's pressing into my upper thigh. I take my time with him, kissing, licking, biting as I expose his partly scarred skin to me. After we strip each other I worship his form from head to toe, licking and nibbling every part of him except his gentiles. When I reach his feet I grab his pants and dig out his wallet, fishing through it for supplies and stop at his facial expression.

"We don't have to," I assure him, placing them in his hand, as I stand, kissing his forehead.

He doesn't respond at first. When I hear the condom rip, I mentally curse his past only to be surprised to feel the condom being placed on my cock. My eyes meet his, and all he whispers is, "Please."

Stunned, I take the lube packet and open it, coating my fingers and gingerly circle his puckered hole. Finger play isn't anything new to us. Alec has always enjoyed it, so I wasn't pushing any boundaries, yet. As I begin to stretch him, my confidence starts to falter even with his moans of approval. My mind is conflicted, but all thoughts cease the moment I feel my latex-wrapped cock being slathered in lube. "Please," he whispers again. Before I can think clearly, I have him lifted in my strong arms and his back pressed against the wall. I slowly position him perfectly and press into him even slower, giving him every opportunity in the world to change his mind. He doesn't. Instead, he starts begging, "Fuck, Bobby! More, faster, harder."

I let out a small chuckle as I still inside of him, causing him to squirm. "I don't think you are in any position to be making demands, Alec."

His eyes widen and just when he's about to argue, as he always does when he knows he's lost control of a situation, I slip my tongue into his mouth to silence him, moving ever so painfully slow inside of him while I do it. When I break the kiss, my lips are on his ear. "Relax. Enjoy this, enjoy us," I encourage. "We have all night, love. Treasure this, let me worship you." His only response is a moan. My lips move from his ear to his cheek, his forehead, down his nose, past his lips, down his neck. His moans soon turn to whimpers, and I find myself pinning his wrists to the wall with one hand, in attempt to keep him from gaining leverage on my shoulders. He doesn't fight against me much, except for arching his back, causing me to still within him, meeting his eyes. He narrows his at me before he relaxes and lets me continue worshiping him with my mouth.

"Please, Bobby, I need more," he begs after a short amount of time passes.

Frustrated, I pull him to me and walk out of the hall and into the bathroom, not saying a word as I gently push against his chest, causing him to lean backward. He follows my lead, quickly discovering my purpose as his hand finds the bathroom sink, though I am still holding most of his weight. I continue the slow pace I have started and let my free hand glide across his beautiful body. When he tries to quicken the pace, I smack him on the ass, expecting him to stop. Instead, it only encourages him. After a small amount of time, I give up trying to keep it slow and adjust him by the hips until his face shows evidence I found his sweet spot. I give a sly smile, letting him know he may be getting what he wants, but I'm still in control. I start a frantic pace, slamming into his prostate over and over.

"Fuck Bobby!" he gasps, arching his back as sweat pours out of his body. I know the signs well. He's holding back, waiting for me. And truth be told, I am holding back too. I want this to last. I wrap one arm around his waist as I continue to pound into him, stroking his cock with the opposite rhythm, causing him to whimper. I am not going to make this surrender easy on him, and the moment our eyes meet, he knows my desire. I want him to cum before me.

I can read the resistance at once, but I am not deterred even when he squeezes his eyes shut. "Look at me, love," I whisper. When his eyes meet mine, he discovers nothing but love and trust, for I have no challenge in them. I'm not going to push him into anything he isn't ready to give. My hand continues to pump and spread his pre-cum around, causing his eyes to roll back into his head. Then it happens with one loud scream. I feel my cock being squeezed and warm cum covers my hand. The surrender is welcome, yet surprising, and I am not far behind him in our bliss. My lips find his as we ride it out, and I gently slip my softening cock out of him, still holding onto him. "I love you, Alec," I whisper in his ear at last.

"Just as I love you, Bobby," he responds, dropping his legs from my waist. "Now, let's clean up so I can make you beg."